IN A FLASH

MIDLIFE IN AURA COVE BOOK 5

BLAIR BRYAN

To Adrienne, Brenda, and Stacy
A triad of brilliant women educators I adore.
May your passion for education continue to illuminate
minds and hearts, forever shaping a brighter tomorrow.

READ MORE BY THIS AUTHOR

Use the QR code below to access my current catalogue. **Teal Butterfly Press is the only place to purchase autographed paperbacks and get early access.** Buying direct means you are supporting an artist instead of big business. I appreciate you.

https://tealbutterflypress.com/pages/books

Also available at Barnes and Noble, Kobo, Apple books, Amazon, and many other international book sellers.

Find My Books at your Favorite Bookseller Below.

Books by Ninya

Books By Blair Bryan

ONE
1985

Madonna's *Material Girl* blasted from the speakers in Sebastian Kincaid's photography studio in downtown Miami. He hated the bubblegum pop hit, but it helped the models move in front of the lens, and he was always willing to sacrifice for his art. Music was one of the most useful tools he employed to put every rail-thin wannabe supermodel who strolled through the doors with stars in their eyes at ease.

During the past five years, his career had exploded, and Sebastian Kincaid was at the top of his game. The evidence of his success resided on shelves installed on the exposed brick walls of the downtown loft. There, golden trophies shimmered under spotlights, and framed covers of his most prestigious fashion magazine assignments graced the walls. The shelves also held his most prized possession, a vintage camera collection passed down from his father on the day he graduated from the Brooks Institute of Photography. His father had *wanted* to be a photographer, but Sebastian had actually become one.

He wasn't afraid to push society's boundaries and create outrageous images that got tongues wagging and established his artistic genius in the world of haute couture. It was a close-knit judgmental monarchy that bowed at the altar of the superficial, and by the time he was twenty-seven, Sebastian was king.

His avant-garde photographs were seen by millions in magazines, on billboards, and even plastered on the sides of buses. Each commission was a feather in his cap and added to his prestige, allowing his rates to skyrocket into the stratosphere. His work had been published in every reputable fashion magazine on the planet, and commissions coming in from luxury brands doubled every month.

The upcoming spread in Harper's Bazaar was his highest paid yet and over a year in the making. He finally achieved the pinnacle of success he'd been working toward, becoming the most sought-after fashion photographer in the industry. It was a verifiable fact that made his dick so hard he could cut diamonds with it.

As the song's chorus ramped up, he tuned out the music and tuned in to the gaggle of long-limbed women he eyed through his viewfinder. He pressed the shutter instinctively, like the camera was an extension of his arm, focusing on their lithe bodies cavorting in front of his lens. As he captured each breathtaking image, his zeal renewed.

"Arch your backs," he suggested, and they rushed to comply with his command, setting off a heady swell of power flooding through him. It never got old. The most beautiful women in the world submitted to his instructions instantly, like they were dripping from the lips of a Greek god. After using the last frame, he handed the spent magazine over to his assistant.

"Reload it, Ronnie," he demanded, completely dumbfounded when a reloaded Hasselblad film back was laid in the palm of his hand without delay. It usually took several minutes to reload film, and he'd grown accustomed to waiting in between rolls.

"How did you…?"

"I started counting the frames," Ronnie offered in explanation.

"My man!" He clapped the younger man on the back with the palm of his hand. "You're indispensable!"

"That's what I was hoping you'd say," Ronnie said with a capable nod. "And you'll also be pleased to learn I've taken the liberty of calling in our sandwich order."

"Anticipating my needs before I do?" Sebastian raised a brow. "Wow! Above and beyond the call of duty. I should give you a raise."

"You should," Ronnie agreed, offering Sebastian a crooked grin, then asked, "Did you want me to grab them while you wrap up the shoot?"

"Sounds like a plan." Sebastian turned his full attention back to the models sashaying his way. They ambled toward him, forming a circle, on long legs that stretched for days and towered over his slighter stature. "Last chance to make some magic, ladies." He tipped his chin up to look in their eyes. One of the girls reached out and squeezed his bicep, and he savored the contact. It was one of his favorite perks of the job.

Sebastian knew his limitations. He wasn't conventionally attractive, but he wasn't ugly either. His wavy mullet was gathered in a ponytail at the base of his neck. He had a strong nose, broken a time or two from mouthing off, and an intense gaze from his piercing blue eyes could make any woman feel like the only one in the room. He dressed like a New York artist, always in black from head to toe, a look that allowed him to recede into the background yet look professional. It was leagues away from Ronnie's sloppy t-shirt, jeans, and well-worn tennis shoes.

In school, one of the most important lessons he'd learned was that his camera was a powerful equalizer. With it, he could transform the life of any model who walked in front of it, and that was an incredibly attractive quality. Andy Warhol understood the concept better than anyone.

His technical prowess behind the camera and growing client roster afforded Sebastian many delicious nights with the girls smart enough to understand how the system worked. Being flirty with the photographer virtually guaranteed more photos would be taken and increased their representation to fashion houses. From this exposure, there would be runway offers and flights to Milan and Paris to work with the best in the business. Sebastian wasn't the type to spell it out or make demands, but he never turned down their advances. He'd always been the type of man who took advantage of opportunities he was presented with and relished the power that came with being pursued by beautiful women.

The session continued, with flashes popping off sporadically, like a late summer thunderstorm. Getting the shot was similar to harnessing lightning in a bottle. He always knew the moment of conception because it was accompanied by a surge of adrenaline that roared through him more powerful than any aphrodisiac. "Got it!" he shouted with glee, waving the camera in the air triumphantly, as blood rushed to his nether regions. "Great job, everyone."

The photo session had gone so well, he decided to go for extra credit. "If you ladies could indulge me, I have one more concept I'd like to try with you. It's not for the squeamish, but a personal project inspired by Stephen King's *Carrie*."

"Ooh! I'm in!" Melania enthused, the excitement on her face palpable. "I loved that book."

"Coolio." Sebastian turned to Ronnie who'd just returned with their food. "Let's lay down the sheets of plastic and prep the buckets of blood."

Two hours later, the models left after using the shower in the full bathroom in the studio loft. The red-dyed corn syrup dribbled and hugged every one of their curves, and the results on the Polaroids sitting on his desk were jaw-dropping. The photographs walked the delicate line between gore and eroticism, and he instinctively knew that when they hit the mainstream, his name would be seared into the memories of every fashion house in the world.

"You're a genius," Ronnie praised after the studio was cleared out, handing over Sebastian's pastrami on rye.

"All it takes is ten thousand hours in the pursuit of any skill to master it," Sebastian lectured, wondering if Ronnie was smart enough to appreciate the nugget of greatness he'd just been handed. He ripped open the parchment paper his sandwich was wrapped in and took a bite.

"Hey, I was thinking, instead of that raise you were talking about, I was wondering if I could work on my portfolio here," Ronnie asked. "On my own time, of course, and I would provide all my own film."

Sebastian mulled it over, pleased that his brilliance hadn't been wasted after all. It was the kind of arrangement he would have tried to secure for himself when he was a student. Ronnie had gumption; he saw a reflection of his former self in the younger man. The shoot had gone so well that he was feeling generous. "I'll make that deal as long as you clean up after yourself and work around my shoots. They always take precedence."

"Goes without saying." Ronnie grinned and took huge bites of his sandwich to finish it as fast as possible. He cleaned up the studio, popping the flashes before unplugging the lights like he'd been taught to protect their delicate tubes from being blown by a power surge. He rolled up the cords and pushed them to the edges of the infinity cove, a white corner-less wall of vinyl that was the background for many of Sebastian's photo shoots.

Sebastian watched the younger man work, pleased with his attention to detail. "Ronnie, your performance today solidified my decision. I'd like to offer you a position as my permanent assistant."

"Really?" Ronnie grinned, in shock at his good fortune.

"Really," Sebastian confirmed. It felt good to reach a hand back to help another person on the path to success. He could already tell Ronnie wouldn't be a threat to his career. He was too simple-minded and gob-smacked in the presence of beautiful women. Ronnie didn't understand they were a distraction that would render his creativity impotent when most of his blood was summoned elsewhere. He also lacked the vision that was as central to Sebastian's makeup as his DNA.

Looking around the studio, Sebastian realized every goal he'd set for himself as a student at Brooks had come to fruition, and he could confidently say he now lived a lifestyle he'd only dreamed about. His star was rising high in the sky, and the perks were far better than he ever imagined—sexy trysts with up-and-coming models in the industry, a little coke, and a flashy red Corvette he'd purchased last month after a record-breaking quarter of commissions. He was living high on the hog and enjoying the fruits of his labor.

In the summer of 1985, Sebastian Kincaid was becoming a fashion photography icon, but in just a year, three hundred and sixty-five short days, his career would be destroyed. He would swing from the highest high to the lowest low. His public fall from grace would be epic, and the worst part was, it would completely blind side him.

Two

The late October sunset reflected through the tinted windows of Kandied Karma as Yuli flipped the sign to closed after another long day. She untied her fuchsia apron and dropped it into the dirty pile for the cleaning service, taking a second to tighten the sash of the loose-fitting eggplant-colored peasant dress she wore. Glancing through the plate glass of the front window, she watched the ordins file past and into the quaint shops and eateries surrounding her building.

"They are always in such a hurry," she muttered to herself, watching the square fill with the early dinner crowd lured in by happy hour specials. She tilted her head, a crease appearing between her narrowed eyes as she observed the colors around her intensifying and the smell of cocoa beans and espresso becoming more pungent. The incoming auditory and visual stimuli overwhelmed her, and she quickly closed her eyes to contain them before shifting into receiving mode. The vision came a few seconds later. She saw herself closing a book and putting it on a shelf. Then another visual came in quick succession. She saw herself walk through a door filled with warm golden light and shut it behind her.

With a jolt, she re-opened her eyes, marveling at the magic that always seemed to find her at Kandied Karma. Surveying the artisanal chocolate shop with fresh eyes, she felt a surprising but not unwelcome warm gush of bittersweet longing fill her.

The store had become a beacon of Karmic rebalances, and the sight of golden sparkles and colorful aura shifts were becoming more frequent than ever since her granddaughter, Katia, turned fifty and experienced her awakening. Now, with the existence of three generations of supernatural women, the air tingled with purpose and the golden sparkles that accompanied it more often than not. Yuli had long abided by the principles of Karma, letting it guide her decisions and, though there had been some harrowing journeys lately, the mortal coven had only become stronger. She mused over a question that had been at the forefront of her mind since Katia's awakening. Who lived to almost one-hundred without a long laundry list of regrets?

"No one. I'm a lucky lady," she whispered with gratitude as she let this truth fill her for a moment before turning back to her closing tasks. Too exhausted after the long day on her feet to explore the messages she received from Karma, she filed them away to digest later and absentmindedly kneaded the tight muscles in her lower back. She didn't even pause when the amulet at her throat tingled, and instead, she brushed the pesky sensation away. Ready to head home, she gathered the container she'd filled with the few remaining truffles from the case and walked to the kitchen to put them in the chiller.

When she laid eyes on Zoya on the other side of the door, she lurched in surprise and lost her grip on the box. The truffles scattered to the floor, rolling under the marble workstations. Frustrated, she bent down to retrieve them. "Jeepers! You startled me. Now we can't even give these away! What a waste."

"Sorry, darling." An apologetic expression settled on Zoya's features as she swept the full skirt of her cloak to the side with one gloved hand and bent to help retrieve the candy. Yuli noticed her irritation quickly dissolve by the helpful gesture and instantly be replaced by confusion. It was the state she most often felt herself gravitate toward around Zoya lately. They'd been tentatively building a bridge toward each other, and while Yuli found their new dynamic a vast improvement from the bitterness of the past, it was confusing as all get out.

Two versions of Zoya existed in her mind now. One had loomed large in her childhood, cruel and neglectful after her mother died giving birth. The other was softer and apologetic, trying to earn her reincarnation to reunite with the love of her life, Salvatore Lombardo, when the next generation of supernatural females in their lineage was born. It was difficult to reconcile these two vastly different people.

"I'm sorry to drop in and surprise you, but I just received some important information you should know about." Zoya's skin glowed with the translucence of youth, evidence of her rigorous beauty routine in the meditation chamber. Dressed from head to toe in a deep teal-cloaked dress with a plunging neckline, her eyes shone with anticipation. Her long white hair was gathered in a loose braid that spanned the length of her back.

"And you decided to share it with me *voluntarily*?" Yuli's white eyebrows shot to her hairline. Her grandmother, Zoya, had a long history of wielding knowledge as a weapon, manipulating anyone she came in contact with without remorse. But she'd witnessed several recent shifts in her behavior, and Yuli had to admit, the change was astonishing.

Zoya chuckled. "I did, in the spirit of full transparency and to show you I am now a reformed witch. A team player, if you will."

Intrigued, Yuli chuckled at the idea Zoya would call herself a team player. She dropped the candy in the trash and leveled her eyes on Zoya's green ones. "Okay. I'll bite. Out with it."

"I've received confirmation the next generation has been conceived."

"What?" Yuli sat down on a stool in shock, taking in the revelation. "When? Katia has said nothing of the sort."

"I suspect she doesn't know," Zoya said, and after a long pause added, "Yet." She tugged out the stool next to Yuli and pulled off her gloves that provided a protective layer around the ordins. Sitting down, she gathered her elegant hands with long tapered fingers into her lap. "I thought it was important to confide in you first. After thinking it over, I don't believe the announcement should come from us. After all, the birth of the first grandchild is a momentous occasion, but if you feel we need to inform Katia, then I will support your decision."

Yuli cackled and held up a hand as she was overcome by this change in Zoya. "You are going to need to give me a minute. Normally, this is the type of mind-bending secret you brandish like a gladiator."

Zoya grinned. "This is the kind of secret I *used to* brandish like a gladiator. Like I said, changed witch."

Yuli let her bold declaration go in one ear and out the other, and instead focused on what was important. "A baby," Yuli murmured as she sat stone still, musing over the shocking information. "You're sure?"

"Yes," Zoya confirmed. "The dog noticed a change in Lauren's pheromones and leveraged the information to gain his freedom."

"Ah." Yuli let the truth settle deeper. The visions she'd just received came into clearer focus and now made total sense. Karma was telling her it was time to move on, that the changing of the guard was imminent. Yuli was lost in thought as Zoya continued to explain.

"At the Autumnal Equinox, Lauren and Tom

couldn't keep their hands off each other. I did the math, and it's a stretch, but it's possible."

"What do you mean?"

"She would have to deliver two weeks late, but a July 1st birthdate is not out of the question."

"Wow."

"I know," Zoya mumbled, and the silence that stretched between them lengthened as the room darkened.

"Thank you for being forthcoming with this information." Yuli said, "It is definitive evidence of your desire to change, and I appreciate it."

Zoya nodded. Words of praise from Yuli were few and far between, and the honesty rendered her speechless.

"You never answered my question. Do we keep Katia in the dark until Lauren and Tom make the announcement?"

"I think that is for the best." Yuli nodded, thinking. "It would be unfair for us to spoil it for her."

"Agreed," Zoya said. "But we have to prepare. You will have to transition as well. Are you ready for your rebirth?"

Yuli thought about it long and hard. She dragged a loose white hair from her cheek and tucked it into the bun at the base of her wide neck. "I always knew it would happen *one day*, but knowing one day is no longer theoretical, the notion it is happening soon is sobering."

Zoya nodded in agreement, for once taking the back

seat. She pulled her black gloves from her handbag on the counter and tugged them on, preparing to leave.

"I will have the legal team begin preparing the necessary documents to transfer the ownership of the compound," Zoya announced.

Yuli waved it away. Owning the exclusive resort-style property wasn't even a blip on her radar. Truth be told, she mourned the need to leave her current home. She greatly appreciated the smaller footprint and didn't have a need or want for servants to help her maintain a property like the Casanova Compound. Instead, she focused on the ramifications the birth of the next of their supernatural lineage would have, and what it would mean for their mortal and eternal covens, where every woman in their bloodline gathered for eternity.

"How will we teach Katia everything she needs to learn in such a short period of time?" The sheer volume of ancestral wisdom needing to be transferred was overwhelming.

"I think it's important to remember her abilities have revealed themselves at an astonishing rate already, and Katia will mature in her supernatural powers even more rapidly as I decline."

"That's true. Energy is neither created nor destroyed," Yuli mumbled to herself the universal principle.

"Yes. She will evolve at the exact right speed and at the exact right time. Nothing is left to chance. I believe Karma and the eternal coven knew the abbreviated timeline far before we were made aware," Zoya mused.

"Don't worry. You will still have decades to help shape her skills at the compound after I've passed."

Standing to leave, she cupped her gloved hands at her hips. Glancing at her, Yuli was surprised at her calm countenance and lack of reaction.

"You're taking this all in stride? Going with the flow? That's not like you at all!"

"Old witch, new trick." She offered Yuli a shrug and a self-deprecating grin.

"Are you afraid?"

"Only of not being allowed to reincarnate. The possibility of reuniting with Sally…" She sighed as her tone turned wistful and girlish, filled with longing. "It's all I've ever wanted and worth whatever price I will have to pay to earn it." She glanced at Yuli. "I do, however, have one request."

"I'd be surprised if you didn't." Yuli met Zoya's gaze, waiting for her to explain.

"Would you be open to the idea of opening your home to me? Resting inside your sacred circle during this transition will slow the transfer of power and give us more time to educate Katia on the finer points of our abilities together."

"Of course," Yuli said without hesitation. "It makes the most sense." She barked a spontaneous chuckle that morphed into a loud guffaw.

"What is so funny?"

"If you would have told me we'd be roommates someday, even a year ago, I would have called you certifiable."

Zoya's full lips curled up into a smile. "It's true." She looked back at Yuli, and with vulnerability softening the harder edges of her voice, she added, "I do appreciate your capacity for forgiveness. It far surpasses mine."

"Maybe that's one lesson you still need to learn to earn your reincarnation?"

"Perhaps," Zoya considered. "But I don't have to tell you, forgiveness has never been my strong suit."

"It's like a muscle. The more you use it, the easier it gets," Yuli added teasingly.

"Then it's settled. We'll wait for Lauren and Tom to make the announcement and, in the meantime, prepare for the succession."

THREE

Halloween in Aura Cove was one of Katie's favorite nights of the year, especially beggar's night when the neighborhood's children dragged their parents out onto the sidewalks for an evening of twilight trick-or-treating. In preparation, she'd spent the last hour stringing purple spider lights around her front door frame and draping wispy white spiderwebs from the door trim to the windows. She stacked white pumpkins with goofy painted faces on the steps among planters of colorful gourds and golden prairie grasses. Then she had filled a cooler with ice and chilled single-serving glasses of wine and green bottles of Heineken that she tucked into the corner for the adults. Finally, happy with the decor, she rushed to get herself ready before the first costumed child rang her doorbell, demanding one of the full-size candy bars she religiously gave out.

In her bathroom, Katie stood in front of the mirror

applying white face paint with the tips of her fingers. Once she had a good base established, she washed the greasy paint from her hands, pulled on a skullcap, and then topped it with a pastel rainbow wig. With a makeup sponge, she added shimmery pink and lavender eyeshadow to her lids and cheeks and attempted to glue on long eyelashes that tickled her brow bone every time she blinked. The final touch was positioning a clear elastic around her head to hold her shiny opalescent unicorn horn in place in the middle of her forehead.

In her walk-in closet, she tugged on the white unitard she'd ordered online, having to contort her body like a circus performer to smooth it over her curves. Then she tied a pastel rainbow-colored tutu around her waist with a long curly ponytail at her backside that shimmered in the light.

"There," she said to her sparkling reflection admiring the transformation when the doorbell chimed. Confused, she glanced at the watch on her wrist. "It's too early for trick-or-treaters," she mumbled out loud, a habit that had become more frequent since Zoya released her rescue dog, Arlo, from servitude, and he'd been transformed back to his human form.

Katie found the silence deafening without a creature to share her home with, and she was still struggling to find ways to fill it. The doorbell rang again, and she hustled to the front door and pulled it open to see Tom and Lauren waiting on her front step, holding a carved pumpkin.

"Surprise!" they chorused together full of smiles.

Seeing her oldest child and the man she loved, Katie grinned and let out a playful, "Ncigh," as she dragged her hoof on the ground. Hearing her serious daughter chuckle at her cheesy attempt at horsing around made Katie's heart swell. "Come on in."

Tom carried the large pumpkin inside and Lauren followed close behind, buzzing with barely contained excitement.

"Did I forget you were coming over tonight?" Katie was confused by the impromptu visit and even more rattled by the couple's keyed-up energy. Since her awakening, her natural intuitive empathy magnified, and she was still adapting to the stronger ability. It was sometimes difficult to navigate what felt like an intrusion of privacy on those closest to her.

"No, we just wanted to stop by with a special delivery." A smirk sneaked across Lauren's glossy lips before she pointed to the jack-o'-lantern that was now sitting on the island.

Katie glanced over at the face carved into it. With large eyes and a full open mouth twisted into a joyful smile, it was a happy pumpkin, the type she favored. Studying it more closely, Katie said, "Wait… I think there is something inside it." Distracted, she took a step closer, lifted the top by its scratchy stem, and peered inside. Nestled in the fleshy bottom was a much smaller pumpkin.

Katie wrestled it out of its clammy confinement and held it close to her face. This pumpkin had the same eyes, but where the mouth should be, the outline of a pacifier filled the space. "Aww. That's sweet, honey. A mama and a baby pumpkin." Oblivious, she placed the tiny pumpkin next to the bigger one and grinned as a swoony memory surfaced from Lauren's childhood. She remembered the kitchen table in their tiny New York apartment, covered in newsprint and small fistfuls of slimy pumpkin innards, and the nutty flavor of crunchy roasted pumpkin seeds. Carving pumpkins had always been one of her favorite traditions when Callie, Beckett, and Lauren were young, and she insisted on carrying it out annually until they'd left for college.

"Thank you," she whispered as her eyes misted. But out of the corner of her eye, an impatient exchange between Lauren and Tom got her attention. "Wait…" she said, reading their skittish energy and seeing an orange aura. Her eyes darted over to them as they fidgeted from side to side. "Is this what I think it is?" She picked up the baby pumpkin and held it between her hands, turning her hopeful gaze back to the couple.

Lauren bobbed up and down eagerly. "We know Halloween is one of your favorite holidays and thought we would take the opportunity to tell you we are expecting our own little pumpkin."

"Oh, honey!" She gingerly set the baby pumpkin on the table next to its mother and pulled her daughter into her arms, squealing with joy. "Congratulations!" Pulling back, she cupped her daughter's face in her hands, appraising her with a practiced eye. "How are you feeling? Are you having any morning sickness?"

"No, not at all." She pressed her palm to her

abdomen, which was still flat, but the overprotective gesture tugged at Katie's heartstrings. "Just tired, but other than that, I feel great." She added, "Basically, I have been eating like a pig and cannot drink enough chocolate milk."

"And I'd just like to say that, although it was very unexpected, I promise I'm taking great care of your daughter," a nervous Tom interjected, and Katie tuned into his tingle of fear of her possible judgment about their unplanned pregnancy.

"He is," Lauren agreed, reaching out to take Tom's hand to reassure him.

"This is fantastic news!" Katie gushed, trying to ease his worry. "Life sometimes likes to flip the script and send you on a new trajectory." It was a lesson she'd learned herself since she'd awakened. "I, for one, am absolutely thrilled for you both, and this is one lucky baby to get to have two parents who will love them so much!" Katie cried, happy to see Tom's shoulders relax in the presence of her excitement. "Do you know your due date?"

"June 17th."

Trepidation filled Katie as she swallowed hard. The date instantly commanded her full attention.

Lauren and Tom gazed at each other as dreamy expressions settled on their features, both already so in love at the prospect of becoming parents. "We're kind of hoping he, *or she*, comes late and shares a birthday with you and Yuli. I mean, how cool would it be to have three generations of our family born on the same day?"

Lauren raved.

"The coolest," Katie answered as her mind spun with the ramifications. If the child was female, she would be the next in their supernatural line. Though it would be decades before the child would awaken to her powers, she knew it would start a chain of events into motion that she wasn't sure she was ready for. Trying to shake off the worry, she beamed at the ecstatic couple. "This is the best news I've heard all year!"

The doorbell rang in quick, punchy succession.

"Uh oh! Sounds like the natives are getting restless." Tom chuckled. "We'll get out of your hair before you have a mutiny on your hands. Besides, we need to get over and tell Mom."

"Be sure to give Rox a hug from me," Katie said. "She is going to be over the moon with joy."

"I definitely will," Tom agreed. "Man! This baby hit the jackpot in the grandma department!"

Katie grinned and hugged Tom and Lauren goodbye, then walked them to the door where a gaggle of children in costumes waited. She quickly deposited candy bars into plastic pumpkins the enthusiastic trick-or-treaters lifted up, distracted by the news. Over their heads, she watched Tom settle Lauren into the passenger seat of the car and then pull slowly away, skillfully dodging groups of trick-or-treaters lingering on the sidewalks.

"A baby!" She felt the amulet at her throat warm and tingle as her mind spun on the new information. There was another lively knock at the door, and she grabbed the bowl of candy and opened it wide to see Yuli and Zoya standing on her doorstep.

"Oh!" Katie said, "Another surprise set of visitors! Come on in."

"I'll take this." Zoya pulled the bowl from Katie's hands as she walked through the door. While in the kitchen, Yuli made a sign on a piece of cardboard. "Honor System. Take One Please." Then they deposited the sign and the bowl on the front step, locking the door firmly behind it.

"Hey! Handing out the treats is my favorite part," Katie complained.

"We have much bigger fish to fry, Katia," Yuli stated, her tone dismissive. It was a rarity that made a tingle of fear reverberate through Katie. Since the women in the mortal coven were all gathered together, their amulets vibrated at their throats and glowed brighter. The beautiful purple light softly illuminated their surrounding skin.

"And you just missed Tom and Lauren," Katie added, using conversation to chase away her rising anxiety. She didn't want to be the one to spoil Tom and Lauren's surprise, but as she watched Yuli make her way to the mother and baby pumpkin, the shock she expected to register on her grandmother's face never did. Instead, she pursed her lips and picked up the tiny pumpkin in her hands, showing it to Zoya, who nodded.

"She knows."

"Wait. Did you already know they were expecting?" Katie's brow crinkled in confusion.

"Yes. I told Yuli the news," Zoya admitted after a long pause. Her jarring honesty made Katie flinch.

"How?"

"Arlo used it as leverage to earn his freedom."

"Seriously?" Katie had been missing her dog since he had been restored to his human body, but Zoya had not chosen to share all the gory details. Frustrated, knowing she'd been kept in the dark on purpose, she rankled at the admission and boldly addressed Zoya. "What about being more forthcoming with the truth and earning your reincarnation from the eternal coven by changing your ways? Unbelievable!" She strode over to the fridge and pulled out a bottle of tequila, pouring herself a small nip before throwing it back. The alcohol burned as it made its way down her throat, scorching in tandem with the anger coursing through her veins. "That dog!" she huffed as she poured another and knocked it back. "He should have told me first."

"Katia, that would have ruined it for Lauren," Yuli reasoned. "Becoming a mother is a life-changing event in a young woman's life. I'm sure that's why Zoya didn't think we should mention it to you."

"You're defending *her*?" Katie's voice trembled, sounding pitchy with outrage. "What is happening? Did I fall into an alternative universe where you two are besties?"

"Katia." Yuli tried to smooth her ruffled feelings. "Please be reasonable."

Zoya jumped in to help explain, grateful for Yuli taking the initiative to pave the way. "It's true. Yuli and

I decided to wait until Lauren and Tom made the announcement, and now that they have, we are all up to speed!" She clapped her hands together as if that erased all the deception.

"I hate being kept in the dark," Katie grumbled. "But you might have a point." Her lips curled up at the corners as she glanced over at the tiny pumpkin still cradled in Yuli's hands. She thought the news of a grandchild's arrival would fill her with wonder and joy, but it also ushered in apprehension. "She's due June 17th," Katie shared then switched to snark. "But you probably already know that, too." After the dig left her lips, she felt guilty about it. "Sorry."

"No apology needed," Zoya responded softly as she sat on a stool at Katie's island. "It's official. She'll be the newest member of the mortal coven." Zoya's voice was filled with awe as the amulets on their throats brightened to confirm the information. "And the day she arrives, I will be forced to exit."

Katie swallowed the lump in her throat. She was filled with conflicting emotions. "But we just reconnected…" It was a bittersweet reality they would all be forced to accept.

Zoya offered her a wan smile. "There is much to teach you before that happens. Brace yourselves because you'll be seeing a lot more of me."

"Oh, goodie gumdrops!" Yuli deadpanned, and they chuckled.

"Come on, I'm not that bad!" Zoya cried.

"Mmm?" Katie quirked her head to the side and

made a high-pitched noise from the back of her throat, indicating doubt, and breaking the tension. A long silence stretched out before she dared to ask Zoya, "Am I allowed to be happy that my first grandchild is on the way when it means the end of you?"

"Of course, you're allowed, darling! I've lived a long life. The birth of the next supernatural generation *is* a momentous occasion worthy of celebration," Zoya declared as she walked over to the liquor cabinet and pulled out the Horilka Katie kept on hand for Yuli and two more glasses.

"A toast." She poured two fingers of the Ukrainian liquor into the crystal tumblers. "To the end and to the beginning, may they both teach us the lessons we need to learn."

Four

The next afternoon at Kandied Karma, Katie was about to sit down with Yuli and Zoya for an after-shift espresso when Davina appeared at the door. Seeing her former lawyer waving through the glass, Katie grinned. Rushing over to open the door, she welcomed her inside.

"This is a pleasant surprise!" she exclaimed, tuning immediately into Davina's frenzied energy.

"I know, I know. Always straggling in at closing time." Davina apologized with a tight smile as she smoothed a blonde flyaway hair from her crisp asymmetrical bob with her fingers. Around her, an orangey-red aura rippled, and Katie instantly picked up on her heightened stress level. "Kandied Karma has bewitched me. I can't get your amaretto creams out of my head."

"No one can." Katie laughed. "But all our stock is in the chiller at the moment. Can you give me a minute?"

"Of course." Davina smiled. "You're the one doing me a favor. I think the last batch helped me seal the deal at an important mediation. Kandied Karma's truffles are magic!"

Katie barked an awkward laugh. "You don't know the half of it!" A flurry of dinging notifications rolled in on Davina's phone, eliciting an anguished groan from the attorney, and she reluctantly pulled out her phone to answer them.

"This instrument is the bane of my existence," she muttered under her breath, engrossed in tapping out answers while Katie stepped away and pushed through the swinging door that connected the shop to the kitchen where Yuli and Zoya were seated. Their conversation came to a screeching halt when Katie entered, her nerves making her bubble with enthusiasm and pace in front of their table.

"Davina Thorne is here. The last time she was in, I received some flashes. I think she's connected to my next assignment from Karma."

"Ooh!" An over-enthusiastic Zoya jumped to her feet, eyes dancing, clapping her hands together. Her curiosity was like a ferocious lion demanding to be fed. She took a step closer to Katie, eager for more details. "I could see if I can glean any information under the guise of meeting her," Zoya offered, already turning toward the door.

"Wait." Katie considered her suggestion but dismissed it quickly. "I think I'd like to carry out this rebalance as much on my own as possible." She gained confidence in her decision as she explained, "Though I appreciate the offer, a time is coming when I won't have the luxury of being able to rely on you and Yuli."

A disheartened Zoya reluctantly returned to her seat more glum than she'd been a minute ago. "Fine." Witnessing the determined set of Katie's shoulders, she added, "Good on you, Katia."

The praise fortified her resolve enough to add, "Please don't intervene unless I explicitly ask you for help." She eyed Zoya, who was often guilty of inserting herself. "Can you promise me?"

Zoya met her discerning gaze, unblinking for several long seconds before she answered, "I give you my word."

"Okay, then." Proud of herself, Katie tugged open the cool stainless steel handle of the chiller and quickly boxed a dozen amaretto cream-filled triple chocolate truffles. A few minutes later, with the golden box glistening in her hands, she returned to the front of the shop where Davina was waiting. "Do you have time for a cup of coffee?"

Davina consulted her watch with a wince. Knowing Davina needed a little extra nudge and wanting to test out the strength of a new ability she'd been working on in private, Katie yawned into her balled fist. "I know *I* could use one." Katie forced herself to yawn again, locked her eyes on Davina, and felt a satisfied thrill of accomplishment when Davina mimicked her. The influenced gesture grazed the delicate line between free will and mind control, and Katie pushed the residual guilt away, telling herself it was an insignificant bump to break down Davina's fortress of self-protection. She hadn't changed the outcome of anything significant. It was merely a harmless nudge to inspire a deeper connection. What was the harm in it?

"You know what? I got a ridiculously early start today. An espresso is just what the doctor ordered." Davina gave in, oblivious she'd been influenced into compliance.

"Have a seat and I'll be right back."

In a few minutes, Katie returned with a tray holding an assortment of truffles and two cups of coffee. The awkward silence stretched longer than Katie wanted as she searched for a connection point to begin a productive conversation. "I just realized you know so much about me, but I know very little about you. Do you have a big family?"

"Just a sister now. She's the principal of Aura Cove High School," Davina offered tentatively, unaccustomed to sharing personal information with former clients.

"Adrienne Thorne? Of course. I can't believe I didn't put it together before. Mine graduated before she took over, but I know for a fact the community holds her in high esteem." Davina glanced down at her cup, and Katie felt the distance between them grow. Unable to stop herself, she asked, "Are you close?"

"No. We're seven years apart, so she was eleven when I left for college." Davina stared into the cup, lost in thought and unable to make direct eye contact when expressing her feelings. Being vulnerable was a side of

Davina that Katie had never seen before. She was
astonished to learn that underneath the carefully curated
image of the tigress in the courtroom was a woman not
unlike herself. A woman who didn't have all the
answers, but who always did her best. After a long
pause, Davina cleared her throat and offered more
information to fill the void. "Our mom passed last year.
At her funeral, we made a pact to spend more time
together, to get to know each other as women, but life
has gotten in the way."

"It happens," Katie commiserated. She reached out
to offer the chocolates to Davina, deliberately brushing
her fingertips as she handed them over. Her vision
blurred as the colors intensified. She blinked a few
times, and when she regained focus, a murky indigo
aura surrounded Davina. Bracing for the message from
Karma she hoped would come, she felt a tingle and a
zing of current flow from her fingers, up her forearms,
and out into the branches of the scars that remained
from her last rebalance.

The terrifying ordeal she'd suffered after ingesting
the Recurring Torment Rum Truffle still affected Katie.
The scars were forever etched into her skin from the
lightning strike she'd endured when Zoya and Yuli used
their collective power to bring her back from Rox's
stream of consciousness. The trauma she'd survived was
imprinted on her flesh, and Katie wore it with pride. It
was a badge of survival. The scars reminded her of how
far she'd come and the lengths to which the women in
her family were willing to go to save her.

Katie tuned in, amazed at the clarity with which the vision came through. She was startled to realize the visions were more than mere flashes; now, they morphed into the equivalent of streaming video. Katie saw a podium where a beautiful woman stood. Dressed impeccably in a power suit and towering in heels, her long limbs implied the grace of a dancer. In front of her, a group of men and women sat conducting a school board meeting.

Then, the scars on her forearms warmed. Katie felt woozy, under the influence of alcohol almost as she stumbled around, feeling exposed with eyes boring into her body. She felt fingers brush her breast before an embarrassed laugh left her lips that didn't sound like her own.

When she pulled back from Davina, the sensation faded in a flash. She felt discombobulated as she tried to save face and recover from the intensity of the troubling vision.

Katie breathed a sigh of relief when she realized Davina had continued to speak during her reaction as if nothing happened, her stare vacant and focused on the window, avoiding eye contact. Her obvious regret at the current state of her relationship with her sister made her attempts at connection with Katie stilted and awkward. "I should have tried harder, done more for her after I left for college, but I was too busy trying to live my own life. So self-absorbed and consumed by my own goals, I didn't have the capacity for her struggles. It's easier to stop caring when you have the luxury of distance. "

Grateful the vision passed and Davina was none the wiser, Katie leaned in and offered her support. "That's normal behavior in your twenties. You were not at fault for trying to figure out your own life," Katie offered, then added gently, "But what about now?" The question captured Davina's full attention.

"I think I'd like to change the dynamic, but I don't know how." She took a sip of coffee and snorted at her own shortcomings. "Pretty pathetic, huh?" She choked out a throaty chuckle. "Listen to me! What a sap. God, I must be getting weaker in my old age!"

"No. Vulnerability is not weakness," Katie explained. "It's becoming wiser. Opening your heart, knowing it could be hurt, is one of the bravest things you'll ever be asked to do."

"Maybe," she acknowledged as she finished her coffee and stood. "I'll get out of your hair now. Thanks for the chat." She gathered the box of truffles and quickly shuttered her feelings, again deflecting with humor. "You should start a new service here, Truffles & Therapy with Katie Beaumont."

Katie chuckled. "You might be on to something."

The influx of caffeine restored Davina's sarcastic skepticism. "I guess we're all just bruised and battered, trying not to re-open old wounds and survive the hellscape known as human emotion."

Her cynical view of the world made Katie sad as she walked Davina to the door and watched her cross the street, headed toward her Aston Martin. Once inside, she popped on a pair of sunglasses, whipped away from the curb and down the street, and disappeared into traffic.

Katie locked the door to the shop behind her and headed back to the kitchen where Yuli and Zoya were still gathered.

"How did it go?" Yuli asked.

Katie wrinkled her brow as she searched for the right words to describe the visit. "She's closed off."

"She'd have to be to deal with the depravity the woman is exposed to day in and day out," Zoya said.

"You two are alike in that respect," Katie said. "Walls for days. Never let anyone get close enough to see the real you."

"It's a protective instinct. If you don't let anyone in, then you can't get hurt." Zoya said, "I subscribed to that philosophy my entire life, but recent evidence shows it might be flawed thinking."

Yuli quickly agreed, "You *are* opening your heart." She smirked as she pinched her fingers together to indicate the shift had been infinitesimal. "It's screeching in protest and behind a wall as high as the clouds, but that old ticker of yours *is* making an appearance."

Zoya's cheeks flushed with embarrassment. "It still counts!" All three women laughed and then let out a sigh at the same time that only made them chuckle in unison again as the amulets at their throats tingled.

"There was something odd about this message from Karma," Katie finally offered, eager to get their take on it.

"How so?"

"The flashes are more theatrical than they have ever been. Immersive might be a better word." She tried to explain, "It was like the vision was happening to me."

Zoya and Yuli exchanged furtive glances.

"What?" Katie asked.

"It seems your last rebalance might have opened up a new ability that neither of us has experienced without first consuming the truffle." Concerned, their eyes leveled on Katie's, which were widening with fear. "Consciousness Transferal."

"Your reaction is scaring me," Katie admitted.

"Never be afraid of your supernatural powers, darling." Zoya winked.

Yuli jumped in, "She's right. You must understand and then embrace your abilities in order to utilize them for the greatest good."

Katie shivered, remembering what transpired the last time she entered the consciousness of another being. "What if I get stuck again?" Her forearms throbbed and the branches of her scars pinked up. She held them up for Yuli and Zoya to see.

"I don't believe you will," Zoya said, examining Katie's arms. She brushed her thumbs against the scars, noticing they were raised on the surface of Katie's skin. Where their skin touched, Katie felt a surge of strength from every brush from Zoya's fingers.

"What is happening?"

"The transfer is beginning," Zoya offered as an explanation. "Your powers are strengthening, absorbing a bit of mine, and that is why I am certain you will not be stuck again."

When Katie met her gaze, she noticed for the first time a smattering of crow's feet at the corners of Zoya's eyes. They were mere inches away when Katie detected Zoya's normally flawless skin was showing its first crack in the foundation. Doubt filled her. Had they been there all along? Katie wasn't sure, but she couldn't spend any more precious brain power on her great-great-grandmother's aging process. It was all superficial anyway. Right now, she needed to focus on her next assignment from Karma.

FIVE

"Sweet Jesus," Frankie said, dropping the cardboard box to the ground in her kitchen. "What are you hiding in here? A body?"

Harry laughed and pointed at the label. "You should have left that one for me, silly." Written in neat penmanship, in black marker in the upper right-hand corner of the box, was the word *Books*.

She collapsed on the sofa in exhaustion, and a few seconds later, Harry dropped onto it next to her. His muscular thigh aligned with hers as he wrapped his arm around her neck to pull her in for a squeeze. Exhausted, they both took inventory of the living room that was stacked to the ceiling with boxes. "It looks like an episode of *Hoarders* in here," he remarked. "But at least everything is in one place."

"Yeah, at least." Frankie laid the sarcasm on thick as the back of her head lolled against the microfiber sofa.

"Having second thoughts?" Harry asked tentatively,

and once again, Frankie was struck by his openness. He boldly covered the terrifying terrain of authentic human emotion with the unfettered innocence of a child. Frankie was often wary, approaching it more like immersive shock therapy. Necessary but brutal.

"About moving in together? No." She surveyed the mess and mountain of work in the boxes in front of them. "About finding a place for all your stuff? Definitely."

"We're going to both have to do a purge." He leaned forward and grasped a kitschy knick-knack made of seashells with crudely glued-on eyes covered in a layer of dust that was on the coffee table. "What in the hell is this?"

"I'm sentimental," Frankie said. "Callie gave it to me for Christmas when she was fourteen."

"You are not," Harry shot back.

"Okay, maybe I'm just lazy." Frankie smirked.

Harry got to his feet and walked over to her bookshelves that lined the living room. Filled to the gills with wrinkled, well-loved paperbacks, most of them featured glistening six-pack abs attached to headless men. He pulled one off the shelf and held it up to make his point. "Why do publishers do this?"

"What?" Frankie asked, standing, taking a step closer to enjoy the man's muscled physique.

"Cut off their heads?"

"At least they kept the head most men think with," Frankie teased adding a comedic drumroll. "Da-dum-dum!"

"Hey!" Harry said in mock offense as he studied her collection. Laughing, he pulled another paperback out and then bent down and rifled through the box at Frankie's feet and pulled an identical paperback from it. "Maybe we need to have a moment of silence for smut authors everywhere, reflecting on the fifty percent fewer royalties they will be receiving from now on because of our sacred union."

Frankie shook her head at him. "Sacred? More like our unholy union." She laughed. "God, you're such a dork."

"Here's the big question. Can you get a tax deduction if you donate cliterature to charity?" he asked, wrinkling his nose. "Not sure the Salvation Army or Saint Vinnie's had *"Taken by the Mermen"* in mind when they said they would gladly accept donations of books in good condition."

"I look at it as bringing solace to the lonely," Frankie corrected, "and that, sir, is an official act of charity."

"You would!" He laughed, pulling her into his arms. "Let's go get some oysters and beers, then we can come back and try to conquer Mount Saint Hoarder."

Six

On the other side of town, crammed into an eighties Florida ranch that his mother kept too warm due to her total reliance on social security, Denny cruised the internet chat rooms. Normally, the ferocious appetite and penchant for sharing among his fellow chat room enthusiasts guaranteed an around-the-clock visual buffet of the young and beautiful from any computer in the world, but that night, all the usual players were silent.

He didn't feel ashamed about his practices anymore. After all, men were visual creatures, and who was he to try to fight centuries of conditioning? It wasn't as if he went trolling for kindergarteners. He had a standard. Sixteen was old enough, and it turned out twenty-two states in America agreed with him.

The first time he crossed the line was the hardest, but each time after became easier and easier, as if the highway to hell was greased into a frictionless pathway to depravity. Knowing he was breaking the law added an element of addictive danger to his practice that hit like a high, and he was forever craving the next one.

To quell his frustration, he lit a cigarette and took a drag, then stubbed it out into the tray before blowing the smoke out of a cracked window. In the bedroom below him, he heard her muffled movement, and then the attic door creaked open and her voice filtered up.

"Are you smoking up there again, Dennis?" She coughed a wet, raspy hack that instantly incensed him. "You know I can't handle cigarette smoke with my asthma."

"No, Ma," he shouted in response. "It's all in your head. Remember, the doctor said it's a case of lingering Phantosmia from when you had Covid last winter."

"Oh, yeah, that's right." He was grateful her stroke last year ended her ability to climb stairs easily. It kept her from his attic lair on the second floor. It was the one place he was free from her hyper-vigilant surveillance. During her hospitalization, he helped himself to her financial records and discovered his childhood home and the remainder of his father's pension would be his after her demise. Attempting to speed up the process, he'd tried to convince her to give him power of attorney, but the old bat refused. It was obvious she would be stubborn until her last dying breath—a breath he hoped she'd take sooner rather than later.

"Don't stay up too late." Her condescending, smothering tone instantly added to the pit of bitterness that resided permanently in his stomach.

He'd moved in after the stroke to help get his mother to her doctor's appointments. With him living there, she could stay in her home instead of going to assisted living. At least that was the cover story he told his last blind date that had been a total bust. After ponying up the dough to buy a steak dinner for a woman who wouldn't even register above a four on the hotness scale, he'd been enraged by her instant decline to his offer for a nightcap at his place.

She'd wrinkled up the nose on her pudgy face and actually recoiled from him. Her! A fat pig with an admin job at an auto parts store! Curvy girl, my ass! She was a delusional liar, fully ensconced in the obese category.

"When your belly extends out further than your tits, honey, you're fat!" he shouted as he ran alongside her Uber that sped away, but not before groaning as it sank under her weight.

Denny's rage simmered as he walked the mile back to his mother's house, following sidewalks and crossing busy intersections, hands balled at his sides. There was a chip on his shoulder that grew heavier with each unsuccessful interaction with a female, and he yearned to make someone pay.

As his social failures piled up, bitterness swelled in the pit of his stomach. A seed of hatred was planted deep in his soul, nurtured with every dis and rebuff that happened. Now it was a mighty oak swaying in the breeze, and his emotional trunk was warped and permanently scarred by their disgust and pity.

In his early sixties, his once thick wavy hair had

receded and thinned. In denial, he refused to cut it and instead religiously wore it in a limp gray ponytail held together with a hair tie at the base of his neck. A particularly bad break to his nose had healed at an unfortunate angle, making it hard to breathe, and his bright blue eyes became dull and wary.

In another life, Denny had been an accomplished photographer until the MWACs (moms with a camera) descended like locusts and destroyed his precious industry. He was reduced to hawking his fine art floral photography at pop-up shows that catered to the moneyed retirees in Florida.

It was a feast or famine existence he supplemented by working part-time for Precious Momento, shooting family portraits on the beach—the most cliché of all family portrait locations. A few nights a week, he lowered the bar of his beloved craft, pasted on a smile, and mingled with happy families while he snapped their photos, hating himself a little more with each click of the shutter. With every session, a little of his greatness drifted away like a puff of smoke. Wasted.

Denny dared to take another drag on the cigarette and then covered it with a blast of lemon-scented air freshener when a *whoosh* sound from his cell phone notified him of a new message. It was from his favorite anonymous chat app, WhisperHub. Hearing the sound, a thrilling tingle surged through him, and like Pavlov's dog, he began to salivate.

Someone had made a new post in the encrypted chat room. Though end-to-end encrypted chat was originally created to help keep login credentials, health records, and credit card information secure, it didn't take long for the dirty underbelly of the internet to find its own alternative use for the technology. It was a veil of anonymity that allowed you to remain hidden, often in plain sight, and to carry out your fantasies without fear or repercussions.

His handle was twistedsnaps69. Denny logged in and tapped to open his inbox where one of his favorite members, 1_bad_influence, posted a short video clip and a message.

"How to Make Six Figures in Thirty Days."

Instantly intrigued, Denny tapped on the video to watch it, and while he definitely enjoyed the content due to its graphic and salacious nature, evidenced by the painful erection in his pants, he was more motivated by the promise of riches.

Twistedsnaps69: Enjoyed the skin-ema. Teach me your ways, oh wise one!
1_bad_influence: 5 Easy Steps to Financial Freedom

1. Create a profile and befriend your target on social media.
2. Slide into their DMs, pouring on the compliments and expressing romantic interest.

3. Exchange selfies. Make it a game. Dare them to record themselves doing dirty things to send to you. Entice your target to push their boundaries and send as many explicit videos and photos as they can.

4. After you've collected the collateral, it's time for your pay day. Contact your target via email with instructions on how to keep these photos and videos private with your bitcoin address.

5. Stalk their accounts, find their family members online, and threaten to send the material to them unless payment is made. Any girl will pay dearly to keep her dad's eyes away.

Twistedsnaps69: Does this really work?
1_bad_influence: You'd be surprised how well.
Twistedsnaps69: Diabolical! I love it.
1_bad_influence: You'll love the money more. I promise.
Twistedsnaps69: What if I already have a collection? I might have access to a private inventory I've personally curated over the years.
1_bad_influence: Then you can skip straight to step 5! You are sitting on a goldmine, my man! Track them down and rake in the cash. Maybe you'll get lucky and one of your beauties will be in the public eye, or better yet, be married to a

pastor! All you have to do is send a sneak peek, apply the pressure, and wait.

Twistedsnaps69: You're a legend.

1_bad_influence: How about you show your appreciation and share the most depraved photos in your collection? Daddy needs a taste.

Twistedsnaps69: Coming right up.

He spent the next hour crawling through his collection of solid-state hard drives containing his most debased digitized content. They were meticulously organized and carefully concealed in the back of his closet in a large lockbox. The collection in its entirety was always a tantalizing sight, but now he was pining for the financial windfall. The ones and zeros stored there represented an untold fortune, and thanks to 1_bad_influence, all the wrongs in his life would now be made right. Denny was finally going to level back up into the kind of lifestyle he deserved. The tide was turning and his ship was coming in.

SEVEN

Adrienne Thorne pulled into the beautifully landscaped and well-maintained parking lot at Aura Cove High School and parked her reliable Camry in the designated spot. She pulled her bag and the Pyrex container she'd filled with fresh-baked banana nut muffins from the back seat and walked into the darkened school. She was often the first one in and the last one to leave. Over the last seven years as principal, the school had quickly become her second home.

Dressed in a cobalt blue power suit with a pencil skirt that hit just below the knee of her long legs, the Converse sneakers on her feet made her more approachable to students. They were also infinitely more comfortable than the heels she stashed in her backpack for the meeting with the school board later that evening. At forty-seven, her classic beauty still turned heads, and she knew how to dress herself to play up her attributes. Thanks to good genes, an efficient metabolism, and a natural knack for makeup application, she easily passed for early thirties.

Juggling her keys and the muffins, she swiped her key card to open the door at the faculty entrance. She quickly navigated the darkened halls with ease and turned on the lights in the main office, taking the time to set a warm muffin on a napkin in front of her secretary's computer. She pulled out the thank-you card she'd hand-written and set it in front of the muffin.

Her secretary, Dory Miller, was an invaluable member of her staff, and Adrienne never missed an opportunity to show appreciation for her hard work. Desperate for caffeine, she stumbled into the teacher's lounge and made herself a steaming mug of breakfast blend that she brought back to her office. She sipped it slowly, savoring the final moments of calm before the storm of students rushed through the doors before classes began.

She tucked a thick chunk of her blonde, highlighted hair behind her ears as she logged into her computer to take a look at her email. Drumming her red lacquered fingernails on the desk, she culled through the thirty-three emails she'd been sent since seven p.m. last night. Keeping her inbox under control was a constant chore. As a result, Adrienne developed a habit of checking it and responding several times each day. Her email was often under siege by over-involved helicopter parents typical of the affluent school district she worked in.

A few minutes later, Dory arrived and ducked her

head in Adrienne's office, holding the muffin aloft. "Thank you."

"You're welcome. I know who keeps this school running and my schedule manageable. I never want you to ever feel your contribution around here is unappreciated."

"You're the best boss I've ever had." Dory's gray hair was pulled into a bun at the base of her neck, and she wore a conservative blue cardigan sweater with a long skirt. She pulled the liner from the muffin and took a bite, murmuring with pleasure. "You know, if this principal gig doesn't work out, you would have a real future as a baker."

"I'll keep that in mind." Adrienne grinned as she checked the watch on her wrist. She spent the next ten minutes prioritizing her schedule, and at precisely seven-fifty-five, she walked to the front entrance of the school and stood in the sun-soaked atrium. A few minutes later, like a well-oiled machine, a bright yellow school bus yawned open its door, releasing a flood of teenagers. They made their way to the front entrance, moving slowly as they stared down at their phones in the palms of their hands like zombies.

"Good Morning, Sam." Adrienne was on a first-name basis with every student in her school. It was one nonnegotiable habit she'd acquired in her first school and it stuck. Each fall, she gave herself two weeks to learn the names of all the incoming freshmen. The small gesture endeared her to her students almost immediately, as well as her penchant for throwing outlandish challenges at them.

So far, her losing streak included having to shave her head three years ago when the matriarch of the Wilson Family (and head of the PTA) was given a stage-four breast cancer diagnosis. She challenged the students to raise the funds necessary to send them on one final family vacation. It had been worth it when Parker Wilson, a junior at Aura Cove High School, accepted the check on behalf of his family with tears in his eyes.

At their Carnivale night last spring, she'd spent the better part of two hours being thrust into freezing water from the dunk tank after the baseball team scored the highest on their yearly state assessment tests. With their frightening accuracy, she spent more time submerged in the water than she did on the platform, but she didn't mind at all. Adrienne was the type of leader who would do whatever it took to keep her students properly motivated.

She glanced at the watch that circled her wrist as she made her way down the halls, stopping every once in a while to greet students. The halls were buzzing with the chatter of teenagers beelining to their lockers while talking to their friends. Other students were solitary, wandering the halls, looking down at their phones with the cord attached to white earbuds snaking up their torsos. At the art room, she stopped to talk to Mr. Lorraine, a rail-thin man with a shock of red hair and a manicured goatee. He wore an apron over a pair of worn corduroy pants and a button-down shirt with the sleeves neatly folded to his elbows.

"We're almost to midterms. How's it going?"

"Good," he confirmed. "But there is one student I'm concerned about. Do you have a minute?" He walked her into his classroom, lowering his voice.

"Of course." He shut the door behind them for privacy and continued. "Maisy Duncan has several incompletes, and I talked to the other faculty members and discovered she's been performing the same way in their classes."

"And I am assuming this is a new pattern of behavior?"

"Yep." He explained, "She's normally very conscientious about completing her assignments in Art, but during the last month, she's been checked out. It's like she's just going through the motions."

Adrienne nodded. "I appreciate how plugged in you are with our students, Graham." She thought for a minute. "Is anything happening at home?"

"Not that she's openly speaking about."

"Are there any other warning signs?"

"Other than her drastic change in appearance, but to be honest, you could say that about any art student. Their body is their canvas."

"True story. We have to be detectives most of the time. What's changed about her look?"

"Darker mostly, cruising toward gothic punk, which isn't alarming on its own, but basic grooming has taken a hit. It's just a feeling I have."

He walked over and tugged open a large horizontal drawer that contained her limited portfolio. "There's definite dark themes in the few assignments she's chosen to hand in." He pulled out two pieces, both self-portraits depicting beautifully executed pain. In one, her mouth was covered by a metal gag with a padlock dangling from it. In the other, horizontal lines covered her skin and her mouth was open in a scream.

"Whoa," Adrienne said. The sheer agony of the pieces rendered her speechless.

"It's probably nothing," Graham began. "She's like most teenagers, trying to find her own voice and thinking she has to shock us to do it."

"But it *might* be something," Adrienne admitted as she studied the art. "Could you give her an assignment to depict joy or love instead, even if it is just a palette cleanser to placate us?"

He grimaced. "I can try, but I think she's putting a premium on feelings of angst at the moment."

"Are you concerned about her safety?"

"No."

"Are there any other mitigating factors?"

"No unexplained marks that I can see. Maisy is bright and talented, but handicapped by the anxiety that plagues this generation." He shook his head.

"Your intuition is usually spot on, and I trust your judgment," Adrienne praised. "I will pull her in for a chat today during her free period."

"I think it's a good idea," Graham said.

"Thanks for keeping me informed about Maisy. By

the way, I brought your favorite muffins." Her voice adopted a warm sing-song tone. "They are in the teacher's lounge."

"Better grab one before they're all gone." He smirked and they left the art room together.

She continued down the hallway, stopping to check in with other teachers in the west wing of the building until the bell rang, signaling the beginning of first period. Back in her office, she settled into her chair and began to plan the upcoming teacher development day. It was a day to assess what was working and chart a plan for greater success in their school, and she was eager to brainstorm with her staff. Teacher in-service days gave them valuable time together, and she typed out a loose itinerary in an email and sent it to Dory to send to the rest of the faculty.

An hour later, she was pulled into a meeting with the athletic director to discuss the academic eligibility policy and changes to the activities handbook. By lunch time, her stomach was growling as she made her rounds in the cafeteria. Budget cuts meant she often had to wipe a table or sweep up after the students, menial tasks she never minded and the reason she was still rocking her Converse until the end of the school day.

In the late afternoon, the school counselor, Rebecca White, entered her office with Maisy and closed the door behind them.

"Please come in and have a seat." She offered them both a warm smile. A hesitant Maisy glanced at her and then looked away. "You're not in trouble." The statement allowed Maisy's shoulders to relax, and she folded one leg on top of the other and swung it up and down.

"I wanted to pull you for a chat, Maisy. Your teachers are concerned about you and asked me to speak with you about some recent observations they've had."

"Okay?" Her tone shifted to wary and she tapped her foot even faster. It was becoming clear that the walls Maisy had built around herself were a fortress of self-protection that would not be easily dismantled.

"You've been a great student here at Aura Cove High School for the last two years, but recently, there has been a run of incomplete assignments. Your teachers have voiced their concerns about your lack of focus in the classroom. Can you give me some insight into why this is happening and what has changed? We want to rally around you and find the best way to support your success."

A long, drawn-out silence lingered. Seeing the dark circles under her eyes, Adrienne asked, "Are you getting enough sleep at night?"

"Does any teenager?" Maisy asked, thrusting her thumb into her mouth and ravenously chewing at the nail bed.

"That's valid." Adrienne grinned, trying to win her over. Her expression was stoney, and Adrienne knew she had to dig deeper. "I really want to help you, Maisy."

"I'm bored. High school just seems like such an arbitrary waste of time."

"I remember feeling the same way when I was a sophomore. If it wasn't on the pages of a fashion magazine, I wasn't interested."

"You?" She scoffed at the idea of her principal pouring over "Vogue."

"Yeah, me!" Adrienne grinned. "I bet you'll never believe I wanted to be a model when I was your age! I had big dreams of walking the runway in Milan and Paris. Thought I was going to be the next Christy Turlington."

"Who's Christy Turlington?"

Adrienne chuckled, realizing she'd aged herself with the reference. "One of the first supermodels."

"That seems pretty sketchy, Ms. T." She wrinkled her nose. "No offense."

"None taken," Adrienne admitted. "My point is that you only need to find the one thing that lights you up inside." She turned to the counselor. "Mrs. White, what was your one thing?"

"Helping people." In the chair, Maisy tried to conceal her annoyed eye roll, but Adrienne caught it anyway.

"You have to say that. You're a counselor," Maisy argued with Mrs. White. Then, directing her teenage venom at Adrienne, waving her hand behind her, she indicated the office. "If fashion was your one thing, I'd say you settled."

"Hmm." Adrienne considered her brash statement. "I can see why you'd say that." Her skin was thickened from years of working with at-risk youth, so the criticism slid off her like she was made of Teflon. Usually, their barbs were weak attempts to get a rise from a person in authority. Settling back into her chair, she explained, "Fashion became a hobby and an artistic form of self-expression, which I think you might know a thing or two about."

Maisy's current look featured a black spiked choker and corset dress that contrasted against the elaborate henna designs covering her wrists and forearms. A silver ball piercing in the middle of the dimple in her cheek winked when the overhead light kissed it.

"I know our upcoming production of *Alice in Wonderland* could use your makeup and set painting skills. Would you think about participating?"

Maisy shrugged, brightening up only slightly at the compliment.

"There is also a pilot program at Central Florida Community College that would give you college credit. It's in the fashion and textiles program."

"Would it get me out of here?"

"For a few hours a week at least," Adrienne answered. "Man, I wish these types of programs were available when I was in high school. I would have jumped at the chance."

Maisy sniffed. "I didn't say no."

"You have to submit a portfolio and maintain a B average to qualify," Adrienne said, dangling the prize. "You're brilliant. You could plot a course now to meet with your teachers and dig yourself out of this hole you've made." She paused then continued, "It would take some work, but you can do it. I'd even write you a letter of recommendation once you've completed your missing assignments."

Maisy's wary eyes slid to meet Adrienne's before a tiny grin threatened to breach the scowl on her face. "Why is it so hard to say no to you, Ms. T?"

Adrienne flashed her a triumphant grin. The rush of purpose she always felt when she connected with a student who was in jeopardy filled her with giddy joy. "Good." She stood. "Meet with your teachers, and I'll check in with you in a few days." Walking her to the door, Adrienne added, "Mrs. Miller will give you a hall pass."

Back in the room, Mrs. White said, "Well, that went better than I thought it would. What a great opportunity! Do you think she'll take it?"

"She's certainly capable of turning this around, but is she willing to do the work?" Adrienne thought for a moment and then shrugged. After a couple of decades in education, she'd learned not to get her hopes up too high. "Time will tell. All we can do is plant the seed. It's the student's job to tend the garden and prepare for harvest."

Later that evening, she slipped on her heels, buttoned her jacket, and strode into the school board meeting. The room was buzzing with tension as the board members filed in, each taking their seat at a large conference table. Above them, a banner that spanned the wall read, "Aura Cove Community School District. Nurturing Tomorrow's Leaders since 1986." A projector screen displayed the meeting agenda, casting soft light across the room, while the board members sorted through a stack of documents, exchanging furtive glances and occasionally jotting down notes. Behind a podium, a closed circuit camera recorded the session and streamed it on the school's YouTube channel. The meeting was quickly called to order by the current Superintendent, Dr. Charles McGrath. Dressed in an olive-colored suit, he tapped the gavel on the podium to quiet the room before speaking. In the following silence, the shuffling of papers and creaking of chairs underscored the seriousness of the meeting.

"Esteemed colleagues and parents." His voice projected authority as he continued. "Tonight's meeting is crucial in determining the future success of our school district. It's time for me to step down and hand the mantle over to the next generation. During my time as your leader, I've tried to lead by example and put the needs of the Aura Cove Community School District, its parents, and our students first. I am proud of the work we have accomplished together and look forward to placing the helm of this vibrant organization into the hands of its next capable leader. I'll now open the floor for nominations."

A stern-looking woman seated at the head of the table raised her hand. "I'd like to nominate Principal Adrienne Thorne."

"Ms. Thorne, do you accept this nomination?"

Adrienne stood tall and proud as murmurs of agreement filled the room.

"I would be honored to be the next Superintendent of Aura Cove Schools."

"Are there any other nominations?"

The room fell silent.

"I nominate Dr. Douglas Randall," a small voice said from the other end of the table.

Adrienne's heart dropped. She'd been one semester away from her doctorate when she was offered the principalship at Aura Cove High School. The new position came with a punishing learning curve so she'd put her plans to graduate on hold. Now, it looked like that decision was the one thing standing in her way of stepping into a role she never dreamed she'd be offered.

"Let's open the floor for discussion," Dr. McGrath offered.

Adrienne barely heard a word as Dr. Randall's praises were itemized and accounted for passionately over the next ten minutes. Next, her champion addressed the board members. "I've witnessed firsthand the positive changes Principal Throne has brought to Aura Cove High School. She's innovative and truly cares about the success of every student. She is a collaborative communicator with a proven track record of success. Look at how our test scores have skyrocketed in the last seven years alone!"

Murmurs of agreement from the parents in attendance intensified, and Adrienne glanced behind her shoulder, flashing a smile to her crowd of supporters. In attendance were every member of the current faculty at

Aura Cove High School, and their support shored up her desire for the appointment.

"Now let's hear from the nominees. I'd like to invite Ms. Thorne to the podium first."

Adrienne stood and tugged on the bottom of her jacket before striding confidently to the podium. She adjusted the microphone and spoke in a powerful voice.

"Thank you, Dr. McGrath and members of the school board, for giving me this opportunity to address you today.

Over the last seven years, I have witnessed the incredible dedication and passion that our educators, staff, and students bring to our schools. I stand before you today, not just as a principal but as someone deeply invested in the success of every student in the Aura Cove Community School District."

She paused long enough to catch her breath and offered a relaxed smile as she made her promises. "As your next superintendent, I vow to be a unifying force. I will work tirelessly to ensure that our district is a place where everyone feels heard, valued, and empowered.

"My vision for our schools revolves around creating an inclusive and diverse environment that nurtures each student's academic success and personal growth. I am committed to fostering innovation in teaching methods, embracing technology, and adapting our curriculum to prepare our students for the challenges of the future. At the same time, I promise to efficiently allocate resources to ensure our budget reflects our vibrant community's priorities."

She paused and then addressed the elephant in the room. "Though I have not achieved the same academic heights as the other nominee, I believe I am the better choice. What I lack in pedigree, I make up for with passion. I bring a deep understanding of the unique challenges our district faces. I am not just familiar with the strengths and opportunities that exist within our schools, but am also attuned to the areas that require strategic attention and improvement. Thank you for your consideration."

She was stunned as the room burst into applause behind her when she finished speaking. As the noise died down, she pivoted to take her seat. Adrienne exhaled a warm breath. She'd done her best to convince them. If this was the next challenge life was presenting her, she was ready to step up to meet it. She waited as Dr. Douglas Randall made his way to the podium and struggled to clearly define his wins as Vice Principal of Aura Cove Middle School. Yes, he was a respected doctor and educator, but she had the better track record. He rambled out a dry, emotionless speech that lasted far too long and was greeted by tepid applause.

"Thank you, Douglas." Dr. McGrath waited until he reached his seat. "Now that we've heard from all interested parties, I would like to call for a vote. All in favor of appointing Principal Adrienne Thorne as the next Superintendent of Aura Cove Schools, please raise your hands."

Hands shot up around the table. Six out of seven members voted yes and the sea of support overwhelmed

Adrienne as she stepped forward to accept the appointment to thunderous applause. The vote was such a landslide that he didn't even call a vote for the other candidate. Dr. McGrath banged the gavel on the podium.

"Congratulations, Ms. Thorne. We will begin the transition process, and you will take office at the first of the year. Meeting adjourned." As the crowd got to their feet and streamed toward the exits, he handed the well-worn gavel over to her with a congratulatory smile. Leaning in, he lowered his voice. "You were the right choice. It brings me great joy to know that the Aura Cove Community School District is in such good hands."

Adrienne floated to her car slowly, constantly stopping to receive congratulations from parents and teachers and especially her staff. It would be bittersweet to step away from her day-to-day involvement at Aura Cove High School, but she was thrilled to tackle a new set of challenges as Superintendent of the Aura Cove School District. As she drove home, she was flooded with gratitude at the path her life had taken, marveling at the way the universe worked. It might not have been the path she'd wanted when she was fifteen, but this one felt right.

EIGHT
1989

Adrienne walked through the mall with the carefree exuberance of a fifteen-year-old. It was her favorite hangout and an easy bus ride from school, and more often than not, she found herself lured there by the glamorous painted ladies at the makeup counters dressed in the latest fashion.

In the public bathroom, she'd ditched her boring school uniform for an off-the-shoulder, body-conscious, coral-colored dress and black lace fingerless gloves. Pulling out the makeup she wasn't allowed to wear at home, she swiped glittery eye shadow on her eyelids and pouted to outline her lips with a coral-tinted shimmery gloss. Feeling more like herself and ready to cut loose, she slung her backpack over her shoulder and strolled out into the main mezzanine of the Tampa Bay Mall.

Her yellow Sony Walkman spun the latest Wham! CD, and she hummed along to "Wake Me Up Before

You Go-Go" as she meandered toward the food court. Having worn out the smash hit by listening to it on repeat, she knew every word by heart. She be-bopped through the mall, letting the chorus take her away, crooning in concert with George Michael.

Adrienne was standing in line at the Orange Julius when she felt a tap on her shoulder. She turned around and pulled off her headphones, letting them rest encircling her neck. Her brow knit up as she surveyed the man behind her with wary interest.

"I bet you hear this all the time, but you could be a model," he said behind neon green and black wraparound sunglasses.

"Really?" Adrienne smiled at the compliment that destroyed her defenses.

"Truly."

He pushed the sunglasses on top of his dark wavy hair that was cut in a shaggy mullet. Dressed head-to-toe in black, she guessed he was almost thirty. The dark hair of his mustache twitched as he pulled a business card from an inside pocket of his jacket and offered it to her.

She took it and read the information on the card, and a thrill tingled through her belly.

Chroma Vogue Studio
Denny S. Kincaid
Fashion Photographer

An appraising gaze from his piercing blue eyes

flicked down her long legs. "You have the height and bone structure, but I won't be able to really tell until we get you under the lights and do a few test shots. I've been working with some of the best agents in the biz." He rattled off names that Adrienne didn't recognize, but she nodded like she did anyway. "Have a look." He opened a black leather portfolio and started flipping through the acetate pages. "This could be you one day." He pointed to a photograph of the striking Iman in black satin and gold cuff bracelets. When he pulled out a tattered copy of *Harper's Bazaar* with the same photograph on the cover, Adrienne squealed with delight. "This was a cover I did for *Harper's* a few years ago," he declared with such bold confidence, Adrienne was sure he was the real deal. "I have connections throughout the industry. If you're interested, we could start with a photo shoot. If it goes well, I could set you up with a go-see."

"A go-see?"

"It's an informal meeting where you bring your portfolio to a modeling agency and meet the booking agents. If they like you, they will take some polaroids and refer you to designers." He leaned closer and lowered his voice into a warmer, conspiring tone. "Just six months ago, I scouted Jules Chamberlin at a mall like this one, and now look at her."

Adrienne's eyes widened in awe. Jules Chamberlin had just landed the cover of *Marie Claire* and was scooped up for a Maybelline Fresh Faced campaign.

"She's in Milan right now, and I'll see her next

month at Fashion Week. Jules is walking the runway with Linda Evangelista and Cindy Crawford and, at fourteen, is the youngest model I've discovered to date."

"Wow." Adrienne was amazed, daring to dream she would be next.

"If you don't mind me asking, how old are you?"

"I'm fifteen," Adrienne offered.

"Perfect! Most models get their big break around fifteen. This is your time! You can't afford to wait."

Adrienne felt the effervescent sensation of joy well up in her core. She longed for more, to leave behind her small life in Bradenton and step into a career in the fashion industry. To be able to live a jet-setting lifestyle while modeling designer clothes in front of the camera would be a dream come true.

"Can you come to the studio for a screen test?" he asked, licking his lips, and when she hesitated, he was quick to add, "I'd be happy to talk to your mother and father about this opportunity and address their concerns. I bet they will have some reservations."

At the mention of her mother, Adrienne's joy completely fizzled out. Her mother, Alice, would never allow her to be photographed. Adrienne had been an unplanned, surprise addition to an already broken family unit. The seven years between Adrienne and her sister, Davina, created a distance between them they'd never figured out how to bridge. The only thing that united them was a shared aversion to their mother's doomsday personality that seemed to intensify after their father left. Alice was an anxious woman who saw danger lurking around every corner.

It was a stifling dynamic that left Adrienne and her sister feeling suffocated as they grew up. Often, after her third glass of wine, Alice would drone on and on about worthy pursuits. According to her, fashion and makeup were dead-ends filled with uncertainty and would destine her for destitution. Instead, Alice counseled her daughters to chase the more stable pursuits of nursing, accounting, law, or education.

Alice was especially pleased when Davina followed her sage advice and made the announcement she was pre-law before she escaped to Stanford. The school was prestigious, but more importantly, it was as far away as Davina could physically be from her helicopter mother and still be in the continental United States.

Davina never looked back. She never came home, never called, and she left a hole in Adrienne's heart a mile wide. Though they'd never been as close as Adrienne wanted because of the age gap, the unbroken bond formed by siblings from shared childhood experiences bound them together. The day Davina packed her few worldly possessions into her hatchback and drove away was the first day Adrienne felt truly lonely. She was stuck at home, alone with her hovering mother.

Adrienne found solace in the library where she devoured fashion magazines. Swiping through their slick glossy pages filled with glamorous models, she imagined a bigger life. One that included beautiful clothing and travel to exotic locations far from the melted concrete and punishing humidity of summers in Tampa Bay. She was looking for any ticket out, and when she shot up almost six inches the summer after seventh grade, instead of studying, she practiced walking around the house with a book on her head while her mother was at work. She spent hours in front of the mirror, teaching herself to apply the makeup she kept hidden between her mattress and the wall.

The card she now grasped between her fingers was her ticket out, but after years of safety programming, her first instinct was to refuse. To subscribe to the same fear that kept her mother paralyzed.

"I don't think my mom will let me," she admitted sadly, attempting to hand the card back to him.

He gently pushed her hand away. "Why don't you keep it and see if you can figure something out? I believe you have that star quality every agent is looking for, and I am never wrong."

His bold confidence in her shattered her fears. She always felt she was destined to fly when all Alice wanted to do was clip her wings and keep her grounded in the name of safety.

Adrienne tucked the card in her pocket. "I'll see what I can do."

That a stranger saw valuable qualities in her was a thrilling departure from her dull reality. Adrienne dreamed of the day she would be discovered, and now the golden ticket was in her pocket. As she watched him stride confidently away and disappear into the crowd, she had to fight the urge to punch her fist in the air in victory. When he turned the corner, she gave in to her excitement.

Floating on cloud nine, she pulled the card out again and gazed down at it. The thick cardstock felt legitimate in her inexperienced hand. In bold block letters, his phone number was printed at the bottom. This was the proof from the universe she'd been looking for. Instead of floating through life, this card was a solid vote for the future she'd been dreaming about. A model! She was going to be a model! She tucked it away into the hidden compartment in her wallet. She'd find a way. After all, when your destiny called, you needed to answer.

———

Two weeks later, she was hyperventilating in the dressing room of his downtown studio. At first, she'd been awestruck and speechless as he led her through the studio to the dressing room. Her backpack was slung over her shoulder, jammed full of makeup and an outfit she'd agonized over choosing with the tags still on. She took it all in, her gaze lingering on the stand where the camera waited as her eyes adjusted to the huge bank of soft lights in front of an infinity cove. In movies and on television shows, fashion sets were portrayed as teeming with people, from the designers to the photographers and their technical assistants. Her first niggle of doubt crept in when she realized they were alone. The distinct absence of noise made her insecurities well up, and she struggled to silence them.

Adrienne busied herself and set down her backpack in the dressing room. Her heart dropped when she got a glimpse of the garment rack pushed against the wall. It was filled with hangers draped with lingerie and bathing suits. The hangers screeched in protest as she rifled through the options one by one embarrassed at the minuscule strips of fabric that composed them.

A soft knock at the door startled her and she heard Denny's voice through it. "Is everything okay in there?"

She opened the door a crack and peeked out. "Um…" She wasn't sure how to voice her discomfort without sounding like a petulant child.

"I thought you might be thirsty. Here's a Coke." He passed a glass filled with brown liquid to her hand. "If you're nervous, I can add a little Jack to help loosen you up."

"Jack?"

"Jack Daniels." He pressed a finger to his lips. "It will be our little secret. Jules needed a nip for encouragement, too. It's perfectly natural to feel self-conscious your first time on set."

Relieved she wasn't alone, she quickly agreed and opened the door further. "I guess if it worked for Jules, I'll give it a try." He pulled a flask from his pocket and tipped a little of it into the fizzy drink. When she took a sip, she wasn't prepared for the bite of the liquor, but a few minutes later when she felt her hard edges soften, her limbs lengthen, and her fists unclench, she was grateful she'd decided to take him up on his offer.

"Why don't you pick out what you'll be most comfortable in and we'll get started whenever you're ready." His voice was infused with calm professionalism. "Heels too."

"Okay," she agreed and shut the door behind him. Scanning the options, she picked out a tiny bikini, tying the Day-Glo pink strings behind her neck. She'd developed early and easily filled out the top, and her hips curved in ways that belied her fifteen years. Pulling on a pair of white stilettos that pinched her toes, she teetered out into the studio where Denny was testing the flashes. Unsure where to put her hands and feeling exposed, she hugged her arms to her chest.

"You look sensational in person. Let's see how it translates on film. Stand here." He turned on music and demonstrated a gentle sway. "Just move your body to it. Do what feels natural."

None of this feels natural, she thought as she fought through her fears.

This is your ticket out of Bradenton and out from under your mother's thumb. Even Davina will have to pay more attention to you when you're walking the runways.

Quelling the fear that threatened to destroy her big break, she closed her eyes and began to rock to the beat, letting the music transport her. She felt warmth flood through her as she threw her shoulders back and then clamped one hand on her hip and rolled it seductively toward the camera like she'd practiced a million times in the bathroom she shared with her mother. Behind her closed eyelids, the flashes registered.

"Great work," he praised as another string of flashes popped, and she felt her inhibitions weakening. "Now, let's try a few with your eyes open." Then, with a slight grin, he gave her directions. "Stare down the lens of the camera." She followed his instructions to the letter as a series of flashes burst in quick succession. "Uh-huh, hmm. That's good. Give me more." The positive reinforcement of his murmured approval emboldened her further. She rocked her body forward and then turned away from him, cranking her head over her shoulder with a playful expression she'd spent hours practicing in the full-length mirror at home.

"That's it," he encouraged, and she felt the last of her fears melt away. The fear and anxiety that were forever present in her mind flitted out the window thanks to a few kind words from a stranger and the power of her new friend Jack. She felt warm and pliable like she was made of taffy.

"Outfit change," he declared, resting the camera on his thigh. "Let's try something from the lingerie options in the dressing room."

Adrienne gulped and her palms moistened.

"There is nothing to worry about, sweetheart. I am a professional. When I look at you, it's about the art and the connection with the camera. I am trying to pull the greatness I see in you out for the world to see."

She felt her cheeks flush warm but nodded anyway.

"I can tell you're nervous, but I'd really like to see you push past it. When you are in Paris at the House of Gadot, modeling lingerie on the runway, this will be an everyday occurrence. I am giving you the perfect opportunity to get your jitters out before your career blows up."

"Okay," she conceded. It made sense, and she was determined to acquire the skills she would need as a professional model.

He walked over to the bar cart and emptied another Coke into a clean glass then held it up for her. "Maybe another visit from our friend Jack would help?"

"Yes," she agreed and was grateful when he put the drink in her hand. This time, she didn't have to fight to swallow it. She welcomed the bitterness, knowing it would help her relax. *Just this once. Next time, it won't be so difficult.*

"Choose whatever lingerie you wish from the wardrobe cart and come out when you're ready."

Adrienne walked back into the tiny changing room and sorted through her options. She pulled a black lace teddy from the rack, based solely on the fact it had the most fabric of the choices in front of her. The discovery it was entirely see-through when she put it on sent initial shivers through her. To combat them, she picked up the glass and guzzled the remains of the drink. A few minutes later, she felt her thoughts slow down and the sensation of ease increase. She tugged the strap of the teddy over her shoulder. It was cut so high on her hip, her legs seemingly stretched on forever. Gazing at her reflection in the mirror after she'd added a lush red lipstick, she had to admit the transformation was stunning. A full-blown woman reflected back at her, and she forced herself to align mentally with this new version of herself.

Adrienne rooted through the available shoes, then pulled a pair of black sky-high heels from the bottom of the wardrobe rack and stepped into them. Then she opened the door and strode out into the studio where Denny's eyes lit up when they landed on her.

"Is this okay?" she asked shyly.

"Perfect choice. It really shows off your legs." He directed her in front of the bank of soft lights, and she felt the awkwardness dissipate. She moved more confidently now, thrusting her hips from side to side and laughing into the rafters. She welcomed the ease as her confidence soared.

"Gorgeous!" He coached her from ten feet away. "You're incredible!" The compliments shored up her resources, and she started to enjoy the experience.

"Drop the strap," he directed. "Now give me that drop-dead gorgeous look. Yes!" The lights snapped in rapid succession as Adrienne felt herself channeling power from within. Her expression changed rapidly from flash to flash. One moment, she was doe-eyed and innocent, the next, she was a playful vixen, and the next, she was a sultry vamp as she bit her bottom lip. Encouraged by his admiration, she continued to prance and twirl and laugh for the camera.

He lowered the light and walked closer until she

could feel his breath on her face. He reached up to smooth a wayward hair from her cheek. "Baby, you are beautiful. I think once the art directors see these test shots, there is going to be a bidding war to see who will represent you. Pack your bags because you are going places!"

"Really?" She felt a giddy effervescent thrill rush through her.

"I wouldn't lie to you." He tipped his chin to the side and studied her, hemming and hawing for a minute before deciding to speak. "I have a contract with a jewelry designer, but they have a special request. I'm not sure if you are up for it." He dangled the assignment like an irresistible carrot, and she was too inexperienced to understand it was poisoned. "It's a skin campaign. They want the jewelry to be the focus."

Her brow wrinkled, not quite following him.

"It would require you to be au natural."

"Naked?" She gasped.

"Yes. Wearing just this." He walked over to where a black velvet case held strings of black pearls. Layered in an array of sizes, it created a scarf effect when he pulled it from the case and held it up in the light.

She tentatively took the pearls from him and held the strings up to her chest. A couple of strands grazed her nipples, and the cold pearls raised gooseflesh on her arms. She reasoned her initial discomfort away, looking down at her lace-covered torso. "I guess I wouldn't be much more exposed than I am right now in this lingerie."

"Exactly." Denny grinned.

"Okay," she heard herself agree from farther away. She tried to fasten the clasp of the pearls around her neck and couldn't make her fingers work. Noticing her struggle and ever the gentleman, Denny pulled them from her hands.

"Need a little help?" he asked, his voice stretching long and languid. A few seconds later, she felt his warm fingers brush her neck, a not altogether unpleasant sensation. He took her hand and tugged her gently to the set where a soft fur rug was spread on the ground. She stumbled and laughed when he caught her in his arms.

"Can you step out of the lingerie?" she heard him ask, and her fingers, feeling thick and rubberized, tugged at the straps ineffectively.

"Need more help?"

She nodded and giggled again as a floating sensation disconnected her from her body.

"After these get out, baby, you can write your own check. Paris, Milan, New York? They will all start calling."

She let out a fluttery breath and followed the rest of his directions for the next several minutes. On her knees, she sank deeply into the thick fur rug on the floor. Then she fell down onto her bottom and her eyes grew heavy. All the while, the flashes kept popping. The last sound she remembered was the popcorn sound of pearls bouncing on the hard floor around her and the hum of something she couldn't identify.

"I'm sorry," she mumbled as the pearls rolled away to the darkened corners of the room.

"Nothing to worry about. You be a good girl and take a nap. I'll make sure you get back on the bus after you're rested."

She felt fingers brush her skin and fought the heaviness of her eyelids. The hairs on the back of her neck stood up and her fight or flight instincts kicked in, but the liquor dulled her mind and the heaviness overtook her. She closed her eyes, having no choice but to give in to sleep.

NINE

At her beach house in Aura Cove, Katie was rushing around looking for a missing sandal. She was running late for her weekly dinner date with Frankie. "Dammit, Arlo." She muttered, irritated as she got down on her knees and yanked up the comforter to discover her chewed-up shoe mingling with the dust bunnies underneath her bed. Using a hanger, she'd just fished it out from its hiding place and held it up when the doorbell rang.

Katie let out an exasperated sigh, brushed the dust from her hands, and got to her feet when the bell rang again. Hustling to the front door, she yanked it open to reveal a man she didn't recognize standing there.

"Katie? You're a sight for sore eyes." Looking relieved, he ran a hand through his curly, caramel-colored hair that was laced with strands of white at the temples. He lurched forward and tried to pull her into his arms.

"Whoa, dude," she said, blocking him with her hands and sidestepping the awkward advance by the eager stranger. "Have we met?" A sensation of Déjà vu welled up that left her disjointed and unsettled.

"It's me," he said, his warm toffee-colored eyes beseeching her confused green ones as he glanced behind her into the house. "Is anyone else home?"

"I'm not answering that question, weirdo. Back up and give me some space or I'll have to call the police."

Desperate to connect with her, he added, "It's me… Arlo." His gaze locked on hers, and she felt something click internally.

"No way," she said, astonished, stumbling back a step as her hand flew to her mouth. The man in front of her was claiming to be her former rescue dog. The dog she'd adored for years and then discovered he'd been planted by Zoya to spy on her during her awakening.

"It is." He rushed forward again, attempting to grasp her hands in his. Her eyes widened and she tucked her hands behind her hips, afraid to touch him.

"Prove it," she dared.

"Your best friend is Frankie, and you have three children—Beckett, Lauren, and Callie." He rattled off their names in quick succession.

"Anyone can find that information on social media."

He scrubbed his scruffy jawline with his fingernails, considering his next move, then snapped his fingers. "You're the third generation witch in a supernatural lineage and only discovered you have powers on your fiftieth birthday."

Stunned, her jaw dropped open. When she recovered, she yanked him inside her home. "Shhh! Someone could overhear you!"

Once inside the house, he closed his eyes and deeply inhaled as a soft smile tugged at the corners of his lips. "God, I missed this place." He opened his eyes. "But I missed you most."

"Save it." Katie's anger reared up. Her eyes flashed at him, darkened by the frustration she felt.

"You have every reason to be angry with me. I should have told you Callie was pregnant. I'm so sorry."

Gob smacked by his obvious mistake, Katie shook her head in utter confusion. "What? Callie's pregnant? No." She dismissed the comment instantly.

"Oh no," he cried, stunned that he'd dropped the ball again. "You didn't know."

"No. You've got it all wrong. It's not Callie who's pregnant; it's *Lauren*." She quickly tried to set him straight. This time, it was *his* brow that knit up in confusion and *his* chin that jutted back in disbelief.

"What? Lauren is pregnant, too?" He paced the length of the great room, mumbling to himself as he tried to come to grips with the news.

"You better start talking," Katie warned him as she fired off a text to Frankie to reschedule their dinner.

"Shortly after the Autumnal Equinox Ball, Callie popped in for a visit, and I detected a distinct change in her pheromones. I believed revealing her pregnancy was my only chance to earn my freedom from Zoya," he explained as he paced the floor in front of the island, stopping every few feet to wring his hands. "You know how desperate I was to return to human form, and how she'd dangled it in front of me, only to take it away. It was the only secret I knew she wouldn't be able to resist."

"Callie?!" Katie was awestruck. "I can't believe it."

"Yeah." Arlo whistled under his breath. "Wow." He scrubbed his hands over his face in shock as he took a seat. "I'm certain I would have detected it in Lauren, too, but she doesn't visit as frequently."

"Are you *absolutely* sure?" Katie asked, still trying to wrap her head around the fact she had two grandchildren on the way instead of one. The concept made a nervous belly laugh bubble to the surface. Astonished by her reaction, she clamped both her hands over her mouth as joy fizzed through her.

"Yes. I am sure. Congratulations on becoming a Gigi twice in record succession." He offered a quick smile, then shifted to an apology. "I should have come to you first like I promised before I used the information to gain my freedom, and for that, I am truly remorseful." Her focus shifted back toward his transgressions.

"You made a promise and you broke it." After a long pause, she added, "Again."

"W-wait," he stuttered. "I can explain."

"I'm done with your explanations," she said in admonishment. "Do you remember what I told you last time?"

He nodded sadly, remembering the conversation by

heart, "You said, 'I'll give you a second chance, but you won't get a third.'"

"Exactly."

"But we're soulmates," he cried, scrambling to find the right words to connect with her.

"Soulmates don't lie to each other."

"Katie, please." He reached out and tugged at her arm, begging her with his eyes.

"Take your hands off me," she spat at him, and when his cheeks flushed red with embarrassment, she felt guilt well up inside her gut.

"I'm sorry." He backed up to give her space. "For all of it. But you have to understand, I wanted the opportunity to be with you on a level playing field. I wasn't content to just be your dog. I wanted to know you as a man."

"There were other ways to go about it. You, of all people, know how important trust is to me after what happened with Jeff."

He hung his head and sighed. "You're right. I do."

Katie walked over to her wine chiller and pulled out a bottle of wine. Taking her frustration out on the corkscrew, she twisted it with extreme angst. The popping noise when she uncorked it was the only sound that breached the silence followed by the *glug-glug-glug* of her pouring it into her glass.

"I could use one of those," Arlo muttered, trying to lighten the mood.

"Now you're really pushing your luck!" Katie snorted in outrage. "I should serve it to you in your dog dish." She drained her glass, refilled it, and then reluctantly returned to the cabinet to pull out another wine glass that she filled and then slid over to Arlo with her fingers.

"Thank you," he whispered after a long, awkward pause.

"This is so wild." Katie felt her anger start to diminish with the wine. "I am sitting in my kitchen... enjoying a nice glass of chardonnay... with my *dog...*" she chuckled at the ridiculousness of it as her smirk became a snicker,"...who thinks he's my soulmate." She pressed her lips together to hold in the raspy giggle lodged deep in the back of her throat. Her mirth at the bizarre situation kept bubbling up as Arlo took a sip of the wine, unamused.

The absurdity of it finally hit her full force, and her shoulders started to heave with the effort of repressing her laughter. The harder she tried to hold it in, the more she tittered and snorted, which only made her laugh harder. Crossing her legs and squeezing her pelvic muscles to prevent a leak, she dissolved into a heap of crazed giggles in front of him. The unhinged reaction made Arlo's eyes widen, unsure how to navigate this shift in her. Katie laughed until she cried. Then she wiped the tears from her eyes and propped her chin up with her hands as her gaze leveled back on Arlo.

Letting out an exasperated breath, she offered him the smallest concession, "The first thing that has to go is the name."

It was a baby step, and Arlo took it as a good sign.

"Agreed. I was thinking Loran. Kind of an homage to becoming a new Arlo."

"Nope." Katie dismissed it immediately. "Loran and Lauren? Too close for comfort." She burst into giggles again, now on her third glass, feeling the warmth from the alcohol hitting her senses.

"That's fair." Arlo nodded, then said, "How about Roland? It has all the letters."

"Declined. Roland is a middle management dolt who still lives with his mother. I can't call you that. Quit trying so hard to be clever."

"You pick it then," he offered, trying to be accommodating.

She eyed his shaggy hair and tanned skin. "You have a middle-aged surfer vibe. Bohdi? No. That's not it." She cocked her head to the side, studying the smattering of freckles meandering their way across his cheeks and nose. Her eyes locked on his, and she leaned closer, examining the starbursts of gold and green surrounding his black pupils. Katie felt a trickle of warmth bloom in her center and fought against it.

She remembered the last time she spoke to him when she asked how she'd recognize him when he returned. "You'll know when warmth floods your heart and it feels like Déjà vu." Against her will, the warmth was there. Although she couldn't fully give in to it, she felt her resolve soften.

"How about Brody?" she suggested.

"Brody," he repeated, the corners of his lips twitching up in a small smile. "I like it." He reached out to touch her but stopped himself just short to honor her desire for boundaries. "Mostly because you gave it to me." He paused, then asked the question he needed to ask, "Does this mean you're open to getting to know me?"

"Perhaps." She drained the last of the wine from her glass, adding, "But only as a friend."

He opened his mouth to speak, then decided against it. Katie saw the tendon in his jaw tighten.

"Take it or leave it." She offered her hand to him to shake, And when he pressed his warm palm to hers, it felt oddly familiar and eerily comforting.

"I'll take it. If that is the only way I can be in your life right now, it's a good place to start."

"It is," she agreed and stood, gathering their glasses to wash in the sink.

He pulled out his new cell phone. "Can I have your number so I can message you?"

"Sure," Katie said, rattling off the digits as she plunged the glasses in warm, soapy water.

After he left, she tapped his message and added him to her contacts as Brody. Another frizzle of laughter at the ridiculousness of the situation overwhelmed her. "Gosh, this magical world never disappoints."

TEN

After school, Maisy punched the code into the keypad at the garage door to let herself inside her darkened home. She flopped her messenger bag onto the first flat surface she could find and then bent down to unzip her black leather boots. Their rubber soles hit the floor, and she continued to leave a trail of her belongings as she walked through the great room to the kitchen in search of a snack.

A wall of windows that encompassed the entire back wall of the great room offered a spectacular view of the ocean, but Maisy was immune to its beauty. It had been the hard-won prize of her parents' contentious divorce. The modern design of the oceanside property lacked warmth but maintained the austere sterile appearance that her mother, Tricia, a surgical nurse, insisted on. She often worked sixteen-hour shifts or was on call, coming home well after midnight most nights, and Maisy had learned to fend for herself.

Maisy's stomach growled as she yanked open the refrigerator door to survey the contents inside. Each label was facing forward, a requirement Tricia gave the housekeeper during its weekly cleaning. Disregarding the full refrigerator of healthy snack options like apples and berries that had been washed and stored in color-coded Pyrex, she decided nothing was even remotely appealing. With a dramatic sigh, she slammed the door shut and continued her search for palatable offerings inside the cabinets. She finally decided on Ramen noodles again, as they required the least amount of effort.

She turned the gas burner on the Viking cooktop, and it crackled to life. She was briefly enchanted by the blue flame, a welcome respite from her racing thoughts. Maisy couldn't remember exactly when they began to speed up, but she thought it was somewhere around the time her parents divorced. It was as if her brain was overcompensating. Drowning out the viscous nightly arguments with a barrage of useless information and anxiety her brain created.

Maisy attempted to distract herself with music and art, and her earbuds became a permanent fixture in her ears. Nightly, the Ramones spooled out on repeat, keeping her company. She had recently developed a new love for Screamo, an angsty rebellious soundtrack that drowned out the loudest trains of thought.

She dumped the square of freeze-dried noodles into the boiling water, and after a few minutes, stirred to separate them. Her stomach growled again as she poured them into a bowl, added chili crisp and the seasoning packet, and headed toward her bedroom at the end of the hall.

Setting the bowl down, Maisy opened her nightstand and pulled out a lighter. With one roll of her thumb, a flame shot out of it, and she held it at the end of a stick of incense until the metal of the lighter was too hot to handle. A tendril of smoke wafted up, making lazy loops and smokey curves that dissolved into the fog of orange-scented cleaner the housekeeper used that afternoon.

Maisy flicked the Bic again, this time grabbing a stubby candle and tipping it to light the blackened wick, ignoring the sooty ring around the rim. She watched the flame crackle to life. Fire had become mesmerizing to her, and she had recently begun experimenting with it as an artistic medium, using it to burn the edges of her artwork. The flickering candlelight cast dancing shadows across the walls adorned with posters of her two favorite bands—Panic! At the Disco and The Banshees. As it was with any teenager, her bedroom was her sanctuary. It was a haven of darkness, with heavy blackout curtains in a deep shade of blood-red drawn together to shut out the outside world. The walls were midnight black, a color her overachieving mother hated but used as a reward to motivate her daughter to do better in school. The floor was covered with clothing in various dark shades, mostly black, and her punk accessories. It made it a challenge to cross her room without stepping on something sharp.

Nestled in a corner was her vintage desk. It was

cluttered with sketchbooks that spilled open, revealing intricate charcoal drawings and half-finished art projects scattered amidst a sea of pencils and tubes of dried paint. Balls of paper ringed her trashcan where she'd flung the rejects.

Tonight, however, her usual refuge felt empty, and a sense of restless unease gnawed at her insides. Turning on her computer, she delved into the digital abyss of social media, scrolling and scrolling on her phone while her favorite true crime YouTuber delved deep into his latest tale of horror on her laptop. Her eyes flicked back and forth from her phone to her computer several times before she let out a heavy sigh of utter frustration. Maisy was bored.

Looking for something to fill the hours, she decided to make some content for her TikTok. She turned on her ring light and pulled out her favorite makeup palette. In the chair, Maisy sat up taller and pressed the record button before she dabbed on pale foundation with a blender sponge. Next, she drew on sharp cat eyes with inky black eyeliner, her hand shaking from the Monster energy drink she'd guzzled on the way home. Surveying her results in the mirror, she smudged shimmery charcoal eyeliner under her lashes for a smokey eye. She pressed the red button to stop recording, pulled out a makeup wipe, and wiped it all off. Her face was red and irritated by the cleanser, but she grabbed the candle and pressed record again, holding the candle in the darkness under her chin. She was pleased to see the shadows swallow up her entire face, giving it a horror story vibe, and for the next several takes, she made exaggerated, screaming faces into the phone. She doubled down, really getting into it, contracting her neck to force the veins to surface in her throat. The result was edgy and raw, and when she was done recording, she swiped and pinched the footage together on the timeline, editing her series of video clips into sixty seconds of sheer madness. The music track she chose pulled the video together. When she posted it to her TikTok, the flood of approval in the form of likes, hearts, and glowing comments triggered the dopamine centers in her brain, and she felt a burst of joy thrum through her. One by one, strangers validated her skills and creative talents far more than her mother ever had.

There was a ding before a red dot on her inbox appeared. She slurped up a forkful of noodles and then tapped to open it, desperate for an interaction that would make her feel something. Anything. The world had become so dim and gray lately. Every day, a little of its luster wore off. Maisy was floating in a sea of apathy where nothing really mattered anymore. She was searching for a spark, a heady rush of adrenaline that would ignite the darkness surrounding her and set her soul on fire. Lately, she'd been stuck, engulfed by smoldering ash.

The loneliness was suffocating. It was a silent shadow that haunted her incessantly, yet a constant companion she'd come to rely on. When she'd first arrived at Aura Cove, she'd felt like an outsider. The privileged children of the uber-wealthy had an entitled energy and shiny glow created by a life of unfettered ease. Often, their biggest complaint in life was that they were being gifted a new Acura instead of a Range Rover.

Her mother was doing well financially but didn't subscribe to the same theory about giving children everything their hearts desired like most parents in the district did. In comparison to the kids at her school, she might as well have been on food stamps. She had nothing in common with any of them, leaving her to feel like an outsider looking in on an unfair world. The only way to accept it was to pretend she didn't care, to numb herself to it. Eventually, all that apathy became a dull ache that was an easier burden to carry than the anger and disconnection she felt.

She tapped on her inbox where a message from a user she didn't recognize named justapunk16 awaited. Opening the message, she felt a surge of excitement well up, a welcome departure from her usual numbness.

justapunk16: You are a dark goddess. That video? Flawless. What doing?

Maisy felt her stomach flip. She tapped on the profile where a photo of a crow was sketched.

macabremaze: your profile photo is stunning, Poe influence?
justapunk16: it's a charcoal I did last semester

before I dropped out… good eye… yeah…
definite fan here
macabremaze: of school?
justapunk16: nah
macabremaze: me neither…how old are you?
justapunk16: sixteen
macabremaze: me too…Not fair…You've seen
me, but I don't know what you look like
justapunk16: add me on snap? same name
macabremaze: K

Maisy hurried over to Snapchat, searched for the
username, and added it as a friend. While she waited for
a notification indicating she'd been accepted, she
drummed her fingers on the top of her sketchbook as her
room darkened and the day shifted into night. She
flipped the switch on the black light on her desk to make
the posters over her bed glow. They turned blue and
florescent green under the purple light.

Finally, a notification rolled in and she tapped on it,
letting out a squeal when she got her first glance. A
photo opened up of a dark-haired guy with a red-tipped
mohawk wearing a long black trench coat. His dark eyes
were soulful, and the smudged eyeliner he wore only
made him hotter.

justapunk16: thoughts?
macabremaze: you are a beautiful man
justapunk16: i think we belong together

macabremaze: meant to be… what do you do to pass the time in this ugly void

justapunk16: classic horror movies that make me question reality… finger picking on the guitar… and summoning spirits with the ouija board

macabremaze: those things freak me out

justapunk16: you just need a guide. your darkness is beautiful. it's what makes you special… send me a selfie that you've never sent to anyone else.

Maisy pursed her lips into a deep pout and sent one over, anxiously waiting for his approval.

justapunk16: you're enchanting…need more… embrace your shadows, sweetheart

Maisy felt her nerves tingle through her. The use of the word 'sweetheart' sent a shiver of pleasure down her spine. What was the harm? The photo would disappear automatically anyway.

She pulled off her shirt down to her black bra, tugged down one strap, and vamped for the camera. It took ten attempts before she had a photo that was hot enough to send. Quickly, she edited it on her phone, increasing the contrast and making her skin glow almost translucent and white. She overlaid the photo with text and added a series of seven black hearts.

justapunk16: we're 2 lost souls drifting in the same sea of despair… let me see all of you.
macabremaze: patience
justapunk16: not my strong suit
macabremaze: it'll be worth it
justapunk16: i have no doubt

Maisy felt joy fizz through her. It was a rush, like a roller coaster inching up to the top before the split-second of weightlessness when it went screaming back down.

macabremaze: tell me more about you
justapunk16: what do you want to know
macabremaze: everything

The next four hours passed in the blink of an eye as she exchanged texts with him. Each new message made her more giddy with excitement. At midnight, she heard the front door open followed by footfalls as her mother made her way down the hallway toward her bedroom. Maisy quickly jumped into her bed and slipped the phone under her covers, pretending to be asleep.

"Jesus." Her mom sighed as she walked to the desk to blow out the sputtering candle. "She's gonna burn the house down someday."

Maisy felt the phone vibrate in her hand again and she itched to respond. Every cell within her body lit up and fired sparks of happiness. She waited several agonizing minutes as her mother walked back down the hallway and shut the door to her own bedroom. There was the sound of water rushing through pipes as she used the bathroom and brushed her teeth, and when the silence finally dragged out as her mother settled in for the night, she pulled the phone back out.

> **justapunk16:** have you heard of the concept of twin flames
> **macabremaze:** no
> **justapunk16:** i have a feeling you could be mine… read up & message me tmr. Goodnight, goddess.
> **macabremaze:** night

Maisy hugged her phone to her chest as adrenaline rushed through her body. There was a beacon of light in the darkness now. He'd pierced the veil of blackness she hid behind and caught a glimpse of her, and he actually liked what he saw. Her body chemistry changed as the thrill of him fizzled and bubbled up inside her chest, fluttering like a horde of butterflies trapped within her ribcage. This might actually turn out to be something. A reason, and she'd needed a reason so badly.

ELEVEN

Later that week, Katie stood at the back door of Kandied Karma, ready to insert her key when she heard a giggle and a cackle from inside. Confused by the sound since she often opened the shop alone, she entered the kitchen to see Yuli and Talulah LaRue sitting on stools enjoying a cup of coffee together.

Katie arched an eyebrow toward Yuli, questioning the pairing, but Yuli just smirked back as if she were any normal visitor and not a famous clairvoyant who'd popped in for a visit.

"What an amazing surprise! It's great to see you again," Katie gushed. A little starstruck, Katie quickly joined them and offered an engaging smile, waiting for Talulah's violet eyes to meet hers. "Can I give you an update?"

"Please do," Talulah said, her eyes twinkling. "It's my favorite part."

"Well, after our reading, my mom and dad sorted through the collection of pennies Grandpa mentioned." Katie leaned closer, her words rushing out in excitement. "It seems one of the coins was incredibly rare, and when they took it to a coin shop, they discovered it was worth ten thousand dollars!"

"Wow." Talulah whistled through the gap in her teeth appreciatively. "You were right." She turned her head to address the space next to her as if someone was standing there. "I know. I won't," she muttered out of the side of her mouth, then turned back to Katie and Yuli. "I can't take credit for that discovery. It was all Otto. I was simply the messenger."

Yuli couldn't let her be so humble. "No. You have a pure gift."

"And so do you… *both* of you." Her eyes twinkled with electric understanding that stunned them both as she pointed back and forth between them.

Katie pressed her lips together to avoid blurting out a confirmation. Being outed made her fear rise up, even if the outing was only by the most gentle clairvoyant on the planet. Talulah took another sip of her coffee, resting her elbows on the marble countertop before she continued, asking Yuli, "But your daughter doesn't know, does she?"

"Know what?" Yuli asked innocently.

"That you're witches," she whispered. "The magic, the supernatural abilities, it's a bold feminine energy that swirls and gathers around the two of you, but not the others in your family. You're different. Beyond the veil, in the astral plane, I see you cloaked in golden sparkles and light."

Katie could see the gears turning in Yuli's head and was grateful the question was not directed at her. She patiently waited for Yuli to confirm or deny the allegations. Talulah turned away, her lips moving as she mumbled as if she was carrying on a conversation with someone next to her.

"Otto says there's no sense in arguing with me," Talulah said matter-of-factly as she leaned closer. "He says you can trust me."

"Is he there?" Katie asked in awe, shocked her grandfather was coming through again. "Standing next to you?"

"Standing isn't exactly the right word, but yes. He appeared at your mother's reading and never left."

Yuli reached out to touch the air next to Talulah. Closing her eyes, she tried to make contact with his spirit. "I wish I could feel him near like you do."

"I know." Talulah reached out to pat Yuli's hand, a comforting gesture that made Katie like her even more. Then she muttered again out of the corner of her mouth, "I know, I know! Give me a minute." She returned her gaze to Yuli and said, "Your third act is coming. Is there a big life change on your horizon?"

Katie felt Yuli's remaining walls disintegrate as she opened up to Talulah and nodded. "There will be an ending with a new beginning happening soon. I will be essentially starting over."

Talulah clapped her hands together. "How grand! Can I offer a bit of advice?"

"Certainly."

"Do it on your own terms," she suggested. "Supernatural gifts are so draining. It's a calling for sure, but it is not for the weak or weary. Find a place to start over that restores your spirit." She brushed back her thick, lavender-tinted hair and smiled. "It's why I have my treehouse in the Everglades. It's in the Ten Thousand Islands and hidden by a grove of Palmetto bushes and Kudzu. The treehouse is an introvert's absolute paradise." She sighed with pleasure at the thought of it and grinned at Yuli. It bestowed on her an aura of childlike innocence that made her radiate with joy. "Giving readings and working with people who've lost loved ones is rewarding, but it will all drain you dry if you let it. I have to escape there to keep my sanity."

"Sounds divine." Yuli considered her advice. "I might need to join you."

"Actually, we were hoping you'd say that!" Talulah grinned. "Chakra and I have become a little too feral, and I'm concerned we're one eccentric misstep away from being on the front of the tabloids."

"But I thought the Ten Thousand Islands were uninhabited. How did you end up there?" Katie asked.

"You're right," she confirmed with a wink. "Mostly. We travel by boat, and I live off the grid. A dear friend deeded me a family property years ago."

"Off the grid?" Yuli asked with a wince. "That's usually a pretty primitive setup, isn't it?"

"Solar power and battery back-up have come a long way, but there are simple sacrifices required, like proximity to a grocery store and access to a washer and dryer. I find the silence and peace it offers far outweigh any inconvenience."

"How long have you lived there?"

"I acquired the property in the eighties," Talulah answered, "but didn't move there full-time until ten years ago."

"All this time, you've lived there alone?"

Talulah reached down to scratch Chakra's furry chin, the dog preferring to gather at her feet. "We feel we are being nudged to a new beginning, too, don't we, girl?" Chakra's eyes narrowed into half-slits as she enjoyed the gentle nuzzling in one of her favorite spots. "I recently began construction on a small raised bungalow with fewer steps for Chakra and me since we're both old girls now," Talulah explained. "I always thought it would just be the two of us, but after the reading, Otto has been hounding me day and night. He has this idea in his head…" She chuckled at her own odd little metaphysical joke, "…I mean, his soul, that we'd be compatible roommates and he's suckered me into offering you an invitation. The man can be quite persuasive, as I am sure you know."

Yuli grinned, the action rewinding years off her face as it always softened when she thought about Otto.

"As we get older, I thought it might be nice to have someone to rely on. Someone who knows the signs of a stroke and how to call for a life-flight," Talulah added with a disarming grin. "Chakra here is the best roommate in every way, except for her lack of opposable thumbs." She scanned Yuli's face, trying to decipher her reaction. "I've been asking the universe to send me a sign, and a few weeks ago, Otto appeared, holding an actual sign, that said 'Roommate wanted.'" She laughed. "Men. They are such literal creatures."

"They are." Yuli nodded.

"Well, at any rate, think it over, and I'm sure Otto will let me know when you've made a decision." She stood to stretch. "I better skedaddle."

"How about some Tahitian vanilla caramels for the road?" Katie asked.

"I would adore some."

Long after she left Kandied Karma, taking a little of the magic with her, Katie found the words to broach the subject with Yuli.

"What do you think about her offer?"

"It's very generous," Yuli admitted. "Shrinking my world down was one of the most difficult parts of this transition for me. I am used to having a loud, funny bunch of people around. The idea of eating a chicken leg alone on Thanksgiving was depressing, but necessary, to keep our supernatural secrets intact. But now, I am being nudged toward a better option with a built-in support system. Maybe it's the next right place for me to go."

"I have to admit, I love the idea of you not being alone," Katie said. "It seems like you and Talulah are built from the same unconventional cloth."

"I would agree."

"And it seems like Grandpa is paving the way for you."

Yuli's eyes glistened with tears. "He always did consider it his highest responsibility to take care of me. That's how I know it's for the best. He never had a bad bone in his body." Yuli brightened at the idea. "I'll sleep on it, but it is looking like the Everglades could be my next home."

"Things are really going to change around here," Katie mused out loud. Sadness filled her at the prospect of the day-to-day contact with her grandmother ending.

"In some ways, yes, but in others, they will remain the same." Yuli told her, "You'll have to come to me."

"You never even considered living at the compound, did you?"

Yuli let out a chuckle. "I didn't realize I was that transparent."

"Will Zoya be disappointed?"

"Perhaps, but she'll get over it." She explained, "It's too extravagant. It will be a place we visit, but it's too enormous and opulent to consider home."

"What will you do with it?"

"I don't know. The right path will be revealed when the time is right." A crease appeared between her brows as she picked up on Katie's hesitation. "Don't worry, dear, there is far too much history there for it to not remain in the family. But perhaps it could be utilized in a better way. Let's noodle on it and figure it out later. There's no need to rush into a decision now."

The door swung open, and Yuli teased under her breath as Zoya rushed through it without knocking. "Well, speak of the she-devil and she appears."

Zoya took the reference as a compliment as she sailed into the kitchen, her black cloak sweeping into the room. "Darlings, my ears were *positively* burning. Did you mean to summon me?" Their amulets brightened into shining luminescent purple as she tugged off her gloves. She glanced from Yuli to Katie and back again. Narrowing her green eyes, her discerning gaze landed on Katie. "You." She took another step closer, sniffing the air. "I smell a secret."

The door whipped open again, and Frankie breezed in her eyes wide. "Did someone say secret?"

"Jeepers! It's like Grand Central Station here today!" Yuli remarked.

Katie gulped and cast her gaze down. She'd been sitting on the knowledge of Callie's pregnancy for days, waiting for her to make an announcement.

Zoya closed in, ready to suss it out, wagging her finger at Katie. "What are you hiding?"

Katie pressed her lips into a hard line, not wanting to break her daughter's confidence. She knew, however, that she needed the matriarchs of the mortal coven to know the transfer of power to the next supernatural generation would be more complicated than they thought.

With a heavy sigh, she reluctantly began. "I've been meaning to fill you in on some recent developments. Arlo paid me a visit a few days ago."

"What?! Is that why you blew me off?" Frankie blurted, shaking her head in shock that Katie's former rescue dog had shown up on her doorstep.

"He decided he wants to be part of my life."

"Oh, I bet he does!" Frankie snorted. "He wants to get *right* in there. Probably doggy style." She shimmied her shoulders and laughed at her own joke as Katie choked on her espresso.

"That's a hard pass," Katie said sternly, wagging one finger to shush Frankie. "He's been relegated to the friend zone, but we decided to give him a new name. He's now Brody. It would just be dangerous otherwise in front of the kids."

"Smart," Zoya said.

Katie let out a pained exhale before revealing, "That's not even the most important part. He let a secret slip."

Frankie leaned much closer, her eyes widening. "And…?" She circled her index finger. "You better spill it."

"It seems Callie is pregnant, too."

"What?! Callie? Are you sure?" Yuli muttered in total shock. Zoya's chin jutted back in surprise.

"He swears up and down. She was emitting the pregnancy pheromones, and he used the information to earn his freedom."

Zoya stood and paced, stuttering in shock. "I… I assumed he meant Lauren."

"Well, you know when you assume, you make an

ass out of…" Frankie added, trailing off at the end when Zoya shot her a glare.

"It had to have been the Equinox Ball," Zoya declared. "The security eagles alerted me to a consensual coupling between her and Christos. I thought she was just blowing off steam."

"Christos?" Katie asked.

"A very sexy Greek who really knows his way around…" Zoya's expression turned dreamy.

"Nope! I can't! La-la-la!" Katie cried, covering her ears to stop the deluge of intimate information.

"It's just sex, darling." Zoya was clearly amused by her discomfort. "You'd do well to get your pipes cleaned now and then."

"Pipes cleaned?" Frankie chuckled. "Yes, she would! I tell her that all the time! And this is why I love you!"

"Enough! Both of you deviants need to calm down." Zoya and Frankie exchanged amused glances. "Let's get back to the matter at hand," Katie said, trying to get the group to focus. "You knew?" Katie asked Zoya.

"Not much happens on the compound that I am unaware of. She's not a child. Callie is a consenting adult and allowed to have a little fun now and then."

"Obviously, it was a mistake and completely unplanned, but looks like it is happening just the same," Katie reasoned.

"There are no mistakes," Yuli muttered, still in shock. "Two babies?"

"One is destined to be the next supernatural

descendent and join the mortal coven," Zoya added. "The other will be an ordin."

"Wow." Frankie blew out a sharp whistle. "Never saw that coming."

"Me neither," Katie agreed. "She's got to be scared. I'm sure that's why she's kept it to herself. God, it takes me back to the day I was staring down at a positive pregnancy test as a sophomore in college. I was terrified." Katie was locked in the memory for a minute. "It was the day everything changed. At that moment, my life unfurled out in front of me as if every decision I would ever make was already decreed. I had to let go of my future and embrace motherhood instead. Don't get me wrong, I love my children and would have chosen them every single day, but I want Callie to have more options."

"She will," Frankie assured her friend. "She is surrounded by love and support."

"But it begs the question: which one of them will have the supernatural child?"

"It could be either." Zoya sounded unsure. "We won't know until she arrives."

"Or until she has an ultrasound."

"Lauren has already told me they've decided to wait until the delivery."

"I guess our only recourse is to prepare for both," Yuli said. "Like it or not, our destinies are marching forward and a changing of guard is imminent." She sobered up. Turning to Zoya, her resolve strengthened.

"I received an offer to move to the Everglades when it is time for my transition."

"Gator bait?" Frankie asked. "Not exactly the kind of retirement community I thought you'd choose."

"What about the compound?" Zoya asked, clearly disappointed.

"It's not the second life I want to live. You were given the choice, so don't you think I should be offered the same?"

"Yes," Zoya answered softly.

"There is one disturbing detail we need to discuss. To not arouse suspicion at our incredible longevity, I will need to die an ordin death," Yuli explained.

"What? No!" Katie said, "I need more time with you. I've only just begun to learn."

"Your studies will still continue," Yuli said. "But far away from the life we live here in Aura Cove."

Zoya stood. "There's no time like the present. Since time is of the essence, we can fly back to the compound together tonight and resume your training."

"Can I come?" Frankie asked, never one to miss out on a trip to a luxurious island with a sugar sand beach.

"I'm sorry, dear, another time. Yuli and I need to teach Katia about hexes and curses."

Frankie's face fell, but she understood. "I've got to get moving. One more late punch-in at work and I'll be put on probation." After Frankie left, the kitchen was silent. Each of the supernatural women was lost in her own thoughts.

"Higgins will fetch you later this evening," Zoya

confirmed, then disappeared as quickly as she had come, and their amulets dimmed in response. Katie glanced at Yuli, who offered her a tight smile.

"You're going to be okay, Katia," she said, reading her mind. "I will always make sure you are safe."

Katie's heart tugged and the doubts cued up.

"Even when I am not physically present," Yuli added, intercepting her thoughts. "Shall we?" She stood and pulled out a clean apron and offered it to Katie before tying one on herself. Her words calmed Katie's racing thoughts, but she never let her grandmother out of her sight. She would be forced to do that soon enough.

TWELVE

Katie woke up with a start, forgetting where she was for a moment until she looked out the window of her suite at the Castanova Compound. Stretching her arms above her, she put her feet on the ground and padded across the plush carpet to look out the window.

It was a picturesque day at the lavish oceanside estate. The soft aqua-colored waves churned at the shore, playful in their game of cat and mouse with the sand. Seagulls circled and congregated on the sand, swooping down for the occasional fish that dared to swim too close to the surface. A collection of palm trees dotted the shore, swaying in the sea breeze. Standing there, Katie felt a calm serenity settle into her heart she'd never experienced previously.

A soft rap at the door interrupted her reverie. She crossed the room to open it, finding a maid who offered her a curt smile then walked into the room. She set a tray of fruit and coffee on the bed.

"Is there anything else I can get for you?" The maid made quick work of pouring a cup of coffee. "Two sugar cubes and a dash of cream?"

"How did you know?"

"Madam Castanova knows you well, miss."

The comment tugged at Katie's heart. All the little details, it was evidence that Zoya was paying attention, even when they thought she wasn't. Katie accepted the steaming cup of coffee, grateful for the jolt of caffeine it would provide.

After a leisurely breakfast and a long shower, Katie was ready to get their day of training started and was led down the marble hallway by Zoya's dog servant, Terrance. Stopping in front of a closed door, he barked once and a few seconds later, Katie was surprised to see Zoya open it. She caught a glimpse of Yuli already seated with a cup of tea, and she brightened instantly when Katie came into view.

"Ah, darling, you've awakened. Good, we must continue your education. Today you'll learn about cursed objects." Zoya beckoned her inside the room, leading her to the center where a golden camera sat on a marble pedestal encased in glass. Katie felt a strange magnetism to it and studied the camera with an unexplainable fascination. She bent forward, focused on the lens that looked like an eye, and when it actually blinked, she jumped and laughed when her nose bumped the glass. She was grateful Yuli appeared at her side and tugged her away from its alluring pull.

"Cursed objects must be handled with care," Yuli warned. "But there's a distinct difference between curses and hexes. Do you know what it is?"

"No," Katie admitted.

"*Objects* are cursed. *People* are hexed," Zoya answered.

"So, this is a cursed camera?" Katie regarded the instrument with more awe.

"Yes. It was rumored to be found at the scene of the Manson family murders in 1969." Zoya confided, "I acquired it for our private collection in the eighties after it passed through the hands of several unlucky souls. For ordins, its ownership brings violent murder, madness, and illness in swift succession until it burns a family tree to the ground and renders it into smoldering ashes."

"What does it do to supernaturals?" Katie dared to ask.

"It's become a powerful tool of retribution," Zoya offered cryptically.

"Too powerful," Yuli added. "That's why it is stored here. In the wrong hands, it would be deadly."

"What does it do?" Katie asked.

"That's the fun part." Zoya waggled her eyebrows up and down and laced one gloved hand through Katie's to pull her over to a gallery. On display, across the length of a limestone wall twenty feet long, were gold leaf frames that depicted violent works of art. Katie stepped closer to get a better look at the photographs. When her eyes locked on the subject in the photo, the amulet at her throat warmed and the image drew her in. Behind her, Zoya added, "This is my private collection, titled Suspended Libertines." She waved a gloved hand back at the mural and it began to glow. In the photograph, a portly man was stripped naked as a horde of people surrounded him, pointing and laughing.

"Please." Katie jumped when she thought she heard a man cry as he begged. "Please release me from this shame."

"Riveting, isn't it?" Zoya's eyes glittered with evil mirth.

"How?" It was the only word Katie could think to articulate what she was seeing. Each golden frame held a moment suspended in time. Like a debased boomerang, the moment played sixty seconds on a loop when a supernatural being laid eyes on it.

"Am I seeing things?" Katie shook her head, focused again, and then looked at another frame. This one depicted a disheveled man shoveling fistfuls of cow manure into his mouth while an unsuspecting herd grazed in a pasture. "Eww." She shuddered.

"Don't stare too long, darling, or you will unlock the scented version."

"Yuck." Katie took another step and got an eyeful of a gray-haired man on his knees with a ball gag in his mouth.

"That's a personal favorite." Zoya strode closer to the frame. When her gaze tangled with Katie's, the vision intensified and two women massaged peanut butter over the man's naked body, attracting a pack of growling and snarling wild dogs.

"Ugh!" Katie said. "I think I'm going to be sick." Leaning forward on her knees, she took two deep breaths to center her queasiness.

"Don't worry," Zoya offered, "you get used to it."

"That's what I'm afraid of, getting used to the violence." She shuddered. "How do you stomach it?"

Yuli took a step closer to Katie, pulling her away from the gruesome tableaus, as Zoya offered an explanation. "I understand you're conflicted, Katia, but each of these men deserved the fate they received." She paused for a moment as if she were deciding how much information to share. "To tell you the truth, it began as an experiment." Zoya beckoned them. "Follow me." She walked Yuli and Katie down a darkened hallway lit by the warm glow of wall sconces that illuminated their way. One by one, they magically lit up the darkness as the trio closed in on a hidden alcove. Katie sniffed the air, noticing a lingering musty scent, and when the final lamp brightened the end of their path, it illuminated a library of ancient books. Their peeling leather covers and yellowing pages were curling in the elements, giving a hint about their advanced age.

"What are these?" Yuli asked, her tone wary.

"Shortly after you departed the island for good, I was exploring the compound one day and found an enchanted passageway that led to a vault. Inside the vault were hundreds of volumes of ancient texts. I had them moved and did what I could to restore them. There is an entire education waiting for both of you that will serve you well when I earn my reincarnation."

Zoya walked over to a large green leather-bound volume. She pulled it off the shelf and placed it on a bookstand. When she opened it up, Katie gasped. Light flowed from the pages as Zoya flipped through the thick tome. When she found the page she was looking for and stopped, the words projected from the page into the air. "Evil Entrapment."

"Let me show you." She led Katie over to the pedestal where the golden camera was displayed, pulled a key from her pocket, and inserted it into the lock. It made a clicking noise when the lock disengaged and she opened the glass door, pulled the camera out, and placed it in Katie's hands.

The camera was hot and heavy, and her skin registered a shock and tingle when she turned it over in her palm. "Ouch!" When the shock strengthened, she almost dropped it. Her heart raced as the jittery sensation of electric currents circuited through her body.

"Careful," Zoya warned, pulling it out of her hands and into her gloved ones. "This was my first success at enchanting an object." Zoya gazed with pride at the golden camera.

Katie felt a chill trace down her spine.

"Objects hold energy," Yuli explained softly, holding out her hands. Zoya handed it to her granddaughter, who gasped when she held it. "The terror." Yuli blanched as she clutched it tightly. "It's palpable." She shivered and, eager to free herself from the oppressive energy, quickly handed it back. "Why do you find endless ways to embrace the darkness inside you?" Yuli asked while she shook out her wrists, wiggling her fingers.

"I've always been an exceptionally curious witch," Zoya admitted with a shrug. "You can't accept yourself fully if you don't embrace the darkness along with the light. They both exist to bring out the fullness of the other."

"Hmm." Katie considered her response.

Zoya turned to Katia. "To give you a complete education, you are going to need to learn about both." She turned to Yuli. "Do you not agree?"

Reluctantly, Yuli nodded. "I suppose, in order to have a well-rounded education in the supernatural arts, that is true."

"I don't know if I want it," Katie balked, taking a step closer to Yuli. "You've lived without darkness, so maybe I can, too."

Zoya's tone sharpened. "Going uneducated in the dark arts exposes the mortal coven to greater risk. One of you is going to have to push past your discomfort and learn." Her eyes narrowed as she challenged them.

"We'll learn together," Yuli decided for them, and it put Katie back at ease.

"I suppose that is acceptable." Zoya continued. "I will tell you a physical barrier of some kind is very helpful." She wiggled the fingers of her gloved hand.

"How does it work?"

"It took seven years of concentrated effort to infuse

enough evil into this camera to entrap an ordin. I put the effort in long ago. The power of it will ebb and flow like the sea. The closer we are to a full moon, the more attractive and intense its effect becomes. The camera mesmerizes ordins, and they are driven to their own self-destruction to possess it."

Katie leaned in closer to the cursed object, drawn in.

"It must be given as a gift that the ordin must freely accept."

"Free will again?" Katie asked.

"Yes, Katia," Yuli said, confirming the supernatural laws would remain intact.

"It cannot be forced. There is a sacred covenant required between the camera and the subject that must be entered into. But when they do!" An evil grin snaked across Zoya's lips and she licked them in anticipation. "Oh, the fireworks!"

"Can it really be considered free will then?"

"What else would you call it?" Zoya contested Katie's question. "It's only the ugliest parts of the human soul—greed, vanity, and depravity—that it magnifies. We aren't doing anything more than amplifying what is already in place. It picks up on the energy and motivations of the beholder and uses their weaknesses against them."

"What happens next?"

"The camera sees everything. Once it is focused on the dark and dirty soul of an evil-doer, all that is required to activate its response is the energy of a supernatural to take the photograph. It steals the soul of the evil ordin and locks them inside a permanent purgatory loop of a painful and shameful incident for eternity."

"Whoa." Katie stared at it with increased reverence.

"Whoa is right," Zoya agreed as she returned it to its display cabinet and locked it inside with the key.

Katie walked back over to the wall of black and white photographs in gold frames. "So, it's a prison," she added as she paused at each one.

"Yes." Zoya walked over to where the largest framed portrait hung. Staring into it, she added, "Don't fret too much, darling. They are only getting what they deserve." Her shoulders stiffened as she locked eyes on the subject of the photograph. "This one was my first attempt," she mumbled. Katie felt herself drawn closer, and Yuli followed behind. When all of their eyes were on the image, the amulets at their throats hummed and the image shifted.

"Is that... Is that who I think it is?" Katie stuttered in fear with a flash of recognition as she stepped closer to the photograph where a man was strapped to the electric chair. There was a power surge and the lights dimmed while his body convulsed in the deadly chair.

"Ted Bundy," Zoya confirmed as she cocked her head to the side, enjoying watching the last seconds of his life play out on a loop in front of her. "I was closing in on him when he was finally arrested. Ordin justice creeps along at a snail's pace. I sent him the camera, and he used it to document his crimes. It was recovered in the trunk of his car."

"How did you trap him here?" Katie was still astonished.

"There is a divine moment at the end of ordin life, when the soul and the body exist on multiple planes. I was present for his execution on a press pass, and when I pressed the shutter, it was at that precise moment of transmutation." She leaned closer to Katie. "I'd like to take full credit, but the truth is I simply got lucky."

Katie flinched as he was electrocuted again in front of her. A trail of smoke rose into the air from his leg. His head slumped forward, his mouth covered by a thick leather strap.

"So, you're some kind of supernatural vigilante?" Katie asked.

"Only when circumstances require it." Zoya turned toward Katie and the photograph stilled.

"Have you ever made a mistake?" Katie asked. She had real reservations about becoming judge, jury, and executioner.

"The spell is only effective on guilty ordins," she explained. "The innocent have nothing to fear." Turning to Katia and Yuli, she asked, "Which one of you will carry on my legacy?"

Katie gulped; she didn't know if she would ever be strong enough.

"We will carry on, but in our own way," Yuli insisted. "No two hearts are the same. They are shaped by life experiences. Your tremendous pain cried out for retribution. I believe there are more diplomatic ways of restoring order and balance."

Yuli's explanation put Katie's skittish heart at ease. "I agree with Yuli."

Zoya waved one gloved hand at the photographs. "You'll learn," she rebutted knowingly. "After one hundred and thirty-four years on earth, my heart has hardened. Diplomacy is overrated. Darkness responds only to darkness."

Thirteen

The next morning, they were drinking one last cup of coffee at the breakfast table when Katie dared to ask Zoya a question that had been on her mind since her fiftieth birthday. Knowing the oldest member of the mortal coven's days were numbered, she knew it was time to start asking the hard questions. "What was your awakening like?"

Yuli's surprise registered instantly on her features as Katie glanced from Zoya to Yuli and back again.

"Honestly, darling, it was a traumatic time. Sally had just been taken from me, murdered in cold blood on our front steps, and my memories from that time are murky at best."

Katie nodded. "Losing the love of your life will do that to you." She thought for a minute. "What about the archives?"

"Why do you want to go back to that moment?"

Zoya asked. "Surely, there are others you've never experienced that take more precedence."

"You don't know who you are if you don't know where you came from," Katie explained.

"It wasn't exactly the lesson I had in mind for today, but I suppose you have a valid point." Zoya picked up a little bell sitting on the table next to her coffee mug. She jingled it, and Terrance, her current dog servant, ambled out to the dining room.

"Yes, my queen?"

"We're finished with breakfast," she told him, adding, "We're headed to the archives, but tell the cook we'd like sea scallops and squid ink pasta this evening when we return, and if the papaya is ripe, we'd also enjoy a nice sorbet."

He rocked forward into a full bow of downward-facing dog and then scampered away to fulfill her requests.

"I am going to miss the ease with which I travel through this life after my reincarnation," Zoya admitted with a sigh as she stood and clapped once. "Follow me."

Ten minutes later, they zipped past palm trees in the golf cart, heading down the curving pathways to arrive at the metal building that housed the archives. Once inside, instead of locating the memory box herself, she turned to Katie and said, "Come child, it's time you learn how the archives work."

"Oh!" Katie was surprised by the offer, but eager to learn.

"The first step is to visualize the date you want to

access in your mind's eye. In this case, we are looking for July 1, 1938." At their throats, the amulets warmed and began to glow. Zoya closed her eyes, and sparks flew from her fingers, circling together to create a golden ball of crackling light. She spun her hands in circles and the rows of shelves lurched into movement, picking up speed in rhythm with the cadence of her rotating palms. The breeze from the fast-moving tracks blew Katie's white hair back from her face as they sped by and then lurched to a stop.

"See?" Zoya said. Katie reached out to grab a circular box glowing on the 1938 shelf, when the shelves abruptly shifted before speeding up again, flying by in a total blur until they chugged to a stop in 2010.

"What are you doing?" Katie complained, "It was right there."

"Did you think I would make it that easy on you?"

"Of course not." Katie laughed as she answered herself.

"Now, you do it."

Katie exhaled an anxious breath then closed her eyes and locked the date in her mind. She spun her hands in a circle like Zoya had minutes earlier, but Katie felt nothing.

"Focus, darling. Think of your own awakening. Your first taste of the truffle."

Katie's fingertips warmed to the touch, and when she sneaked a peek with one eye, she saw two sparks form and fall to the ground. She pushed her fists together, amazed at the resistance she felt; it was as if they were frozen. A bead of sweat broke out at her hairline as she labored to move her fists forward. She bore down and gritted her teeth as she felt the first nudge forward, and then there was a screeching sound like trains lumbering slowly on an ancient track.

"That's it!" Yuli said. "Faster now, Katia."

Emboldened by her grandmother's praise, she continued to spin against the resistance, feeling the momentum gathering. The first blast of air from the moving shelves felt triumphant on her face. "I'm doing it!"

"You are, indeed!" Zoya said. "Faster!"

The shelves raced by for several long minutes, then slowed and finally shuddered to a complete stop. When Katie saw 1938 carved into the side, she let out a squeal of delight. "What?" She became self-conscious when she saw Yuli and Zoya exchange pointed glances.

"Nothing." Zoya shrugged off her reaction. "You're a quick study is all."

Yuli pulled the glowing orb off the shelf and handed it to Katie.

"Aren't you coming with me?" Katie asked.

"This is a journey you must take alone. We've lived it," Yuli explained.

Zoya surprised them both by adding, "It brings back painful memories for us, darling, and I do not wish to subject Yuli to any more of them."

Yuli was taken aback by Zoya's desire to protect her. "Thank you," she finally uttered.

"Okay. I'll go it alone." Katie exhaled as she held

onto the sphere that tingled in her open palms. The crank on the side of the instrument was made out of obsidian, and when she turned it, the top opened. With a flash of energy, she was tugged up and into the air, flying toward the compound where she landed on the white sand in a tumble.

Confused by the location, she got to her feet and glanced around, trying to get her bearings. Katie was certain she was at the compound but totally confounded by the more humble home that sat at the edge of the ocean where the estate should have been.

She felt tugged toward it and let the instinct carry her along. Hearing voices inside the dwelling, she pressed the door open with the palm of her hand and ducked inside, looking for shadows to hide in.

A much younger Zoya stood at an ornate table in front of a box she'd recently opened.

"Taste and see who you were meant to be?" She read the words aloud from a folded piece of parchment and then breathed out a heavy sigh. "It's much too late for that." She walked to the wall of windows that looked out onto the sea.

"Following directions has never been your strong suit," a craggy voice said from the doorway.

Katie's head whipped over in surprise to see Olena, the diminutive little person who was Zoya's grandmother and her great-great-great-great-grandmother make an appearance.

"What the hell are you doing here?" Zoya asked, "How did you know where to find me?"

"You can't be that daft, dearie!" Olena chastised. "Think!"

"*You* put the keys on my doorstep? How? Why?" Zoya was flabbergasted.

"What are the chances another anonymous benefactor would just come out of the woodwork to save your candied ass?"

Zoya sputtered in response, completely dumbfounded.

While she waited for Zoya to collect her thoughts, Olena pulled a pipe out of the breast pocket of her tailored jacket and struck a match to light it. A few long inhales later, the orange glow of the pipe ignited and a curl of smoke drifted up.

"Disgusting habit," Zoya groused as she shuddered in repulsion. "Reminds me of father."

"A worthless creature, even if he did share my DNA," Olena agreed bitterly. "But I'm not here to talk about the past. Instead, I must awaken you to the future."

"Awaken?" Zoya asked again, confusion coloring her features. "Why must you always speak in riddles?"

Olena balled her hands on her hips and spread her legs apart in an attempt to take up more space. "Why must *you* always fight me on everything?"

They both folded their arms across their chests, disgusted with the combative dynamic they were stuck in yet again. Scowling at each other, their genetic predisposition for stubbornness was on full display.

"Where is the child?" Olena demanded.

"Yuli's probably reading again or out on one of her beach walks."

"Good, because what I am about to share with you will not do well with little ears around."

"Get to the point," Zoya spat.

"The candy in that box, when ingested on your birthday today, will set a chain of events into motion. You are the next generation of powerful supernatural females in our bloodline. Now that you are turning fifty, the second half of your life can begin."

The darkness that had filled her since Sally's murder cleared for a moment, and she felt a shaft of hopeful light touch down. "A rebirth?" Zoya was intrigued by the concept. Eager to shed the dark skin that no longer served her, she strode over to the box where the candy awaited. Without pause, she popped a dark chocolate truffle into her mouth, only chewing it twice before she swallowed. Her eyes bugged out and she clawed at her throat as the truffle burned all the way down.

"Jesus. Pace yourself," Olena muttered, watching the spectacle. "Ever hear the phrase, slow and steady wins the race?"

Ignoring her grandmother's warning, Zoya reached down and grabbed two more candies, inhaling them just as fast. She fell to the ground and writhed around as they were ingested.

"Get out!" Zoya screamed at Olena as she felt the rage lodged in her gut transform into a furious ball of manic energy. She crawled back to the box on her hands and knees, her eyes glazed with greed, and devoured the rest. Orbs of bright red energy converged over her body into one aura that rippled with red and black. Olena sighed in frustration then shook her head.

"GET OUT!" Zoya shrieked as she continued to convulse on the floor.

"You'll never learn." Olena stepped over her body that had stilled momentarily before it started convulsing and seizing again. Frustrated with her granddaughter who refused to listen, she walked away from the howling and screeching woman. Zoya was a loose cannon. She was dangerous, and now that she'd been awakened, there was no telling just how powerful her rage would become.

Olena hurried to the waiting boat. At the shoreline, she hesitated when she saw the outline of the ten-year-old little girl she'd loved as a baby. She hated to leave Yuli there. Her heart was torn in two, but the terror she just witnessed unfolding left her no choice. Zoya was a woman consumed by ownership and power, and like it or not, little Yuli was hers.

FOURTEEN

A week later, Maisy's phone stayed glued to her hand day and night as she exchanged thousands of texts with her new admirer. Each one set off a flutter of butterfly wings in her core. Even the school day was more tolerable, knowing that she'd have hours of uninterrupted time afterward with a boy she now knew was named Garrett. Lost in their back-and-forth messaging, he sent her poems and tentatively asked if she was falling as hard for him. She was, and though she'd never admit it to him, he was the first boy to declare his undying love and affection. He valued her opinions on his artwork and they sent ironic song lyrics to each other.

Every morning she woke up to kissy face emoticons, and every night she fell asleep with her phone still clenched in her hand. He hated speaking on the phone as much as she did, and when he asked her to video chat, her shyness won out and she made excuses. Instead, they embraced a modern twist on classic romance inspired by Mr. Darcy and Elizabeth, where each text became a secret promise, igniting vivid fantasies of each other. Maisy lived and breathed for them all day long.

After school, Maisy walked down the hall with her backpack slung over her shoulder and clutching a plate with two slices of pizza. Once in her room, she inhaled the pizza, then pulled out a makeup wipe and removed all her makeup before discarding it into the trash. She tapped the record button on her phone and squirted foundation that was two shades lighter on a sponge blender. Dabbing it onto her skin, she meticulously covered the freckles peeking out like clouds on a perfectly sunny day. Ringing her eyes in heavy eyeliner, she added a set of thick lashes and a metallic gunmetal shadow to her eyelids. Before applying each product, Maisy flashed it at the camera for viewers to see, hoping one day a makeup brand would reach out for a collaboration and she could monetize her content.

She turned her chin from side to side as she surveyed the progress in the mirror. Then she pulled out a pencil and made a series of small lines, darkening the blonder hairs of her eyebrows to blend with her current black hair color.

Yesterday, she'd added streaks of dark red to her roots, a color influenced by the bra she'd lifted at the mall. It cost seventy-two dollars, and the rush she felt when she exited the store wearing it underneath her clothing came second only to the interactions she'd been having all week long with Garrett. The allure of danger was intoxicating, and her pilfered Victoria's Secret sparked a flurry of exhilarating euphoria inside her.

Back in her bedroom, Maisy took a series of photos and videos with her phone, spending the next twenty minutes pouring over them, analyzing her attributes with a critical eye, and then editing them with apps on her phone. With a few swipes and pinches, her cheekbones became more prominent, her eyes wider and more sparkly, her skin pale and effervescent. A notification popped up and she tapped to open it with a giddy rush. Seeing his handle, bliss quivered through her.

justapunk16: hey beautiful.
macabremaze: i have a surprise for you
justapunk16: aww…and it's not even my birthday

She attached one of the new photos wearing only the bombshell bra, feeling daring, and when she tapped the button to send was instantly rewarded with a barrage of black heart emoticons. The rush of endorphins from his lavished adoration raced through her.

justapunk16: 1 more? just the choker?

Maisy didn't hesitate. She whipped off her shirt and flung it onto the floor, then removed the push-up bra. It was the recklessness of pure teenage rebellion charging through her bloodstream that egged her on. She didn't even think twice, eager to please Garrett, growing more bold and uninhibited as she continued to click photos of herself. When she caught her reflection in the mirror, she quickly lit a few more candles. Then she pulled out the vial of costume blood she'd used for Halloween and let it drip from the corner of her mouth, knowing his obsession with vampires and blood rituals would give her the appreciation she craved like a drug.

justapunk16: you are a dark gothic princess and you are mine… lucky me

Maisy squealed as another delightful surge of dopamine fizzled through her blood stream.

justapunk16: touch yourself and pretend it's me.

She tapped a reply then deleted it, then tapped another and deleted it too.

justapunk16: Send me a vid

Maisy hesitated only briefly, unafraid and unaware of any long-term ramifications. It was just a rush, a naughty game, a bold departure from the mundane, and it felt decadent. With a wicked grin, she complied. It took seven tries to get a good angle and after she hit send, she panicked briefly as she picked at the black nail polish on her thumbnail. She awaited his reaction with eager anticipation, her eyes glued to the incoming text bubble.

justapunk16: your body is fire… damn baby

Maisy felt herself flush hot with pleasure from head to toe. The warmth felt welcome and spurred her on. Over the next two hours, she got even more brazen and bold, following his explicit directions to the letter, then basking in the praise he gushed over the results each time.

Around midnight, she heard the front door open and hastily sent Garrett a text goodnight before throwing on a t-shirt and climbing into bed. When her door creaked open and her mother walked across the room to blow out the candles with another pained sigh, it took everything in her to lie still as her heart hammered in her chest. Her mother stopped for a second, surveying the room in the dim light.

"She's cleaning it tomorrow," she mumbled under her breath and then blessedly turned on her heel and walked away, shutting the door behind her. Maisy waited a few minutes in case she returned, and when she finally looked down at her phone, Garrett's last message melted her.

justapunk16: you r mine 4ever

FIFTEEN

I n mid-November, Adrienne was sitting at her desk going over the latest benchmarks and aptitude test scores. She had already appointed her replacement, and the school board voted unanimously to accept the new principal. Adrienne made copious notes she intended on leaving for her successor so the students and faculty at Aura Cove High School could transition to their new leader smoothly. She decided to take a break and stood to stretch her arms overhead when she caught a glimpse of Maisy through the glass of the door. She quickly crossed the room to open it.

"Please come in," Adrienne said with a welcoming smile. The carefree Maisy that strolled into her office was lighter, a total departure from the previous version. There were even a few reluctant smiles that dared to dart across her face. Adrienne offered her a seat in front of the desk as she sat back down in her own chair. "I've been eagerly anticipating your status report since our last meeting."

Maisy bit on the inside of her cheek, playing with the earring that was centered there twinkling in the light.

"I checked in with your teachers, and they collectively agree there has been a positive shift in your attitude and grades. Can you fill me in on what you've been doing right?"

Maisy nodded and squeaked out, "I'm handing things in and stuff. I made up two quizzes and have a test to retake next week."

"That's fantastic progress! I am proud of you." When Adrienne's warm gaze landed on the girl, she shrugged off the compliment, looking down at the ground. "Look at me, please." Maisy's eyes shifted from the floor to meet Adrienne's. "Always celebrate your successes, no matter how small they seem. It's how you build momentum and create long-term change." When Maisy blinked, she added, "I *also* have some fantastic news."

"What is it?" Maisy was wary.

"I've been keeping track of your progress since our last visit, and this morning, I made a few calls to Central Florida Community College to get some details on the Fashion and Textiles program."

On the outside, Maisy seemed unimpressed, but when Adrienne saw her lean forward slightly and her shoulders clench tighter, she knew it was just an act. "They have never accepted a junior into the program, but I got them to agree to make an exception." She continued, "The course is two days a week from nine to noon. Now, I know how much you love being here," Adrienne's tone took on a teasing, sarcastic one, "but somehow, I think you'll manage to push past the deep-seated feelings of sadness and regret and find a way to enjoy it anyway."

The sarcasm connected, and Adrienne was rewarded with a wide grin that spread across her face, the grin disappearing just as quickly. "Now, it's not guaranteed. You'll still have to submit a portfolio to the entrance committee as a condition of acceptance."

Maisy curled her bottom lip into her mouth and started to chew on it. "No need to get nervous. Mr. Lorraine showed me some of your newest pieces. The raw talent is there. He said he'd be available to talk through the concepts and requirements with you any time before or after school."

"Why?" Maisy asked, wary of her good fortune.

"We want to see you succeed," Adrienne answered. "Our main goal here at Aura Cove High School is to turn out students who are confident enough to chase their dreams and contribute to the world in their own special way. There is greatness inside you just waiting to be unlocked. At this stage of your life, you can do anything. You can *be* anything. It's the time to be bold and take risks." Adrienne delivered the information passionately. It was easy because she tapped into what she'd longed to hear when she was a high school student.

"I've been working on a few sketches since we met," Maisy admitted, shyness evident in her voice.

"Ooh!" Adrienne enthused, clapping her hands together in excitement. "Would you feel comfortable sharing them with me?" Maisy didn't answer the question verbally; she simply bent down, unlaced her black corset bag, and fished out a sketchbook. Her cheeks pinked up as she slid it slowly across the desk with two fingers. Adrienne flipped to the first page where a charcoal sketch of a woman was poured into a corset with a structural neckline of poofy tulle rosettes. A pair of skin-tight leather pants and black stilettos completed the edgy rocker look.

"This is fantastic!" Adrienne didn't have to fake her enthusiasm. The lines were confident and showed incredible promise. She flipped to another page where a twiggy model was outfitted in a navy blue micro-dress, and elaborate organic designs embellished the rest of her exposed skin.

"It's henna," she offered and tugged up her own sleeve to reveal the same designs drawn on her arm. "It helps calm the anxiety."

"Beautiful," Adrienne said, flipping to another page. "Maisy, I'm impressed. You have a remarkable ability to blend edgy creativity with wearability. It's captivating!"

Maisy soaked up the praise, growing more animated than Adrienne had ever seen her.

"Remember, talent gets beat seven days a week by hard work."

"What if I bring the talent *and* the hard work?"

"That's what I hoped you'd say!" Adrienne grinned then added, "If you have both, you could become an unstoppable force."

"An unstoppable force," Maisy repeated softly, letting the words seep in and claiming them by the second. This was the moment Adrienne savored, when a student put the pieces together themselves that would set them on a trajectory to the life they desired. It was a pivotal moment in a young person's life, and Adrienne felt fortunate to have shared in hundreds of them over the years as principal.

"I don't know if you've heard, but after the first of the year, I'll be taking a new position in the district as the Superintendent of schools. Maisy's face fell and Adrienne quickly tried to assuage her fears. "Don't worry, this school will be left in capable hands, and I will personally see to it that you get enrolled at Central Florida Community College."

"Really?' Maisy asked, and Adrienne got the sense that not many adults in her life followed through with the promises they made to her.

"I give you my word." Adrienne extended her hand and Maisy shook it. "Now keep up the good work." She stood and walked Maisy to the door, melting when the teen abruptly turned to thrust an impromptu hug on her.

"Oh!" She let out a surprised gasp as Maisy pulled back and pinked up. "Remember, you can do this. Believe it."

Adrienne watched her walk away, thrilled with the progress she'd witnessed. She returned to her desk and fired off replies to the thirty-two new emails that flooded in since the early morning, and then spent the rest of the afternoon conducting observations in the science and math classrooms. Sitting in the back, she took detailed notes about what each teacher was doing right and then outlined three things that could be improved. At lunchtime, she warmed up a cup of soup in the teachers' lounge and sipped it gently while reading a book. Autobiographies were her favorite. She learned so much through the lens of another person and found it inspiring to bear witness to the true story struggles and transformations of many of the memoirs she read.

At four p.m. she followed Dory out to the parking lot. "Another great day at Aura Cove High School," she said. "I sure am going to miss this place."

"Don't start with that already." Dory waggled her index finger at Adrienne. "I can't imagine this place without you."

Adrienne was touched by the sentiment. "You can't get rid of me that easily! As superintendent, I'm sure I'll be able to find a million excuses to visit."

"You better!"

Adrienne drove home to her condo in Aura Cove. It was the only real estate she could afford in the school district, and as principal, she was required to live there. She threw on a pair of shorts and a t-shirt and drove out to the beach to clear her head. The sun was setting as she wandered down the shoreline, lost in thought. She'd given almost a decade of her life to Aura Cove and to start over in a new capacity was thrilling, but it also came with jitters. She brushed them away and, as she looked out at the expansive sea in front of her, she welcomed the shift. She'd become complacent in the last few years and had settled into a routine. In six short weeks, she'd be launched into a whole new world, with new challenges to solve and new mountains to climb. As she watched the waves rush in at sunset, she realized she was just like Maisy, being nudged by the universe toward a bigger, bolder future.

Sixteen

Hours later, Adrienne was freshly showered and sitting in her bed with her laptop open and her reading glasses perched at the end of her nose. She yawned as she clicked on the last email message of the evening that opened in a new window. Confused by what she was seeing at first, she clicked to enlarge the screen. It was a blurry photo, startling in its familiarity, that made her breath catch in her throat when it came into focus. Her eyes darted away from it in shame as she scanned the body of the email, her lips moving as she read each word.

Greetings!
I must share bad news. I've recently acquired a series of scandalous photographs of you from several years ago from a like-minded friend on the internet. After a reverse image search, I was delighted to discover your identity, as well as

your well-documented and celebrated career in the public education sector.

I've attached one of the tamer photos to prove to you this is not an idle threat. The remaining photos in the series are much more graphic. Your face *is* recognizable. You appear naked in the series with the exception of a string of black pearls around your neck.

Unfortunately, in light of your recent appointment as the Superintendent of Aura Cove Community Schools, having these photos shared publicly would result in a scandal that could be detrimental to your career. I would assume we are united in our mission to keep these photos private.

Let's resolve this dilemma in the following way:

You must transfer .25 bitcoin to my account below (bitcoin equivalent based on the exchange rate during your transfer), and after the transaction is successful, I will proceed to delete all the photos permanently and without delay.

Send to bitcoin wallet: 1B5ic9iPpyadTEfWx-WM4Xq6PkzbickrL4g1

If you doubt my serious intentions, remember it

only takes a couple of mouse clicks to share
these photos with your friends, relatives, and
colleagues. I have the contact information of Dr.
McGrath and the rest of the school board, as
well as the closest news outlets to you. I truly
believe you would not want this to occur, as it
would decimate your career in education. You
have seventy-two hours to comply with my
request before I make them public.

Adrienne's fingers trembled as she closed the vile
window. It was a futile protective measure and
accomplished nothing. The photograph had already
seared itself into her consciousness. Its impact was
indelible; once seen, it was impossible to forget, and a
pit of dread formed in her stomach. Through hot tears,
Adrienne pulled up her bank accounts to learn she had
just enough savings to consider paying off her
blackmailer. She'd scrimped and saved for years, and
the twelve-thousand-dollar balance had been earmarked
to pay for a trip to Bali to celebrate her fiftieth
birthday. After reading *Eat, Pray, Love* she'd been
tucking a little bit of money away every year, longing
for a life-changing experience in the rainforests of Bali.
Now, the balance in the account offered a different type
of life-changing experience. It could be used to erase a
terrible mistake she'd made in her youth and secure her
future.

Panic swelled as Adrienne opened the email again
and enlarged the photo of herself. She was so young and

naive in it. Wracking her brain, she tried to recall the photographer's name. Was it Darren something?

"Think!" She said frustrated as she hit her forehead with the palm of her hand. Looking at the photograph, she felt dirty. Registering a glimpse of one nipple through the pearls made her face flush hot with shame. Her heart hammered in her chest as she jumped up and paced the length of the floor next to her bed. Her drowsiness completely dissolved as panic flooded in.

She'd relegated the failed photoshoot to the far recesses of her mind for decades and now struggled to recall the details. There was a swath of time at the studio she couldn't account for. She remembered his offer to include her in the jewelry campaign, and then her next foggy memory was sitting on the bus, then trying to sneak into her darkened home.

When she climbed in through the window, her mother was seated on her bed waiting and she'd been grounded for two months. Under constant surveillance, and more desperate than ever, she still held out hope the modeling portfolio would be her ticket to the life she wanted. It took several weeks for Adrienne to find an opportunity to call the number on the card she'd squirreled away in a secret pocket of her backpack. When she discovered it had been disconnected, it was a sucker punch. Unable to believe he'd disappeared, she skipped out during a sleepover and traveled back to the studio, only to see it was vacant with a FOR LEASE sign in the window. He had evaporated into thin air along with her dream of being discovered, and she felt like an idiot.

Unable to stop herself, Adrienne clicked on the photo again, looking for clues, and the visual unlocked a memory. His clammy fingers on her skin, the smooth pearls cold against her breasts. Sickened by the memory, she rushed to the bathroom and vomited. Kneeling on the cold porcelain, she trembled and retched until her stomach was completely empty.

Adrienne stumbled back to her bed, spent and trembling. In the darkness, sleep was elusive as her thoughts spiraled down, drowning her in a sea of guilt and shame. For two hours, Adrienne agonized over the decision to get her sister involved. Having no other recourse, she finally pulled out her phone and dialed. An annoyed Davina answered on the second ring, with a tone that wasn't the practiced professional one she'd adopted for the courtroom. Instead, it was disjointed and edged with exhaustion.

"Davina." Adrienne breathed into the silence that lingered, emphasizing the wall that always felt insurmountable between them. "I'm sorry to call so late, but I need your help."

After a loud sigh, Davina cleared her throat. "What's going on?"

"Can you come over?"

"Adrienne, it's late. Can't you just give me the cliff notes version over the phone?"

"This is really difficult, but I'll try." Adrienne's thoughts raced as she tried to figure out the place to begin. Knowing Davina was direct and appreciated a factual approach, she went right to the heart of it. "I'm being blackmailed."

"What? You? The squeaky clean high school principal? That's absurd."

"Someone obtained compromising photos of me and is threatening to send them to the school board if I don't pay."

"It's probably some whack job lying to you. Ignore it."

"I can't. He sent a photo." She shuddered. "It's obvious, it's me."

"How in the hell did he get it?"

"It's kind of a long story. I had some headshots taken and…" Her voice cracked in shame. Hot tears gathered at her lashes and she balled her hands into fists, determined to get through the rest of the conversation. "I…" She started again and was unable to continue the explanation. "Can you please… I just need…" A choked cry she tried to keep locked away finally escaped, and Davina's exasperation morphed into genuine concern.

"I'm on my way."

Thirty minutes later, Davina was sitting in her living room reading the message on Adrienne's computer. "My God, how old were you?" In shock, she enlarged the photo, trying to get an objective opinion on whether her sister was recognizable in it. With a heavy sigh, she immediately closed it down, unable to look at it any longer.

"Fifteen." Adrienne's eyes loomed large in her face.

She wrung her hands in her lap, wanting to reach out to Davina to squeeze her hand but fearing rejection.

"This crosses the line. We need to report this scumbag." Davina was disgusted. "I want you to start at the beginning and tell me everything." She pulled out her phone and waved it in the air. "Are you comfortable with me recording this conversation so I can review it later?"

"I'm a huge fan of anything that spares me the need to repeat this story ever again." Adrienne offered her a pained smile as Davina pressed play on the recording app and slid her phone closer.

"Tell me what you remember."

"A man approached me at the mall one day. He handed me his business card and asked if I'd ever thought about becoming a model." She pursed her lips. "You know how obsessed I was with fashion back then."

"Were you?" Davina's question highlighted their disconnect in a way that was a sucker punch to Adrienne. "I don't remember that." Her ambivalence caused a lump to form in Adrienne's throat.

Davina cocked her head to the side, studying her sister as if she were a stranger. Glancing around her home, she saw the stack of fashion magazines on the coffee table. At the door, a trench coat and red pumps reinforced the notion.

"It's okay. You were busy with your own life, starting college, and focused on your future." Davina nodded and avoided eye contact for a long moment, acknowledging her statement. Adrienne reached out to squeeze her forearm. "I don't blame you for not paying attention."

Clearing her throat, Davina swallowed hard and continued, "Then what happened?"

"He offered to take test shots for my portfolio and told me about his connections with modeling agencies. There was talk of sending me on go-sees, and he dropped a few names of newly discovered models that, in my teenage brain, legitimized his claims. He even showed me the cover of a magazine with one of his photographs on it. I thought he was the real deal."

Davina muttered a slurry of curse words under her breath while she listened.

"Hearing myself now, I get it, but back then, I wanted out from under Mom's thumb so bad. I thought he was my ticket out of Bradenton and into the big-time." She paused, remembering the thrill and how validated she felt when she'd been approached.

"Did Mom know?"

"Of course not," Adrienne cried. "She didn't understand. She would have never let me go."

"For good reason," Davina muttered, then quickly apologized. "I'm sorry. That was unnecessary."

"Do you remember how hovering and controlling she was?"

Davina nodded. "I do."

"Did you ever want something so much you were willing to do whatever it took to get it?" Adrienne whispered, feeling her eyes fill with tears.

Davina pursed her lips considering the question, then shook her head no. "I'm not built that way. I'm all the way on the other side of the spectrum, self-protective to a fault." Her admission increased the isolation Adrienne felt. Completely oblivious to her lack of empathy, Davina yawned into a balled fist. "We need to stay on task. I have an early start tomorrow."

"Sorry."

"No problem. How did you get to the studio?"

"I lied to Mom and said I had a study group, but that night, I took the bus."

"By yourself? That was dangerous."

"I thought I was being resourceful."

"Ah, the ignorance of youth," Davina added.

"When I got there, I was so nervous," Adrienne whispered. "I remember seeing the rack of bathing suits in the dressing room and panicking. I was intimidated and didn't want to seem like a child. The photographer realized I was rattled and offered me a Coke. Then added some whiskey to help calm my nerves."

"Jesus." Davina pressed her palms to her face, scrubbing it in frustration.

"He told me Jules Chamberlin needed it, too. I wanted to be a model so bad; I knew if I could just overcome the jitters, I'd be golden." She gulped then continued. "We did some portfolio shots, and then he said he'd just been approached by a luxury jeweler who was looking for a fresh face and offered me the opportunity to test for it. I was so green, totally out of my depth, I would have agreed to anything just to have the chance to live my dream." The childish desperation she'd felt at the time was a distant memory. "I didn't think it through."

"You were incapacitated. There is no way you could give consent in the state he put you in."

"He showed me the pearls and, after a second drink, I agreed. I don't remember much after that." She buried her face in her hands and sobbed. "It's all a blur of sound and sensation, murky memories where I thought something might have happened, but I couldn't prove it. The details were fuzzy." She shook her head in disbelief. "Now, I *know* he violated me." She waved one hand at the screen. "It's right there in black and white," Adrienne cried. She was shell-shocked as her mind scrambled to piece together the fragmented events of the night.

"Who was the photographer? We have to start there. If we can find him, he can lead us to the extortionist."

"I don't know," she answered. "I can't remember. I think the name of the studio was Vogue something." Her recollection of the events that happened and the days after was muddled. "He disappeared and I was too ashamed and confused to try to find him."

"Forward me his emails and any future correspondence you receive from him."

"I think I should just pay it," she said. "If he follows through, my career is over. There is a morality clause in my contract."

"No," Davina said. "You pay it and he will keep coming back for more. Ignore him. Nine times out of ten, these bastards are on a fishing expedition. He's trying to intimidate you into complying with his demands. Do not respond."

"What happens if he follows through and leaks them?"

"We'll cross that bridge when we get there." Davina dismissed her concerns. "You're an accomplished administrator. If push comes to shove, your impeccable professional record will serve you well. Besides, this event happened when you were a minor. You cannot be punished or held responsible for an illegal act that occurred when you were underage."

"But the superintendent is an elected position. The board can call for my dismissal."

"Do not respond," Davina insisted. "He'll go away. Trust me." She stood and Adrienne followed her to the door. With one hand on the handle, she abruptly turned around. "I meant to call you more after Mom died."

"I know. You've always had good intentions," Adrienne said, not as a dig, but an observation, yet Davina recoiled from the statement as though it hurt.

"I'll do better."

"I'd like that," Adrienne said softly, giving her an awkward hug that involved a lot of pats on the back as if to say *'Okay, I'm done now.'* Davina offered her a tight smile and then walked away as she locked the door. Adrienne lay in bed but didn't sleep a wink, dragging herself to work with the sunrise, wondering if this week would be her last at Aura Cove High School.

SEVENTEEN

Denny fished his key to the climate-controlled storage unit out of the pocket of his faded Levi's. He unlocked the padlock, rolled the metal door up, and slipped inside, pulling it down behind him. Then he crossed to the battery-operated bank of LED lights and clicked them on, letting his eyes adjust to the darkened area after being blasted from the morning sun on the drive over.

The pungent tang of photographic fixer still lingered on the darkroom equipment he couldn't bear to get rid of. Its monetary worth vanished when digital technology came screaming to the market. Its sole significance now lay in sentimentality. The cracked leathery bellows of the enlarger and scratched metal easels were relics from his past, reduced to obsolete knickknacks. Metal shelves held his lenses, developing trays, and a bucket of stainless steel film reels and tongs. The storage unit had become the professional graveyard of D. Sebastian

Kincaid and told the story of his meteoric rise and fall in the field of fashion photography.

Typically, being surrounded by the tools of his trade brought him peace, but instead, he was restless. To take the edge off, he opened the soft-sided cooler he'd brought and cracked his first beer, guzzling it down.

On one side of the storage unit were metal filing cabinets that housed negatives. He tugged out one drawer, the rusty tracks screeching from years of humidity. In the back of the drawer was an old copy of Luxe Mode, a European fashion magazine, the only one not too prudish to print the Carrie-inspired photographs in 1986. On the cover, a twiggy blonde, an Amazonian brunette, and a feisty redhead who appeared to be wearing nothing but blood gave him 'come hither' eyes. He'd known the magic happened the second he clicked the shutter, but none of the usual players were interested in the spread after the accusations.

Staring down at it, he scoffed in caustic frustration, knowing if he were to approach the same magazines today, they would probably tell him the photographs were too tame. That is if they were even in existence at all. Digital photography and the internet shuttered the lion's share of publications, leaving only a few holdouts remaining. It was obvious that civilization was going to hell in a handbasket, and his timing was never quite right to capitalize on its descent into depravity.

Eager to relive his glory days, he pulled out a manilla folder and tugged out glossy contact sheets. A Polaroid fluttered to the ground and he bent down to pick it up. In it, he was surrounded by two models on each side, all grinning ear to ear, and on the periphery was his assistant, Ronnie.

"Asshole," he whispered under his breath. The bitterness crept in the longer he looked at it. He scowled as he ripped the photograph in half, removing Ronnie. "There, that's better." He set it upright on the desk. Then he spent the next several minutes tearing the remainder into tiny bits of confetti. Shredding Ronnie's face into indiscernible chunks was the most satisfying part of the process.

He opened another beer and studied a dusty set of trophies in the corner. They mocked him with their plaques: "Fashion Photographer of the Year" and "Hot Shot Award 1985." Denny chugged the beer and sat down in an old director's chair facing the corner. He'd been down this road many times, but he could never stop himself from another trip when he was surrounded by the rubble of his old life. It was masochistic in a sense. He was punishing himself but unable to stop the madness.

It started out as murmured rumors. One day, he was Sebastian Fucking Kincaid—the East Coast's fashion photography wunderkind, living the good life. The next, he was black-balled by the biggest fashion houses, tucking his tail between his legs, and telling people to call him Denny. His fall from grace happened so fast it was almost comical. First, his phone calls went unreturned. His favorite models then began refusing to work with him, offering excuse after excuse. When he finally figured out what was happening, it was too late. His reputation had been destroyed by a man he'd thought was his friend.

His assistant, Ronnie, had taken the liberty to install hidden video cameras in the changing rooms, bathrooms, and showers at the studio, recording the models without their permission. It was such a horrific violation of privacy when the truth finally came to light, and as the studio owner, Sebastian shouldered the blame. It was simply a case of guilt by association.

Ronnie was a coward and fled, fearing legal prosecution, but Sebastian was foolish enough to stay, thinking it would all be brushed under the rug after the next scandal happened. Though Sebastian was legally cleared of any wrongdoing, the damage had been done. Overnight, Sebastian Kincaid was black-balled by the fickle industry, when every model flat-out refused to work with him—even the no-name ones. Every door he knocked on was slammed shut in his face. He quickly learned the fashion industry on the East Coast was an incestuous, elite group. When you were in, you were IN, and when you were out, you were OUT.

For the next six years, he desperately tried to claw his way back to the top. He scouted the Tampa Bay area for the next big thing. Spending his time cruising the malls and boardwalks, he was desperate to find the face that would save him. Naive enough to think that was all it would take.

Denny had the talent, but his access pass had been declined. It had been a long downward spiral since then.

He eventually traded the models for still-life photography, preferring florals with their universal appeal and lack of vocal opinions. Under the Sebastian Kincaid brand, he was slowly eking out a living, selling his intimate floral studies at art shows across the country and supplementing this stream of income with other portrait photography gigs. He was the prize-winning quarterback benched at the Super Bowl, never able to recapture the magic of his heyday.

For the next several hours, Denny went through his inventory of abstract florals. They were oddly erotic yet innocent at the same time, and he thrived on the attention docents of the area museums lavished on them. They called the images groundbreaking and a burst of fresh air. He just wished they'd put their money where their mouth was. He was tired of piecing together a meager existence. He deserved better.

With a heavy sigh, Denny wiped the sweat from his brow with the back of his hand and opened up another drawer of negatives and contact sheets from 1989. One folder labeled Candice Wright caught his eye. She was the pious wife of a newly elected conservative senator from Pensacola.

"Holy shit," he whispered under his breath. He'd completely forgotten he'd photographed her. After being punished for Ronnie's misdeeds for years, he began to think *Why not?* If he was going to do the time, he might as well have done the crime.

Denny studied the contact sheets, hearing a cash register *cha-ching!* in his mind. Thanks to

1_bad_influence, he now saw the collection with fresh eyes. It had the potential to be a literal treasure trove, and he made a plan to mine the collection for all potential golden nuggets.

He whistled while he got to work, indulging in a hearty jaunt down memory lane. He'd forgotten how many girls he'd approached and won over at the mall. The younger ones were easy pickings, eager in their desire to believe they could be models. Wielding their broken self-worth like a weapon against them, his flattery often won them over instantly. With their naivety and innocence, it was easy to love-bomb them with compliments and then dangle the prize. Over the years, it had evolved into a game. How much farther could he push their boundaries? How far could he go?

Denny wasn't an idiot like Ronnie. He was careful, targeting only the girls who cruised the mall alone. The ones who dashed outside to smoke a cigarette in between laps around the food court or dared to give themself a five-finger discount at Claire's Boutique while the sales girl was busy re-stocking shelves. Denny used these actions as a qualifying barometer and often spent up to a month surveilling potential candidates. Then, only when a girl met the criteria, would he pounce.

Denny pulled out his phone and checked his email, looking to see if Adrienne Thorne had responded to his request. Still nothing. Her lack of acknowledgement made him stiffen and his anger formed into a pit of self-righteous rage. The tension mounted as he sought a lever that would instill enough terror in her to ensure compliance. He was running out of time. Denny needed that money. He *deserved* that money. It was his ticket back to the lifestyle he wanted to live, and he would do anything to cash it in.

He glanced at his watch, annoyed by the passing of time. Unfortunately, he had back-to-back family portraits scheduled at the beach that evening. He hated debasing his art, but it kept his skills honed, and he'd promised himself when his other endeavors proved more profitable, he would leave it behind. It was just so tedious to be surrounded by all those happy families on vacation, recording their stupid, perfect lives.

Denny indulged in one final lingering gaze at the trophies before he pulled the accordion door down the tracks and locked it with the padlock. He had to find a way to turn up the heat and get Adrienne Thorne to pay. On his way home, he stopped at McDonald's to connect to the Wi-Fi and fired off another email. He would not be ignored.

EIGHTEEN

The next morning, as Adrienne was rushing to her car, her phone vibrated. She pulled it out, relieved to see Davina's name on the caller ID. She tapped to answer and sandwiched the device between her shoulder and cheek as she walked to her car, already late for school.

"He sent another one," Adrienne blurted. Opening her inbox was becoming a torturous exercise she found herself avoiding like the plague. She hated that the blackmailer was affecting her day-to-day life, and she was desperate to put an end to the intrusion.

"He's just throwing his weight around," Davina counseled. "Again, I would advise you to ignore him."

"It's impossible. He keeps threatening me. I am mortified at the idea of anyone seeing those photographs. Just knowing you have is… it's… beyond upsetting." Her voice cracked. "As a public figure in education, my reputation is paramount, and like it or not, I am held to a higher standard. If they get leaked publicly, no one is going to understand or even care that I was exploited and manipulated. It will destroy the life I've built."

Davina's advice was crisp and detached as she adopted full-throttle counselor mode. "Most of these cases are just idle threats. The worst thing you can do is engage with this person."

"But I have the money," Adrienne said, desperation making her voice waver.

"No," Davina cut in. "Do not, under any circumstances, open a dialogue with this whack job. If he knows you're good for it, the harassment will never end. Trust me. He will keep coming back for more."

"I just want this all to go away," Adrienne cried. "I am supposed to start my new position at the first of the year. Right now, I need to focus on the transition and getting my replacement prepared to step into my role, instead of this nightmare. I'm so exhausted. I didn't sleep at all last night." She let out a frustrated breath and pinched the bridge of her nose with her fingers, leaning back in the seat of her car. The walls were closing in, and she was feeling more suffocated by the second.

"I've been thinking about it," Davina reasoned. "He's got to be local, or at least have ties in the area. Otherwise, how would he know about your appointment to the school board?"

"True," Adrienne agreed, and then she had an epiphany. "What if we use that to our advantage? How about we orchestrate a rendezvous to lure him out of hiding?"

"No way," Davina insisted.

"Hear me out. I could play dumb and tell him I don't know how to obtain cryptocurrency and instead offer to pay him with cash. If this is purely financially motivated, it will be hard for him to resist an untraceable payday."

"I don't know." Davina was wary as she turned it over in her mind. "It's risky."

"Since when were you ever afraid of taking a risk?" Adrienne asked with a knowing grin. She drove herself to work, grateful to have a glimmer of hope to believe in. Ever since the first email, she'd been stuck in defensive mode, waiting for the axe to fall on her career. To take back her power recharged her depleted batteries and restored enough hope to help her get through the day.

———

"I can't believe I let you talk me into this," Davina complained the next afternoon, sitting in her car next to Adrienne. She glanced down at her phone while they waited. "More importantly, I can't believe he agreed to meet up."

Adrienne looked down at the backpack in her hands, a decoy filled with small-denomination bills. "I don't feel good about this. I think I'm going to be sick."

"I guess that officially releases you from the guilt of

calling in sick today," Davina said, trying to bring some levity to the tense situation, but failing miserably. "Look, he's obviously desperate if he's willing to meet in person. At least we have that going for us." A text notification rolled in. "Okay. Max is in place at the drop site. Are you ready?"

"As I'll ever be," Adrienne mumbled as she opened the car door and stood. Every nerve was frayed as she tugged on the front of her jacket. Adrienne settled a pair of sunglasses on her nose, grateful to have them to hide behind.

"Text me if there's an emergency. Otherwise, I will pick you up at the coffee shop around the corner from the drop. You're going to be okay. Max will handle it. You're in good hands, and soon, this will all be over."

"Good. I'd welcome the chance to get back to my mundane life. This feels too much like I'm stuck inside an episode of *Law and Order*."

Adrienne shut the door and swung the backpack onto her squared shoulders. Walking down the street toward the bustling downtown area during the noon hour, the sidewalks were filled with people hustling to their business lunch appointments. It was surreal, navigating the busy sidewalks with the future of her career hanging in the balance. Suppressing the rising tide of terror, she honed in on her breath, counting in and out as she crept forward.

The bag felt heavy on her shoulders. It was supposed to be a decoy with fake currency, but she'd gone against Davina's wishes and withdrawn the cash he'd requested. It was banded together inside the largest compartment. Adrienne's glance darted from side to side before she navigated across the street and stopped in front of a series of steel storage lockers next to a bike rack. Inside locker fourteen was an open padlock she was to use to lock the box. She pulled it out, tucked the backpack inside the metal cage, and fastened the padlock on it. The metal click felt ominous as she stepped back and tugged, testing the lock. She stood for a moment, gazing in disbelief at the locker that held her entire life savings. Then, before she could change her mind, she turned and started walking slowly away. As she continued toward the coffee shop, her eyes swept the two city blocks she passed for suspects, hoping to come in contact with the man who was blackmailing her, but everyone seemed uninterested in her and the lockers. A man wearing a ball cap with dark glasses passed by her, just suspicious enough for Adrienne to turn the corner and hide behind it. Her eyes were glued to the storage lockers, unable to take her eyes off number fourteen.

In front of the lockers, the man in the ball cap glanced behind him. Left then right, and seeing nobody watching, he pulled a key out of his pocket, shoved it into the padlock, and opened the door, reaching for the backpack. Max sprinted from his concealed spot in the alley and lunged, pushing him up against the lockers.

"Hey!" the man shouted in protest as his cheek was shoved tight against the cold metal.

"Shut up! I will do the talking." Max snarled as he

rammed the man's shoulders harder into the lockers with one thick, meaty forearm across the back of his neck. Adrienne ran over, eager to reclaim the backpack Max had yanked away. She was only able to fully exhale when she held it in her hands.

"You think you can shake down an innocent woman for money?" Max spat at the back of his head which was still lodged against the cold metal.

"You got the wrong guy!" he shouted, the words muffled against the lockers.

"Nice try, asshat! If you're the wrong guy, what are you doing here?" Max pressed the man's face harder into the front of locker fourteen, and Adrienne heard bones crack.

"Ahhh! Please, you're hurting me," he whimpered.

"Good, because *you're* hurting *my* friend," Max spat back. "I think that makes us even."

"I'm just the delivery service. I had no clue what was inside the bag."

Max whipped him around by the throat to face Adrienne. The imprint of the metal made a repeating hexagon pattern on his cheek. "We're going to need more details."

The man trembled, his eyes wide with a mixture of fear and awe, clearly intimidated by Max's sheer size and physique. At six-feet-three and two hundred and seventy-five pounds of muscle, Max would strike fear into any man. Max leaned closer to glare at him, then released his choke hold. As he retreated, the coward stumbled backward, crashing into the lockers with an audible clang. With no escape route in sight, he scrambled to offer an explanation that would appease the formidable Max standing in front of him.

"Someone contacted me on social media and offered me $200. All I had to do was come here at noon, remove the contents of the locker, and return it to where I got the key. He said it would take less than an hour of my time, and an envelope of cash would be waiting. It was supposed to be a cakewalk."

"Pull out your phone," Max demanded, and the man rushed to comply. "Send the messages and all the correspondence you had with this person to this number right now." He rattled off the digits.

He swiped and tapped feverishly on his phone, and within minutes, a series of notifications rang on Max's phone that was concealed in his pocket. "Good man. Now, if he contacts you, I would encourage you to be forthcoming and forward me those messages, too." He waved his phone in the air. "Or I will have to pay you another visit." Max leaned closer. "Have I made myself clear?"

"Crystal," he said. Max took a step back, and Adrienne watched the man scurry away without a backward glance.

"I'll walk you back to Davina."

"That's not necessary," Adrienne replied.

He laughed as if she had told a joke. "You don't know your sister very well."

A few minutes later, Adrienne slid into the

passenger seat of Davina's car and let out a long, agonizing sigh.

"Well?"

"It was a dead-end." Adrienne sighed. "It wasn't him. Max got the details." She fell back into her seat, letting her head loll against the seat rest. Tears rushed down her cheeks and she turned her head away to hide them from Davina.

"Give me a moment," Davina said, getting out of the car. Through the windshield, Adrienne watched her speak with Max.

When Davina returned to the car, Adrienne quickly swiped her tears away with her fingertips and forced on a pained smile. In her pocket, an email notification dinged on her phone. Adrienne pulled it out and felt her stomach lurch to her feet when she opened her inbox to find another scathing email waiting inside.

> You must think I'm an idiot. I told you to come alone, but instead, you brought Jack Reacher with you. Now the cost is double, and you have twenty-four hours before I release the photographs to the public.

Adrienne read it aloud to Davina. "What now?"

"I'm going to get the messages Max gave me to my expert and see if he can help us lure him out of hiding," Davina explained. "But from you, no reaction is still the best reaction. He'll calm down and this will just fizzle out. Trust me. Men like him are all talk, no action."

"It doesn't matter anymore. Even if I wanted to pay up, I couldn't afford to now." Adrienne exhaled a weary breath. She couldn't bring herself to ask her sister for a loan. Davina was adamant it was the wrong move. Asking for the money would add another layer of awkwardness to their already strained relationship.

They sat in silence as Davina drove her home.

"Try not to worry, and get some rest if you can," Davina told her. "I'll call you in the morning."

"Easier said than done," Adrienne mumbled, offering her sister a small wave when Davina eased away from the curb. Frustrated, she let herself into her darkened condo and made a meal, but she couldn't eat more than two bites. Her nerves were shot. The next twenty-four hours were going to be absolute hell.

NINETEEN

The next day, Adrienne assessed the bags under her eyes from another sleepless night. She'd tossed and turned and finally gave up at four a.m. when she got up and took a shower. Her stomach was sour and nothing sounded remotely appetizing, so she made her favorite childhood comfort food. She popped a couple of pieces of bread into the toaster to brown them. Five minutes later, she was seated at her dinette with a small tea plate filled with buttered toast sprinkled with brown sugar and cinnamon and a cup of black coffee. She picked up a slice and bit into it, crunching as she opened her laptop where her usual email routine beckoned.

She hesitated for the briefest moment before entering her password and quickly scanning her inbox. Another fifty emails awaited her response, but one got her full attention. The one with the subject line: Do not ignore me

A wave of nausea rolled through her as she tried to still her rapid heartbeat. She clicked on the message to open it, and a more offensive photograph was attached. In it, her eyes were closed slits while hands outside the frame ravaged her body. She gasped, unleashing a startled cry that pierced the air, then quickly forwarded it to Davina with tears in her eyes before focusing on the email.

Will you create your own happy ending, or will I have to destroy your life because of your stupid decisions?

Just so we're clear, you live at 4319 Palmetto Drive in Aura Cove. If you do not successfully comply with my demands, be advised that I plan to upload nearly a hundred photos like the one attached here to WhisperHub and other NSFW websites all over the internet, along with your current photo, school contact information, and home address.

You have twelve more hours before I detonate a bomb in your life.

Adrienne slammed her laptop shut and hastily got ready for her school day. Preoccupied, she pulled into her parking spot at Aura Cove High School and spent the next few hours trying to focus on the never-ending meetings that filled her schedule. First, she met with the

Student Council about plans for the upcoming Winter Formal Ball and then approved a fundraiser for the outdoor kitchen the PTA wanted to install near the football field for team-building events. She also got pulled into a heated argument between the speech teacher and the academic decathlon leader about which one deserved a motor coach for their upcoming state contests.

Having work to focus on was a blessing as it kept her fears at bay and gave her tasks to focus on. At lunch time, she sat at her desk to catch her breath and pulled out the avocado egg salad sandwich she'd packed along with bright orange carrots and a container of peppercorn ranch dressing.

Opening up her inbox again made the fear well up in her gut. She braced for another message as she glanced down the list, feeling the sandwich transform into lead in her stomach when she saw it. The subject line simply stated: Your last chance

She clicked on the email to open it up and quickly glanced at the message. No longer wordy and awkwardly cheerful, it had been reduced to the facts and a recap of the threats.

I can see you are not taking me seriously. To
help you understand the urgency, here is a link to
the gallery of photographs I possess in its
entirety.

Without payment, this link will be provided to

Dr. McGrath and every member of the school
board in Aura Cove, as well as every news
station in the Tampa Bay area. You have the
power to stop this from happening.

With a trembling hand, Adrienne forwarded the
email to Davina. She waffled between her desire to see
all the photographs to grasp the extent of the impending
damage and relief that she could not view them during
the day on the school's network. Clicking on the link
would alert the IT department, who would have lots of
questions, and it might lead them to open an
investigation. The thought of her colleagues scrolling
through a gallery of racy photos turned her stomach, and
the doxing was a chilling intrusion. It was a flagrant
breach of her privacy and security and left her feeling
violated and exposed a second time. She closed her
laptop. It sat there like a ticking time bomb waiting to
be detonated, and her eyes subconsciously flicked over
to it again and again until her lunch break was over.

She watched the clock all day. Finally, when the last
bell rang, she gathered up her messenger bag, tucked the
laptop inside, and shut off the light in her office.

"You're out of here early today," Dory remarked.

"I have a doctor's appointment," she lied, eager to
leave the school and lock herself in her bedroom. She
had the sensation of being naked in public, where every
flaw was raw and exposed as she scrambled for cover.
"Have a good night."

Not even waiting for her response, she hightailed it

out of the school, speed walking to the car and driving straight home. She ordered greasy Chinese food and polished it off with chocolate almond ice cream, piling carbs and sugar precariously on top of the fear. Ravenous in her desire to consume enough to make the gnawing anxiety from impending disaster in her belly disappear, the influx of calories only made her feel more miserable. Moaning, she got into her bed early, resolving to set her alarm an hour early and climb on the treadmill in her spare bedroom to undo the damage. She glanced over at her bag that contained the laptop. Afraid to touch it, yet oddly attracted at the same time, she got out of bed and padded over to the bag. Sitting back on her heels, she opened the bag and tugged it out, hugging it to her chest as the cool metal of the computer warmed up in her hands.

Needing to know, she yanked it open and typed in her email login and password without thinking. She clicked on his last message and hovered over the link for a long moment before clicking on it, then chewed on her thumbnail as she waited for the high-resolution images in the gallery to load. At last, the first photograph appeared and she gasped, instantly recognizing herself from decades ago. Her fly-catcher bangs were sky-high and the permed back exuded the epitome of 1989 glamor. Its impressive volume was a testament to genetics and helped along by Aquanet. Her skin was ivory and flawless, and her cheekbones were chiseled with the tightness of youth. Though she'd aged gracefully, there was no denying the subtle softness of her middle-aged jawline and the delicate sag that could now be seen around her eyes.

The photographs were raw and straight out of the camera. With legs that seemed to stretch on forever in stilettos and adorned only by a string of pearls, the light skimmed across her body, revealing a mound of blonde pubic hair she couldn't bear to look at. Her cheeks flamed crimson with a mix of embarrassment and shame. Adrienne shook her head to clear it, but the thoughts were swimming and swirling on top of themselves. A veritable crescendo of humiliation stuck on repeat in her mind.

The photographer had captured her eyes half closed, and instead of looking inebriated, she skewed toward sultry. Her wide mouth, instead of gaping open from being on the verge of passing out, looked eager and wanting. Taken out of context, the photographs would be difficult to excuse and impossible to explain. She scrolled and scrolled, stuck inside a gallery of degradation that seemed to go on forever. As she got further down the page, the acts became more brazen and pornographic in nature. She slammed the screen shut, noticing for the first time her cheeks were soaked with hot tears.

When the phone on her charger rang, she was relieved to see Davina's name on the caller ID.

"Did you see them?" Adrienne's voice croaked out and her heart cracked open with a sob.

"Yes," Davina whispered.

"I'm so ashamed. I feel violated."

"That's because you were," Davina said, validating her, and Adrienne gulped. The knot in her throat tightened and threatened to choke her.

"There are only a few hours left before he leaks the photos." Adrienne insisted, "I can't let that happen. It will destroy me."

"He's playing chicken and probably shaking down twenty other women as we speak. Stay strong. He'll move along to an easier target soon. These types of guys always eat the low-hanging fruit."

"I don't know if I can."

"You can," Davina said, building up her confidence. "We are going to track down this guy and hold him accountable. I promise you."

"How?" Adrienne asked. "It happened thirty-five years ago. The statute of limitations expired eons ago."

"Leave it to me," Davina said. "Promise me, you will not give in to this scumbag."

"I promise."

———

Adrienne toiled in agony as the final minutes of the deadline ticked down on the clock sitting on her bedside table. Forcing herself offline, she waited as a pit of dread filled her stomach. At 7:01 pm she logged into her computer with her heart pounding up her throat. Opening her email, she scanned down the length of messages in her inbox, and then her phone began to ding incessantly with notifications.

Ding-ding-ding!

Her eyes widened and waves of panic rolled in, crushing her with their intensity and dragging her into the undertow.

Ding-ding-ding!

Email after email filled her inbox as more notifications flooded in.

Ding-ding-ding!

She scanned the screen, noticing she had been blind copied in a series of thirty emails that included attachments.

The ugly subject line was a headline of horrors. Adrienne Thorne: Aura Cove's New Superintendent of Schools Exposed.

What kind of role model is Adrienne Thorne for the youth in our community? The headline screamed above one of the photographs.

(Click to see the complete gallery of photos.)

Adrienne's head pounded as her phone rang and more notifications flooded in. Then came a series of texts. The constant dinging notifications resembled a busy pinball arcade and only ratcheted the tension exploding through her. She pressed the buttons to shut down her phone so hard her fingers ached, in a desperate attempt to staunch the incessant flood of messages.

"I can't go in tomorrow," she mumbled to herself,

reaching for the offensive instrument her laptop had become. Adrienne logged into the absence management program and put in for a personal day, then crawled back into her bed and sobbed. She punched the pillow on her bed and pressed her face into it to scream. The act only made her feel marginally better and her throat hoarse. She lay there for hours, shutting out the world. It took two doses of sleep-aid for her to finally settle down enough to fall asleep.

———

The next morning, she felt like she was walking through mud. Her limbs were heavy and she was still drowsy from the sleep-aid. From faraway, an unrelenting knock pounded on the door, and she rolled over with a groan and ignored it. A few minutes later, it only increased in painful unison with the pounding of her head where, behind her eyes, a migraine was gathering strength. She sat up and squinted against the brightness of the morning light streaming in from the window. Desperate to get the noise to stop, she stumbled out to the door and pressed her left eye to the peephole. Seeing it was Davina, she unlocked the deadbolt, quickly opened the door, and ran into her sister's outstretched arms. Adrienne tackled her, heaving and sobbing, resting her chin on Davina's bony shoulder.

"I was worried about you. I called and called," Davina said, her face pale. "I'm in shock. I can't believe he went through with it. I'm so sorry." She smoothed her sister's hair while she awkwardly tried to provide comforting noises. "We need to get out in front of this," Davina coached as Adrienne pulled back with panic in her eyes.

"How? He emailed the entire school board, sent the photos to all the major news outlets, *and* published them online. It's only a matter of time before they call for my resignation. My career is over."

"You were a victim, not a criminal," Davina argued. "Trust me, I will get to the bottom of this and we will make him pay. Get dressed. I'm taking you to the police station to file a report."

"No. I just want to crawl back into bed and forget it ever happened." She said.

"I understand, but we need to go on record," Davina reasoned. "I will take you in myself and be your advocate."

"You have time for that?"

"I'll make time."

Adrienne showered quickly and got dressed. Her face was pale and her eyes were swollen from tears. She felt wooden and detached from her limbs, going through the motions and letting Davina put her in the front seat of her car. When they arrived at the Aura Cove Police station, they were promptly shown to a private room where an officer joined them after a twenty-minute wait.

"I'm Officer Harrison Willey. Thank you for waiting."

Annoyed, Davina glanced pointedly at her watch. "Does it normally take this long to file a report?"

"Sorry, ma'am, the station is swamped today." He pulled out a clipboard and a pen and was poised to write notes. "Tell me why you're here."

Adrienne led the conversation, explaining the extortion attempt and the blackmail scheme. Officer Willey listened patiently, nodding from time to time, and scribbled notes onto a paper. When she'd finished the tale, her mouth was dry and her tongue felt thick.

The officer stood and said, "Thank you for coming in. I'll get this information to one of our detectives, and if they need to speak to you, they will reach out."

Confused, Davina's expression soured. "That's all? You have got to be kidding me."

Officer Willey sat back down and leaned closer, his voice filled with compassion, a rarity in the field of law enforcement. "Unfortunately, in cases like this, that's all we can do." He paused before adding, "I must temper your expectations here. Cyber-crimes are tough to prosecute. Legislation has not kept up with the technology, and it is very easy for the perpetrator to remain anonymous. We will likely hit a dead end."

"She was a minor when this crime was originally committed," Davina said. "Even if we can't charge him criminally for possessing the photos, I believe a federal case can be made in regards to distribution." Her directness silenced the officer's doubts.

"Possibly."

"We need to find the photographer. Chances are, if he violated Adrienne, there are others. People like him don't just stop. Once they get a taste for it, they are likely to become repeat offenders."

"You are right, unfortunately." His tone grew more serious as he leveled his eyes on Adrienne. He glanced over his shoulder before secretly handing her a thick card with his contact information on it. "I'm not supposed to do this, but this is my direct line." After a long pause, Officer Willey's face darkened and he shared an explanation, "I believe my twin sister, Jessica, was victimized by a predator. She was abducted when we were seven."

Adrienne immediately gasped and apologized. "Oh my God. I am so sorry for your loss."

He gave a curt nod. "Thank you, but I don't need the sympathy. I wanted you to understand why I have a vested interest in your case. She's the reason I became a cop in the first place. Helping other women in crisis makes me feel closer to her." He offered her a sad smile. "I couldn't help her, but I *can* help you. Please forward me the chain of communication you received, and I will personally follow up with the detective assigned to your case."

"We appreciate that, Officer Willey," Adrienne said and stood to shake his hand. He led them out to the front door, and they exited the building as the sun darted behind the clouds and a gentle rain began to fall.

"You were too docile with that over-sharer in there," Davina criticized.

"Don't be so cynical. Everyone knows you catch more bees with honey than vinegar."

"We're not catching bees," Davina said. "We're trying to catch a predator."

"I am fully aware," Adrienne stated. "But now we have an ally in Officer Willey, and that might come in handy. You don't always need to be the steamroller. Sometimes, connection and compassion can go a long way."

TWENTY

A week later, on Thanksgiving afternoon, Katie pulled the golden turkey out of the oven to let it rest before carving. Next to her, Yuli was loading yeasty rolls into a bread basket, and Frankie and Harry were standing at the drink station topping off everyone's beverages.

"Can you believe what's happening to Adrienne Thorne?" Beckett asked, sipping on his rum and Coke. "The guys at work got their hands on the photos from some dark hole on the internet, and I had to remind them that, even though she's an adult now, in them, she was underage." He scowled in disgust. "Sometimes, I'm ashamed to be a man. I think about how I'd feel if it were Callie or Lauren in her place, and it makes my blood boil."

"It's so sad," Katie said. "That poor woman. Being exploited as a teenager was bad enough, but seeing her reputation get demolished on top of it is sickening. It's all anyone has been talking about at Kandied Karma." She glanced over at Harry, who shifted uncomfortably, averting his eyes to the floor.

Frankie blurted, "Hey, Willey, didn't you take her report at the station last week?"

Harry tightened his lips, shooting Frankie a warning glare, silently urging her to stop speaking. It was a subtle signal she ignored and soldiered on. "Photos of the high school principal in a compromising position being leveraged for cryptocurrency? And here, I used to think that nothing exciting ever happened in Aura Cove."

"Frankie…" Katie cautioned her filter-less friend.

"What?" she asked, totally oblivious, glancing around the room in confusion.

"Adrienne Thorne is a good person who was violated in the most public way possible." Harry reluctantly chimed in to set the record straight. "I wish I had better news for her, but blackmail and extortion on the internet is a tough nut to crack. The bad guys hide in plain sight under the cloak of anonymity."

"To think, Adrienne has dedicated her life to serving her students and the Aura Cove Community School District, and in one second, her unblemished record was destroyed," Katie commiserated. "The fact that presidential candidates are held to a lower moral standard than a school superintendent is insane to me."

"Me too," Lauren agreed.

"I have a feeling she'll come out of this better than

ever." Katie felt confident they should look on the bright side, knowing Karma was on her side.

"No offense, Mom, but you live in la-la land sometimes," Lauren said. "She'll have to get her vindication in court. Sue the pants off that vile scumbag."

"Tommy, can you help her?" Rox weighed in, trying to be helpful.

"I'm in family law, Mom. A law degree is not a one-size-fits-all solution. Besides, her sister is Davina Thorne. She has relationships with attorneys at all the major firms in Tampa Bay. When they find him, Davina will make sure he is punished to the fullest extent of the law."

"Ha! A woman after my own heart," Rox said, letting out one of her trademark laugh assaults, hoisting up her Blue Moon for emphasis.

"Davina will get it done," Katie agreed, careful not to cross into her own history with the lawyer. Eager to divert everyone's attention away from the painful discussion, she turned to Lauren. "Can you mash the potatoes, sweetheart?" Lauren nodded then blanched white, her eyes widening as she raced to the bathroom with her hands clamped over her mouth, only to return a few minutes later.

"You poor thing." Katie pulled her close for a side hug. "Morning sickness?"

"Lucky for me, it lasts all day," Lauren groaned, wiping her mouth with the back of her hand.

"I can take over," Yuli offered. "Why don't you and Tom find your seats at the table?"

Lauren nodded, still a little green around the gills, as she let Tom lead her to the elaborate table that was set with bouquets of lush flowers, crystal glasses, and bone-white china.

"I think that's everything." Katie surveyed all the plated dishes. "If you could help me get all the bowls and platters to the table, I'd appreciate it."

"Of course." Kristina handed a bowl to David. Katie smiled gratefully at her parents.

"Katie, I'd like to say something before we dig in." Tom stood and every eye darted to him as he reached into his pocket and pulled out a tiny aqua-colored box from Tiffany's. Lauren gasped as he got down on one knee in front of her and his warm gaze tracked across her face.

"What is happening?" Lauren's voice bubbled with a mix of anticipation and curiosity. Animated and slightly nervous, her gaze flitted around the room, alighting on her mother's face before settling back on a steadfast Tom.

"Lauren Elizabeth Beaumont, you're my best friend. You've proven to me what it means to be a partner during one of the darkest times of my life."

He glanced over at Rox, who was tearing up at the reminder of the challenges they had all just endured together when Rox was accused of embezzlement.

"I don't know how I could even begin to articulate what your support meant to me during that time, but I know I want to spend a lifetime trying to show you. You're brilliant and tough and tenacious, and I can't wait to see all of those qualities take root in our child. There is no one else I want to walk through life with, so before our dinner gets cold, would you do me the honor of agreeing to become my wife?" He pried open the box, and resting on a bed of white satin was an enormous diamond sparkling from its platinum setting. Lauren squealed and nodded excitedly as he pulled the ring from the box and placed it on her finger. Then he stood and pulled her into his arms for a hug as elation spread across his rugged features.

"But you didn't answer him!" Callie shouted, getting caught up in the anticipation buzzing around them all as they waited for her response.

"Yes!" Lauren cried, "Yes! Yes! Yes!" Tom cupped her face in his hands and kissed her tenderly while the guests seated at the table around them burst into spontaneous applause. There was a screech of chair legs on the travertine as the group got to their feet to congratulate the newly engaged couple. Katie beamed at Lauren and squeezed her tight. The couple's bright yellow aura filled her with joy.

"I'm thrilled for you both," she said. "You are going to make a beautiful bride." She remembered the premonition she'd had almost a year ago of Lauren on her wedding day. To see it come true and confirm her supernatural abilities was sobering. At her side, Callie reached up to offer Lauren a hug, but when she pulled back, her smile faltered and her face paled.

"I don't feel so good," Callie whispered as a vacant expression settled on her features. Katie turned toward Callie just as her knees buckled and she fell back into Beckett's arms. He quickly wrapped his arms around her and carried her to the sofa to lay her down.

"Cal?" Beckett said as he patted her cheek to try to wake her up. Her eyes fluttered open, and she was disoriented for a moment before she realized what happened.

"Did I ruin it?" Callie blurted to Lauren, her eyes wide with fear. Lauren gathered close to the sofa Callie rested on with Tom in tow.

"Of course not, silly," Lauren said, holding out her hand and gazing at the stunning ring that now adorned the fourth finger on her left hand. "Nothing can ruin this day! I'm engaged!" She squealed with joy, waving it in the air before turning to her sister, her voice filled with compassion. "But are you okay?"

"Of course. I must have overdone it with the girls last night," Callie admitted sheepishly.

"Ah, the perils of single life!" Katie mused, lying to help Callie cover up a secret her daughter was obviously afraid to reveal.

"How about some hair of the dog?" Beckett asked, always eager to help.

"No, that sounds revolting," Callie said, wrinkling her nose. "Just water for me. You can all stop fussing over me. Let's eat! We have an engagement to celebrate!"

Later that afternoon, one by one, the members of Katie's family cleared out of her beach house, their arms laden with Tupperware filled with leftovers. Callie was the only one who remained, and after the kitchen was cleaned, Katie found her curled up on the sofa napping. Her dark hair was smooth and her cheeks flushed pink. She dozed peacefully with a thick, chenille throw wrapped around her. Katie watched her daughter sleep, seeing her chest rise and fall, waiting for her to wake up. A few minutes later, she stirred. Then Callie's eyes fluttered open and she struggled up to a seated position.

"Hey, Mom." She offered Katie a sweet, drowsy grin. "How long was I out?" She stifled a yawn with a balled fist. "I'm just so tired lately."

Katie stilled her mind, searching for an inroad into Callie's thoughts, wondering why Callie was keeping her pregnancy a secret. The first whispers were filled with fear.

She knows something is up. I should just tell her.

"You know I love you, honey? Right?"

"Of course."

"And you know I would move heaven and earth to see you happy," Katie added, her voice softening, the love she felt for her daughter evident. The sentiment made Callie crumple as her defenses were still down from her nap. Katie moved closer to her and reached out a hand to squeeze Callie's warmer one. "There is nothing you can say or do that would change that."

"Mom?" The word came out like a whimper as she instinctively pressed her palm to her belly. "I'm…" She struggled to complete the sentence as her eyes filled with tears. "…pregnant." She finally choked the word out.

"You are?" Katie said, reacting with surprise, knowing it would confuse Callie if she didn't.

Callie nodded as one fat tear rolled down her cheek.

"Are we excited about it?"

"More like terrified," Callie admitted. "I feel like I let you down."

Katie spent many hours lecturing her kids about condoms and safe sex when they were teenagers. Having had an unplanned pregnancy herself that changed the trajectory of her life forever, she wanted her children to make better choices.

Callie burst into tears and her shoulders trembled. "Christos wore a condom! I know they aren't 100% effective, but I still can't believe this is happening."

"Oh, honey." Katie pulled her in by her shoulders and kissed her forehead like she had every night when she tucked Callie into bed when she was little. Then she grasped Callie's hand in hers and smoothed the top of her palm with her thumbs. "You could never let me down. I love you." Callie whimpered and Katie continued, "How far along are you?"

"Almost the same as Lauren. It happened at the Autumnal Equinox Ball. I had a little too much fun with the man I met there."

"What do you want to do?" Katie asked.

"I've been waffling back and forth, but after weighing the pros and cons, I decided I want to keep it," she said.

"Then that's what we will do. I will be there every step of the way to help you. Being a single mother isn't easy, but you have a big support system you can lean on. We all love you and we will love this baby."

Tears rushed down her cheeks and Callie brushed them away.

"Can I ask you something?"

Callie gulped and nodded.

"Why did you wait to tell us?"

Callie sighed as relief settled in. "I was going to tell everyone today, but I didn't want to spoil Lauren's big moment." Callie's voice sounded small and childlike. Tears coursed down her cheeks as she began to tremble. "I didn't think I deserved to celebrate when I was so irresponsible."

"Oh, sweetheart," Katie murmured. "Quit beating yourself up."

Callie sighed and then added, "The timing is terrible. My life is a mess. I had to turn down the offer at Pixar." She picked at her nail bed, unable to make eye contact. "They don't offer remote employment."

"Oh," Katie whispered. "I know how much you wanted that job. I bet you were disappointed. I'm so sorry, honey." She reached out and squeezed her hand.

"I looked at it from every angle." Callie seemed resolved in her decision. "It sounded like the career opportunity of a lifetime, but outside of the work, I realized I would be all alone. I would be starting my life over from ground zero. The decision was hard enough to make when it was just me, but a few days later, I took the pregnancy test and it became simple. I want my son or daughter to have a close relationship with you, and to be razzed by Uncle Beckett, and eat Yuli's truffles."

"I am sure that was a difficult decision, but I am proud of you for making it."

"You are?" Callie's voice cracked. "I thought you'd be more disappointed in me."

"Are you kidding me? You get that notion out of your head right now."

Callie brightened, gulping down the remainder of her fear. She brushed the rest of her tears away with the pads of her fingertips and sat taller. "Okay, it looks like I am having a baby."

"Okay, then." Katie nodded, then asked, "Will Christos be in the picture?"

Callie blushed. "No. He is not interested in being a father at all."

Katie was dumbfounded but didn't want to pry, Callie's state was already fragile. "No worries. You have all the support you need already. When are you going to tell the rest of the family?"

"Soon. But instead of a grand announcement, I would like to keep it more low-key."

"Okay," Katie said.

"Will you come with me to the ultrasound?"

"Of course. Ultrasound, Lamaze, whatever you need, honey, I will be there," Katie promised, reassuring her timid, overthinking daughter. Katie witnessed the relief wash over her in waves and calm Callie's jumpy heart. She tuned in to Callie's train of thought to be sure.

What a relief. What was I so worried about?

"I should head home, but I'll call you later." Callie stood and hugged Katie tight. "If I can be half the mom you were to us, it will be enough."

"You will be," Katie said. "Everything will work out the way it is supposed to. You'll see."

"I hope you're right." Callie let her mother walk her to the front door, and she welcomed the brown paper bag of leftovers that was put in her hands. A few minutes later, Callie pulled out of the driveway and headed back to her apartment, and Katie waved until she couldn't see her car anymore.

Two. Two babies were coming, and life as they knew it was going to change forever.

Twenty-One

Thanksgiving at Adrienne's condo was quieter. By the time their little roasted chicken was ready, Davina and Adrienne were deep into their second bottle of wine. It had been a last-minute, awkward invitation, and she was surprised when Davina agreed to come over.

"Have you heard anything new from the detective assigned to your case?"

"No," Adrienne said. "Officer Willey warned us it could be a dead end."

"I refuse to accept that." Davina leaned back in her chair. She had ditched the suit and heels for jeans and a white button-down shirt that hugged her thin frame. Across from her, Adrienne was wearing an ancient Eagles concert t-shirt over a lacy camisole and a pair of black skinny jeans. Her bare toes were accentuated with red polish.

"You always were more of a fighter than I ever

was." Adrienne poured the remainder of the bottle into their glasses. "But that killer instinct has served you well in your career."

"It has, and I plan on putting it to full use when we catch him." Davina's voice deepened with resolve.

"Can we take a break from this nightmare for one day?" Adrienne asked. The scandal and its fallout had cast a dark pall over her life, and she was eager to escape it for a few hours.

"Of course," Davina agreed, and in the silence that lingered, she fumbled for her glass and took a sip in an awkward attempt to fill it. Adrienne stood and gathered the two dirty plates and walked them over to the sink. Davina trailed silently behind her, eager to have another task to focus on to stop her from needling Adrienne about the investigation.

"Do you ever wish you'd gotten married and had a family?" Adrienne asked her sister after their plates had been scraped and were resting inside the dishwasher as she cut thick slices of pumpkin pie.

"Hell no," Davina admitted. "It comes with the territory. I think you'd be hard-pressed to find any divorce attorney gleefully jumping on board the marriage bandwagon."

Adrienne let out a somber chuckle. "So cynical."

"Is there any other way to be?" Davina asked with a shrug and a sarcastic grin curling up her lips as she squirted a layer of whipped cream so thick over her pie it became a shapeless white blob on the plate. She swiped one finger through the cream and licked it off with glee. This carefree child-like version of Davina was so different from the one she presented to the world, and Adrienne was captivated by it.

"I used to think so," Adrienne finally answered. "But maybe there's a reason we're both old spinsters alone at Thanksgiving."

"Hey!" Davina reached out to shove Adrienne's shoulder. The wine they'd consumed made her typical formal personality softer around the edges. "Speak for yourself. I am alone by choice. It suits me."

"Mom scarred us both for life," Adrienne declared. "God, I loved her, but that woman was a worrywart."

"She played too small," Davina agreed. "I was determined to be the polar opposite of her. I wanted to walk into a room and own it, not cower in fear in the dark corners like she did."

"You have done that," Adrienne assured her. "And Mom was proud of your accomplishments." A pained expression burrowed into her face, becoming a grimace. "God, it's a good thing she isn't around to see the disaster my life has turned out to be."

"Disaster is a bit harsh. One day, maybe this will prove to be a simple course correction." Davina was trying to cheer her up, feeling partially responsible for the current state of Adrienne's career.

"There is nothing simple about this situation."

"Agreed." Davina blew out a hot, frustrated breath between her teeth. "Unfortunately, adversity can only be truly appreciated with the passing of time and from a new viewpoint. When you're three bites deep in a shit sandwich, the time to appreciate it comes long after you swallow."

Adrienne snorted. "Your colorful anecdotes are something else!"

She waved it off with a smirk and a chuckle. "I might be a little inebriated and lack my usual panache and sophistication, but the sentiment still holds true." A relaxed smile played across Davina's features that Adrienne had never seen before. Why had she never seen it before?

"I like seeing this side of you," Adrienne said softly. Knowing she was just buzzed enough and still raw from the recent nightmare, she dared to voice her question aloud. "Why aren't we closer?"

Davina pursed her lips as a swell of conflicting emotions battled inside her. "I don't know," she answered truthfully. "I guess I didn't think you needed me."

"You're my sister," Adrienne reminded her. "I'll always need you."

TWENTY-TWO

The next morning, Adrienne received the phone call she'd been dreading. Seeing the name "Possible Dr. McGrath" on the caller ID under a number that seemed vaguely familiar made her stomach flutter in panic. Her lips formed a tight circle as she let out a quick series of bursts of hot air to calm her nerves before forcing a sunny smile on her face and answering the call.

"This is Adrienne Thorne."

His usually amicable tone was replaced with a pinched one, and his use of formalities set off the first alarm. "Ms. Thorne." She felt her mood wilt as he continued. "In light of the leak of the explicit photographs to the media, the board feels the best course of action is to put you on administrative leave until this scandal dies down."

She cleared her throat, blanching at the idea of the

board seeing her naked body. "Can I ask what this means about my appointment to my new post?"

He let out a frustrated sigh. "You can step down, or we can let you go. I believe it will bode better for your career if you choose to resign. It will give the district some time and distance from the scandal, and who knows, maybe next year we can take another look at your performance and decide if you meet the criteria."

Disappointment flooded through her. "I would caution you to remember I was a victim here." With the risk of losing the career she'd worked toward her entire adult life hanging in the balance, she refused to go down without a fight. "I was taken advantage of as a minor with photographs that I did not consent to have taken nor released to the public. You know we would rally around one of our students if this happened to them."

"Of course we would," he scoffed. "But the unfair reality is that we hold faculty and administration to a higher standard. Their actions matter, and we simply cannot afford the backlash we will be exposed to if we carry on with your promotion. I'm sorry, Adrienne. I really am, but I am sure you can see my hands are tied."

"What if this happened to your daughter, Charles?"

"It wouldn't."

"Why not? Because she came from a prominent family?" Adrienne continued, "Sextortion is a cybercrime that is on the rise. It crosses all socioeconomic boundaries. *Any* woman can be a victim."

"The decision has already been made," he stated,

ignoring her argument. "The school board had a closed-door emergency meeting and the vote was unanimous. We are offering the superintendent position to Dr. Randall. I'm sorry."

"That's the thing, Charles. I don't think that you are." Adrienne couldn't help herself. "I love the Aura Cove Community School District, but this is wrong."

He ignored her pleas and cleared his throat. His tone was adamant. "You're on administrative leave until January thirty-first."

"And then what?" she dared to ask.

"And then we will need to examine the evidence and make a decision in regards to your future at Aura Cove Community Schools."

"Wow." Adrienne was floored. "The board should be ashamed. I gave my life to Aura Cove Community Schools and have a perfect track record of service. After my administrative leave expires, *I* am going to have to reevaluate if this district is the best decision for *my* future. Good day." She ended the phone call and threw the phone across the room where it landed on the sofa. The interaction made her whole body tremble from pent-up nervous energy. She shook out her quivering hands as tears washed down her face and the stored humiliation and outrage rushed to the surface. She waited until she was under control again to phone Davina.

"They are forcing me to step down," she blurted the minute Davina answered the phone.

"We'll fight it," Davina told her, her conviction

strengthening the resolution in her tone. "And we'll win."

She breathed out an anguished moan. "To be honest, I don't know if I *want* to fight it."

"No," Davina said, making up her mind for her. "You do not get to lose your career and your livelihood over a mistake you made when you were a child. I will hold them accountable. I will hold them *all* accountable," Davina repeated. Then she quickly shifted to damage control, strategizing her next steps out loud, and Adrienne zoned out, only responding with an occasional *uh huh* to the one-sided conversation. Her mind flitted away, and she found she was mentally drained from the weeks of sleepless nights and the what-ifs that spun on a continuous circuit in her brain. Now that the worst she'd imagined had come to pass, all she wanted to do was sleep, to pull the covers over her head and hide away from the world.

"Are you there?" Davina asked after a long silence.

"Yeah," she mumbled. "I'm tired. Can I call you later?"

"Of course." And then Davina said something completely out of character. "I'm sorry. I let you down, but I *am* going to fix this."

"I'm not sure you can, and honestly, I'm not sure I want you to anymore." Her voice cracked and she whispered, "I've got to go." Hanging up the phone, she walked to her closet and pulled on a fresh pair of cotton pajamas. It was only ten am, but as far as she was concerned, the day was over, along with her life.

Twenty-Three

The following Monday, Davina sat in her office enjoying the quiet that came at the end of a long day. She kicked off her Louboutins and padded across the cool marble floors to the bar cabinet she'd installed to help celebrate important wins and commiserate over difficult losses when she'd become a partner at the firm. She poured herself a whiskey neat and tossed it back, then poured another that she walked back to her desk. She was using the booze to take the razor edge off the guilt that overwhelmed her, sending her brain down rabbit holes of doubt.

Davina was frustrated. She had built her reputation by settling tough cases, giving respected advice, and negotiating the best outcomes for her clients. The fact that she'd failed her only sister hit hard, and without the churn of her workday to distract her, she felt the disappointment well up in her gut. Eager to figure out a way to salvage her sister's career, her mind spun on possible solutions when a soft knock on the door startled her.

"Come in." She glanced up, pleased to see Niles enter her office. He had an impressive skill set in hacking and navigating the dark web and was a freelancer she'd worked with on other tough cases. Niles avoided eye contact altogether and made a wide enough berth to discourage a handshake, choosing his usual chair. The one that sat perpendicular to her desk with its smooth surface. She knew fabric irritated and distracted him, and Davina required his full attention.

His hair was gelled and smoothed back from his head and his sneakers were immaculate. In all their years working together, she'd never seen him wear a different pair of shoes. Intrigued, she'd asked him once about it, and he answered, "Simple. I own thirty-seven pairs."

When her brow knit up in astonishment, he launched into a strange, yet logical explanation. "Each shoe will last me approximately four hundred and twenty-seven days. The actuary table calculates my earthly demise at seventy-nine years old. As such, I should never need to purchase another pair." He pushed up his glasses by the nosepiece and offered her a satisfied grin and a fleeting split-second of eye contact.

He was on the autism spectrum, a fact he'd boldly disclosed to her like he had brown hair during their first meeting. Davina took the honest admission in stride. His references were impeccable and his results were even harder to discredit regardless of his perceived disability.

To her, his hyper-focus and genius mind were distinct advantages.

She asked, "Can I get you a drink?" It was just a polite formality, as he never took her up on her offer.

"No," he answered, pulling his glasses off of his face and polishing the lenses with a square of microfiber material he pulled from his shirt pocket. "I've had my daily allotment of brown liquids already." She was used to his odd answers to her questions and the unconventional way his brain worked. "You said you wanted to speak to me today." He avoided looking at her almost completely, seemingly focused on the window behind her.

"Yes." Davina sat down, getting right to the heart of the matter. "Can you find the identity of an individual using only an email?"

"It depends," Niles offered. "Did this person go to any lengths to conceal their identity?" He continued on without taking a breath, his words stuttering for a long moment before bolting out of his mouth in a fast-paced informational stream. "They could use a VPN, or a proxy routed through an international server, even just the public Wi-Fi at an area business. There are a myriad of ways to conceal the country of origin of a particular email if you are smart enough." He started to rock forward and back slightly in the chair as his explanation sped up.

His eyes darted up to hers then away again as he held up one finger. "But all it takes is one slip up. One time when he or she forgets to use the VPN. There is a digital footprint a user leaves behind that we can track. If we wait, often they will get sloppy and make a mistake. Human error is usually their downfall."

"Wait? What if I don't want to wait?" Davina sighed the words out in one long breath. She abhorred waiting. "Do you know anything about an app called WhisperHub?"

"It's an anonymous chat service." He explained, "They claim support for user privacy, but most companies like WhisperHub track their users and keep user data they can leverage to sell targeted advertising."

"That's great news, but how do we locate him in their sea of users?"

"Any online service that allows cross-device login must authenticate users to recognize them on multiple devices. Lots of social apps help connect users geographically, and use the phone's location to find nearby contacts unless the privacy modes are configured correctly." He let out a distressed groan and rocked faster in the chair. "You... You can... You need an IP," he started with a stutter. "Ugh! An IP address is like the address of your house. If we can get his IP address from WhisperHub, or track his emails to an IP address, then a physical address can be pinpointed."

Davina stood and handed a thumb drive over to Niles, carefully avoiding physical contact that had the potential to make him uncomfortable. "You'll find all correspondence with him here. I want you to do a deep dive and find out everything you can about the emails and messages included on this drive. We need to know who this is and where to find them, as soon as possible."

She reached into her purse and pulled out a thick wad of cash. "Your deposit. I have brand new bills as you requested, and I made sure the teller wore white gloves to handle them." He took out a cloth and wiped the envelope down before depositing it into his briefcase. "The remainder will be paid when you present your final report."

"Yes. Yes. That is the way I prefer it." He stood looking at the floor and then picked up his briefcase and strode out of her office.

"Thank you," Davina added, and she wasn't surprised when Niles kept walking. The only indication he'd heard her was the one-handed wave he raised behind him as he disappeared down the hallway. For the first time since this nightmare had started, Davina felt they were on the right track. Niles was a miracle worker, a technological savant. If anyone could flush this spineless weasel out of hiding, it was him.

TWENTY-FOUR

L ate the next evening, Denny was signed in to his profile and trolling the chatrooms. Seeing the handle **1_bad_influence,** he sat up and fired a private message off in WhisperHub.

Twistedsnaps69: I followed your advice, but she refused to pay up.
1_bad_influence: Well, it's time to reassess your approach. You must not have hit her button hard enough.
Twistedsnaps69: Hit her button? That's what she said. LMFAO.
1_bad_influence: I bet you made the classic mistake all rookies make. How old was the target?
Twistedsnaps69: Late 40s (I think.)
1_bad_influence: That's your first problem. The younger, the better. It's easier to scare them into

complying. Move on to another target. If at first
you don't succeed, try, try, again.

Twistedsnaps69: You should have been a life
coach.

1_bad_influence: I don't have the stomach for
fire walking. Besides, this was much more fun.

1_bad_influence sent you photos.

Practically salivating, he clicked on the attachment,
and his screen filled with a thin, dark-haired nymph. In
one image, a trickle of blood was artfully placed in the
corner of her mouth that matched the crimson streaks in
her hair as she eyed the camera topless. Her skin was
pale and smooth as if it had been airbrushed, and
covered in elaborate designs that reminded him of
henna. On one cheek, in the center of a dimple, a shiny
piercing caught the light. A candle provided dim
ambiance, and the photographer in him appreciated her
artistic use of light and smoky incense for mood. As far
as selfies went, this one was top-notch.

Twistedsnaps69: I humbly bow to the master.

1_bad_influence: Part of the fun is seeing just
how far you can push your target. I've set the
hook with this one. Now it's time to reel her in.
After a few weeks, I have her eating out of the
palm of my hand. She's a poor little rich girl
with too much time on her hands, stuck in her
beach house with a mother who doesn't pay

attention. Add in some daddy issues and she was ripe for the picking.

Twistedsnaps69: I understand.

1_bad_influence: Never forget, love is the greatest lever of all. Most people will do anything for it. Now get back out there and don't come back until you have something worth showing me.

Twistedsnaps69: Aye-aye, Captain.

Denny wasted the rest of the evening. Unable to relax enough to fall asleep, he conducted a web search for Adrienne Thorne. His leak of the photographs to the press resulted in a series of articles and YouTube links to news stories. He read through each mention, line by line, feeding on her misery and savoring the endless array of judgmental opinions from the armchair crusaders on social media. Cruelty was their specialty, and they didn't disappoint. The hours he spent reading their scathing vitriol lifted his spirits and restored his faith in humanity.

"Oh, how the mighty have fallen!" he said with glee. Clicking on a photo, he read about her resignation from her newly elected Superintendent of Aura Cove Schools appointment. As he studied her face, a sneer curled up his thin lips. She had matured since he'd photographed her, but she was still beautiful and he hated her for it. The world was unfair. Beautiful people got a pass. Their playing field was vastly different than the one he was forced to play on. They had better opportunities and were baked in riches, and Denny was sick of it.

It had been so gratifying to break her down, to humiliate her and tarnish her image forever, like his had been tarnished so long ago. The destruction he'd been able to unleash in her life was thrilling and an excellent consolation prize. He might not have gotten the big payday he'd been hoping for, but he'd gotten something of far greater intrinsic value. He'd gotten to witness the total destruction of another human being, and it made him feel like a god.

Twenty-Five

Adrienne's head pounded when she awoke the Monday after Thanksgiving. She wasn't proud of it, but she'd spent the long weekend wallowing. Her mouth was dry and her tongue thick from the wine she'd overindulged in. Reluctantly, she opened one eye to glance over at the clock on her nightstand that held the evidence of her favorite coping mechanism—binge eating. A bowl with sticky melted ice cream rested atop a pizza box where half of a congealed pizza sat when she couldn't bring herself to walk it the fourteen steps down the hall to put it in the fridge.

Reality flooded into the brightly lit room and she recoiled from its assault. She'd become so accustomed to having a packed daily schedule; she didn't have time to eat a proper dinner or even take a bathroom break most days. Now, she had huge swaths of unscheduled time that seemingly rolled out forever, and she didn't know what she was going to do with herself.

Out of habit, she reached out to pick up her phone and swiped through the last forty-eight hours of notifications and texts. The list went on forever, and she balled one hand and rubbed her eye socket in a pitiful attempt to massage away the tension lodged there.

With a heavy sigh, Adrienne put her feet on the floor and walked out to her kitchen to brew a cup of coffee, continuing to scroll through the messages on her lock screen. She poured heavy cream into the cup and added a sugar cube, lodging her phone between her cheek and shoulder while she absentmindedly listened to her voicemails play.

The third message was from her former secretary, delivered in a hushed whisper that made her freeze and drop her cup. It cracked into sticky shards and coated the countertop in a caramel-colored liquid she tried to mop up with a handful of paper towels she ripped off the roll with one hand.

"It's Dory. I know I am probably not supposed to be doing this, but Maisy Duncan tried to commit suicide tonight. She was unsuccessful, thank god, but I know you two had a special bond and you'd want to know."

Stunned, Adrienne froze as she watched the coffee stream down her cabinet doors and pool on the floor. A few seconds later, Dory continued.

"I am just sick about those photos that were leaked and the spineless administration that forced you on leave. If there is anything more I can do, please reach out to me at this number. Since you don't have access to PowerSchool, Maisy's mother's name is Tricia and her cell is 641-555-1678."

Adrienne scribbled down the phone number on the back of the receipt as Dory continued.

"If anyone finds out I did this, I will lose my job, but getting you connected to Maisy is more important than any stupid privacy policy. If this goes sideways, I guess it's time for early retirement. Merry Christmas, Adrienne. I hope to see you back at school after the holidays."

Grateful for the information, but incredibly sad she had to use it, Adrienne sopped up the puddle of coffee with another handful of paper towels while she hastily dialed the phone number Dory left her.

The woman's voice on the other end of the phone was beaten down.

"Mrs. Duncan, this is Adrienne Thorne. I wanted to reach out and inquire about Maisy's wellbeing."

"It's Tricia," she corrected dully. "Adrienne Thorne… Why does that name sound familiar?"

"I am…was her principal at Aura Cove High School."

"That isn't it," she mumbled.

Adrienne was mortified. Instead of waiting for her to put the pieces together, she ripped the band-aid off and offered an explanation. "You might have seen my name in the newspaper or on the news. Some explicit photos of me as a teenager were leaked to the media recently."

"Oh no. Teenagers can get into all kinds of trouble if they have too much time on their hands."

Adrienne felt the sting but pushed past it. "Is she still at the hospital?"

"Yes. She's at St. Thomas's for observation. There are plans to release her tomorrow, and then she will be enrolled at an out-patient mental health program after the holiday is over." Tricia added, then her voice caught, and Adrienne got a glimpse underneath her well-polished professional veneer. "I don't know what happened. She has been given everything she could ever want, so much more than I ever had as a child. Why would she want to take her life?"

"I don't know," Adrienne commiserated, answering as honestly as she could. "Maisy is a bright and talented young woman. We were monitoring her progress closely at school, and she was making great strides. Something must have gotten in her way."

"I should have paid more attention."

"Please don't blame yourself," Adrienne said. "Parenting teenagers in this age is brutal. Cell phones, the internet, and social media have only increased the anxiety and bullying that young people face, and

COVID added fuel to the fire. We are in a full-blown mental health crisis in America with unprecedented numbers of children being affected." She then shifted gears. "Are you comfortable sharing more details with me? It takes a village, and the more insight I have into what is happening internally with your daughter, the more I can support her." She paused then added, "That is, if you'd let me." Adrienne didn't know how she'd be able to help Maisy now that she wasn't welcome at school, but she was resolved to find a way.

"I'm an ER surgical nurse and have been working a lot, but Maisy has always been an independent child. When I come home at night, she's already asleep, most of the time with candles still blazing in her room. I always worried she'd burn the house down. But this? This, I never saw coming."

"Is her father in the picture?"

"Not anymore, but his absence definitely left scars."

Adrienne thought about the scars her own father left behind and felt a kinship with Maisy. His absence left her feeling unworthy. It colored all her future interactions with men and was likely the reason she remained single. How could he just walk away? Adrienne bit on her lip, grateful when Tricia continued, and she didn't have to face the truth of how deeply it hurt.

"I don't know what happened," Tricia cried. "I was completely in the dark. And this just feels so far out of left field for Maisy."

"Have you talked to her friends? It's natural for teenagers to pull away and for their friends to become more important as they get closer to adulthood."

"She's tight-lipped," she explained. "I think there was some kind of falling out with her friend group recently."

"Hmm," Adrienne mused, going over the information. "Was she dating anyone?"

"She was becoming more secretive, but I think there was someone, by the lovesick way she was acting. The constant attention to her phone. It was always in the palm of her hand."

"I would bet you'll find answers if you search her phone, especially her social media accounts."

She sighed. "I know this sounds stupid, but it feels like a breach of privacy to do so. I wouldn't want anyone going through my phone."

"Normally, I would agree with you, but in crisis mode, our main goal is to keep her safe. Sometimes to accomplish this, it requires temporary unrestricted insight into her activities, especially if she is unwilling to be forthcoming with the truth."

"Could you talk to her?" she blurted, clearly embarrassed, but desperate enough to ask anyway. "I don't have anyone else to turn to."

"I absolutely would," Adrienne answered, grateful to have something to focus on outside of her own problems. "Are you getting some support?" She asked. "Having a child in crisis puts a lot of pressure on a mother. You have to take care of yourself so you have the resources to help Maisy navigate this."

"I'll look into it," Tricia said, dismissing the idea immediately. Adrienne made plans to come by for a visit the next afternoon and ended the call. This was not going to be an easy conversation.

TWENTY-SIX

The next afternoon, Adrienne pulled into a parking spot in downtown Aura Cove and closed her eyes to inhale the scent of cocoa beans and browned butter. Through the plate glass window, she could see the shop had emptied out from its typical morning commuter rush where a long line often snaked down the sidewalk. Grateful she'd timed it just right, she hid behind a pair of enormous black sunglasses and quickly exited the car, hoping to make the stop unrecognized. The idea of being confronted by an Aura Cove High School student or parent was more than her fragile heart could take. She walked into Kandied Karma where a beautiful woman with luminous green eyes and thick white hair that was gathered into a ponytail offered her an approachable smile.

"Can I help you?"

"Yes." She returned the smile. It was the first one

that didn't seem forced since the news had broken, and she asked, "Can you recommend something to help butter up a teenager?"

"Whew! That's a tall order! They *are* the toughest critics." She laughed, then confided her biggest frustration. "How can they be so jaded when they haven't even experienced the worst life has to offer yet?"

Adrienne chuckled at her observation and watched the woman deftly fold up the sides of a golden box. "My sister is addicted to your truffles," she said to make conversation. It was second nature for her to always look for a positive comment to share when meeting someone new.

"We love hearing that, don't we, Yuli?" The woman turned her huge grin of undeniable pride toward an older woman seated at a small bistro table surrounded by paperwork. The lines of her face were deeply etched into her softening skin, but there was no denying their genetic link. They shared the same luminous green eyes and white hair. She looked up from her stack of paperwork, accepting the compliment with a warm smile.

"Who is your sister?"

"Davina Thorne."

"Oh, yes!" The woman's warmth tripled with this new information. "Davina was actually my attorney in my divorce. That woman is a powerhouse! Be sure to tell her Katie Beaumont says hello."

"She is and I will." Adrienne felt herself relax.

Katie started layering the bottom of the box with rich dark chocolates with caramel centers and a pair of crunchy turtles with pecans. At the register, she wrapped the box in a fuchsia bow and handed it over to Adrienne. Her cool fingers gently pushed Adrienne's hand away that was offering her credit card.

"Your money is no good here. These are on the house."

Adrienne felt a little jolt of static electricity pass between them when their skin connected and she jumped.

"Sorry to shock you! This cold snap has us running the furnace more than usual and it's so dry," Katie explained as her eyes bored into Adrienne's.

Adrienne's gaze darted away. She busied herself putting her card away and pulling a pair of fingerless gloves from her handbag. "I feel your pain! Don't tell anyone, but I keep these bad boys in my purse for days like this." She looked down at the beautiful gold box. "Thank you for being so kind. I have a feeling these will do the trick."

"How are you holding up?" Katie's voice was kind, yet Adrienne flinched when the salt hit her wound. She'd convinced herself that Aura Cove Community School District was a tiny ecosystem, and the dismissal from her appointment as Superintendent of Schools was already yesterday's news. A tight knot formed in her belly, and she felt the shame coloring her cheeks a scarlet red.

"Oh no! I'm sorry, I didn't mean to pry," Katie apologized.

"No. It's okay," she said, dismissing the painful topic of conversation. "I am going to have to get used to speaking about it." She heaved a heavy sigh. "It's been rough. I never in a million years thought I would be unemployable in education." She quivered as a tremor of humiliation passed through her. "I feel so violated."

"Of course you do. I am so sorry," Katie empathized.

Her lips tightened and a grim expression settled on her face. "I always told my students, 'Be careful what you share online and on your devices. One poor decision as a teenager can impact the rest of your life.'" She shook her head and offered a worn, self-deprecating grin. "I'm finding this slice of humble pie particularly hard to swallow." Katie's warm gaze held hers for a long moment.

"We're huge believers in Karma, aren't we, Yuli?" Katie said, and the old woman grunted in agreement as she continued to sort through the paperwork in front of her. "At Kandied Karma, we believe the universe has a way of righting its wrongs and bringing even more success and favor to good people than it ever takes away."

The warm sentiment calmed Adrienne's shame and doubts, and she held the beautiful box of truffles aloft as she said goodbye. "I'm going to hold you to that! Thank you for the candy and the cheering squad."

"You can't hold a good woman down," Katie

encouraged. "You wait and see." The door jingled as Adrienne walked to her car lighter than she'd been when she got out of it. She punched Maisy's address into her GPS and navigated toward the house.

She drove through the iron gate and turned down a winding street of impressive homes lining the beach. Massive palm trees ringed the impeccably landscaped yards in the pristine subdivision. At her destination, Adrienne pulled her car into the driveway and made her way to the front door. She pressed the doorbell and waited, and a few moments later, a middle-aged woman opened the door with a weary smile. Her lined face was plain and unassuming, with gray hair cropped close to her head, and she was dressed in flowy linen pants and a baby blue tunic.

"Yes?"

"I'm Adrienne," she said with a bright smile, offering the box of chocolates to Tricia with both hands. "Thanks for letting me visit today. Maisy was one of my favorite students."

"She was?" Utter shock walked across Tricia's features and settled in. Adrienne could read between the lines; this was a woman who wasn't used to school officials saying anything positive about her daughter.

"She's got a brilliant, creative mind," Adrienne gushed. "We were working together to get her enrolled in Central Florida Community College's fashion and textiles program. Maisy seemed excited at the prospect of earning college credits while still in high school."

"Oh, yes, she did mention that. It's the most excited

about school she'd ever been, and then this…" The rest of the sentence faded away in the awkward silence. "I'm sorry. Where are my manners? Please, come in."

Adrienne followed her into the sunny entryway. "You have a beautiful home." She glanced around at the minimalist interior where not a single item was out of place or a stitch of clutter was visible. The house was painted in cool ocean tones with an impressive two-story bank of windows offering a panoramic view of the sea. It was difficult to imagine Maisy's gothic punk aesthetic being embraced by her mother's adoration of modern coastal design.

"Thank you," Tricia said, then abruptly turned and shouted down the hallway where faint music could be heard. "Maisy! Ms. Thorne is here to see you!" She turned to Adrienne. "Sorry. It's the only way I can get her attention."

A few minutes later, a pale-faced Maisy stumbled down the hall wearing a pair of sweat pants and a wrinkled concert hoodie. Her face was devoid of any makeup and she looked much younger than the version she presented at school with the full lashes and eyeliner that added years and a theatrical quality to her look.

"Why don't you two sit on the lanai?" Tricia offered. "I'll bring out a tray with some lemonade."

One of Maisy's natural brows arched up, and she narrowed her eyes at her mother, scrutinizing the offer.

"Fresh air sounds great," Adrienne agreed, eager to bridge the obvious divide between them. "Right, Maisy?"

"Fantastic," Maisy muttered under her breath as she led Adrienne out the door to an all-weather wicker patio set that overlooked the ocean. Only a hundred yards out, the aqua water tickled the white sugar shore. It was a spectacular view.

A few minutes later, Tricia appeared with a silver tray of cut crystal glasses and an ornate plate of truffles. She set the tray down and quickly left them alone.

"So…" Adrienne began, unsure where to lead the conversation. "How are you today?"

"Better than a few days ago, I guess," Maisy said, her cheek twitching nervously. The stud in the valley of her dimpled cheek jostled around as she bit at it and rubbed it with her tongue. She thrust a hand into her mouth and began chewing on the remnants of her fingernails. Katie could tell it was a self-soothing tic that had been used often to curb her anxiety as they were worn down to peeling nubs.

"Things haven't been so great with me either," Adrienne started to explain, finding common ground with the teen. "I'm sure you've heard all the rumors," she mumbled. Surprised by the truthful admission, Maisy's glance darted over, her interest piqued. "It's been a bit of a nightmare, to be honest." Maisy, who wasn't used to the concept of unbridled truth coming from the mouth of an adult, was bowled over by it. "I'm on administrative leave pending a full investigation. Looks like we both have some extra time on our hands."

"They weren't photoshopped?" Maisy asked, stunned.

"Nope. The photographs were supposed to be part of a modeling portfolio. I made a poor decision and trusted the wrong person when I was your age, and it caught up with me," she offered in explanation.

"Are you getting fired?"

Adrienne decided to be frank with her, hoping it would encourage her to do the same. "I'm not sure, but I had to relinquish my appointment as superintendent because of the controversy."

"You did?"

"It was the right thing to do," Adrienne admitted sadly. "I love the Aura Cove School District. Ultimately, I had to put it first."

"What are you going to do now?"

"I don't know." Adrienne looked out at the ocean. "Right now, I am just going to have a day. It doesn't have to be the best day of my life, but I got up, I took a shower, and I got some candy for a friend. And now I'm sitting in the sun, looking at the waves, having a conversation with someone I care about. So, as far as days go, this one is better than most of last week already."

The beginning of a grin twitched at the corners of her mouth. Maisy pulled one of the chocolates off the plate and peeled off the liner before sinking her teeth into it. She chewed slowly, letting the sugar flood her bloodstream. Adrienne pulled a dark chocolate caramel off the plate and popped it into her mouth, letting it dissolve on her tongue while she waited for the teen to speak.

"Something kind of similar happened to me." When Maisy finally spoke, the sentence was barely above a whisper. Now that she was opening up, Adrienne was afraid to say anything to spook her, so she waited for her to continue. "A guy contacted me on Snap, and we started messaging back and forth." Her gaze darted away, and she swiped a tear from her cheek before letting out a wry laugh. "He told me I was beautiful." She said the word so wistfully that Adrienne instantly knew why it hit so hard. The melted chocolate on her chin reduced her to an innocent child, and it broke Adrienne's heart.

"No one has ever called me beautiful before," she whispered, her eyes filling with tears. "He started asking me for selfies and I sent them. It was exciting to be wanted. It kind of felt like a high, you know?"

Adrienne nodded.

"I thought he was in love with me. He kept asking for more skin. It was kind of fun at first, and I knew it was wrong, but that was part of what made it thrilling." She sniffled. "It wasn't just me sending photos. He did, too," she admitted as she pulled another chocolate off the plate and popped it into her mouth.

"Then he sent me a naked one and dared me to text one back. I tried to stall, but he wore me down. It was easier to just do it instead of arguing with him why I shouldn't. He said it would be our little secret."

Adrienne felt her stomach churn as she sat there listening to Maisy being groomed by a skilled predator. It was sickening.

"Then he wanted me to record myself... doing things."

"Oh, honey." Adrienne reached out and squeezed her hand, and a fat tear rolled down Maisy's cheek.

"He made me feel wanted... and... sexy, I guess?" She looked down. "He kept pushing me farther and farther until I told him no and that's when he changed."

Adrienne waited, already knowing the direction this was going and unable to stop her heartbreak.

"I didn't realize he'd been recording the screen the entire time. Saving every photo and video I ever sent. It was Snap, so they were supposed to disappear," she cried, her cheeks red with embarrassment.

"He knew where I lived. He sent me a list of students at Aura Cove he was going to send my photos and videos to if I didn't send him more explicit ones." Her voice deepened. "Then he threatened to share them on the internet, and with my mom and my grandma unless I gave him some money."

"Did you comply?"

"At first, but he kept coming back for more. Threatening me, telling me he was going to sell my videos to the highest bidder on WhisperHub, and leaking them to my friends. I just didn't see another way out." She hugged her knees to her chest and gently rocked forward and back as she sobbed, trying to self-soothe. Adrienne's heart was broken for the young girl. The name WhisperHub made goosebumps break out on Adrienne's forearms. She tucked the information away, eager to share when Davina came by tomorrow after work.

Turning her full attention back to Maisy, she leaned closer and said, "I am sorry you were manipulated."

"I was such an idiot. God, I wish I could go back and block his first stupid message in my DMs." She sniffled as she picked at the arm of the wicker chair. "I tried to forget about it, and I thought I was getting better, but every day my mind got caught up in the worry and the fear. The idea of my mom seeing them? It made me sick." She trembled as more tears coursed down her face. "What if he posted them online and my future college doesn't accept me? I had a pit in my stomach every day, and it seemed like the only way out was a permanent one."

"I understand exactly how you feel," Adrienne said. "I felt hopeless too, but I am so glad you were unsuccessful."

"I'm not," she admitted and burst into tears, covering her face with her hands.

"Do you have a plan to try it again?" Adrienne had to ask. She was terrified for the girl.

"No. I just want to run away and hide, but I can't. I hate myself for being so stupid."

Adrienne exhaled a hot breath. "I wish I had a magic pill to make this all go away, but I will tell you that one day you will feel better. My sister is helping me understand that you and I were victims. We didn't do anything wrong except trust the wrong people."

"I hate myself, and when I think about it, I feel terrible."

"Me too," Adrienne empathized. "You feel exposed, like you are naked in public and everyone can see."

"Yeah," Maisy croaked out, brushing hot tears away.

"When I was violated, I didn't report it, and because I didn't, it destroyed my future. I don't want that for you Maisy." Adrienne reached out her hand. "Do you think you could be braver than I was and file a police report?"

"No." Maisy was panicked at the thought of voluntarily entering a police station. "I can't." She wrapped her arms around her middle in a defensive position.

"I don't blame you. I couldn't either. But because I wanted to hide my head in the sand and pretend nothing happened, he probably did it to someone else. When we are silent, they continue. They get even bolder and hurt more women. I am asking you to be stronger than I was, and I promise I will stand next to you, shoulder to shoulder." Another fat tear slid down Maisy's flushed cheeks. "Please think it over."

Maisy nodded slowly, and Adrienne backed down. She didn't want to add to the fragile girl's pain.

"The only way out of this nightmare is to walk through it. And, although there are no shortcuts, I would like to help you." She held out her hand. "When you are having a bad day and you feel your self-worth slipping, I want you to reach out to me. What's your phone number?"

Maisy rattled it off, and Adrienne fired a text over to

her. "Day or night, you call me and I will talk you through it. Promise?"

Maisy nodded. The heavy conversation cast a pall over them both, and to shake it off, Adrienne changed the subject.

"Now, let's dry our tears and eat chocolate until our bellies ache in the Florida sunshine," Adrienne offered. "It's time to put down the shame we're carrying and forgive ourselves for the mistakes we made."

"I'll try."

"That's all I'll ever ask you to do."

"Ms. Thorne?" Maisy said, "You're a good person."

"So are you, Maisy." A full five minutes passed while they sat in the sun. When Maisy spoke, her voice was so soft Adrienne had to strain to hear it.

"Okay. I'll go with you to the station."

TWENTY-SEVEN

The next evening, Davina was exhausted from a long day at court and on her way over to Adrienne's condo. She parked in the driveway and sat in the car for a long moment before working up the nerve to press the button on her sister's doorbell. While she waited, she unbuttoned her jacket and tugged it off, draping it over her forearm as she suffered a hot flash. Fanning her face with her free hand, she was relieved to step into the glorious air conditioning of Adrienne's home.

"Need a glass of wine?" Adrienne asked

Balancing on a single leg like a flamingo, Davina peeled off her six-inch power heels, one at a time, before descending onto the cool travertine flooring of Adrienne's entryway.

"More than I need air right now," Davina answered, following her into her tidy kitchen. She waited, sitting on both the information she'd promised to share and one of Adrienne's wooden stools while her sister uncorked the bottle and poured two glasses.

"You're stalling," Adrienne assessed accurately as she handed Davina her glass.

Davina took a long sip of the wine and then said, "I wish I had better news for you. The initial search has been a dead end so far. He did a respectable job covering his tracks. All the emails were sent over a VPN that looks like it originated in Croatia."

"Croatia?"

"Emails sent through international servers in foreign countries are typically untraceable and are often used to conceal a person's identity."

"Damn," Adrienne whispered.

"I also consulted with another firm who is well-versed in sextortion and blackmail schemes." Her lips straightened into a grim line. "They painted a pretty bleak picture. That's why so many of these cases go unsolved. It's incredibly difficult to accurately identify the perpetrators and bring them to justice."

"So, he just gets away with it?"

"That's not what I'm saying. I always tell my clients to hope for the best but prepare for the worst," Davina said, backtracking.

Adrienne saw red. Her words became bullets that shot from her lips. "He gets to hide in the shadows and destroy my life, and nothing can be done to stop him from doing this to someone else?" Adrienne was justifiably outraged with no place to put her frustrations.

"We're going to find him."

"How can you be so sure?"

"I just am. One way or another, I promise we are going to flush this maggot out of hiding and make him rue the day he met you." Davina took another long sip of the wine, noticing for the first time Adrienne was dressed in a pair of high-waisted, fitted slacks with two rows of gold buttons and a pristine white t-shirt. "You're dressed. That's an improvement!"

"Gee, thanks!" Adrienne's lips quirked up.

"I know you've been depressed since the news broke. It's nice to see you looking more like yourself."

"I didn't have a choice. One of my former students had a mental health crisis after getting caught up in a similar scenario, and we went to the police station to file a report today."

Davina cocked her head and her eyes narrowed. "Similar? How?"

"She was being manipulated to trade explicit photos and videos on Snap with a guy she met on social media. But when she got uncomfortable and refused to comply with his demands, his attitude changed. She learned he'd been secretly recording and screen-capturing them all along without her knowledge or consent."

"Wow," Davina said. "I'm glad phones didn't exist when I was young and stupid."

"Get this." She became more animated, talking with her hands as her words crashed over each other. "Then he began blackmailing her, demanding payment or threatening to send the photos to her entire list of contacts. He even went so far as to threaten to post her actual address online alongside the photos and videos on…" she paused for emphasis, "wait for it… WhisperHub!"

"What?!" The hairs on the back of Davina's neck stood up and she jumped to her feet. "Did you say WhisperHub?"

"Yes!" Adrienne confirmed. "It gave me goosebumps when she said it. Do you think there is a connection?"

"Maybe." Davina mused it over as she paced. "At the very least, we need to shut down that cesspool."

"We do," Adrienne agreed. "Platforms like WhisperHub need to be held accountable."

"You're absolutely right."

"Maisy thought the only way out of the nightmare was to take her own life."

"Oh my God. That's terrible," Davina said.

"Luckily, she was unsuccessful, but we have to do more to protect young women like Maisy. I know better than anyone that one stupid mistake can impact your life forever." She let out a disgusted chuckle. "I'm the walking poster child for stupid teenage mistakes."

"Hey! You don't get to talk about my sister like that," Davina said wryly, trying to inject some levity into the shameful situation.

Adrienne's lips turned up into a small smile in spite of herself. "You know what? You're right. This pity party ends now." Looking for the silver lining, she said, "We have to do something. We can't let them win."

"Agreed. We won't." She downed the last of her

wine before she had a burst of inspiration. "I might have a way you can take some of your power back."

Intrigued, Adrienne cupped her chin in her hands. "I'm listening."

"I have a client that knows Melanie Stevens."

"From the morning show? I love her!" Adrienne gushed.

"I am going to ask for an intro and see if she wants to do an exclusive interview. It would give you the chance to clear your name and educate the viewers on the dangers of online extortion. If it can happen in Aura Cove, it can happen anywhere. Maybe Maisy could be part of it?"

"I'm in," Adrienne said without hesitation. "But I don't want to re-victimize Maisy. Her mental health is far more important."

"True. But I would argue the same applies to you." Davina was leery.

"I have thicker skin. Besides, what could it hurt? My reputation is already destroyed."

"I would want to be there," Davina demanded, her capable, overprotective side emerging in full force. "I will also request a list of the interview questions in advance so we don't get hit with any surprises."

Adrienne nodded, picking up on the guilt Davina was trying to assuage by seeing around corners and being on the lookout for possible pitfalls. "I don't blame you."

"I know," Davina whispered.

"Let's do it! Education is always key. Even if the

ones who victimized us are never discovered or brought to justice, if I can stop one teenager from this hell, it is worth it."

"True, and while that is a very noble stance," Davina said, "forgive me for wanting retribution. I'm still out for blood." She stood to leave. "I better go. I've got an early appearance in the morning. Thanks for the vino and the update."

"Anytime," Adrienne said, rinsing out their glasses. Davina hurried to the car, eager to touch base with Niles. She didn't want to get Adrienne's hopes up for nothing, but there had to be a connection. She was now more certain than ever that WhisperHub was the answer.

TWENTY-EIGHT

Katie walked right by a window display filled with stunning family beach portraits taken at sunset. Then she circled back and ogled them for several long minutes before entering the bright modern studio in downtown St. Pete's Beach. On the exposed brick wall, life-size portraits were lit by overhead spotlights. The display had an art gallery aesthetic, and the high ceilings with lofty exposed ductwork and steel beams painted a stark black only further enhanced it.

Artfully arranged on one wall were murals of families walking on the beach. Dressed in their soft pastels that echoed the colors of the sea at sunset, they all donned wide smiles and clasped each other's hands as the white surf nibbled at their toes. Another wall was filled with ornately carved frames, including mats and filigree liners surrounding timeless portraits of babies. Looking at them, Katie envisioned two of them hanging in her beach house already. They were artistically rendered, and the babies were often photographed in the nude. The collection was tasteful and sweet with a distinct nod to Anne Geddes's whimsical style.

On the back wall, three antique curio cabinets housed a collection of vintage cameras. Katie was immediately drawn to it, recalling Zoya's notorious enchanted camera locked away at the Casanova Compound. The enormity of the collection was impressive. It ranged from old wooden view cameras, to twin lens reflex cameras with multiple lenses, to a rugged Hasselblad—just like the camera that recorded Neil Armstrong's first steps on the moon. All of them were painstakingly merchandised amid flourishing succulents and stacked fine art photography books. It was an impressive display purposefully curated to appeal to an older demographic, and Katie ate it up.

A few moments later, a beautiful young woman walked into the reception room to greet her.

"Welcome to Precious Momento." The woman's shiny flat-ironed hair swung gently at her waist. "I'm Raquel." She extended her tiny hand and pressed it into Katie's thicker one. She was svelte and immaculately dressed, wearing flowing garments and nude heels. Chunky modern jewelry adorned her neck and wrists, a contrast that emphasized her birdlike frame.

"I'm Katie." She pointed over at the cameras as her curiosity won out. "Are you a collector?"

"No," she confided with an open smile. "They are a little too old and musty for my taste. It's the private collection of my freelancer, Denny. I believe they were passed down from his father. When we were in the final stages of design, he offered them to us on loan, and the designer thought they added a certain vintage vibe."

"They *are* beautiful," Katie said, appreciating their gleaming focusing rings and metal cranks. She had a weakness for vintage décor, and at Precious Momento, it was done well.

Bored and eager to get back to business, Raquel blinked then nodded politely, and asked, "What brings you in today?"

"Well, I've probably walked by your display a million times but now that my family is expanding, it's become more important to have a record of the changes and new additions. I love your work," Katie gushed, pointing back to the family photos on the beach. "You're geniuses at capturing emotion."

"We believe capturing the love you feel for each other is our highest calling." She leaned in. "Family is everything and we strive to document what makes yours unique. Not just a physical representation of your faces, but we endeavor to capture your very souls."

Katie listened to her over-the-top sales pitch, amused by the similarities. Zoya's camera at the compound had the same goal, but it was far more sinister.

"Can I offer you something to drink?"

"No, thank you," Katie declined politely.

"You mentioned your family is expanding. Can you tell me more?"

"I don't even know where to start! I've got two grandchildren on the way and a wedding happening all in the next six to eight months. Do you have some sort of frequent flyer program?" She chuckled at the reference as she watched Raquel's eyes widen, and her tongue darted out to lick her lips in anticipation.

"Congratulations! You are smart to start now to secure the right photographer early. We often book up to a year in advance, but I am sure we can squeeze you in. Do you have a few minutes to discuss some specifics?"

"Sure," Katie said as Raquel led her into a consultation room. She sank into the plush sofa in front of the large screen and waited for instructions.

"Just enjoy the show, and if something catches your eye, make a mental note and we'll discuss your preferences when it's over." Katie leaned back as the room darkened and dramatic music cued up that gave the theatrical soundtracks of her favorite movies a run for their money. The show lasted less than ten minutes and purposefully tugged at her heartstrings. When the room lights came up, Katie laughed at herself as she swiped tears from her eyes. "Tell me I'm not the only one who is moved to tears by other people's photographs."

Raquel smiled wide and leaned in with a conspiring whisper, "You're not alone. Our clientele places a lot of importance on family and creating a visual legacy. Never be ashamed of letting your love for your family show."

Next, she spent thirty minutes walking Katie

through the portrait and video options available. Raquel used words like visual legacy and artistic rendering to set the tone and justify Precious Momento's astronomical rates.

"The Heirloom Collection is our starter plan that includes a yearly photo session at the location of your choice, and we build family portrait albums that grow as your family does. It's an artistic archive you can pass on from generation to generation that only grows in value as the years go by."

"I love that idea," Katie said, drinking the Kool-Aid. "Both of my daughters are currently pregnant."

"Oh! Congratulations!" Raquel segued right into maternity sessions without delay. "Imagine your daughters at sunset at Siesta Key, with yards of flowing satin billowing around their burgeoning bellies. I am certain they are stunners like you!" She was laying the flattery on thick, and Katie saw through it, but it didn't make her any less excited at the prospect. Raquel was a hustler, a genius in the art of persuasion, and Katie respected her drive and ability to instinctively pull her emotional levers. "And you mentioned an upcoming wedding, too?" Raquel gushed at the prospect, her well-trained expression shifting appropriately to dreamy. "You need us!"

Katie smiled. She was putty in Raquel's capable hands, realizing for the first time she desperately yearned for a visual record of the years that were coming. She knew from her own experience, motherhood was a blur of constant motion, and she wanted to stop time. "Children change so quickly, especially in the first year of life."

Raquel nodded in agreement. "You are so right! Not many clients understand that."

Ready to sign a contract on the spot, she listened to Raquel detail their extensive portrait plans and what was included with each investment level. The word choice was not lost on her. This wasn't a package of sheets of photos from a mass-produced chain store. What Raquel was proposing was one-of-a-kind and completely tailored to reflect her family's values and interests, and Katie fell for the presentation—hook, line, and sinker.

"We want to be the one you call to record every milestone in your family's life. From weddings to the birth of grandchildren and every step in between, we want to be your lifetime photographer."

"Are you the one who will work with us?"

"If you chose the Legacy Collection, then yes," Raquel started in. "It is only reserved for our most discriminating clients and requires two photographers. I will be on hand to capture the candid, unplanned moments in a documentary style. I find that some of the most tender moments happen in between the clicks of the shutter. My associate, Denny, is an accomplished portrait artist. He will focus on creating your formal groupings, turning them into precious family keepsakes that will last generations."

"You mean he'll turn them into Precious Momentos?" Katie joked, getting swept up in the excitement.

"Exactly."

"A week after each photo session, we invite you back to the studio for your viewing and selection appointment. It's a truly magical event when you sit down on this very sofa and get to experience the love you have for each other documented forever in the most beautiful and timeless way.

"We walk you through the selection process, guiding you to select the right size photographs for your display space." She waved a hand behind her where a series of beach photos was displayed in gorgeous frames that almost glowed under the lights. "We guarantee all of our art meets archival standards. We also offer a full line of frames, ensuring that your portraits have the same time and attention to image preservation that fine art deserves. This is especially important with the higher levels of harmful UV rays found in the Florida sun."

"Of course." Katie nodded. "Do you think you could squeeze us in before Christmas? I know it sounds silly, but I'd like our first family photo taken before the babies come. It will be our last one before we expand."

Raquel gave her a wince. "We are fully booked for our heirloom packages, *but* I might have an opening available for the Legacy Collection. We keep a couple of slots available every month for our members that invest at the highest level."

"Then that's what I want," Katie said as she pulled out her credit card to make a healthy deposit on the plan. She signed a monthly agreement that was roughly more than her first house payment in Aura Cove.

She hadn't found anything worth splurging on with the money she'd squirreled away from her divorce. But when she walked out of Precious Momento with a family portrait appointment for the following week, it felt like an unseen force was guiding her. She just didn't understand it was Karma.

TWENTY-NINE

The next morning, Katie honked her car's horn from Frankie's driveway, and ten minutes later, the front door opened and Frankie drifted out into the mild December sunshine. She offered Katie an apologetic half-wave and hurried over to the Beetle dressed in a long flowing skirt, a purple tank top, and a pair of well-worn Birkenstocks. She was getting settled in the passenger seat of the convertible when the screened front door slammed and Harry flew out of it, dangling her keys and clasping a light jacket.

"Thanks, hon! You, sir, are a prince among men." Frankie grinned, holding her palm out, and Harry dropped the keys into it. He bent down with the jacket and kissed her goodbye, and she reached up to cradle his face in her hands. Katie watched their display of affection, feeling a tender tug at her heartstrings. There was an inkling growing inside her, a hint of wanting that she'd been pushing away, afraid of where it would lead.

"Well, someone's got to look after you," he said. "Don't forget, I've got a double, so there is no need to come rushing back home." He pulled back and said to Katie, "You two have fun at the Farmer's Market."

"There's an art show a few blocks down I'd like to check out, too," Katie said, winking at Frankie needling her. "Especially now, since I know you have the time."

"Dammit, Willey!" Frankie cried, thrusting one fist up in the air in mock frustration as they watched Harry reenter the house. She buckled her seatbelt, then turned toward Katie and whined, "Do we have to? Those things are always filled with hoity-toity snobs discussing things like the use of light and the symbolism of the subject. I'd rather stick needles in my eyes!"

"Consider it your penance for making me wait, you drama queen!" Katie laughed at Frankie's semi-accurate description.

"Please address me as Your Highness," Frankie teased, folding her arms across her chest playfully. Huffing in frustration, she quickly accepted her fate. "Fine, but you're buying me margaritas before exposing me to the torture."

"Deal."

Frankie grinned and took a quick journey down memory lane. "Remember that time you dragged me to the Dali Museum? God, that man was a nut ball."

"But you love nut balls!" Katie said. "Of all the balls, they are your favorite."

"Second favorite." Frankie snickered.

"Eww." Katie chuckled. "You should thank me.

Being exposed to art makes a person more cultured and well-rounded. I thought you, of all people, would appreciate Dali's delightful eccentricities… The waxed mustache, the melting clocks? What's not to love?"

Frankie laughed in agreement. "Dude was a flamboyant legend, but to be honest, I was hoping the show would have focused more on the orgies."

"Orgies?" Katie questioned, and her face flushed a pretty shade of pink in embarrassed surprise.

"Yeah, he was famous for hosting them. Did you know Cher was invited to one once? Apparently, she picked up a painted rubber fish with a remote control that wiggled back and forth when she clicked it on."

Frankie lowered her voice several octaves, trying to channel her inner Cher. "She said, 'This little fishy is funny. Uh-huh.'" Frankie smirked, flipping her frizzy red hair over her shoulder. It was a dreadful impression, mimicking the singer's contralto tone. "Dali didn't skip a beat and answered, 'While it might look like a children's toy, I've heard it's quite delightful when placed on your clitoris.'"

Katie burst out laughing, which made Frankie snort. "You made that up!"

"I did not!" Frankie said, making a cross over her heart with her index finger. "It was a true story they told us at the yearly kick-off meeting during my brief stint as a sexual health and wellness consultant at Pure Seduction."

"Oh my God!" Katie laughed. "I forgot about that!"

"It was short-lived," Frankie admitted. "Maybe I can

unload some of the vibrators I still have at Lauren's bachelorette party."

Katie laughed. "She would kill you. And I'd probably let her."

Frankie rolled her eyes. "At least, at the Dali museum, we can entertain ourselves by counting the penises."

"Um, I believe they are called phallic symbols."

"See? That's what I'm talking about," Frankie whined. "I like to call 'em like I see um. Phallic Symbols? Pfft!" She huffed her outrage. "They are wieners. Schlongs. The Ye Olde Grande Meat Sword."

Katie laughed at her vivid description of male genitalia. "I am simply trying to educate you in the arts and expose you to culture."

"Harry already has the exposing thing covered," she said with a snort.

"Of course he does," Katie remarked, giving up on her attempts to reason with Frankie about the value of appreciating art. "I *will* say the man has done a number on my best friend. I don't think I've ever seen you this relaxed and happy."

"It has taken some getting used to, that's for sure," Frankie agreed.

Katie hit the gas when the light turned green, and the breeze blew their hair back as they whipped down the roads toward downtown St. Pete's Beach. It was a glorious warm winter day where the sun glinted over the rippling water like cut diamonds.

"Has Arlo, er, I mean Brody come back around?" Frankie asked.

"No," Katie admitted, realizing that the statement made her a little sad. "Just a couple of texts. He's giving me the space I asked for."

"Do I detect a bit of regret?" She looked at her friend knowingly.

"Would it be weird if I said yes?"

"Not to me," Frankie said. "Weird is where I excel. I live for weird."

Katie laughed. "Maybe it's a calculated move, you know, the whole absence makes the heart grow fonder thing?"

"He was always pretty intelligent, apart from barking at every little sound he heard." Frankie leaned in and studied her best friend. "Do you *want* him to come around more?"

Katie chewed on the corner of her lip, considering Frankie's question. "I might."

"Then why don't you reach out to him?" Frankie asked. "Men appreciate a straightforward approach. Maybe he's sitting around waiting for a sign?"

"It's just…" Katie hesitated. "I don't want to get his hopes up when I don't know what I want our relationship to be. If I even want it to be anything."

"Ooh!" Frankie picked up on the shift in her demeanor. "Your relationship? I thought he was regulated to the friend zone."

"He is," Katie quickly backtracked.

"Life is short, babe. When you are offered a chance at happiness, you should take it."

"I know you're right. I just have too many conflicting emotions, not to mention the lingering weirdness about the idea of falling in love with my former dog."

"He loved you then as that creature, and he loves you now as a human," Frankie reminded her., "What more proof do you need of his love and devotion? It spans species *and* lifetimes!"

Katie laughed at the grandiose stance on the topic Frankie was taking. "For someone more cynical than I was, you sure have come around."

"That's what love does to you." Frankie smiled dreamily. "It changes everything."

Katie parked the car and pulled out two canvas bags she threaded over her shoulder, and they started walking down the sidewalks toward the sound of a strumming guitar. The crowd thickened as they neared, and Katie inhaled the scent of caramelized onions from the street vendors who were cooking up tacos for the early lunch crowd. Cafes' patios were filled with people and spotted with dogs lying on the bricks soaking up the winter sun. Katie stopped to chat with a few of her favorite vendors and added a bunch of organic kale, papery bulbs of garlic, and spring onions to her canvas bags. Frankie hit up her favorites, too. First, the sugar cookie baker, and then, the kettle corn vendor, and they passed an open bag of kettle corn back and forth as they walked down the street, stuffing handfuls of it into their open mouths.

"Such a beautiful day," Katie remarked, closing her eyes and tipping her face up to enjoy the rays of the sun. She stopped at a table filled with lemons and other various citrus. Picking up a plump orange, she sniffed it and said to the vendor, "I'll take a dozen."

They stopped for a kebab and continued down the side streets, darting around a man crooning into a microphone as they nibbled and giggled like teenagers catching up on each other's lives. At a taqueria, Katie handed Frankie a margarita, a preemptive strike against the whining, and they stood on the crowded patio at a tall table and ate their weight in chips and salsa. "After this, you owe me a slow sojourn through the art festival."

"Can we compromise on a medium-paced one?"

Katie raised her plastic glass and tapped it against Frankie's. "Deal."

They dropped off their heavy bags of produce at the car before heading down the street in the opposite direction. Under a multicolored balloon archway, the art show was already in full swing. They cruised down the blocked-off street, and Frankie followed without complaint, dawdling a few steps behind. At a jewelry vendor, Frankie stopped short and actually paused, bending down to look at a selection of handmade rings. Lit by a single spotlight, she leaned closer to them as a beautiful blonde asked, "Would you like to see anything from the case?"

Realizing Frankie had stopped following her, Katie turned, surprised to see her best friend browsing the stock of men's rings. In shock, she rushed over and asked, "Is that what I think it is?" Frankie was holding a thick men's band made out of a deer antler, studying it as if her life depended on it. The question made her cheeks pink up immediately.

"May-be?" Frankie's response was uncharacteristically sweet and unsure, and it made Katie's hand clamp over her mouth in shock. "We've been talking about it for a while now."

"You have?" Katie flung her arms around her friend and pulled her in close for a hug. "Why didn't you tell me?"

"I didn't want to jinx it." She picked the band up between her thumb and forefinger and held it in the light.

"Gosh, they grow up so fast," Katie cried, mocking her with glee as she pulled back and bit one of her knuckles theatrically, "You're making me tear up." She let out an exaggerated distressed yelp, then began to blubber, and collapsed into another fit of giggles.

"Knock it off." Frankie rolled her eyes. "And help me pick one."

"Wait. You're serious?" Katie's eyes widened and a huge smile washed over her features.

"I'm going to propose."

Katie shrieked, "What? You Are? Oh my God!"

"Shhh! You're creating a scene!" Frankie's face blazed red; even the tips of her ears were crimson.

"Go with your first choice," Katie advised when she finally gott her excitement under control. Frankie studied it in the palm of her hand for a long moment before saying, "I'll take it in a ten."

"What? You even know his ring size?" Katie was astonished. "You *are* serious! Holy cow!"

"It's not rocket science, woman." Frankie explained, "I put a string around his ring finger when he was asleep."

"Who are you?" Katie was taken aback.

"Still the freak you know and love." Frankie offered the artist her credit card, who swiped it through a device and wrapped her purchase. Frankie tucked it into her purse and walked further down the street as if nothing important had just occurred. It took an astonished Katie a bit longer to pick her jaw off the concrete and join her friend. She laced her arm through Frankie's as they strolled onto the next street that was lined with artists' booths.

"A wedding?"

"Cool your jets," Frankie warned. "We are not the wedding kind. We both decided an elopement was more our style."

"Really? Where?"

"Well, Vegas is on the table."

"Let me guess, at one of the drive-through chapels?"

"Maybe or an Elvis impersonator."

"Honestly, that seems perfect for you both."

"Yeah, throw in a Burlesque show, a crazy buffet with all-you-can-eat crab legs, and it's my perfect day."

"You know what?" Katie told her, "The big wedding

is overrated. I love that you want to keep it simple. As long as I get to be one of the witnesses."

"You know it!"

Katie stopped in the middle of the sidewalk and hugged her friend tight. "Look at you. Going all in. I never thought I'd live to see the day. I'm thrilled for you."

Filled with happiness, they walked further down and Katie stopped at a booth where a man with thinning gray hair pulled into a skinny ponytail was speaking to a group of younger men in suits. "It's transcendent." He waved an arm back toward his booth, which was covered from top to bottom with luscious floral photography. Intrigued, Katie felt herself drawn closer to investigate why the men were so enraptured by the art.

"I need a new piece for my bedroom," she mumbled to Frankie, who quirked her head to the side as her brow scrunched up in confusion.

Studying the photographs, Frankie spoke in hushed tones out of the corner of her mouth, "These don't remind you of anything?"

Katie took a step closer to study a soft flesh-colored rose photograph. It was a limited edition and signed in graphite by the artist. The petals were curvy and layered in an oval opening that repeated, and the soft light made each petal luminescent and practically glowing. "What do you mean?"

Frankie dragged her by the arm over to one that was pink with a tiny circle at the top of the oval. "I can't believe you can't see it." Frustrated, she circled her hand near the plum-pink circle of the engorged bud. "The little man in the boat?"

"What!?" Katie took a step back, horrified. "That's ridiculous. You see genitalia everywhere you look, you dirty bird!" She feverishly scanned the images closest to her. "No!" She walked around to the other side of the booth, desperate to find a photograph that conflicted with Frankie's theory. An ebony-colored rose with a bright red "boat" made her cheeks flash bright red in embarrassment.

"These are floral va-gines," Frankie hissed, her eyes dancing with unconcealed mirth. "Maybe I *am* a patron of the arts after all." Katie tittered with laughter and Frankie snorted, leaning closer to each one to study them more closely. "He's pretty good."

Katie was intrigued and stepped closer to the artist, who was wrapping up a sale to a well-dressed businessman. "Be sure to take a photo of the installation and tag me on Instagram."

"Hello there," he said, turning to her with a tight smile and offering her his hand. Katie pressed her palm into his, and when it connected, the colors of the photograph intensified. She was temporarily blinded by several pops and bursts of light. It took a second for her eyes to acclimate to the vision that spun forward like a movie. She glimpsed the exposed back side of a young woman, who arched her back and glanced over her shoulder, biting on her bottom lip. Feeling dirty, Katie yanked her palm away from his, eager for the image to dissipate. She laced her hands behind her back to avoid any further contact.

"Are you okay?" he asked her. Katie blinked several times, trying to clear the offensive flash from her head. Stepping back from him, she swallowed what felt like the bitter burn of whiskey in the back of her throat. She was grateful when another group of men wandered over, drawn to the photographs like moths to a flame. Sensing Katie wasn't going to be opening her wallet anytime soon, he quickly moved over to an easier target. "Greetings, my good men."

Katie wandered back toward Frankie. "He's part of my assignment," she whispered, her lips close to Frankie's ear.

"Really?' Frankie asked. Katie reached down and pulled a card from the stack on the table. On it was a formal portrait of the man she'd just met with the name D. Sebastian Kincaid listed underneath it. There was a QR code that led to his website and his social media handles. Katie folded the card and dropped it into her handbag to research later, eager to put some distance between them.

"Let's get out of here," she said, walking back to the car. Each step she took eased the load of bricks stacked on her chest.

"You're so preoccupied," Frankie remarked. "What did you see?"

"It was a photo session, I think," was all she could bring herself to say. She needed to do more digging and didn't want to speculate around Frankie.

"He gave off huge creeper vibes." Frankie chattered as usual as they slid into the car and started the drive home. "Obviously, he's very in tune with his target market." Frankie made a gagging face and scrunched up her nose. "Pretentious douchebags are his specialty."

———

Later that evening, Katie pulled the card from her bag and scanned it with her phone. The QR Code led her to a minimalist website with a rotating slideshow of his best work installed in opulent homes and modern offices.

She clicked on the tab labeled "About the Artist." The page loaded, revealing a black and white photo of him standing ankle-deep in the ocean leaning on a view camera mounted on a tripod. The photo was taken probably ten years prior when his hair was significantly darker and thicker than she remembered it being that afternoon.

Next to his name, a quote appeared in tasteful italics.

"Kincaid has unlocked the portal to an erotic realm where flowers and femininity entwine, transcending the societal boundaries of sexual norms."

Meet D. Sebastian Kincaid: A Maestro of Arboreal Allure

In his work, blossoms metamorphose into

symbolic declarations of femininity, capturing the very essence of nature's most intimate secrets.

His large-format photographs, meticulously composed, unfurl with unrestricted grandeur, revealing a secret tango between his lens and the luscious folds of Mother Nature's most guarded treasures. Behold, the orchids that whisper mysteries and the prim and proper tea roses that blush with clandestine tales.

Kincaid's stunning creations are hailed as a testament to the profound coupling between the sacred and the sensual. Each timeless photograph is an explicit pixelated sonnet, capturing the elusive beauty of ripened botanical femininity.

A Collector's Wet Dream

Lord Archibald Wallingsford, a collector of the sublime, declares, *"Kincaid's flora is an exquisite fusion of botanic mystique and visual indulgence, an opus that resonates with whispered sensuality."*

Kincaid has unlocked the portal to a realm where flowers and femininity copulate, transcending the boundaries of society's prudish restrictions.

Whether one views his scandalous creations with awe or bemusement, there's no denying the audacious brilliance that unfolds in each limited-edition photograph—a passionate testimony to the ephemeral beauty of nature and the provocative depths of arousal.

"He's a real piece of work," Katie said aloud, chuckling at the pretentious tone of his autobiography. She fired off a link to Frankie and, in less than a minute, her phone rang.

"Luscious folds of Mother Nature's most guarded treasures?" Frankie barely got through the sentence before snorting with laughter. "Holy shit! I bet he wrote that himself." She started in again, giggling as she delivered another zinger, "Delicate curves of chlorophyll passion? God, that is rich!"

"I know, right?" Katie agreed. "He's ridiculous."

"What are you going to do now?"

"I'm not sure." Katie dismissed the specifics, not wanting to jeopardize her assignment. She redirected the conversation. "More importantly, when are *you* going to propose?"

"TBD!" Frankie cried. "Get off my back, woman! I've only had the ring for a few hours. I haven't figured it out yet."

"Me neither," Katie whispered under her breath.

THIRTY

Davina was sitting in her office at the end of her last long day in mediation before Christmas. The dismantling of lives was a tedious process to witness, and she always marveled more often than not the negotiations stalled out on the tiniest details. She was amazed that it was shared custody of the family pet that got more pushback than the equitable division of million-dollar real estate and retirement investments. Eager to wrap up, she said goodbye to her clients and walked them to the elevator. When the doors shut, she peeked at the gold timepiece on her wrist. Knowing Niles was punctual to a fault, she realized he would be coming by to give a report any minute.

She had barely tucked away the clutter on her desk when her assistant knocked on the door and led Niles into the office. He chose the same chair he always did and waited until the door was closed before he spoke. Sitting on the edge of his seat, Niles rocked back and forth in his chair, a subtle tic that Davina had learned conveyed his excitement. It was as if his body failed to physically contain the energy. Niles pressed his palms to his thighs and rocked faster before a little excited yip escaped his lips. "It looks like Santa came early this year," he began, his attempt at a joke dry but effective.

Davina's eyes sparkled and she wanted to lean closer but forced herself to maintain the distance he preferred, not wanting to distract him and get the meeting off-track.

Niles rocked faster and yipped again. "I received a technological gift last night."

Davina pressed her lips together, breathing out of her nose as she felt her heart beat faster in her chest.

"I think we got him." His eyes darted up to hers, offering a small smile, then skittered away. "Yep. We got the bastard."

Davina felt a surge of joyous vindication threaten to overtake her, but she squelched it down and forced herself to remain calm. Overt displays of emotion could make Niles spiral, so instead, she asked, "How?"

"I discovered an unpatched security update that exposed vulnerabilities in WhisperHub's backend. Then I wrote a bit of malware code that exploited a flaw in their users' browsers, forcing their computers to reveal their authentic Internet protocol addresses, and ran a script to collect them."

"Wow." Davina blew out a hot breath. In the ethical hacking arena, they were past the point of no return, far from the gray area, and balls deep in the black. Davina knew they had crossed the line but pushed on anyway. She'd always been the type to ask for forgiveness instead of permission and decided she'd worry about how to explain it to the authorities later. Right now, the information was gold, and she was greedy to unearth all of it.

"Over the course of the last several weeks, I was able to collect tens of thousands of IP addresses. Traffic to the site and the number of engaged users tend to ramp up during the holidays as loneliness magnifies addictive behaviors. The hard part was the massive amount of collected data had to be combed through and sorted." Niles adjusted his glasses and then folded his hands together in his lap. After a few distressed yips, the rocking ramped up again, and Davina waited for him to deliver the rest of his report.

"End users are complete idiots. I read through WhisperHub's terms of service, and buried in there is a veiled reference giving them permission to mine data and monitor usage. Most end users never read those things. WhisperHub advertised their platform as private and anonymous, but on the back end, they were gathering as much data as they could to train their algorithm so that when they rolled out their advertising program, they could rake in the profits. The money is always in the data! It is the digital gold of any organization. Meta and Google were among the first to figure that out."

"Free is never free," Davina agreed, hoping to subtly guide him back on track. His excitement was sending him on a tangent.

"Yep, you always pay one way or the other," Niles said. He folded his hands together, and it seemed to calm his rocking.

"Sorting through the data was an absolute nightmare. I had to find his handle among the tens of thousands that use the platform. It was a bit of a needle in a haystack situation until I wrote the perfect program to cull it. I asked the software to search the database for its top one hundred most active users. Then I narrowed it geographically.

"It revealed frequent correspondence between two handles. Twistedsnaps69 and 1_bad_influence."

"Ick," Davina said under her breath as she rolled her eyes at their weak attempts to be clever.

"Ick is right. You'll notice in the messages between them that 1_bad_influence became a mentor to Twistedsnaps69. He provided the step-by-step instruction that led to the blackmail scheme and distribution of Adrienne's photos."

Davina leaned back in her chair and steepled her fingers under her chin. The case was becoming bigger than Adrienne's isolated incident, and as the outrage clawed up her ribs demanding retribution, she vowed to take them all down. Every last demented sicko that frequented WhisperHub and used it to distribute their vile photographs and videos.

"But I haven't told you the craziest part yet."

Davina's eyes widened and she leaned forward, intently waiting.

"They are both right here in the Tampa Bay Area." He let out a little excited yip.

"No shit?"

"Offensive!" he blurted then looked down, his ears pinking up in embarrassment.

"My apologies," she replied, then stood and started to pace the area behind her desk, deep in thought. "I knew he had to have local ties! I'm going to need those IP addresses. All of them."

"They are already in the report." He pulled the thumb drive from the pocket of his button-down shirt and placed it face-up on the desk.

"Niles, you have done it again," Davina praised him. She pulled out a drawer in her desk and removed another envelope of new bills in the requested denominations, sliding it over to him with two fingers. He quickly picked it up and set it down on his lap.

"As usual, I'll keep you out of it," Davina said, picking up the thumb drive and placing it in her desk drawer.

"I don't want to know how you plan to use this data. It's important I can maintain plausible deniability."

"I get it." Davina nodded. "Your secret is safe with me."

Niles stood to leave.

"You're brilliant."

"I know." A quick smile darted across his features. Davina watched him walk out of her office. Finally, they had information that could be turned over to the authorities. They could flush this despicable person who had destroyed Adrienne's life out of hiding and shut down the platform that allowed it to happen.

THIRTY-ONE

The next day, after meeting with a prospective client in Aura Cove, Davina knocked on Adrienne's door. She'd decided to deliver the news to Adrienne in person.

"This is a pleasant surprise!" Adrienne said. "I was just thinking about making some of Mom's special Ruebens for lunch."

Davina pulled a face. "No, thanks. Canned corned beef and processed Swiss cheese don't sound very appetizing. Besides, when you hear what I have to say, you're going to want to celebrate!"

"What? Really?" Adrienne grinned and tugged her sister into the house, eager for an update.

"We got him," Davina said. "I mean, we've got his IP address, and the FBI can do the rest. I left a couple of messages at the field office this morning, but they haven't responded yet."

"Maybe we can take Harry up on his offer? You know, squeaky wheel gets the grease?"

"Won't hurt, I guess," Davina said. Adrienne was already gathering her handbag and keys.

Ten minutes later, they were seated in the folding chairs stationed at Harry's desk when he rounded the corner and joined them, dressed in his black uniform, gun holstered at his hip, and radio squawking at his shoulder.

"What can I do for you?"

Davina immediately took charge. "I recently uncovered some information that I believe will provide a break in Adrienne's case."

"How did you obtain it?" Harry asked, his skepticism evident.

"That's not important," Davina said, expertly sidestepping his question.

"It most certainly is, but I'll play your game," Harry replied. "What have you got?"

Davina pulled out the thumb drive and handed it over to Harry. "On this, you'll find the IP addresses of thousands of users of the WhisperHub app that have been using the platform illegally to distribute child pornography. I have reason to believe the man who targeted Adrienne uses the handle twistedsnaps69, and he was being coached by a member using the handle 1_bad_influence."

"Real original," Harry muttered under his breath, completely disgusted.

"Yeah, but the most interesting part is that both users

have ties to the Tampa Bay area and a familiarity with Aura Cove as I suspected. We need the FBI to subpoena WhisperHub's user database to obtain their physical addresses."

"Wow." Harry stared at the drive on his desk in awe. "This is exactly the kind of breakthrough we've been looking for."

THIRTY-TWO

"You're lucky it's Christmas and we love you so much," Beckett grumbled as he tugged at the neckline of the shirt Katie picked out for their family portrait session.

"I knew it was the only way I could get everyone on board without whining," Katie said. The entire family was gathered in her kitchen, each wearing a shade of beach glass and waiting for the photographers from Precious Momento to arrive. Yuli was dressed in a long, lavender muumuu that flowed to her ankles, talking to Kristina who had donned a white skirt topped with a peach-colored cardigan.

"Mom, what's your secret?" Kristina asked Yuli. "I swear, every time I've seen you in the last few weeks, you look younger."

Katie's heart skipped a beat and her gaze flitted over to Yuli, trying to be objective. She had to admit that Kristina's observation was accurate. Yuli had never looked better. David's sharp eyes also assessed his mother-in-law. "Did you lose weight?"

"No, dear ones," Yuli answered, deflecting their attention. Her eyes twinkled as she shot Katie a quick wink.

Callie reached up to gather her long hair in her hands, and a flash of her abdomen peeked out from under her flowy pink tunic.

"Looks like Callie found Yuli's lost weight." Beckett teased his sister with a soft poke to her belly, then added the trademark "Hee-hee!" from the Pillsbury Doughboy commercials they grew up watching between cartoons on Saturday mornings.

"Dude. No wonder you're still single." Katie leaped to Callie's defense. "The subject of a woman's weight is never up for discussion."

Unable to keep the secret from her siblings any longer, Callie blurted, "Actually, I've been waiting for the perfect moment to tell you all some big news." She paused, and her fearful gaze flicked over to Katie who gave her a tiny nod, hoping to inspire confidence. "I'm pregnant. Ta-da!" She waved jazz hands on either side of her rounded belly.

"You're what?" Beckett's strong chin jutted backward in surprise.

"I'm pregnant," Callie repeated.

Lauren's jaw dropped and Beckett's eyes bugged in shock then darted to her stomach again.

"Congratulations?" He twisted the word up like it was a question, completely dumbfounded as to how to respond to the news. His gaze rocketed over to his mother and then over to Kristina and back again.

Kristina broke the tension with a squeal of joy at the idea of another great-grandchild joining the family and swept Callie into her arms. "This is fantastic news!"

"Thank you, Grandma," Callie said. "I've decided to keep the baby and raise it on my own."

Recovering quickly, Lauren asked, "But what about Pixar?"

"It wasn't the right path for me. The work would have been creative and satisfying, but the thought of moving across the country away from all of you..." Her voice broke.

"Oh, Callie." She reached out to pull her sister into her arms, then laughed when their rounded bellies made the first contact. "Look, our babies' first fist-bumps."

Callie giggled as she swiped the rest of her tears away. "See? How could we ever live without this?"

"When can we expect this unexpected little bundle of joy?" Beckett asked.

"June fourteenth." Callie watched them all mentally calculate the date of conception in their heads.

"Christos?" Lauren whispered and Callie nodded, her cheeks flaming with embarrassment. "Wow! That baby hit the genetic jackpot. He or she is destined to be gorgeous."

"Congratulations, Callie," Tom added, trying to get a word in edgewise, happy to see Lauren thrum with happiness next to him as she warmed up to the idea.

"Ooh! You know what this means?" Lauren

shimmied on the balls of her feet, her wide smile making her radiant. Not waiting for an answer, she added, "We get to raise our babies together! Remember how we swore an oath to do so when we were little?"

Callie laughed. "Yeah, I stuffed a balloon into my t-shirt and walked around pregnant for most of the second grade."

"Oh! And there will be cousin sleepovers!" Lauren babbled on, practically swooning and getting caught up in the excitement. "And Mom can read the babies *T'was The Night Before Christmas* on Christmas Eve and…"

"And I can get a Santa suit and borrow Yuli's sleigh bells," Beckett added, getting swept away with the idea. "The only thing better than being an uncle is being an uncle twice!" He picked Callie up off the ground and swung her around in a circle. "I am so happy for you, loser."

Feeling the flood of her family's complete support and love, Callie burst into tears. "This is such a relief!"

"Why didn't you tell us earlier?" Lauren asked.

"I didn't want to steal your thunder," Callie admitted. "And I guess part of me was ashamed that I got myself into a mess."

Lauren pulled her sister close. "It's not a competition, weirdo. I, for one, am thrilled to become an auntie. There's enough love in this family for both of these babies."

"Yeah, there is. Keep 'em coming!" Katie said.

"Whoa! Slow your roll there, G-Mama." Beckett smirked at her excitement. "Two is enough for now."

"For now," she agreed, then took a last glance at her family, inspecting their clothing. "Everyone looks so great."

Beckett laughed. "Great? We look like sorbet."

"He's not wrong." Lauren laughed, looking down at her baby bump making its first real appearance through a pink cardigan. Tom hugged her from behind, both of his hands protectively gripping her belly. He made affection look easy as he relished it on his grinning fiancée.

"How have you been feeling, Cal?" Katie asked, always conscious of Callie doing it on her own, knowing it was harder.

"This is the first week I haven't puked, so I am considering that a win." She offered her mother a wide smile as she reached down to tug her soft blue cardigan into place. The color contrasted beautifully with her shiny dark hair. "It's getting harder to keep this thing covered." She pointed to where a small patch of skin was visible under her swollen belly.

"How about we check out the maternity shop next week and get the mamacita-in-training a few wardrobe staples for the next few months?" Katie offered.

"That sounds great," Callie said.

"I'm relieved you decided to tell them," Katie whispered.

"Me too."

"The photographers will be here any minute," Katie said, noticing the time as she pulled her watch off her wrist, and crossed the room to pop it on the charger.

Lauren stood next to Callie, and when Katie caught a glimpse of them together, she had to laugh. They both stood with their legs shoulder-width apart while kneading their lower backs with their hands. "You're twinning." She gave the girls a soft grin. "Look at my radiant beauties! Two vibrant and glowing mothers-to-be." Lauren and Callie collectively groaned in response.

"Look away," Beckett directed his mother, before whipping the room into a snarky frenzy. "Mom's gonna blow. First, she'll start sobbing the happy tears. Then, she'll ruin her makeup and we'll all have to come back and re-do the photo session."

"You are being ridiculous. I'm not that dramatic." Katie laughed, rolling her eyes.

"Yeah, you are." Lauren snickered.

A few minutes later, the doorbell chimed. Seeing Katie dashing into the powder room to touch up, Tom crossed the room to open the door. Two people walked into the great room. Katie finished up in time to hear the introductions and quickly made her way down the hall. "Hello, Beaumonts! I'm Raquel from Precious Momento." Behind her, there was a flutter of movement. "And this is my assistant, Denny."

Denny's eyes shifted toward hers and she felt a flutter of Déjà vu when they connected. Confused, Katie said, "You have to forgive me. I swear I just met your Doppelgänger at an art show in St. Pete's Beach. He is a floral photographer from Tampa Bay."

The man chuckled. It was a flat, dry sound that

fizzled out prematurely. "Not exactly," he admitted. "Let me guess. You met Sebastian Kincaid?"

"Yes!"

"That's me. My given name is Dennis, but in the art world, I go by my middle name, Sebastian."

"Ahh! That explains it!" Katie said.

"Denny, can you get the portable flash stand set up?" Raquel asked. "We've got to get started before the light dies."

"I'm aware, Rachel," he muttered under his breath, deliberately mispronouncing her name. Katie honed in on him, wanting to listen, and yet was distracted by the flurry of thoughts from her family members racing around her. The volume in the room swelled from the intertwining voices and deluge of overlapping consciousness. She forced herself to concentrate and took a deep breath to center herself.

Stupid bitch.

Katie heard the phrase and focused on Denny, trying to figure out the source of his rage. His eyes narrowed as he focused on Raquel, who was busy gathering the rest of Katie's family and gently prodding them out the back of the house and down the stairs to the sand.

Making me carry all this by myself! She should be the one assisting me!

The voice was twisted into a mocking tone.

Denny, we've had a few complaints from clients about items that were missing from their houses after our photo sessions. Do you know anything about that?

Denny clearly hated Raquel and the control she wielded like a weapon in his life.

Look at these entitled idiots. Living in one of the most affluent zip codes in the world and no art on their walls? Maybe while they are outside with Raquel, I can use the bathroom and help myself to the jewelry that's bound to be hidden in the master closet.

Katie was stunned by his entitled train of thought.

I'm always waiting for a woman to give me what I deserve. Whether it's the pittance this woman will pay us to capture photographs of her family, or hocking my photos on the art circuit, I'm always the one getting screwed. Such a waste of my God-given talents. I should be photographing the runways of Fashion Week, not this clichéd pastel Norman Rockwell nonsense.

"Ready?" Raquel asked, returning to where Denny was fumbling with the portable flash. The slave on top of the camera refused to fire, and his face was turning beet red with frustration while he worked to troubleshoot the malfunction. "Denny!" She called his name louder this time and he jumped. "Are you ready?"

He forced a smile on his lips that never reached his eyes and nodded. Katie followed behind him down the stairs, afraid to leave him alone in her home.

On the sand close to the shoreline, her family gathered near a patch of sea oats that rippled in the breeze. Katie watched them tease each other and observed Raquel working, snapping photos, and conducting short video interviews with each family member. Yuli wrapped one arm around Lauren and

Callie and squeezed them in close. The moment was more bittersweet than any of them would realize. Knowing it would be the last time they were photographed together, Katie re-centered her focus on the moment. She let Denny guide them into a pleasing composition, and he captured group after group together. Her favorite was the four-generations photo, five if you counted the babies in utero. Then they were instructed to roll their pant legs up to their calves and stroll down the beach.

"Hold hands!" Denny shouted to them over the pounding sound of the surf, and he walked backward, refocusing and clicking the shutter.

"Cheesy!" Beckett said, even though he complied. "And now we are strolling down the shore pretending we love each other so dang much!" He chuckled the words out as he grinned like an idiot, his focus shifting back and forth as Raquel orchestrated their movements.

"You're the king of cheesy," Callie teased him.

"Takes one to know one." He pulled her closer to him and ruffled her hair.

"When are you gonna settle down and find a queen?"

Katie laughed at their antics, jumping onboard with their good-natured razzing of each other. "Yeah, B, when?"

"Jeez! I thought the babies coming would keep the heat off of me!" Beckett grinned. "I have no idea when the future Mrs. Beaumont will make her appearance, but right now, I am going to bend down and pick up this rock and then fling it to the sea, hoping it skitters across the surface of the water in the most picturesque way just to make my sappy mom happy."

"Laugh at each other!" Raquel shouted over the surf, directing them as she and Denny snapped away.

"It's so easy to laugh at you when you look like that!" Callie sang out, ribbing Beckett who laughed right back.

"You mean chiseled and brooding, like the cover of those spicy books Aunt Frankie is always reading?"

"Yes!" Lauren laughed. "But without the six-pack and more mentally challenged!"

Katie laughed at their banter, soaking it in. She played along with them in the sand and surf as they made their way down the beach. Everyone's moods were lighter and more playful as the last rays of the warm winter sun faded and the sun drifted to the horizon line.

The day turned into night and she caught Yuli's eye. There was a tenderness there as she watched her grandmother drink in the faces of the family she'd adored. Katie felt the same bittersweet tug in her own heart. Knowing it was all coming to an end made tears well in her eyes. When Yuli noticed, she offered Katie a warm, reassuring smile.

The photo session ended with a bonfire on the beach where they roasted marshmallows and made S'mores. The warm orange light reflected on their faces as Katie brimmed with joy to have the moment captured forever. Soon, their world would undergo a seismic shift, welcoming new souls into their family while bidding farewell to others on their journey.

This night and the photographs created would serve as a time capsule. A snapshot of who they were at that precise moment in time. Katie glanced up at the moon rising in the darkening sky. In a few months, the full moon at the Spring Equinox would usher in the changing of the guard. Soon, she would be largely on her own, navigating the magical world of Karmic rebalances and helping guide the next generation of supernatural females in their coven. But tonight? Tonight, she would soak up the last meaningful moments they would enjoy together in the ordin world.

THIRTY-THREE

A few days after Christmas, Frankie and Harry were enjoying coffee in bed and arguing over five across on the New York Times crossword puzzle when the doorbell rang. Frankie dragged herself out of bed and to the door.

"Did you do it?" Katie asked with a huge disarming grin, waggling her eyebrows at Frankie.

"Shhh!" Frankie said as she yanked her best friend in by the hand. "I chickened out," she whispered, trying to get Katie to quiet down. A few minutes later, Harry was walking down the hallway when his cell phone at his hip rang.

"Harrison Willey." He walked by Katie with a nod of acknowledgment. "I appreciate the call, Special Agent Coleman. Yes. Adrienne Thorne." He was silent for a long minute, and Katie listened intently, trying to eavesdrop, as she followed Frankie to the kitchen for a cup of coffee. "Right. The blackmail and extortion case.

I wanted to make sure the holidays don't cause the case to lose momentum." His usually sunny disposition faded away as he reminded the detective of the particulars. "Yep. That's the one. WhisperHub. They were using it to communicate and share illegal photographs and videos."

There was another silence at his end. "I know," he said, clearly getting a dressing down from the person on the other end. "Can we get a warrant? I believe there is probable cause." He was quiet again. "Yep. Okay." He hung up the phone and turned to Katie. "Sorry about that."

"Was there a break in the Adrienne Thorne case?" Katie asked. "Last I heard from Davina, it was all dead ends."

"We are narrowing down on a suspect, but I'm not at liberty to disclose further details about the case. I'm sure you can understand."

"But hypothetically, Har?" Frankie voiced the question on Katie's mind, and for once, she was grateful for Frankie's big mouth and outspoken nature.

"Hypothetically…" he paused, considering the ramifications only briefly before adding, "WhisperHub might crack this case wide open. When a user conducts illegal activities on any platform, their identifying information can be subpoenaed by the authorities." His voice lowered into a hushed tone. "Davina somehow acquired user data from the WhisperHub app and discovered it's being used to trade explicit photographs and videos of children. I have a feeling the Adrienne

Thorne case is just the tip of a very ugly iceberg. Only time will tell." He stood, signaling the end of the conversation.

Harry walked over to the sink, taking the last sip of his coffee before he rinsed out his cup and kissed Frankie on the cheek. "Gotta run, gorgeous." He turned to acknowledge her best friend with a smile. "Katie." Then he picked up the keys to his El Camino and left the house.

"I forgot to ask, how did your family portrait go?"

"You're never going to believe this." Katie leaned in. "Remember Sebastian Kincaid?"

"The kinky flower photog? How could I forget?"

"He is a freelancer at Precious Momento."

"No way!" Frankie said. "I bet that was awkward."

"There's more."

"At the photo session, his thoughts were vile. He is a bitter, entitled man with a deep-seated hatred for women. "

"Ooh!" Frankie grinned; she loved getting the inside scoop.

"I'm pretty sure he's the photographer who took those explicit photographs of Adrienne. I did some digging into his background. In the eighties, he was a world-renowned fashion photographer, but there was a scandal at his studio that shut it down."

"What kind of scandal?"

"Models were being secretly filmed in his studio's dressing room and bathrooms."

"Seriously?!" Frankie gasped. "What a tool!"

"He proclaimed his innocence and threw his assistant under the bus, but the damage was done. Sebastian's career was destroyed."

"We have to tell Harry."

"What would that accomplish? It's just a hunch and a few flashes from Karma. Besides, I have no real evidence to corroborate any of my accusations."

"True," Frankie said, musing it over. "What are you going to do?"

"I'm not sure yet." Katie needed to discuss her findings with Yuli and Zoya. Changing the subject, she asked, "What is taking you so long to pop the question?"

Frankie paled as anxiety made her scrub her face with her hands. "There's so much pressure! Now I see why guys avoid proposals like the plague."

"But this is Harry we're talking about. I'm pretty sure, no matter how you ask, the answer is going to be yes."

Her eyes widened. "Do you know something I don't know? Did you intercept his thoughts or something?"

"No, silly."

"Can you?" She bit the inside of her cheek.

"You're being ridiculous," Katie said. "First, Yuli said magic should always be respected. It's not a parlor trick that I should whip out anytime I need an easy solution."

"Ugh!" Frankie cried. "Where's the fun in that?"

"It's a huge responsibility."

"Okay, fine."

"And secondly, Harry adores you. That man will follow wherever you lead."

Frankie grinned. "He *is* pretty smitten." She lit up with joy and hugged herself as her anxiety waned.

"You moved in together. I think the chances of him balking at the idea of making it official are slim and none."

"You make a good point." Frankie nodded. "Okay, I'm gonna do it."

THIRTY-FOUR

That evening, Katie went to Yuli's house where she knew Zoya would be waiting. They sat at Yuli's round table where a bank of fat candles was already lit.

"I know who blackmailed Adrienne Thorne. It's the photographer who took our family portraits," Katie shared. "Denny Kincaid or Sebastian Kincaid, depending on who you talk to."

"I knew it!" Yuli revealed, "There was a darkness around him, and his thoughts were oppressive."

"Sebastian Kincaid? I know that name!" Zoya said, "He was talented but full of himself. After the scandal broke in the eighties, he sent me an enormous wooden crate to get my attention. Inside was an autographed photograph of the controversial cover he did for *Luxe Mode*. I think it's still around the compound somewhere. It's really quite lovely and was groundbreaking for its time." She remembered fondly. "But it was all a desperate ploy to wrangle an invitation to my Equinox Ball and surround himself with models to get back into the good graces of the designers."

"No wonder he's so bitter," Yuli added. "I'm sure that rejection just added fuel to the fire. It takes a long time to nurture a pit of hatred of that magnitude."

"Davina's got the police and the FBI involved," Katie informed them. "It's only a matter of time before they locate him. If we are going to intervene, the time is now."

"Rotting in jail is too gentle of a punishment for a man like him," Zoya mused. "Ordin justice takes far too long and is far too soft. There's no need to rush, Katia. We have plenty of time to deliver his rebalance."

"If you say so."

"I do."

"It turns out he's a collector of many things," Katie added, shifting directions. "Some depraved, but of particular note is his collection of antique cameras."

Zoya's eyes sparkled at the mention. "Are you thinking what I'm thinking?"

Katie nodded with glee. "Suspended Libertines?"

Zoya let out a delighted squeal and clapped her hands. "Love it, darling! It only seems fitting that a man who called himself a photographic genius becomes part of the exhibit." Zoya took joy in the irony. "Creating the tableau will be the most challenging part of the rebalance. So many ideas come to *my* mind, but remember, you explicitly asked me not to intervene."

"I remember, but I don't know if I'm cut out for retribution and revenge."

"You are going to have to get more comfortable, darling. Life is not all rainbows and puppies. You must learn how to shoulder the responsibility of seeking justice for the ordin Karma assigned to you. A mere slap on the wrist is not enough! You will have to learn to stomach the punishment phase to keep Karma satisfied, or she will no longer trust you as her partner."

"I'm not built like you."

"Few women are," Zoya said, taking it as a compliment.

"Katia, there have been all types of judges throughout the ages. Some of them were kind yet fair, while others dominated with terror and revenge," Yuli reasoned. "There is always a choice on which you become."

Katie nodded in agreement as she thought it over. "The punishment should fit the crime." She tried to come to a compromise. "He exposed Adrienne in the most intimate and public way possible. She is the sweetest soul, and he exploited…." Katie stopped short as an idea clicked in her mind. She snapped her fingers, exclaiming, "I've got it."

"Good. I, for one, cannot wait to see what you've decided." Zoya steepled her fingers together and rippled them against each other in anticipatory delight.

"Do I have to enjoy it?" Katie asked, horrified that she would turn into the type of person who would savor another human being's suffering, no matter how repugnant she found him.

"No," Yuli instructed. "That part is optional."

"How do we get the camera to him?" Katie asked.

"Another great learning opportunity has presented itself, darling." Zoya closed her eyes and tried to demonstrate. "Concentration is key. You must see the object in your mind's eye. First, you must focus on the details and feel its weight in the palm of your hand. Rub your thumb over the textured gold ridges on the grip. Hear the click of the shutter and the mechanical sound of the crank when you advance the film inside. Feel the heat that sears your skin where you touch it." Her instructions floated out of her mouth as Katie tried to focus.

Her palms warmed and her breath hitched in her chest as her pulse quickened. Katie floated in a state of altered consciousness as Zoya's instructions took on a dreamy quality. Far away, she heard the mesmerizing twang of a tuning fork before a blast of light blinded her. When her eyes readjusted, the gold camera was clasped in her hands.

"Whoa," she exclaimed, yelping as the heat intensified. "Did I do that?"

"Mostly," Zoya answered with a wink. She was winded from the combined effort.

"Impressive," Yuli said. "It took me the better part of a month to learn that spell."

Zoya stumbled, letting out a whimper as her knees buckled, and Katie rushed to her side. Operating on instinct solely, she scooped Zoya up and was shocked when Zoya felt light as a feather in her arms. Katie walked her over to a velvet sofa and laid her down on it. A few moments later, her eyes fluttered open.

"What happened?"

"Another transfer of power," Zoya said. "It is nothing to fear, darling. All is happening as it should."

Yuli stood and walked to a drawer, pulling out a sheath of papers she handed over to Katie. "Speaking of transfers…"

"What's this?"

"It's a DNR, Katia, and it gives you medical power of attorney for me."

Now it was Katie's turn to yelp in pain. "No," she refused, attempting to push it back toward Yuli.

"Burying your head in the sand changes nothing, Katia," Yuli said softly. She held up her arm where a medical alert bracelet was now fastened. "It's done."

"I know." She swallowed hard against the knot in her throat, willing herself not to cry. Reaching out, she reluctantly accepted the paperwork.

"The Spring Equinox is approaching. That is when our magic will reach a heightened state and the major shift will occur." She pulled out a blanket and walked it over to where Zoya was resting, taking the time to tuck it around her. Before she walked away, Zoya thrust out one hand and grabbed Yuli's.

"Thank you," Zoya mumbled before her eyes fluttered and she fell into a deep sleep.

A few minutes later, as her great-great grandmother

lay snoring, Katie studied her face. There were now deep ridges of crow's feet etched into the corners of her closed eyes and a soft sag underneath her chin that was never there before.

Yuli joined Katie and wrapped her arm around her granddaughter. "It's happening faster now," Yuli whispered in the quiet that surrounded them. "Not unlike an ordin suffering from a terminal illness, she will continually decline. There will be a few bursts of intense energy as her soul prepares for transmutation."

"Do you think the coven will allow her to reincarnate?" Katie asked. "She's desperate to unite with Sally."

Yuli studied her again, taking in the rise and fall of her chest and the softness that sleep brought to her features. "I can now honestly say, I hope so."

THIRTY-FIVE

The next day, in early January, a plain cardboard box was sitting on the kitchen table when Denny arrived home from work. The only indication it was for him was his name scrawled across it in loopy cursive.

"Aren't you going to open it?" his mother asked, her curiosity winning out. She pulled a knife out of the drawer and stutter-stepped toward him with her walker when he cut her off and pulled the knife out of her hands.

"It's addressed to me," he said pointedly.

"Sorrrrry," she muttered under her breath, leaning against the countertop at the kitchen sink. He stalled her, mostly out of spite, while he warmed up a slice of two-day-old pizza in the microwave. She glared at him while he choked it down before he gave in and found a box cutter to slice it open. Nestled inside a thick wad of white tissue paper was a golden camera. His first glimpse of it took his breath away.

"Look." He held the box out for his mother to see.

"Who's it from?"

"There's no return address." Denny was enthralled as he pulled it out. It was a single-reflex vintage camera with gold gears that sparkled in the light and felt weighty in his hands.

"Well, isn't that a dandy?" his mother said when she laid eyes on it. "It's the kind your father would have loved to own." Denny shared a passion for photography with his father. He had grown up in the darkroom next to him, agitating trays of developer and witnessing the blank paper come to life before his eyes. When he'd been accepted to Brooks, his father had gifted him his most prized possession—his antique camera collection.

It was his father, the original Sebastian Kincaid, who cheered the loudest seeing Denny's photographs gracing the covers of fashion magazines. He'd brag to anyone with ears about his son's glamorous life, jet-setting all over the world with famous models. When he'd hit rock bottom and sullied his good name, Denny would never forget the disgusted look on his father's face. It haunted him. His father never lived to witness Denny's redemption, and after his passing, Denny lost the ambition to keep trying.

He turned it over in his hands, examining the golden camera more closely in the light. The longer he held it, the hotter the metal became. It seared his fingers, and he fumbled it, almost dropping the camera like a hot potato before resting it safely on the countertop.

"You always had butterfingers, just like your father."

"Shut up, Ma," he mumbled under his breath with a scowl.

"What?"

"Nothing." He reached for it again. It was warming to his touch, and he found himself oddly drawn to it. His mother tired of the camera quickly and banged her walker on the floor. She forced it away from her body and dragged her bum leg back to it, repeating the process over and over until she'd made her way across the living room.

"Wheel of Fortune is almost on," she announced as she collapsed into her recliner. Denny put the camera to his eye and focused on her through the viewfinder. He turned the focusing ring until she went from fuzzy to tack sharp. Once the shot was composed, he clicked the shutter. A sharp bolt of static electricity shot through him and he jumped.

Across the room, his mother let out a pained yelp and then fell back into the sofa. He clicked the shutter twice more and cranked the release, recording her slack jaw and bugging eyes before he realized there was a roll of film inside it. Recognizing his mother had become incapacitated, he set the camera down and walked over to her reclined form resting on the sofa. Trying to assess her state of consciousness, he pushed on her shoulder with one finger.

"Ma?" He waited for a response. When there was none, he pushed her shoulder harder. Then he waved his palm in front of her face. Feeling no breath coming from her nose or mouth, a sinister smirk twisted up his features. This was the moment he'd been waiting for. He could simply walk away and let nature take its course. When he returned, he could make a valiant effort to resuscitate her… or not. Maybe he could cry a few tears for the paramedics who would come with the coroner to collect her cold body. It would be no different than if he'd been at a photo session or an art show when she'd collapsed at home alone. His mother had lived a long life. She'd had her chance, but now, it was time for him to have his.

He backed away from her slumped form and walked down the hallway to his bedroom. Looking down at his watch, he decided he'd troll the chat rooms for a while and find a decent distraction for the next thirty minutes. Setting a timer on his phone, he worked his way through Instagram, setting up three new profiles with burner telephone numbers and photos he'd scraped from a college website. Shirtless and in the prime of their lives, his new social media profiles listed his first name as Brady, Peyton, and Zander. The names were carefully chosen to reflect the photos he'd downloaded to accompany them.

He found he was halfway decent at flirty banter when the females he catfished were young and inexperienced. 1_bad_influence was right; naive targets were a lot more easily manipulated than the hardened and embittered shrews that were the fish in his more age-appropriate dating pool.

He was chatting with three different girls, sending photos of his six-pack and encouraging them to return the favor. It was a high, love bombing them into submission and gathering up whatever tasty tidbits they willingly sent him, not knowing they would soon be used as leverage. Thirty minutes passed in the blink of an eye, and he stood and stretched then walked back to the living room. In the corner, the television blared as a timer counted down the final puzzle against the festive *Wheel of Fortune* soundtrack. Finally, the contestant said, "I'd like to solve the puzzle. No rest for the wicked."

The letters lit up and he watched Vanna chase after them in her heels and evening gown as Pat Sajak said, "Let's see what you've won! Ten-thousand dollars!" Obnoxious applause from the studio audience filled the air. Annoyed, Denny crossed the room to turn down the TV and then hurried back toward his mother's still form. He reached out to touch her cheek and pulled back in surprise when it felt cooler to the touch. Denny focused on her chest, checking for it to rise and fall, but it was as still as a statue. Waving another hand in front of her face, he confirmed she was not breathing. Then he pulled out his phone and made the call.

"Goodnight, Ma," he whispered. Across the room, the camera shimmered in the light reflected from the television. A quick glance at it and his heart fluttered. The lens shifted into an all-seeing eye, and he would swear he saw it blink, but quickly decided it had been an optical illusion. It was a camera, an inanimate object, for crying out loud, not a living, breathing entity. As the room darkened, and he felt the first prickles of terror walk up his spine, the hair-raising sensation he was not alone overwhelmed him. Laughing it off, he let his nerves settle down. He was, in fact, alone inside a home that was now his, and that fact filled him with immense joy.

THIRTY-SIX

The joy was short-lived when, a few days later, banging on his front door startled him awake at seven am. He opened the door to see three agents wearing navy blue jackets emblazoned with FBI on the back in gold lettering. The sight of them on his doorstep set off an alarm inside his head.

"Dennis Kincaid?" one began. "I'm Special Agent Coleman with the FBI. We have a search warrant for the premises and need to ask you some questions. Can you come to the field office with us?"

"Wait." Denny asked, feigning innocence, "For what?"

"Where are your electronic devices? Computer, laptop, phone?"

"What is this about?" He tried to stall as the agents brushed past him to enter his home, then fanned out and climbed the stairs to his bedroom where they unplugged his computer. As he trailed behind them, a feeling of impending doom spread from his belly to his brain where a tension headache was beginning to form.

"Read him his rights," Special Agent Coleman said to one of the other officers, holding out an evidence bag to collect his cell phone. Denny hesitated and then dropped it inside and let the officer lead him to a dark sedan, grateful he hadn't been cuffed.

Twenty minutes later, Denny sat at the table in the FBI field office. He was impatiently drumming his fingers on the table when Agent Coleman walked in dressed in an ill-fitting suit and carrying a file folder. She was stuffing the remnants of a glazed donut into her mouth, and a look of disgust rippled across Denny's face as he watched her chew with her mouth open. A flake of crystallized sugar was stuck in one corner of her lips, and he couldn't tear his eyes away from it.

"I'm with the Cybercrimes Division. I'd like to remind you you've been read your Miranda rights." The folding chair screeched across the concrete floor as she pulled it out to sit down. "I just need to ask you a few questions."

She glanced down at the folder with brown eyes that were too small and set too close together in her fleshy face. Denny assessed her with his practiced eye that craved symmetry, but Agent Coleman had been hit repeatedly with the ugly stick. Sure, he could use lighting tricks to slim down her face, but the pock marks from old acne scars that covered it would need extensive retouching, and the crow's feet surrounding her eyes were deep. She was a lost cause.

"It says here you're a photographer?"

"Yes. I graduated from Brooks in the nineties. Had my moment as a fashion photographer, then ultimately left it to pursue other opportunities in fine art photography for discriminating collectors."

Her eyes narrowed on his, and he wondered how deep a dive she'd done on him before this interview.

"My wife has been begging for one of your floral studies for over a year now."

His lips quirked up in a smile. This was going to be easier than he thought. "Well, once we finish here, I will go through my inventory and give you a deal on your favorite. How's that?"

"She will lose her ever-loving mind. Thank you. By the way, we stopped by your booth at the Tampa Bay Art Show, but you seemed pretty preoccupied with a group of businessmen."

"I'm sorry. Those events are bananas. My work has been so well received that I practically need a clone to handle the crowd."

Her brow furrowed as she studied him. "If I remember correctly, even when the booth cleared out and we were the only ones in attendance, you wouldn't give us the time of day."

Denny felt the first frisson of fear wind through him. "What? There must have been other extenuating circumstances. I offer my deepest apologies."

"Well, we couldn't afford one of your original giclee prints anyway." She continued to peruse the file folder in front of her then sighed dramatically. "I have some bad news for you today, Denny. Or should I call you Sebastian?"

He cleared his throat. "Denny is fine."

"It seems emails sent from an IP address associated with your residence were used to blackmail Adrienne Thorne."

Terror peaked in his gut, and Denny felt the floor drop underneath him. It was impossible. He religiously used a VPN. Knowing law enforcement's tactic of bluffing, he decided to keep his mouth shut.

"I know what you're thinking," she said with a smirk. "You went to great lengths to conceal your IP address. Using a VPN and routing all your emails through a server overseas. It should have done the trick, right?"

Denny felt his confidence crumble. His lips curled up in a sneer as his hatred for the smug lesbian in front of him grew.

"It usually does, but in the hands of a professional, one who is adept at combing through all the data, you were exposed. You forgot to use a VPN on Thanksgiving." She mimed tipping a bottle into her mouth. "Maybe you hit the sauce too hard at home and got a little lax with your privacy practices? Don't worry, it happens to the best of us."

She closed the folder.

"It's your correspondence with members of the WhisperHub platform that garnered our full attention." She laced her fingers together and leaned back in her chair, wrapping them behind her neck. He was incensed at her obvious enjoyment of his discomfort. "Does the name Maisy Duncan ring any bells?"

"No? Should it?"

"You downloaded a topless photograph of her from WhisperHub. It was an attachment from a user with the handle 1_bad_influence." She cocked her head, studying him, and he tried not to flinch. In his lap, his fingers tightened like a vise around his wrist. "She's sixteen."

He shrugged. "That's legal in some states."

"Not in Florida." She leaned closer. "We've got you on possession and distribution of child pornography. You're also looking at charges for producing and promoting. Each photograph you shared is a punishable offense. It's a second-degree felony, and if the judge chooses to impose the strictest sentence, you will face hellacious fines and significant jail time. I'm sure I don't have to remind you what happens to men like you in prison."

He shivered at the prospect and blinked several long times, letting the terror and the truth sink in. Denny was going away. This nightmare was far worse than when he'd lost the studio. This woman was going to take away his freedom.

"Your actions were despicable, and while I would love nothing more than to lock you up and throw away the key, it seems you might be more valuable to us in a different capacity."

"I'm listening." Denny leaned in, grasping at the only life preserver in sight.

"Be advised, this is a one-time offer that expires at midnight tonight." She pulled out a form from the folder and slid it over to him. "If you agree to actively participate in the ongoing investigation as an informant, we can have your charges reduced so that you'll probably walk out of here with only probation. It's up to the judge, of course, but your cooperation would go a long way."

"What would I have to do?"

"Just continue to live your life. We want you to maintain your frequent habits of participation in the chat rooms and on WhisperHub, so we can build our case and gather evidence on other offenders. We've been investigating WhisperHub for the last several months and think you can offer us the last bullet we need to take them down."

Denny mentally calculated the damage he'd already done to himself on WhisperHub. Somewhere buried inside the digital footprint the FBI was already actively unearthing were records of his wrongdoings, and when they fully came to light, he would go down with everyone else. There was no way he was going to let that happen.

She tapped a fingernail on the document. "This is a consent to assume your online identity."

"Isn't this entrapment?" Denny asked. "What if I consent and you try to use those actions against me?"

She rolled her eyes. "We already have enough to put you in jail for a long time as it is. Any further illegal activity on your accounts while under our control would be granted immunity."

"Aren't you participating in the re-victimization of children by allowing this investigation to continue?"

"So, now you want to take the high road?" She sat back, crossing her arms in front of her while glaring at him. "You're either on board, or you're going to prison... *federal* prison."

Denny gulped at the knot lodged in his throat and began to sweat.

"Do you need some time to think it over?" Agent Coleman asked.

"Nope," he said, choosing self-preservation. "I just need a pen."

"Great decision." She slid one over to him.

Two hours later, he was home after handing his log-in credentials over to all the programs and apps he used. Relief that he'd made a decent deal flooded through him. Sure, he'd have to register as a sex offender, but he'd stay out of prison. Understanding his limited options, it was a win.

THIRTY-SEVEN

A few days later, after Special Agent Coleman called with an official update on the case, Davina stood at the bank of windows in her office, sipping a glass of whiskey while looking out over the water. Failure washed over her, and it was a confusing and novel sensation. Bitterness lingered on her tongue, and when her assistant softly knocked then opened the door and led her sister into her office, she turned and shot Adrienne a wan smile.

"Wow! This place is impressive!" She took in the gorgeous wood-paneled office and modern design. "You've done very well for yourself."

"Thanks," Davina whispered, feeling a tug of regret she hadn't been able to fare as well for her sister.

"Want one?" She held up a highball glass to Adrienne.

"That depends. Do you think I'll need it?" she asked, trying to lighten the mood.

"Maybe." She turned with a sigh and poured two fingers of whiskey into another glass, handing it off.

"Jesus, you're glum. Who died?" Adrienne teased.

"Have a seat." She waved at the chairs in front of her desk.

"You're plying me with booze *and* sitting me down? Now you're really freaking me out."

"I have some good news and some bad news," Davina began. "Which one do you want first?"

"Let's start with the good."

"They have a suspect."

"What?" Adrienne leaned closer, sitting on the edge of her chair.

"His name is Dennis Kincaid. There is concrete evidence that identifies his profile as the one that shared your photos on WhisperHub and sent them to the news outlets."

"How did he get them in the first place?"

"He was the original photographer, and it's apparently not the first time he's been accused of impropriety." Davina took a sip. "Another member of WhisperHub was mentoring him, feeding him step-by-step instructions on how to dox and blackmail young women over the internet."

Adrienne exhaled, feeling a weight that had been lodged on her shoulder since the nightmare began to lift a little. Curious, she asked, "What's the bad news?"

"He's made a deal to become an informant." Davina took a sip and added, "It's pretty normal in cases like this. The FBI will assume his online profiles while they gather information to make cases against a larger group of perpetrators. You won't get the resolution you deserve."

Adrienne's forehead creased in confusion. "That's not bad news at all. If it means fewer children will be victimized and more abusers will be held accountable, that's a good thing." She picked up her glass. "We should toast!"

"What?" Davina said. "Don't you want to see him locked up?"

"Of course I do, but it's too late for me. What's done is done, but I'd love to see more young women like Maisy Duncan protected from this nightmare. Knowing there is a chance she could get justice for what happened to her is good enough for me. You said yourself these crimes are hard to prosecute."

"They are." Davina was astounded by her sister's perspective.

"Then it's definitely a good thing." Adrienne smiled an engaging grin. She settled back in her chair to enjoy the rest of the whiskey. "You really came through for me. Thank you."

"How can you thank me?" Davina said. "I failed you."

"That is not true at all," Adrienne argued, her tone resolute. "You carried me through the darkest time in my life, and I wouldn't change a thing about what transpired. It brought my sister back." Her voice cracked as she leaned forward to squeeze Davina's forearm. "I missed you so much."

Davina felt her throat tickle and a puddle of tears gathering at her lash line as she whispered, "I missed you, too."

THIRTY-EIGHT

I n mid-February, on the day of the full moon, Katie paced the length of a swanky hotel suite in downtown St. Pete's Beach like a caged animal. In contrast, Zoya sat at the chairs and table, enjoying the afternoon tea service. Using a pair of delicate silver tongs, she plucked a cucumber sandwich from the three-tier tray and placed it on a sparkling cut-crystal saucer.

"What if I can't do it?" Katie asked, doubting her abilities, wringing her hands to quell the fear that was rearing up.

"Then you simply ask for assistance." Zoya turned to Yuli, exasperated. "A little help here? She's wearing a track in the carpet."

"It's natural to be nervous, but Zoya is right," Yuli said. "You have to calm down, dear."

"Can we go over the plan one more time?" Katie begged.

"We've been over and over it, darling. You're working yourself into a tizzy. Come sit and have a nibble before he makes his appearance. You'll thank me later."

Katie's skin tingled and the occasional wayward golden spark shot from her fingers toward the carpeted floors before disintegrating in the air. "I'm too keyed-up. Is this normal? My heart is racing."

Zoya yawned and took another calming sip of her chamomile tea with her pinky finger extended. "Yep. It's the shift. You're gaining energy as I lose it."

Katie glanced over, guilt clouding her features. "Sorry," she mumbled in apology for becoming a human siphon.

"It's the natural order of things. There is nothing to be sorry about," Zoya explained.

A playful knock at the door interrupted their pep talk and they exchanged anxious glances.

"It's time." Katie exhaled a heavy breath and wiggled her fingers to release the tension before she walked over to the door and opened it. Holding the box, Denny filled the doorway, and she could feel the greedy anticipation rolling off of him in waves. It colored his aura a rusty brown hue.

"You look familiar," he blurted, cocking his head to the side and scrunching his face up trying to place her. "Have we met?"

"You photographed my family at my beach house a few months ago," Katie quickly explained. "Please, come in."

"Oh, that's right," he said, but their real-world connection seemed to throw him off.

Katie stilled her mind and connected with his train of scattered thoughts.

Interesting. Need to milk this for all its worth. The beach house bitch can afford it. Besides, finding work is going to be impossible when the case is settled.

Zoya slowly got to her feet, and Yuli helped her cross the room.

Is that? Oh my God! That's Ana Castanova! Cha-CHING! Those photos in the tabloids must be hella-retouched! She's really showing her age.

Intercepting his ugly thoughts, Zoya glared at Denny. Reaching out one shaky hand, she clasped a white envelope filled with cash and handed it over to Katia.

"It's the amount we agreed upon," Katie said, offering it to him.

"About that..." Denny hesitated, licked his lips, and then continued. "After you reached out with your generous offer, I took the liberty to do some research on this camera. Between you and me, I thought the price you were offering was too generous for this relic, and I couldn't figure out why you were willing to pay so much to own it." He gripped the box tighter in his hands, almost as if he was afraid to set it down.

"You never mentioned its infamous origin," he said. "After doing a little digging, I discovered this camera was rumored to be recovered at the scene of the Helter Skelter murders in the seventies." He made a tsk-tsk sound with his tongue. "Seems to me its sordid past would put it in the priceless category at auction."

Katie felt a rush of uncharacteristic irritation surge up her esophagus and spill out onto her tongue. Her eyes narrowed suspiciously and her lips curled up in anger. "Is there a question in there, Denny?" Her direct response shocked her. Confused, she glanced over at Zoya, whose eyes danced and grin electrified, relishing the shift taking place in her great-great granddaughter.

He cleared his throat, ignoring Katie completely, which only stoked the rage that clawed up her ribs. "In light of this finding and knowing it is a one-of-a-kind, I believe the investment to own it should be closer to seven figures. Don't you agree, Ms. Castanova?"

Bristling with fury, Katie couldn't contain her frustration. "You want to re-negotiate the purchase at the eleventh hour? Are you an idiot or just a greedy bastard?"

His nostrils flared and his lips pinched together. A flash of disgust panned across his face. Waffling and losing confidence, Katie abruptly whipsawed her angle and softened her approach, deciding to placate him. "Would you mind if I inspect it first before we re-open negotiations?"

"Of course," he said magnanimously. He brushed off the putdowns and handed the box to Katie. She tugged it open and, inside, the camera shimmered. Reaching in, she cradled it between her hands and felt it warm to the touch. As she pulled it out of the box, it felt leaden in her hands. She turned it over, admiring the craftsmanship. "It's really beautiful."

Across the table, Zoya chimed in, "I was wondering… Did you resort to having to convince pre-pubescent girls to remove their clothing for your nefarious photo sessions because adult women find you insufferable? Or was there another reason?"

He stiffened and Katie shot her a warning glare. Zoya shrugged her shoulders and crossed her arms across her chest.

"We know what you did," Yuli said, unwavering.

"Excuse me?"

"To Adrienne Thorne."

"I don't know what you're talking about." He tried to deny it.

"You exposed her in her most vulnerable state and tried to ruin her life."

Sensing the negotiations had come to a screeching halt, he rushed over and yanked the camera back into his hands, preparing to leave. Seizing the moment, Katie raised both of her palms, and shafts of golden light pinned him to the wall.

He let out a roar of anger. "Let me go!"

"We haven't finished conducting our business," Katie said. She turned her hands over and circled her fingers up, repeating the movement until the camera floated from his hands over to hers.

"Sit down!" Yuli demanded, her eyes glowing with fury. "My granddaughter is not finished speaking to you!"

Unable to fight her directions, he obediently walked over to the table and sat down. A confused snarl distorted his features as he tried to battle against it.

"How many other women have you violated?" Katie asked.

"They took their clothes off willingly. I never forced them!"

"You preyed on innocent girls, barely more than children! You manipulated them and used them for your own gratification and financial gain."

"I didn't have a choice. Everything had been taken from me!" He crossed his arms defiantly across his body.

"You're the victim? Please." Katie was disgusted.

"I was! Why would I jeopardize my successful career by filming models without their consent, when all I had to do was ask them to remove their clothing and they would eagerly comply?"

Katie faltered for a single second.

"It was my assistant," he continued. "He destroyed my life, and those hateful bitches would never listen to reason. I was blackballed by association and lost everything. For years, I tried to clear my name, but eventually, I decided if I was going to be punished for a crime, I might as well commit it."

"Unbelievable." Yuli's face wrinkled up in disgust.

"You hate women, yet you are obsessed with us," Katie accused him.

He scowled with hatred, and his lips twisted up in an angry pout. "Women use their assets every day to get ahead. The deck is stacked against you when you've got a cock!"

The outrageous statement tickled Zoya, and a peal of laughter rang out. "Oh yes, please do educate us all on the pitfalls of being a white male in America. A country run by white men, protected by a panel of supreme court judges that are white men, who feel it is their place to tell the rest of us how to live. Yes, darling, you have it *so* rough!"

"Women use their sexuality like currency. I was just helping grease the wheels of capitalism. You all raise your picket signs and declare you want equality! Why are women the only ones who financially benefit from their sexuality? All I was doing was leveling the playing field." He stood to leave.

"Now it's my turn to level the playing field." Katie boldly stepped in front of him, pressed her palms toward his body, and directed her entire frustration and outrage there. The energy surged and the lights flickered and pulsed. There was a buzzing sound as he flew back and hit the wall. Dazed, it took him a full minute to rise to his feet. Again, he tried to run to the door, but Katie concentrated harder, directing even more energy at him. Golden sparks rushed from Zoya to Katie, and she felt herself surge with power. Every hair on her head was electrified, and Katie began to glow as she filled with Zoya's energy. Gold lightning shot from her hands into the center of his chest, and Denny let out a yelp as he flew back into the exposed brick wall of the suite. A trickle of blood snaked down his cheek from where his head connected with the wall. Zoya threw her head back and cackled with delight then staggered to the floor.

Shock registered on Katie's features. She felt vitality and energy flowing through her like it never had before. Astonished at her growing strength, she stared down at her wiggling fingers, now regarding her hands as powerful weapons. Terror registered on Denny's face as he sat propped up against the wall.

"This would typically be the moment I would force you into the body of a Malti-poo or a Chihuahua," Zoya muttered from the floor out of breath, "but I'm a changed witch." Turning to Katie, she demanded, "Katia, finish him."

"Did you say witch?" The last word was a screech as it tumbled from his lips.

"She did," Yuli spoke for her.

"Get undressed," Katie ordered Denny. "I want you in the same state you put your victims in."

His eyes widened as he got to his feet and started to strip down to his boxers. Standing there, he trembled in fear, and a stream of urine trickled down his hairy leg. Across the room, Zoya's nose wrinkled when the scent of ammonia hit her nostrils. "Get on with it, darling. This man is foul."

Katie reached for the camera, feeling its solid weight in her hands. She lifted it to look through the viewfinder, and when her left eye connected with him through it, she felt the sensation of being whipped into a funnel cloud. It spun faster, dizzying with its intensity, and when she tried to tug the camera away to see what was happening in the suite, she was unable to lower it. The wind howled in her ears, and she heard Denny scream as golden bolts of electricity surged from her lens to him. The circuit of energy intensified as the power raced between them. There was a *whoosh!* and then they lurched to the ground in the middle of a crowd of onlookers.

Katie jumped to her feet, energized, and circled the cobblestone street to get her bearings. She took in the sweeping panoramic view of hundreds of people gathered in a town square. In the middle of it, the pool of medieval onlookers surrounded Denny, who stood in front of the group completely nude. He was covered in a viscous, amber-colored substance that made his hair sticky. It dripped down his face and torso and then down the long lines of his legs. The crowd roared with laughter, pointing at him as he stood in front of them flaccid, shivering, and covered in honey.

A hum of insects filled the air just as a swarm circled him, drowning out his screams. One by one, the bees stung his exposed flesh. Some of the children gathered around and picked up rocks. Suspended above his head was a buzzing hornet's nest. They flung stones at it until a swarm of angry hornets flew out, enraged by the destruction of their home. The hornets joined the bees, and the air turned black around Denny as they encircled his hanging body, stinging every inch of his sickeningly sweet flesh. His skin became red and swollen, and it was hard to recognize him after only a few minutes.

"Press the shutter," Katie heard Zoya whisper, and she hoisted the viewfinder back to her eye. Her trigger finger didn't hesitate. Denny released one last blood-curdling scream before he disappeared from her view. There was a suction noise as the camera's viewfinder released its hold on her eye, and then it fell like a stone to her side down to the carpeted floor of the hotel suite. Katie stumbled to the ground on her hands and knees, breathing heavily when a wave of nausea hit her head-on and she rushed to the bathroom to vomit.

"Great work," Zoya praised, sitting up when Katie had returned.

Katie's chest heaved with exhaustion, overwhelmed by the perilous journey she'd undertaken. She was completely drained but filled with pride she'd handled the rebalance on her own. "What happens now?"

"I'll see that his photo gets printed and archived in my gallery, and then I will return the camera to its home at the compound." A shaky Zoya stood, wobbling on her feet. Yuli rushed to her side and helped her over to the bed on the other side of the hotel suite, tucking her in.

"Not until you get some rest."

THIRTY-NINE

A week later, Katie was munching on some toast while getting ready for her shift at Kandied Karma when the story broke.

"Good morning, Tampa Bay." Melanie Stevens' throaty newscaster voice echoed through the house. It was the voice who kept Katie company most mornings as she dressed for work. "We begin today with breaking news out of Tampa Bay. A major victory was won in the fight against online exploitation as the Federal Bureau of Investigation announced the successful bust of a child pornography sharing ring."

Katie immediately stopped chewing and turned up the volume, glued to the broadcast.

The video cut to Davina standing at a podium with Adrienne. "This case began when my sister, Adrienne Thorne, the beloved former principal of Aura Cove High School was targeted by a man on the internet. He'd come into possession of a series of explicit photographs taken of her as a minor and threatened to release them to the public and on the file-sharing app WhisperHub. Last Thanksgiving, she was unfairly forced to resign from an elected position as Superintendent of Schools."

A video clip of Adrienne walking the halls of Aura Cove High School and interacting with students last May flashed on the screen as Davina continued to speak. "Officials have also discovered at least one student from Aura Cove High School was doxed and victimized by users of WhisperHub. Corporations that create applications that allow users to share explicit material must be held accountable when their users commit illegal acts. It is my intention to fight for my sister and for every child who was victimized by this heinous crime."

Then the video segued into a clip from the interview Adrienne gave to Melanie Stevens about the dangers of online extortion.

"Becoming a victim of online extortion myself has opened my eyes to the real dangers children and teens face. It's terrifying to feel so vulnerable, to know that someone you've never met has the power to ruin your reputation, your relationships, and your sense of security with just a few keystrokes." Adrienne paused then continued, "We must educate our young people about the dangers of oversharing on social media and promote responsible online behavior to protect them and their peers from becoming victims of cybercrimes. I want to help lead the charge toward empowerment and online safety."

The video panned back to Melanie, who continued, "Sources within the FBI have revealed that the investigation was several months in the making, involving meticulous planning and coordination with local law enforcement agencies across the state of Florida. Charges are pending against one hundred and twenty-seven individuals currently, and the investigation is still ongoing."

A series of mugshots of disheveled, scowling men flashed on the screen. "In a shocking twist of events, Dr. Douglas Randall, the newly elected Aura Cove Community School District Superintendent, was arrested and charged with distribution and possession of child pornography. The Aura Cove Community School District has declined to comment on the ongoing investigation."

"Wow." Katie was stunned by the findings. "All those children victimized." It was hard to be happy with the outcome when so many lives had been devastated. She found herself sliding into aligning more with Zoya's revenge-based methods of retribution. The depravity Zoya must have witnessed in the course of her lifetime shaped the witch she became. Katie could feel herself being shaped by the events she'd witnessed as well and wondered how different her thinking would become when she was the oldest member of the mortal coven.

"Shoot!" Katie winced, noticing she was now running a few minutes late for her shift at Kandied

Karma. She hopped into her Beetle and drove the short distance to the shop to begin her shift.

The day passed quickly as she filled golden boxes with truffles and overheard the gossip buzzing about the superintendent of schools.

"People live secret lives right under your nose all the time."

"I always knew he was a creep."

"They also arrested an oncologist and the youth pastor at St. Mary's Immaculate Conception. You never can tell about people."

The sting was all anyone could talk about. Ten minutes before closing time, Katie's back was turned when she heard the bell jingle one last time.

"Your favorite five-minutes-before-closing customer is back!" Davina said as she tucked her phone back into her handbag and offered Katie a warm smile.

"Davina!" She flashed her a welcoming grin. "I saw you on the news this morning! You were awesome!" Katie pulled out a box, folded it together, and started filling it with Davina's favorites. "How's Adrienne in light of the arrests?"

"She's doing great." Davina leaned in. "Can you believe those spineless bastards asked her to become the interim Superintendent of Aura Cove Schools?"

"I can, because she's the best choice."

Davina smiled and nodded. "She was."

"Was?"

"She turned them down."

"What?" Katie was in shock, "Why?"

"Between you and me, she's considering her options. One of her former students was swept up in this nightmare, and she mentioned she'd like to create a foundation that helps keep teenagers safe from online exploitation," Davina explained. "The laws haven't always kept up with technology and she'd like to lead the charge for change, and I plan on helping her."

"What a great idea!"

"She's a better person than I am," Davina admitted.

"I doubt that," Katie said. "You just have different approaches."

"She's definitely more forgiving. Right now, I'm pretty disgusted with law enforcement. They might have brought down the ring and levied charges against over a hundred child predators, but Denny Kincaid is still walking the streets as a free man. He was supposed to appear in court today but was a no-show. Knowing he's out there and the rest of them are behind bars facing real jail time doesn't sit well with me."

"I wouldn't worry about him too much," Katie said. "I have a feeling Karma will be like a bee in his bonnet until he's brought to justice." She turned away to hide the satisfied expression that settled on her face. Katie had zero regrets. Denny Kincaid had gotten what he deserved.

FORTY

The morning of the spring equinox, Katie lay in bed, unwilling to get up and start the day she'd been dreading for months. In the weeks leading up to it, she felt ripples of energy flowing through her as she grew stronger. Knowing it was coming at a cost made it harder for her to enjoy the clear-headed thinking, ramped-up accuracy, and increased potency of her supernatural abilities.

Procrastinating, she pulled the remote control from the bedside table and clicked on the news to fill the silence of the morning.

"Decades of tradition come to an end." Melanie Stevens' polished face filled the screen. "Ana Castanova's lavish Equinox Balls have been a social staple for the West Coast Elite for ages. Twice a year, celebrities and titans of industry are escorted by private plane to the Castanova Compound for a long weekend of debauchery, celebrating the changing of the seasons."

She continued her report with a practiced, professional smile. The camera panned over to a beautiful Zoya dressed impeccably, but showing subtle signs of her age. Katie bolted up in bed at the mention of the Castanova name, and she increased the volume, not wanting to miss a word.

"Thank you for having me, Melanie," Zoya said graciously.

"Just like that, Ana? The party of the year is over?"

Zoya laughed a sanitized, practiced chuckle that reminded Katie of the first interview she'd watched filmed from the compound when her ex-husband, Jeff, was actively pursuing Ana and her fortune. "We've had a great run, but I decided a pivot was in order. Moving forward, we are focusing less on philandering and more on philanthropy." Her delightful play on words teased a soft chuckle from Melanie.

"Great sound bite."

"Thank you. But in all honesty, in light of the current climate, it seemed a little self-indulgent to continue. We've had our fun, and now it's time to pass the reins on to the next generation while we focus on leaving a legacy behind."

"That sounds like a noble undertaking."

"The most noble," Zoya said solemnly. "The Castanova Foundation is committed to the health, well-being, and joy of women everywhere, and we will use our resources to their fullest capacity in order to carry out this new mission."

Melanie turned away from Zoya and directed her

gaze into the center of the camera lens. "I, for one, applaud this move and encourage other organizations to follow suit."

Katie studied Zoya's face on the screen for visible signs of deception and was surprised when she couldn't detect any. She had to give it to Zoya, always one step ahead of everyone. A celebrity couldn't just disappear into the ether; she had to say goodbye, and Katie had just witnessed the end of Ana Castanova along with the rest of Tampa Bay.

Unable to put it off any longer, she shut off the television with a long drawn-out sigh and pulled the comforter off. She rose and showered and then forced down a breakfast sandwich before driving to Yuli's house.

They spent their last ordin day together, and as the sun lowered in the sky, Yuli rose and clapped her hands together.

"My dear, it's almost time."

Trying to dispel a surge of nervous energy, Katie paced the sacred circle at Yuli's home. Torn up inside, she felt a knot tighten in her stomach as the minutes sped by faster. The fact that Yuli was in high spirits made the impending physical separation much more painful.

"Can we go over the plan again?"

"Katia," Yuli whispered, her voice softening as she saw the tears track down Katie's face. "You already know it by heart. We've been over it a hundred times." She reached up to brush the tears from her granddaughter's cheeks. "What are you afraid of?"

"I can't imagine a life where I don't see you every day," Katie cried.

"It will be difficult for me, too, but we have ways to reconnect." Yuli wrapped Katie's smaller hand in her larger ones. Her palms felt like well-worn satin, and Katie's heart broke again, knowing the sensation would be one she wouldn't feel as often anymore.

"I've lived my life, really lived it, and now it is time for you to do the same. Out of love, I've become a crutch for you, but I sense you are ready to stand on your own two feet. And now that you *can*, promise me you *will*."

"I promise," Katie whispered. She exhaled one last shaky breath before Yuli began to speak, once again recounting the details of their plan to calm her only granddaughter's jumpy heart.

"I will drink the tea, and the mandrake root will slow down my heartbeat, sending me into a paralytic state. At midnight, when the moon is high and full, you will call the paramedics. Once I have been declared legally dead, they will leave you with instructions to call the funeral home."

Katie nodded as a solitary tear slipped down her cheek. "I know."

"Zoya has arranged for transport to the compound. Now, this is the most important part. I must be revived within five hours of ingesting the tea."

"Five hours," Katie repeated. "Got it."

Yuli stood and walked to a lock box hidden in an alcove of the earth altar. Taking a key from her neck, she unlocked it, pulled out a thick stack of oversized legal documents, and handed them over to Katia. "It's all here. The property deed has been put in your name. The business licenses for Kandied Karma and the incorporation documents as well." Then she tugged the chain with her keys free from her neck and deposited it into Katia's hand, curling her fingers around it. Katie felt the keys cut into her fingers and focused on the sensation, grateful it pulled her focus from the excruciating agony in her heart.

"The kids are going to miss you so much," Katie whispered. "It will be like I'm living a double life, having to keep our secrets from them. I don't know if I can do it."

"You can." Yuli reached up to cup Katie's face between her hands. "You are stronger than you realize, and without me to get in your way, I expect to see you rise to become the most powerful witch in our lineage. Having me around has handicapped you in a way. You haven't had the opportunity to embrace your gifts without training wheels. I cannot wait to see you soar!"

"This is dangerous," Katie reminded her. "What if something goes wrong?"

"Zoya is well-versed in mandrake tea and the reversal of its effects," Yuli reminded her. "You don't need to worry. I'm in good hands."

"If you're certain," Katie conceded. Seeing Yuli

would not easily change her mind, she made a last-ditch effort to persuade her. "Aren't you going to be lonely at the compound?"

"Who says I am staying at the compound?" Yuli asked with a mischievous glint in her eye. "Zoya has made a mockery of the family estate by turning it into a playground for the rich and famous."

"Didn't you see the interview?"

"I did." Yuli nodded. "She had to make a grand announcement to slip out of the public eye, but it is going to fan the flames for a while and I prefer to stay out of the spotlight." She offered Katie a reassuring smile. "Besides, I prefer something a bit more unreachable and remote."

"Ah!" Katie said, immediately understanding. "You decided to join Talulah in the Everglades."

"I have," Yuli confirmed. "And I have big plans for the estate when I am the key holder for the mortal coven. I'm going to fulfill the promise Ana Castanova made to the world this morning."

"Care to share?"

"I will when the moment is right." She smiled, patting Katie's hands soothingly. "I think you will approve."

"But will Zoya?"

A startled laugh bubbled out of Yuli. "Doubt it."

"Now I really want to know." Katie loved this side of her grandmother. The feisty take-charge woman she'd always been had only strengthened with age.

"No more stalling. We must begin." Yuli said, then

stood. She hugged her granddaughter tight once more repeating the words her mother, Nadia, said the night of the *Fioletovy Mahiya*. "I love you, Katia. You are the best of us all."

"I love you, too," Katie repeated, choking on the words as tears flowed down her cheeks. Yuli had to pry herself away. Katie nodded and quickly regained her composure. She walked to the freezer and pulled out the blood-red truffle, placing it on a pristine white plate. With reverence and sorrow, she walked it over to her grandmother and watched Yuli bite into it.

"It's revolting," she muttered as she fought to swallow it. Her gag reflex engaged, and Katie had to look away, afraid she would vomit in sympathy with Yuli. After it was consumed, Yuli led a teary Katie over to the stove where an ancient cauldron sat on the gas burner. She pulled down the mandrake plant from its place on the sunny windowsill then walked over to a drawer and pulled out two heavy pairs of headphones. Setting them down on the countertop, she chanted over them, weaving her hands together in circles as golden sparks shot from her waggling fingertips. After several minutes of infusing her energy into them, she picked up a pair and handed it over to a very confused Katie.

"When we pull the mandrake root, it will emit a high-pitched, blood-curdling scream that will condemn whoever hears it to hell. Put these on and let's see if they block out the noise."

Katie stretched the pair apart and placed one over each ear. When they were secured to her head, the silence was absolute. There was the eerie sensation of burrowing deep inside herself, of being a part of the arteries and veins that pumped blood from her heart and throughout her body. She looked over at Yuli, who cupped her hands around her mouth and screamed as loud as she could. The sound wasn't just muffled; it ceased to exist until Katie tested it by tugging one of the earpads off and Yuli's scream made her jump.

"Anything?"

"No. They are the real deal!"

"Good," Yuli said then started to give last-minute directions. "Pulling it free is going to be a bit of a challenge. You hang on to the pot and I'll do the dirty work." Glancing over at the water in the cauldron that was now at a rolling boil, she said, "It's ready." She pointed to the glowing noise-canceling headphones and put her set on, and Katie followed suit. Nodding, Katie picked up the pot and tightened her grip on the edges as Yuli tried to wrench the mandrake root free. She yanked with all her might, forcing Katie and the pot to stumble forward as she gritted her teeth. Seeing it wasn't budging at all, Katie braced her foot against the wall and yanked back, leveraging her entire body weight against Yuli's, tugging the opposite way. The mandrake screeched a deafening scream that neither woman heard. Yuli bore down, pursing her lips, her chin jutting out, and gave one final hard yank and the root came free. She immediately threw it into the pot, and it hissed then screamed as it boiled. Picking up the heavy cast iron lid that was resting on the countertop, she covered the water as the last piercing screams faded out. She waited one long moment before she tapped her headphones which were losing their shine. At her urging, Katie pulled hers off and placed them on the counter.

Yuli pulled the mitt from the hook on her refrigerator and tucked her hand inside to remove the lid. A cloud of steam billowed out, and the stench instantly made acid lurch up Katie's throat.

"Oh, Lilith! That's vile!" Katie cried, the foul air making her cough. "How are you going to be able to stomach it?"

"I believe I will have to channel my inner Beckett and chug it."

Katie laughed and then burst into tears. She felt time turning into a physical ache in her chest that, as each moment passed, only added to the weight of loss she knew was coming with Yuli's departure. "I'm sorry," she apologized.

"You are going to be okay," Yuli soothed with her calm countenance, then she tapped the purple pendant at her throat. "If you need me, I will find a way. All you need to do is focus your energy on connecting and clasp the jewel between your thumb and fourth finger, and I'll be summoned."

"Now? You're just telling me now how I can summon you?" Katie croaked with a chuckle.

"I can't reveal all our secrets at once." Yuli smirked. "A woman always needs an air of mystery." She ladled out the boiling liquid and Katie eyed the mug.

"Before I drink it, I want to remind you that Kandied

Karma and all its recipes have been deeded to you. But I do not want it to be an albatross around your neck. If you feel life pulling you in a different direction, I want you to know, without a doubt, you have permission to sell the shop and move forward on your own terms. It was never meant to be an obligation. It must be a choice. Do you understand?"

She nodded.

"And I know Brody lied to you more than once, but there is goodness in him. Never turn your back on a man who would move heaven and earth and even make a deal with a she-devil to earn your heart."

Katie laughed again at her reference to Zoya.

"It's all in jest, dear," Yuli smiled, "but I need to know you understand."

"It's just too weird."

"I'd wager it's not the weirdest situation you've encountered since your awakening, and it won't be the last."

"Maybe." Katie still struggled to wrap her head around the mental gymnastics of falling in love with a person who used to be your dog. "It's complicated and awkward."

"Oh, my darling. Who ever said love was simple?" Yuli pulled Katie into her arms once more. "I love you. You can do this."

"Okay." Katie nodded as Yuli reached for the mug and then walked it over to the center of the sacred circle. She wrapped her hands around it and paid homage to all five altars, lifting it up as a sacred offering. "Down the hatch," she muttered to herself before hoisting it up to her lips and gulping it down in one long swallow. After it was ingested, she began to heave. The empty mug slipped from her hand and crashed to the floor, shattering on contact. A loud moan escaped her lips as her stomach convulsed. Katie hurried to her side and helped her lie down, afraid Yuli would injure herself. Once on the ground, her body seized upward several times as she let out a pained shriek. She writhed on the floor for several long minutes until she eventually wore down, making exhausted mews before her body became motionless. Katie watched her chest rise and fall and glanced at the clock.

"Twenty more minutes before I call the paramedics," she reminded herself, glancing at her watch.

The doorbell rang, startling Katie. Another punch of the bell forced her onto her feet and over to the front door. She opened the door, surprised to see him.

"What are you doing here?" Katie yelped and felt herself rush forward and wrap her arms around his torso, resting her head on his chest.

"Yuli," Brody said softly. "She thought you'd need me tonight."

His warm body sheltered hers and she felt a familiar comfort. "She's over here," Katie said as she led him into the room where Yuli was lying on her back inside the sacred circle.

The next twenty minutes ticked by painfully slowly as she stared down helplessly at Yuli's slack form. Her cheeks twitched from time to time, and the vestiges of a frown twisted her lips, and then after a long moment, her face relaxed. Katie bent down, holding a compact in front of Yuli's mouth, registering the breaths that were slowing down. She pressed two fingers to her throat, and it was obvious her pulse was slowing, too. Katie struggled with her inaction. She'd made promises to both Yuli and Zoya to carry out the plan, but that was when it was only a theory. Watching the deterioration of her grandmother unfold with a physical death imminent was much harder than she anticipated.

Finally, the time had elapsed, and she checked Yuli's breath one last time. Her chest had stopped rising and falling, and Katie pulled out her phone and dialed 911.

"Emergency Services, this is Amanda."

"I need an ambulance!" she cried. She didn't have to fake the emotion; she was genuinely tearful and scared. "My grandmother collapsed on the floor of her home." She recited Yuli's address as her hands began to tremble.

"The paramedics are enroute. Is she breathing?"

"I don't think so. Please hurry."

Katie let the capable woman on the other end of the phone coach her through the process of checking her airway. Pretending she was following along, she made all the appropriate noises and asked the right questions, but she did nothing. Katie was relieved when the whine of the siren could be heard in the distance, and then the paramedics burst on the scene. Two men in their twenties knelt down next to Yuli and made an assessment. Seeing the purple bracelet on her wrist, the paramedics exchanged glances.

"She's DNR," the paramedic said. "How long has she been unresponsive?"

"Only about fifteen minutes," Katie said as tears streamed down her face. Brody wrapped his arm around her, and her trembling stopped.

"I'm sorry," one of the men said. "We cannot perform CPR on her." He searched for a pulse and found none, then he leaned his face close to hers. "The airway is open and there is no response to verbal or tactile stimulation." He leaned his cheek closer. "There are no breath sounds." He lowered his voice. "I'm sorry, ma'am. There is nothing more we can do."

Tears spilled down Katie's cheeks as the paramedics performed one last round of vitals to confirm Yuli's state. He pulled a penlight from his pocket and, with one thumb, yanked up her eyelid and shined the light inside. "No pupillary reflex. I'm sorry, ma'am. She's gone."

Katie fell to the ground next to Yuli and clutched her hand, unable to speak.

"What should we do now?" Brody asked, taking over.

"We'll send the coroner, and he'll issue the death certificate. Then you will need to call the funeral home and make arrangements."

"Okay." Brody walked them to the door, and they departed, sirens off. He hastily returned to Katie, still seated on the floor next to Yuli's body. He wrapped a blanket around her shoulders and answered the door when the coroner made his appearance.

In a daze, Katie watched the coroner hastily scribble his report and thrust it into her hand like he was writing a prescription. She was relieved when he left and a white van pulled up in the driveway. Higgins appeared with three burly men led by Zoya with a gurney. They slid the backboard under Yuli's still body and hoisted her up onto it, then rolled her to the van. When Yuli was safely inside, Higgins got behind the steering wheel and drove to the hangar. Katie watched Brody wave goodbye and disappear through the window as they sped away. There wasn't a second to waste.

FORTY-ONE

At the compound, the moon was full and clouds whipped furiously by, their rough edges illuminated by the moonlight. A storm was brewing in the distance, and flashes of lightning lit up the night sky. The electric air was balmy, and the ocean temperature was like bathwater.

"Get her inside the meditation chamber," Zoya ordered, tugging off her long black gloves and removing her black cloak. She pulled her thick, white hair into a ponytail at the base of her regal neck.

"We're running out of time," Katie said. "We only have an hour to give her the antidote."

"I know, dear. Follow me."

Katie raced up the marble stairs behind Zoya. Each minute that ticked by increased the knot of tension forming in her belly.

"Try to relax," Zoya said. "I can almost taste your

anxiety." Her green eyes flashed over to Katie's, locking on them.

"Sorry," Katie apologized. "This feels risky. I never should have agreed to her plan in the first place."

"The time to second-guess is not now, darling. We have to work together." Zoya pulled Katie into the library and pulled a book from the shelf, handing it to her. The book felt like lead, and she almost dropped it. "Focus on your intention to understand," Zoya directed. "Place it on the altar in the meditation chamber. Hurry."

Katie dragged it back to the small, windowless meditation chamber as fast as she could. Near the altar, a series of candles were lit, softly illuminating the space. Finding the book stand, she was eager to lay it down. Enduring the weight of it made her hands tremble and her shoulders shake with muscle exhaustion.

In the center of the padded room, Yuli was lying on her back. Zoya rushed in with two large boxes of salt and quickly handed one to Katie. "Help me pour a sacred circle." She then used her fingernail to pry open the container and poured it out into a perfect circle around Yuli's body. Katie followed her directions in the opposite curve, and in a few minutes, the circle was fully connected.

"To the book," Zoya urged, and she grabbed Katie's hand and pressed it down onto the cover. The contact with the soft leather surface made the first white sparkles dance up to the ceiling from the circle of salt. "That's a good sign." Zoya's features relaxed, and her skin became luminous and dewy. She guided Katie's hand to the edge, and they opened the book together in a focused team effort that made the amulets at their throats brighten. The weight of the cover was surprising as Katie let it go and it clanged and dented the stand it was laying on. "What do you see?"

"Nothing." Katie cried as she studied the blank pages. She whipped through the book, swiping through it right to left with her index finger. Page after page of blank white space mocked her and only increased the panic rising in her throat.

"Focus," Zoya commanded sharply." Focus on your sweetest memories of Yuli. Your intentions must be pure."

"Okay." Katie closed her eyes. She walked through the lifetime of memories they'd shared. The sweetness in Yuli's expression as she gazed down at the precious bundle swaddled in a soft, pink blanket the day Lauren was born. The hours she'd spent at her side, stirring the chocolate in the double boiler into a smooth, creamy consistency.

"It's working," Zoya said.

Katie's eyes popped open, and she looked down at the book. Faint words and drawings were traced as if written in glowing golden ink. Encouraged by the progress, she closed her eyes again and focused on the joy and relief that flooded through her the moment Yuli had burst through the doors and into her arms in the warehouse when she'd been kidnapped. The warmth of safety she only felt around Yuli filled her entire being, and she began to glow with golden light.

"Open your eyes," Zoya directed her. "Read the spell." Zoya knelt down next to Yuli and wrapped her hands on the sides of her face, focusing all her attention on Yuli's still body. When Katie stumbled through the pronunciation of the spell, one painful foreign word at a time, Zoya lit up from within and emitted light. She chanted louder and louder as the white sparkles transformed into yellow glowing vampire moths that brushed their crispy wings against Yuli's pale skin. There was a flutter from the multitude of vibrating wings that made the hairs stand up on the back of Katie's neck.

"Louder!" Zoya shouted as she pressed her lips together, baring down on the energy that shot from her fingertips. It electrified Yuli, and she floated a few inches from the floor. The moths doubled in number and spread over her entire body, leaving no inch of skin uncovered. Powdery trails traced down the paths they made. Zoya's eyes glowed, and a trickle of blood dripped from the corners of her eyes and down onto Yuli's cheek. The moths pounced on the droplet, devouring it and brightening even more as their feeding became more frenzied. Zoya cried out, "Aaagh!"

The energy in the room peaked as Katie howled the spell again. The book was now completely lit up, and the words swirled and whipped by, page by page, as her tone grew more confident. Then, the number of vampire moths tripled and consumed Zoya's entire body.

Another trickle of blood sent them into a feeding frenzy on Zoya's face that swallowed it whole. Their vast numbers completely obliterated the two women for several long moments. Yuli's body convulsed and shook, and Zoya whipped forward then lurched back with her hands clamped down on Yuli's cheeks as her wails of agony intensified. Katie felt a sensation of tearing apart accompanied by a scorching burst of searing heat, and then a gush of release.

The room was thrust into complete darkness and the book slammed shut. Katie crashed to the floor in a euphoric daze. A few moments later, she struggled to acclimate her eyes to the ink-black interior of the meditation chamber. Slowly, she got to her hands and knees and crawled toward the altar, feeling her way through the dark. Her hip wedged into it and she patted the surface, searching for matches, grateful when her palm connected to them. She struck one against the box to light it and then bent to light the wicks of two tall tapered candles with wax already dripping down the sides. She lit two more and then glanced around, able to finally make out the shape of Zoya lying face down on one end of the room, her body unmoving. Facing the opposite wall, Yuli was moaning, and Katie's heart lifted as she raced over to her grandmother's side and pulled her into a seated position. "Thank Lilith!" Katie exclaimed. "I was afraid we were going to lose you." A tiny smile quirked up the corners of Yuli's fuller mouth, and her eyes fluttered open. Confusion washed over Katie as she glanced at her grandmother from head to toe. The shapeless housedress she favored now hung on her much thinner frame. The age spots on her hands had disappeared and the skin was smoother. Katie cradled Yuli's face in her hands and took inventory.

"You're... you, but... much, much younger," Katie finally stuttered, still unable to believe her eyes.

Yuli got to her feet more easily than she had in several decades. She released a charged chuckle of astonished joy.

"Look!" Yuli twirled around and the dress spun out. Katie was utterly transfixed by the transformation, unable to tear her eyes away. Yuli's white hair was thicker and rolled down her back in long waves. Her eyes sparkled and the wrinkles that surrounded them had been smoothed so effectively, they virtually disappeared in the candlelight. To Katie, it was like looking at her own reflection.

"This is so trippy!" Katie said, reaching out a hand to touch Yuli's much smoother cheek. They genetically shared the same sturdy bone structure, and now, with the last forty years seemingly wiped off Yuli's face, they looked like sisters. A moan from Zoya across the room startled them both and refocused their attention.

"Zoya!" Yuli cried out, rushing to her side, so spry it was like she'd floated over. There was a spring in her step and a lightness of being that made each step bouncy and buoyant.

Still dazed from the drain of reading the book of spells and in shock from Yuli's transformation, Katie stumbled over to where Zoya lay on her stomach. After several attempts to work together, they successfully turned her over. They collectively gasped when they got their first glimpse of Zoya's face in the candlelight. Her stunning beauty had completely vanished. In its place, a deep network of lines crisscrossed her leathery face. Her eyes were lidded and sunken in, and her teeth were now yellow and crooked. Her once luxurious white hair was now a pile on the floor underneath her, having been shed like skin. What was left on her head was a dingy gray and so thin that patches of her pink scalp peeked through. Brown liver spots dotted every inch of her shriveled skin. Katie reached over to shake her gently.

"Zoya. It's Katia, wake up."

Zoya stirred, slowly coming to life, and eventually opened her eyes and met Katie's. "Did it work?"

"Yes." Yuli leaned away in an attempt to hide her own transformation, afraid of Zoya's reaction. "But it was not without sacrifice," she added, her voice a low, somber tone.

"What do you mean?" Zoya asked as Katie helped pull her up into a seated position. Catching a glimpse of her hand in the dim candlelight and confused by the knobby knuckles, thick veins, and brown spots, she gasped. She flipped her hand over and then back again, cataloging the changes in the candlelight. She let out an agonized cry and rocked forward on her knees to gather up the strands of her once beautiful white hair. In horror, she began to scream as the gossamer strands drifted between her fingers to the floor. "Give me a mirror," she snarled at Katie, her fingers snapping to demand it be placed in her weathered palm immediately.

"That is not a good idea," Yuli tried to explain from the shadows.

"NOW!" she roared, and Katie rushed out of the room. The door opened and flooded the room with light, and Zoya's eyes widened as they locked on Yuli's. Katie returned a few minutes later with a hand mirror. She averted her gaze, terrified to look Zoya in the eye, as she handed it over.

Zoya studied her reflection, unable to comprehend the dramatic change. Her forehead knit together in bewilderment as she dragged one wrinkly hand across her cheek to her saggy chin. "I'm hideous," she muttered. She turned her chin from side to side, glaring at her own reflection. "The ugliest crone alive." She raked her fingers through her thin hair and whimpered when chunks of it drifted to the floor to join the others. "Disintegrating as we speak." She started to cackle, an unhinged response to the loss of her physical beauty that made Katie's eyes widen in shock.

"And you…" Her thin lips curled into a grimace as she pointed one thin, gnarled finger at Yuli. "You've dropped forty years in an instant. You stole my vitality from me like a leech."

"I can try to heal your skin," Yuli quickly offered, eager to stop Zoya's crazed reaction to their transformations.

"Resistance is futile," Zoya said. "The transfer of vitality is already complete. The die has been cast."

Frustrated, she threw the mirror to the ground, unable to stomach seeing her own reflection any longer. Zoya threw her head back and her piercing scream ricocheted from wall to wall. Her fists were balled into rocks at her waist, and the veins in her head and neck throbbed. Stunned, Katie felt the raw despair roar from her small frame in search of a new home to inhabit.

The ground shook and glass shattered. Fissures and cracks raced across every reflective surface in every room of the compound as her rage rippled from the meditation chamber outward. A few minutes later, worn out from the effort of expelling her vitriol, Zoya crumpled to the ground. Katie rushed over to her, eager to calm her down as she lay motionless with her eyes closed. Her hand trembled as she reached out to smooth Zoya's brow, trying to comfort the distraught woman. Her eyes were closed and a single tear fattened then rolled down the surface of her wrinkled cheek.

"We all survived," Katie whispered. "Isn't that what really matters?"

Zoya's eyes popped open again." Forgive me if I don't wish to look at the bright side. Being an old hag, I now prefer to wallow alone in the dark."

Terrance, her servant dog, pushed the door open with his nose. Seeing his mistress, he whined and circled to lie down on the floor, hiding his eyes with his paws as he trembled.

Noticing his reaction, Zoya let out an anguished exhale. "Get a grip, you superficial canine, or I will extend your sentence."

"I am deeply sorry, My Queen," he mumbled, still unable to meet her watery eyes. She stood and her dress hung on her frame. Her once perky bosom was now deflated, and the exposed skin was paper-thin and crepey. Zoya was skin and bones, completely emaciated, a shell of her former self.

"I need some rest," she declared. "Stay… Go… I don't care anymore," she said to Katie and Yuli, waving them off to discourage any further interaction. She walked away without another word, completely bereft. Terrance's tags jingled together as he leapt to his feet and followed her out of the meditation chamber and then into her bedroom.

Katie helped return the chamber to order, re-shelving the ancient book and blowing out the candles. They worked together in silence, abiding by Zoya's wishes, and left her chamber, deciding to share a bedroom further down the hall. Silently, Katie pointed to the mirror in their ensuite bathroom. It had been shattered into a reflective web where ten thousand tiny versions of their faces reflected back. Shards of the mirror crunched under their feet on the marble floors, disintegrating into powder.

"We all need some rest. Then we can decide what is next," Katie suggested, bone-tired and mentally exhausted.

"All the rest in the world isn't going to help Zoya," Yuli mumbled, and Katie didn't disagree.

Katie let the more rejuvenated Yuli tuck her into bed while they waited for trays of food to be prepared. They ate quietly, the only sound in the room their knives screeching across their plates as they cut through their steaks glistening with thyme and garlic butter. Unable to speak about what they'd just witnessed, they turned out the light and fell into a deep sleep.

FORTY-TWO

The sun climbed on the horizon as they slept fitfully, exhausted from the events of the night before. When Katie finally opened her eyes and glanced at her watch, it was almost noon and Yuli was gone. She sat up in the opulent bed, the lightweight down comforter tucked around her, and glanced around, still drowsy. The room had been thoroughly cleaned as she'd slept, the shards of glass from the mirrors removed, and for a few minutes, Katie wondered if it had all been a vivid nightmare.

She tugged off the blanket and stood, stretching her arms as high as they could go. Every muscle in her body ached, and she bent forward, sweeping her arms down and then around the backs of her thighs, shaking out the tension that remained.

She took a quick shower and then exited the suite, her stomach growling, and followed the scent of bacon wafting up from the kitchen below.

At the table, Yuli was seated and sipping on a cup of coffee.

"Good morning," Katie said brightly.

"That remains to be seen," Yuli said.

"Has she come down yet?"

"No," Yuli answered. "I suspect she's been in the meditation chamber for the last several hours, trying to restore her beauty."

"You would be wrong." A raspy voice drifted down the staircase. Katie's shoulders tensed in anticipation as Zoya finally rounded the corner and swept into the dining room. The sun beat onto the wooden floor through the bank of windows as Katie glanced at the approaching Zoya out of the corner of her eye. She was hunched over and grasping a cane with one gnarled, arthritic hand. Reduced to shuffling her steps, it took much longer to cover the distance than usual, and when she reached her chair, she let out a groan as she fell into it. A sheer black veil draped over her head and obscured the view of her face. Not paying attention to the other women, she hooked the cane on the edge of the table and rang the bell that was next to her empty plate. When nothing happened, she rang it again with more irritation and fervor.

"Finally, you've decided to grace me with your presence," she spat at Terrance, who obediently rushed to his side. "Bring out the coffee and sweet rolls."

"Yes, My Queen." He averted his eyes as he rocked forward into a downward-facing dog position before scampering off to fulfill her request.

She leaned forward, propping up her elbows and steepling her fingers together. Katie was astonished at the frailty of the long skinny fingers and knobby knuckles and the sheer volume of dark spots that now covered the backs of her veiny hands. "Don't stare, darling. It's rude."

Katie jumped and then offered a weak apology. "Sorry."

"I guess life still had one twisted lesson to teach me," Zoya muttered. She gathered the fabric of the veil in front of her and rolled it up, letting it sit on the crown of her head. Katie gulped and had to fight her urge to gasp at the dramatic physical transformation. It had been one thing to see it illuminated by the soft, forgiving light of candles in the meditation chamber, but now, in the bright Floridian sun, the change was jarring.

"What did you expect? I'm almost a hundred and fifty years old! Without the divine magical intervention of the glam chamber, this is the result." Her tone was embittered. "I've become the prime example of the dangers of skipping sunscreen in the tropics."

Yuli started to chuckle under her breath, quivering with repressed laughter. She pressed her palms to her mouth to stop it. The giggles became infectious, and Katie started to titter, and finally, Zoya cracked a smile that revealed yellowing and chipped teeth.

The door to the kitchen opened and a maid pushed a trolley laden with pastries piled high, a silver coffee pot, a plate of sunny eggs studded with ham, sausage, and bacon, and another bowl of brightly colored fruit.

Placing them in the middle of the table, Terrance said, "Is there anything else we can fetch for you?"

"Fetch?" Zoya harrumphed at his choice of word. "No. This is perfect. You may go."

He barked once and then ran away with the maid in tow. Zoya stood to shovel an impressive amount of the steaming egg scramble onto her plate and added at least six strips of bacon. On a separate plate, she piled a cinnamon roll, an apple Danish, and a chocolate eclair. Not bothering to pass the pastries, she bit into the eclair first and sighed in delight. "At least food hasn't lost its pleasure."

Katie picked up the plate of remaining breakfast rolls in front of her, added a caramel cinnamon bun to her plate, and then passed it to Yuli. The women ate in silence for a few long minutes before Katie broached the subject that had been on her mind.

"So, what now?"

Zoya wiped the corner of her mouth with her cloth napkin and then set it next to her plate. "Unfortunately, you will need to carry out the ordin rituals required for death and burial on your own. Are you going to be able to play the part of the devoted, grieving grandchild?"

Katie thought it over with a wince. "The deception that will be required is not part of my factory settings."

"I suggest you upgrade then, dear."

———

"Do you feel that?" Katie asked several hours later, sitting on the edge of Yuli's bed. They'd spent the remainder of the day resting in their suite, and Katie found she couldn't bear to leave Yuli's side. Absentmindedly, she tugged at the purple amulet at her throat that cast a glow of purple light onto her neck. She pointed at Yuli's amulet. "Is mine glowing, too?"

"Yes," she confirmed.

"It's getting warm," Katie said.

"We're being summoned." Yuli got up and lumbered around, looking for her shoes.

"Are you sure you're up to it?" Katie asked, concerned. She was still drained from the events of the last few days.

"I feel surprisingly refreshed, and I can't bear to sit in this bed anymore," Yuli said. "I'd rather be useful."

A few minutes later, they climbed onto a golf cart and Katie closed her eyes and conjured an image of Zoya in her mind, connecting with the flow of energy that was omnipresent at the compound. She turned the key and pressed down the accelerator, being pulled to the path that led to the archives. The cart felt magnetized like it was driving itself to the destination, and Katie let go of the steering wheel to let it.

"It worked like you said it would," Katie said, relieved the amulets connected them to each other, no matter where they were.

Yuli patted her hand. "Of course it did. You can always trust the magic."

At their destination, the cart puttered to a stop. They

climbed out and walked the short distance to the small metal building on the property that contained the archives. Katie pulled the brush away from the door and turned the handle, surprised when it creaked open. It took a long moment for her eyes to adjust, but when they did, she caught her first glimpse of Zoya. The black veil still obscured her face like an evil bride, and she was seated sipping on a vodka gimlet, presumably from the shaker next to her. On the table was a single box and a pile of ashes. A thin, wispy tendril of smoke curled up from the charcoal and remnants of wood.

"What have you done?" Yuli asked, her voice barely a whisper as she walked closer to Zoya.

"Just taking a stroll down memory lane," she answered flippantly, lifting the veil and bringing the full glass to her lips for a long sip. Her words were slurred, and it was painfully obvious she'd been inside the archives for a long time. Another beautiful box glowed with stunning pink light that refracted around the walls of the archives, awaiting its destruction.

Yuli rushed to her side and pulled the box away before she could make another life-altering mistake and destroy the memory forever.

"Hey! Gimme that." She warbled, reaching out to grab the box back, and stumbled when she misjudged the distance between them. "I wasn't finished."

"What memory is this?"

"The day my Nadia was born."

"You can't go inside. You'll destroy it forever!"

"I miss her so much. I wanted to feel the joy again.

Just one more time so I could say goodbye and let her go before I move on to the next place." She crumpled and began to wail.

"I cannot let you do that," Yuli said, guarding it with her life. The thought of losing the archive of her precious mother's birth was a price too high to pay.

Katie bent down next to an inconsolable Zoya. She'd never seen her powerful great-great grandmother so fragile before, and it was unnerving. "Do you need to wear that over your face?"

"I'm disgusting." She sniffled. "I scared Terrance at breakfast and neither of you can stand to look at me."

"That's not true," Katie said as she stepped closer and gently asked, "May I?"

Under the veil, Zoya nodded once. In her lap, her hands were curled into fists. Katie reached forward and gingerly lifted the delicate lacy fabric up over her face and then gently pushed it behind her bony shoulders as another clump of brittle hair drifted to the floor. Zoya's face was a network of lines, as aged and cracked as broken-in leather. Her eyes shone like two jade-colored jewels, and her full lips were wrinkled and loose.

"I think you're even more beautiful than you were the first time I saw you," Katie said, remembering the first real glance she'd gotten of her great-great grandmother at the warehouse.

"You're a liar," Zoya argued feebly.

"For one, you aren't coming in hot with the force of a hurricane and threatening to destroy everyone in your path."

Katie's joke elicited a wary chuckle from Zoya. "Seriously though, the lines add a uniqueness and character that wasn't there before. Isn't it better that your mind is the most beautiful part of you now?"

"I guess." Zoya sniffed. Her usual vanity taking a back seat, she reached behind her head and yanked the veil off, letting it fall on the floor. "It *is* easier to breathe without this thing hovering over me."

Zoya forced herself to unsteady feet and stumbled to the shelves. Then she climbed a ladder while Katie held her breath as Zoya reached up on one foot to access a box on the highest shelf. When she climbed back down and it was still contained safely in her hands, Katie let out a breath she didn't realize she'd been holding.

It was a magnificent butterfly-shaped box. Zoya brushed her hands against it, and it began to brighten and then glow. A soft smile tugged at the corners of her mouth as she reminisced about the memory inside.

She held it out to Katie and Yuli. "This is my most precious memory," she whispered, her voice filled with longing. "I can't go inside or I will lose it forever, but it lives inside my mind and brings me joy whenever I revisit it. Time has blurred the memory and the fine details are harder to recall. Or perhaps, parts of it have been rewritten like your mind does when someone you love passes away. You don't remember the squabbles or the frustrations you had with each other; you only remember the magical moments. The moments you hang on to when the darkness haunts you." Her forehead wrinkled as she tried to explain.

She locked eyes on Katie and Yuli. "Time is running out, and I want you to know me. To really understand the woman I became when love transformed me so you can reconcile that version with the one I became after I lost my beloved Salvatore."

In Katie's hands, the butterfly warmed even more, and she was drawn to the crank.

"Wait!" Zoya pulled a bell out of the pocket of her floor-length black cloak, and a few minutes later, Terrance led Higgins into the room to collect his inebriated mistress. Higgins swept her up in his arms, and over his shoulder, she called out further instructions. "Remember every detail so you can describe it to me when you return." Katie waited until she heard the door latch firmly behind her, then reached out for the silver crank on the side of the butterfly. She gasped with delight when the wings slowly flapped in response, and then the box opened and pulled them both inside.

They floated down into a verdant forest teeming with life at the golden hour.

"This way," Yuli directed as she followed a pathway that seemed to glow brighter with every step they took down it. Her gait was lighter, and Katie had to hustle to keep up with her. They rounded a bend that opened into a field of aspen trees, golden in the fall, their leaves a vibrant yellow against their peeling white trunks.

A small clearing opened up and, inside it, peals of nervous laughter rang out from a younger Zoya. Dressed in cobalt blue, her black hair fell down her shoulders in thick, bouncy curls, and the hereditary white streak darted from her widow's peak and down the middle of her part. Standing next to her was Sally wearing a black three-piece suit with his sunny yellow carnation pinned to the lapel. They were lost in each other like they were the only two souls in the world.

Puffy cumulus clouds turned into cotton candy as the last rays of the sun lowered behind the grove of trees. Its soft light bounced onto Zoya and Sally's faces. On the branches of the trees, scores of brilliantly colored blue butterflies gathered. Their wings were aflutter as they rested on the arms of the branches. It was a surreal experience, seeing so many gathered together, flitting up and down and around as if they were invited guests. Captivated, Zoya pointed up at them. "Look, Sally! Have you ever seen anything so beautiful?"

"Yes," he said, never taking his eyes off of her. "I'm looking at it right now." A soft smile lit up Zoya's features as she reached eagerly for his hands. "This is perfect."

Katie's eyes locked on Yuli, who was as entranced as Zoya by the scene. Yuli couldn't tear her gaze away from Sally, a man who had shown her kindness in her childhood. She hastily swiped away tears that ran down her plump cheeks. Katie wrapped her arm around her grandmother. "I know. It's hard to see him again knowing how it ends, isn't it?"

Yuli nodded. "I never got to see this side of her. She only gave her love to him." Katie squeezed her closer, wanting to heal the crack in her heart. "It's water under the bridge, Katia, and I *have* forgiven her, but darn it if these moments don't still sting."

"That's understandable," Katie murmured. They'd come so far, but it seemed the mortal wounds you received as a child cut deeper. Your scar tissue formed a protective layer around the wound, but you were forever changed. Katie wondered briefly who her grandmother would have been if she'd been as loved and wanted as a child as Katie was.

The leaves of the trees began to glow like they were illuminated from within, and it transformed the curving bank of trees swaying in the breeze into a breathtaking natural cathedral. Sally hummed the bars of a song that felt familiar, but Katie couldn't place the tune. He twirled Zoya around, and her dress fluttered out around her. Laughing, she pressed her lips to his and swayed in the soft breeze without a care in the world.

"Ready?" Sally asked and Zoya nodded eagerly. "Zoya Ana Castanova. My life forever changed the day you stole my wallet, and then my heart."

A soft chuckle escaped Zoya's lips, remembering the moment they'd met.

"You challenge me in every possible way. Tonight, in front of this forest of beautiful witnesses, I promise to love you in this world and beyond. You are my soul mate, my one true love, and whatever this life has in store for us, from this moment forward, I vow to face it with you… together." Zoya's lips curled up as happiness bloomed over her features, making her even more luminescent and beautiful.

"Salvatore Theodore Gabriano," she whispered as tears rolled down her high cheekbones. "You are the one I adore. There will never be another heart as perfect for mine as yours. I promise to love you with all of me, every day, and honor this sacred commitment today and forever after."

He reached into the pocket of his suit coat and pulled out an enormous diamond ring that sparkled when twilight's final rays hit it. Zoya gasped and both of her hands flew to her mouth when she laid eyes on the sparkler. "It's obscene," she declared with a throaty laugh. "And I love it."

He offered her a rakish grin as he pulled her left hand down and placed it on her finger. "This is the real deal, doll face."

"I know." She whispered, her eyes brimming with tears. He laced his fingers through her hair and drew her in for a long kiss. When their lips met, the butterflies launched into the air and began to circle them, funneling up into a swooping helix and then back down again. Their gossamer wings tickled the couple in a sort of choreographed ballet as they spun in a slow circle, their arms wrapped around each other as they kissed passionately. When Zoya finally pulled away, Sally pulled her back into his arms, hugging her to him from behind. The butterflies rushed over and caressed them once more as they both laughed up into the sky, lost in the joy of the moment.

"I will never forget this day, doll face," Sally whispered into her hair as Zoya tugged him by the hand

and spread out a blanket under the first twinkling stars. They disappeared onto it a few minutes later, lost in each other.

Hidden by the trees and the darkening night, Katie reached out for Yuli's hand and squeezed it. "Did you know they married themselves like this?"

"I had no idea," she admitted. "Zoya always liked to do things her own way. Laws of man never applied to her."

"She's an original." Katie barely got the sentence out before she felt the first flutter of butterfly wings brush against her forearm. The sensation tingled where they touched, and she watched in awe as more and more of them surrounded her and Yuli.

"It tickles." Katie giggled as they were swept away, being lifted up by the hundreds of synchronized wings as if they were weightless. They climbed higher and higher as the leaves rustled in the darkness and then dissipated into the starry sky.

FORTY-THREE

They slept for hours, and on their final night at the compound together, Katie and Yuli joined Zoya for dinner. She'd abandoned the funeral attire and the long black veil in exchange for a loose-fitting purple cloak. Her thinning gray hair was now shorn close to her head in a silver pixie cut. Uncharacteristically self-conscious, Zoya pressed her palm to the top of her head and then tucked an imaginary strand of hair behind her ear, clearly a habit she'd acquired that was no longer needed.

Yuli opened her mouth to say something, then closed it without speaking, then opened it again.

"Close your mouth, dear, you'll catch a mosquito. I simply thought it was time for a change," Zoya offered in explanation with a dismissive shrug of her shoulders.

"I love it!" Katie gushed in an attempt to cover the awkwardness. "You look great!"

Zoya laughed at her attempt to fill the silence. "You

might be overselling it a skoosh, darling, but thank you just the same." She eyed them as the maid rolled in a trolley of dishes. Terrance nipped at her feet, racing around the table, directing the placement of the platters.

Rack of lamb with mint jelly and a platter of enormous seared scallops were set at Zoya's right hand. A basket of cheddar and chive biscuits rested on white linen, and pan-seared pork medallions with a mushroom and caper sauce waited on platters next to Katie.

"Dig in," Zoya encouraged as she filled her plate.

"You don't need to tell me twice." Katie plucked a biscuit from the basket and passed it over to Yuli. She broke off a corner of the burnt orange crusty cheese and popped it into her mouth, surprised at the tender texture as it melted on her tongue.

"So?" Zoya said as she speared a slice of the lamb with her fork and slid it into her mouth. "How was the journey?"

"Spectacular!" Katie gushed. "It was like living inside a Baz Luhrmann film!" She shook her head, still gob smacked by the stunning beauty she'd witnessed inside the music box. "I've never seen anything like it."

"Me neither," Zoya admitted. "It's beautiful when life gives you a magical moment like our wedding day, but it's also cruel."

"How so?" Katie asked.

"Because you become addicted to the feeling. Once you know it, nothing will ever compare."

"But isn't it better to have loved and lost than to have never loved at all?"

"Resorting to trite platitudes, are we?" Zoya's sass had returned in full force.

Katie winced. "Sorry." They ate a few more bites in silence when she asked, "If the eternal coven allows you to reincarnate, how will you find Sally?"

"That's the million-dollar question, isn't it, darling?" Zoya asked. "I just know that I will recognize his soul in whatever form I next encounter it."

"How can you be so sure?"

"A soul always recognizes its counterpart." Zoya took a sip of the vodka gimlet that had been set down in front of her. "I've been meaning to speak to you about Arlo."

Katie leaned away and shifted uncomfortably in her seat, raising her glass of wine to her lips to avoid speaking.

"I believe he is your counterpart."

Katie sputtered, choking on the wine. "You're as bad as Yuli. Why is everyone team Arlo... er, I mean Brody, all of a sudden?"

"Katia..." Yuli started in. "Please listen."

"Thank you, Yuli," Zoya said. "Just hear me out. Yes, the quality of loyalty is admirable and its importance cannot be overstated. But you must understand I put him between a rock and a hard place. I knew he loved you, but I also knew he would do anything to be returned to his human form so he could have a real chance at a relationship with you. He was conflicted. He just didn't see another way."

"It's just too weird. Having a romantic relationship

with my former dog? Even if I was able to forgive him, I don't know if I could get past that."

"What if I was able to give you a little help?"

"What do you mean?"

"I could help you forget Arlo and open the door for Brody."

"Hmm." Katie considered her proposal. "Isn't that cheating?"

"Not to me," Zoya said. "Perhaps I had it wrong all along. Perhaps men aren't dogs, after all, but they are the very embodiment of love and devotion."

"I like this softer side of you," Yuli whispered in awe, astonished at the change.

"Perhaps this is another lesson for me to learn. Maybe instead of weakness, vulnerability is true strength." She turned to Katie and reached out to grasp her hand. "To walk through this world without armor is brave and, you, darling, seem to do it with ease." Her tone downshifted to almost a whisper as she leveled her eyes on Katie. "Looks like we have a thing or two to teach each other yet."

She tipped her head and offered a solution. "I could soften your inhibitions, open your heart and your mind, just enough to give you the space to let him in. It would take nuance and finesse and most likely a significant portion of my remaining resources. Truth be told, it might even make me more hideous to look at." She laughed as if she'd told a joke. "But I believe it is worth it. After all, it might be your only chance to feel the sun on both sides."

Katie closed her eyes, thinking Zoya's proposition over. If she was honest with herself, she'd longed for it since the day Zoya shared the concept with her. It was as if a lock inside a hidden chamber of her heart had found a key. Now that it had been opened, the longing was increasing with each passing day. It seemed that all the lessons she'd been learning since her awakening were converging together into the only one that mattered. Love is all there is, and it was worth the risk to feel the warmth that Zoya was offering her.

"I hope I don't regret this." Katie finally gave in when she was able to put words together. "But I want to try."

"Fantastic," Zoya said with a pert nod of her head. The grin on her face made the crow's feet crinkle at her eyes. Katie was struck by the sheer mature beauty of her genuine happiness but knew better than to draw attention to it.

"There is something I need to say as well," Yuli stated as the eyes of the other two women drifted over to her. She cleared her throat.

"What is it?" Zoya finally asked when the silence stretched out too long veering into uncomfortable territory.

"I need to thank you," Yuli finally said. "You sacrificed to save me, Zoya, and have proven to me that you are a changed witch. I didn't make it easy for you to earn my trust and respect, but you have, and I am grateful."

Zoya bit on the corner of one wrinkled lip. Clearly

affected by Yuli's gratitude, she pulled the linen napkin from her lap and dabbed at the corners of her eyes. "I didn't realize how much I needed to hear you say those words until now. Thank you."

The sentiment choked up Katie, who reached out a hand to Yuli. The breakthrough made their amulets glow. The tears falling down their faces worked down their cheeks, to their jawlines, and then changed direction, beelining to their amulets causing them to glow ever more brightly. There was a surge of tingling energy, and Katie felt the urge to stand and pull the other two women into her arms. Once their hands were joined together, the tingle worked its way from woman to woman on a circuit as healing energy snaked through them all. They began to glow and emit light, and Katie had to squint, eventually closing her eyes to shield them from the brightness. In the distance, a tuning fork began to hum and then stilled, and behind her eyelids, Katie noticed the room darken. When she opened her eyes, she felt fully refreshed and completely restored. She gasped in awe when she caught first sight of Zoya's dramatic physical transformation. She'd been rejuvenated into an age-appropriate yet vibrant centurion. The decay evaporated into the ether and her face held a sweetness it never had. Her silken pixie cut was once again a radiant white, though much thinner. The age spots lightened, yet still snaked their way across her skin, but it was her smile that ignited a beautiful light from the inside that took Katie's breath away.

"You did it, Katia," Yuli whispered.

"No, we did it together," Katie said. It was a truth that resonated in her heart and rang so true none of the women could dare to dispute it. "Zoya, now that your heart is your most beautiful attribute, all we had to do was unite and encourage the outside to match the inside. Before, you were physically stunning but your heart was hideous. Your selflessness encouraged the flip, and all our magic did was restore the equilibrium."

Zoya nodded. "I understand now, in a way I never have before." She leaned closer. "Yuli, my beautiful granddaughter, your outside now matches your beautiful, forgiving heart. I hope your next lifetime brings you the peace you deserve."

"And Katia, you are now the strongest and most capable witch in the mortal coven. It brings me great peace of mind and joy to know our bloodline will be protected by your valiant heart and capable hands. Trust your instincts. You have everything you need inside you right now to take this coven to its highest heights."

"Agreed!" Yuli weighed in with a huge smile.

There was a collective exhale from the group, and it was as if a weight they'd all been carrying around for decades had finally been lifted. Katie felt capable and calm. She'd come so far since her awakening and was now confident in her ability to lead the mortal coven. She glanced from Zoya to Yuli and back again, grateful for all the breakthroughs they had together. Her heart filled with a sense of contentment that seeped outward like a warm blanket wrapping around them all.

FORTY-FOUR

The next morning, Katie said her goodbyes to Zoya and Yuli and flew home alone, bracing for the phone calls she would need to make to her mother and her children who would be heartbroken.

She touched down and rolled her suitcase to her green VW Beetle parked at the private aviation company. Then Katie drove in silence past her house and down the streets of Aura Cove toward Yuli's home. When she arrived, she let herself in and began to make the phone calls she dreaded. While she waited for her family members to gather, she straightened up Yuli's kitchen, getting rid of the empty cup of mandrake tea and washing the plate where the vile truffle Yuli ingested had rested.

Her mother, Kristina, was the first to hurry through the door with David on her heels. "Where is she?" Glancing around the circular room, nearing hysteria, Katie quickly ran to her side and led her to a chair.

David's expression was grim, seeing the despair settle on his wife's typically sunny features.

"Hey, Dad," Katie said, walking over to give him a hug.

"Hey, sweetheart." He held her close and then returned to his wife's side, resting one comforting hand on her shoulder.

"What happened?" Kristina asked again, forgetting the details she'd been told over the phone.

"She passed in her sleep," Katie said. "When I found her, she was unresponsive. I called for an ambulance, but she was wearing her DNR bracelet and they could not intervene medically. The coroner is delivering her body to the funeral home, and we will have to meet there to discuss her final arrangements."

Kristina burst into tears and collapsed face-down on the table. "We were supposed to have coffee today."

"I'm so sorry, Mom." Katie knelt down next to her, reaching out to hold her mother's frail hand.

"She was ninety-eight. I knew this day would eventually come, but I was foolish enough to think we had a lot more time." Kristina cradled Katie's face in between her satiny palms. "She loved you most of all, you know."

The sentiment cracked Katie's careful composure. Kristina continued. "Thank you for carrying out her final wishes. I don't think I would have been strong enough to do it myself." She squeezed Katie's hand. "You two were made from the same stock." It was the highest compliment Katie's mother could offer, and Katie nodded, blinking back the tears in her eyes.

"She shared her final wishes with me a while ago."

"She did?"

"Yep." Katie continued, "Yuli wanted to be cremated, and then we are to have a celebration of life at Kandied Karma."

"What a wonderful way to honor her life, it's perfect," Kristina whispered as Katie filled her parents in on the details, hoping Kristina wouldn't demand to see her mother one last time.

She was relieved when Kristina admitted, "That sounds like Mom. I don't want my last memory to be of her dead body. It was her soul that we all loved."

"It was." Katie brushed her tears away and stood.

"Mom was such a force to be reckoned with," Kristina said. "I always felt that my life choices were too small and that I let her down."

"I better never hear you say that out loud again," David warned.

"He's right. Grandma loved you deeply. She was proud of the mother you became."

Kristina's voice cracked and a peaceful expression spread across her face as her eyes took on a shine. "I can almost see it. Mom and Dad are together now. Dancing in heaven. No arthritis, no creaky hips, just floating on a cloud in each other's arms."

"Exactly." Katie knew differently, but the visual of it brought her mother so much peace she had to indulge it.

A cool blast of air cooled the room as Beckett,

Callie, and Lauren entered the small house. They flew into Katie's arms, almost tackling her with their grief. "I can't believe she's gone," Beckett cried.

"She loved you all."

"I can't believe she is not going to be around to meet our little pumpkin," Lauren said, sniffling and rubbing her rounded belly with the palms of her hands.

Callie looked down at her own bump, rubbing it softly. "I can't either," she whispered. A tear spilled down her cheek, landing on her belly, and darkened her shirt where it landed.

"The baby is moving!" Lauren cried. "Mom, Grandma, come feel it."

David led Kristina over to her, and Lauren reached out to grab her mother and grandmother's hands. They waited, collectively holding their breath, concentrating on noticing the fleeting sensation. There was a little flutter, then a gentle rocking movement as the confines of her abdomen stretched, and Katie gasped with delight.

"There! Did you feel it?"

"I think so!" Kristina said.

"Wait," Callie said, her eyes widening. "My little peanut is on the move, too."

"Really?" Kristina stood between them, resting one hand on each of her granddaughters' swollen bellies. For several long moments, she palmed Callie and Lauren's bellies, waiting, concentrating on detecting the tiniest flutter.

Callie pulled up her shirt to expose the skin of her

belly, and a tiny ball no bigger than an inch emerged and poked out.

"Mom! Look!" She guided Katie's hand to it, and when she made contact through her stretched skin, the shape glided down the surface of her belly and then disappeared.

"An elbow, maybe?" Lauren guessed, thrilled for her sister.

"Or a little foot?" Katie added.

"My turn!" Beckett jostled his way inside the tight-knit circle. "Uncle B needs to connect with his two favorite little aliens." His comedic timing was perfect as usual. It was a moment of magic during a dark day that seemed to provide a balm for their broken hearts. Katie bit her lip, hearing Yuli's words whisper in her ear, "You have everything you need inside of you, Katia. You are ready to stand on your own two feet. And now that you *can*, promise me you *will*.""

FORTY-FIVE

On the day of Yuli's celebration of life, Katie donned an apron and passed them out to her kids who had gathered at Kandied Karma.

Lauren tucked her head into the apron Tom held up for her, then let him spin her around to tie the strings behind her back. Overnight, her belly protruded with a roundness that she'd embraced and taken to wearing form-fitted shirts to emphasize it. Tom laced his fingers through hers as she protectively wrapped her hands around her belly and snuggled back into him closing her eyes. Katie watched Callie witness their sweet exchange and headed over to comfort her picking up on a trace of envy. Callie's bottom lip trembled, and Katie pulled her in for a hug. In her ear, Callie whispered, "I'm happy for her, Mom. I am, but I'm also sad for me and my baby."

"Oh, darling girl, it's perfectly normal to feel that way," Katie whispered back. "But I don't want you to worry. Your baby is just as wanted and loved as theirs is."

"I know." Callie smiled. "I'm just so tired. It would feel amazing to have someone around to rub my feet and bring me ice cream. I would love to have a partner to shoulder some of the worry and celebrate every milestone. But please don't tell Lauren I'm having a jealous moment."

"Of course not," Katie promised. "You know you're always welcome at home. If you find after the baby comes that you need more support, you could move in with me."

"I appreciate the offer. Can we see how it goes?"

"Of course."

The front door burst open, and the shop began to fill with Yuli's favorite patrons. On a computer, Beckett played a slideshow of photos he put together that ran on repeat alongside the soundtrack of Yuli's favorite songs. When Queen's *Another One Bites The Dust* came on, there was an awkward silence, but then the filled-to-capacity chocolate shop burst into ripples of irreverent laughter.

"If she were here, Mom would have cackled like a witch!" Kristina said then dissolved into another fit of belly-busting laughter at the hilarious, yet inappropriate twist the universe's playlist served up.

Katie filled gleaming trays of truffles in all the most requested flavors, and she and the kids circulated the packed shop with napkins, offering them to everyone gathered there. There was a steady stream of visitors, each sharing stories about how Yuli touched their lives. By the end of the evening, the love that the community of Aura Cove poured on her family all day took away some of the sting of their loss. Before she turned out the lights at Kandied Karma, she took one last look around the store that held so many memories of her grandmother.

"I'm sure going to miss you around here," she whispered. "You lived your ordin life well."

"She did," a warm voice said from the shadows.

"Who's there?"

He stepped into the light. "How are you holding up? I've stayed away as you wished, but I wanted to pay my respects today. Yuli was always kind to me."

Seeing Brody, her heart clenched and her mouth became parched.

"Please tell me you were able to revive her," he pressed, clearly concerned about Yuli's wellbeing.

"Yes," Katie answered, looking down at her feet, feeling shy. "She's successfully embarked on her second life in the Florida Everglades."

"Good." He nodded.

She paused, then offered him an olive branch. "Thank you for being there that night."

"There is nowhere else I'd rather be than by your side." He sounded so earnest. Katie sensed he wanted to reach out, but instead, he clasped his hands behind his back. "Katie?" Her name on his lips was a whisper, and she pulled her chin up to look him in the eye. "Do you see any future where we end up together?"

"Truthfully?" She was quiet a moment before saying, "I don't know."

The tiniest spark of hope ignited in his warm brown eyes, and a soft smile tugged at the corners of his lips as his eyes locked on hers. Katie's gaze traveled across his face, looking at him with fresh eyes.

"That's good enough for now. Goodnight, sweetheart."

"Goodnight," she whispered as she watched him walk away and disappear into the darkness of the night.

FORTY-SIX

The next afternoon, Harry was sitting at his desk in the Aura Cove Police Department sipping on a cup of coffee when a waif of an old woman floated in. Her long lavender hair flowed down her back, and she was dressed in a cotton tie-dyed flowing romper that cinched at her shoulders and billowed out at the waist, revealing skinny legs dotted with age spots and wearing well-worn sandals.

Her presence ushered in a flurry of murmured and excited whispers that made Harry sit up and take notice. His sergeant, Reggie O'Malley, quickly left his post at the coffee maker and crossed the room over to her. Fighting against his curiosity to rubber-neck the interaction like his co-workers, Harry focused back on the screen in front of him. He had a stack of reports to file before he could leave and was eager to wrap them up. He wanted to get home before Frankie decided to start making dinner.

God, he loved the woman, but she was a disaster in the kitchen. Her latest concoction was accurately and lovingly called The Bucket of Yuck. It was a crockpot dump recipe fail that included a random assortment of canned goods, including watery tomatoes and rubbery boiled potatoes that he'd had to secretly bury deep in their trash can on collection day.

Reggie walked the woman by his desk, and the frenetic energy caught Harry's attention. He offered her a small professional smile as she passed while three other officers brought up the rear of the procession. Suddenly, the woman froze in front of his desk, narrowly avoiding being knocked over by the impromptu entourage walking behind her. Her vision clouded and she zoned out for a second before closing her eyes and taking a centered breath. Feeling the shift in her demeanor, Harry's brows pinched together, concerned for the unusual woman.

"I'm sorry." She turned to Reggie and the officers congregating around her. "Can you give me a moment?"

"Of course," Reggie said. "If you need some privacy, I can escort you to some place quieter."

"That would be great." She pointedly looked at Harry. "But I'd like Officer…" She glanced at his name placard, "…Willey, to accompany me there."

Harry saw the flash of disappointment cross Reggie's features, but he quickly recovered. "I think the conference room is free. Harry, will you show Ms. LaRue the way?"

Surprised he was being given the task, Harry got to his feet and started leading her down the hall. When they arrived at the bright conference room, he was shocked when she entered, tugged him inside by the arm, then pulled the door shut behind them. His skin tingled where her hand made contact with the fabric of his uniform shirt.

"Yes, I understand," she answered like he'd asked her a question, and Harry was instantly confused by the exchange.

"I'm sorry, but I don't," he admitted. "Can I get you anything to drink while you wait?"

"Not yet." She beckoned him closer, tilting her head to the side as she studied Harry. Her lips moved as if she were having a silent conversation with an unseen being in the room. The whole exchange made the hairs on the back of his neck stand up. She extended one hand and introduced herself. "I'm Talulah LaRue."

"The medium?" He blurted, finally putting the pieces together as she beamed up at him. Frankie had regaled him with all the details from Katie's parents' reading months ago, and while he was still a skeptic, it was hard to debunk her abilities.

"Do *I* have any rare pennies in my jug of change?" he quipped. "Because I sure could use an extra ten grand."

She offered him a small smile. "Afraid not, dear."

"Well, it was worth a try," he said. "You're here about the Anderson case, right?"

She nodded. It was a cold case that hit a dead end years ago, and Reggie was willing to embrace unorthodox methods to get new leads so they could bring closure to the family.

"I have a message for you if you are open to receiving it," she gently offered.

"What?" He was taken aback but quickly recovered. "Absolutely!" he accepted, excited by the once-in-a-lifetime opportunity he'd just been given. "Your waiting list is ten years long! Tell me what to do!"

She chuckled softly. "Just try to relax." Talulah closed her eyes and seemed to be straining her ears to listen to something just out of earshot.

"There is a gentleman that will not leave me alone. He's coming through for you very strong. He keeps saying, 'Sorry about the name.'"

Harry laughed. "It's my maternal grandfather."

"He's showing me two halves of something. He keeps repeating, 'There's two.'" Confused, she concentrated harder. She exhaled a heavy breath, shook out the tension in her long arms, and rolled her shoulders. The collection of colorful bangle bracelets on her wrists tinkled together like wind chimes.

"Are you a twin?" she asked, her eyes shimmering luminous pools of lavender that Harry couldn't pull his gaze away from.

"Yeah." He choked on the word as it remained stuck in his throat and then shot out as his voice cracked. "Is my sister there with him?"

She focused, concentrating harder. "Hold on.

There's a room full of souls who've passed. They are all talking over each other. I'm sorry. Let me see if I can calm them down enough to receive the message they are trying to tell me."

She pressed both of her hands to her temples and inhaled deeply then exhaled. After ten long breaths, Harry leaned forward.

"Jessie?" he asked softly.

"There was a traumatic event years ago." Her eyes were still closed. "Gone. They keep saying, 'Gone.'"

Harry cleared his throat where a tickle was lodged. "She disappeared when I was seven," he whispered, then asked the question he was most afraid to ask. "Is she there?" Panicked, he waited for the answer. On one hand, it would be a tremendous relief that she was surrounded by his loved ones and light on the other side. On the other, it would force him to accept the fact he would never see her again, a truth he was not ready to acknowledge.

"She's not coming through," Talulah said. "I'm sorry. I can't connect with her. Wait." She held up one bony finger as she listened in, nodding several times.

"She's alive."

"Really?" He choked on the word again. "I always thought she was. I've been searching for her for decades."

"There's confusion. I feel discombobulated." She pressed a hand to her heart. "I see a puppy. So many tears. Crying a river of tears." She opened her eyes.

"I need more. How do I find her?" Harry begged the

old woman. Desperate to connect to his sister through the medium, he reached out to grasp her hand in his own. The skin-on-skin contact rocketed her body forward, and then she slumped her shoulders forward.

"Willey!" Reggie shouted from the doorway he'd just come through, crossing to where a dazed Talulah now sat in a chair Harry had guided her to. "Take your hands off her."

"Sorry!" Harry cried, instantly upset.

"Are you okay, Ms. LaRue?" Reggie said, firing a glare at Harry. "I'll take it from here, Willey."

"It's not his fault," Talulah defended, trying to smooth the sergeant's ruffled feathers. "The dead aren't always willing to take no for an answer."

"I need more!" Harry cried as Reggie pulled him roughly away from the medium and over to the door. Harry couldn't let it go. "Please," he begged. "She's been gone for over forty years."

Reggie dragged him back to his desk and said, "You're done for today. Go home, Willey."

"But she had information about Jessica!" Harry said. "She confirmed she's alive." He pushed his way to his feet and wrestled out of Reggie's grip, forcing his way back to Talulah. The veins in his neck bulged as he strained under the effort.

"Go home," he repeated gruffly, "or I will put you on administrative leave." He firmly pushed Harry out into the hallway and shut the door. Harry trudged back to his desk and sunk down into his seat, letting the truth settle deep into his bones. He always felt Jessica was still alive and consoled himself that she was somewhere out in the world. To know this wasn't just a dream, but a confirmed reality, albeit by a psychic, renewed his energy. He quickly gathered his keys and drove home to tell Frankie the great news.

He tapped his fingers impatiently on the steering wheel, eager to lay eyes on the woman he loved. Harry parked under the carport and pulled his keys from the ignition, twirling them on his forefinger to expel the excitement that filled him.

"Frankie?" he called out as he walked through the darkened breezeway.

"You're early!" she shouted out. "Hold on for one second."

"I can't! I need…" Unable to wait, he crossed the room when his foot connected with a red rose petal on the cold tile. It squished underfoot, staining the flooring underneath it.

"What in the…?" As he closed in, he noticed more red rose petals underfoot, making a makeshift pathway he followed into the living room. At the doorway, he stopped, in shock at seeing hundreds of unlit candles set up in the living room. The few she'd hastily lit illuminated Frankie standing in the corner, her eyes shiny with tears. In awe, he stepped closer, crushing the red petals under his boots, and landed in front of her with a soft smile on his face. "Is this what I think it is?"

She held one finger to his lips to shush him when his tongue flicked out and licked her finger. "Ew!" She laughed before wiping her finger across his chest and hugging him tightly.

"Harry." She cleared her throat and furrowed her brow, trying to recall the words she'd prepared. Waving one hand from her chest to his, she finally distilled it down to a few words. "This… just works."

He nodded, biting the inside of his cheek. He was a softie, and feeling the tears gathering, he grasped her hands in his larger ones. "It does."

Frankie bounced from foot to foot on the tips of her toes. "If you were being serious about getting hitched, I'm in. I'm all in."

He threw his head back and laughed. "How romantic!" he exclaimed, reaching out to tuck a loose hair behind her ear. "I never thought I'd live to see the day when Frankie Stapleton would be begging to become my wife."

"Begging?" Frankie laughed and pushed his shoulder away playfully. "You smug, over-confident bastard! Go ahead and bust my balls, Willey! But I would like to remind you, I have a long memory and an epic ability to hold grudges."

"Okay, okay." He held his palms up in front of him. Harry knew when he was outwitted.

"Let me finish?"

"Of course," he said, patiently waiting.

Frankie swallowed and started in a small voice. "You are the one I never saw coming. Every day I am surprised that I get to wake up next to you. You disassembled my walls brick by brick, without me even noticing. I want to be yours forever if you'll have me." She fished something out of her pocket and lowered to her knees. She tipped her head back, and when Harry looked down at her eyes, so filled with hope and love for their future, his heart burst wide open. In the palm of her outstretched hand, a ring glinted in the candlelight.

"I promised myself I wouldn't cry," Harry teased, waving his hand in front of his face comically before wiping away the tears and pursing his lips dramatically.

Frankie rolled her eyes as a wide grin spread across her face. "Zip it, joker, or I will find a clown to officiate our wedding service." Terror filled Harry's face. He'd had a raging case of coulrophobia ever since he'd read *Stephen King's It* in middle school.

Frankie took a deep breath and began again, "Let's do this. Let's elope and keep each other forever. What do you say?"

"Can I check out the ring first and let you know in seven to ten business days?"

"You're the worst!" Frankie exclaimed as Harry pulled her up to her feet.

"Okay, fine, you wore me down."

"Is that a yes?" Frankie asked, her tone teasing.

"No. It's a hell yes," he cried and kissed her on the mouth, a deep kiss that was a promise and a vow for their future. When Frankie pulled away, she was in a euphoric daze, enchanted with joy. She grasped the ring between her thumb and forefinger and circled it on his ring finger, pushing it into place.

"Fits perfectly," he said when it was seated on his hand comfortably. "How did you know my size?"

"You sleep like a rock. I could do anything to you in that state and you would have zero recollection."

"Anything?" His eyebrows danced seductively. Frankie rolled her eyes again and tried to push him away, but Harry only pulled her closer. She squealed as he snuggled into her and delivered a series of ticklish kisses on her neck. "This day... might be one of the best of my life."

"Aww." Frankie was taken aback by his sweetness.

"Something big happened."

"I know, silly, we just got engaged."

"That too." He deposited a quick kiss on her lips.

Frankie's brow wrinkled. "What else?"

"I had an interesting encounter." He was still in shock as he glanced down at his hand where the ring now sat.

"With whom?" Frankie was instantly interested.

"Talulah LaRue," he said. "She came to the station to work on a case and had a message for me. Apparently, my grandfather has been adamantly contacting her and demanding that she get a message to me."

"About Jessica?" Frankie guessed, hoping it was true. It seemed like the only logical reason.

"Yes!"

"WOW! She's the real deal." Enthused by this new development, She asked, "What did she tell you?"

"Jessie is alive." He smiled sadly. "I always thought

she was. In my mind, I dared to believe she was living her best life out there somewhere, unaware we were looking for her. I know it's stupid, but that's the story I told myself."

"Did she give you anything to go on? Where to start looking?"

He huffed in frustration. "Reggie pulled rank and sent me home before I could grill her."

"We *have* to get back in contact with her." Frankie had an idea. "I'll talk to Katie. Maybe she has her information."

"Her waiting list is long! It's a one-in-a-million chance."

"That's all we need. I'm not sure if you are aware, but I can be pretty persuasive when I'm properly motivated."

"Oh, I know," Harry said with a wicked grin and a wink. He reached her and wrapped his arm around Frankie's neck, pulling her close and depositing a soft kiss on her temple.

"Case in point."

She pulled out her phone and swiped to her digital wallet where two boarding passes for Las Vegas awaited.

"Next week?" Harry asked, noticing the date.

"Yeah," she said and released an empathetic exhale between her lips, bracing for his answer. "But if you want to wait until we find Jessica, I would understand."

"It could be years before we find her," Harry said. "Being in law enforcement, a lead is promising, but on a cold case this old, it could be another dead end." He pulled her closer and brushed his lips across hers. Frankie circled her arms around his shoulders and looked deeply into his eyes. "You think I am going to take a chance that you might change your mind? Hell to the no! Pack a bag, sweetheart, we're going to Vegas. My only question is should we have fat Elvis or the skinny one perform the ceremony?"

FORTY-SEVEN

A week later, Frankie was snoring in the bed next to Katie in their suite at the Venetian. Across the room, in typical Frankie fashion, her suitcase had exploded and her clothing was strewn throughout the suite. A pair of shoes she'd kicked off remained at the door. In contrast, Katie's empty suitcase was perched on a luggage rack in the closet after the contents had been neatly tucked inside the gold leaf-trimmed dresser.

Soft morning light spilled into the room, and Katie slowly rolled over onto her side, trying to lay as still as possible. Five minutes later, when the alarm clock on the side table trilled, Frankie jolted up in the bed and peeled off her sleeping mask, propping it up on the mass of red hair on top of her head. She balled up her fists and rubbed her eye sockets, yawning for the first few seconds. Then, as if it just occurred to her, she blurted, "It's my wedding day!"

Whipping the comforter off her legs, she stood on the pillowtop mattress and jumped up and down, completely carefree. "C'mon!" she encouraged Katie, who laughed as she bounced in sync, still seated on the bed. Frankie's exuberance was impossible to ignore as she bent down and pulled Katie to her feet. Getting into the spirit of the moment, Katie squeezed Frankie's hands as they both bounced higher and higher on the bed while Frankie squealed with delight.

"Someone call the devil because Hell just froze over," Katie said as she flopped back down on the bed, exhausted from the impromptu exercise session.

"Right?" Frankie finally settled back down next to her, a little out of breath.

"I never thought we'd live to see the day." Katie laughed. "I'm happy for you, Frank. Though I am concerned that, when you walk into the chapel, you might burst into flames."

Frankie grinned. "God help me, it's a risk I am willing to take. Willey is worth it." She exhaled and then let out an anxious laugh as she turned toward Katie, propping herself up on one skinny elbow. "Remember that you said you were happy because I have a feeling that, when I tell you what I did, you won't be happy anymore."

"Oh no!" Katie groaned, instantly suspicious. "What did you do?"

"I might have called Brody and extended him an invitation…" Frankie grimaced.

"Seriously?" Katie sighed, rubbing her forehead with the palms of her hands.

"Come on! You can't be mad at me on my wedding day." Frankie graced her with a lopsided grin, making Katie chuckle under her breath.

"True. But *tomorrow* is another story."

"I'll take it!" Frankie winked and glanced at the clock. "Let's get some room service and then begin the beautification process before we have to head to Graceland on the Boulevard."

There was another knock at the door, and Frankie, still dressed in a bathrobe, opened it clutching a champagne flute of mimosa.

"Delivery for Frankie Stapleton?" the bellhop said.

"That's me!" She held out her hand to receive the garment bag. "Who's it from?"

"Ana Castanova." The bellhop grinned. "Do you think you could get me on the guest list for the next Equinox Ball?"

Katie handed him a tip, knowing there wouldn't be any more of them, adding, "We'll see what we can do." When the door was closed behind him, she hung the garment bag on the hook in the bathroom suite.

"There's a card."

Frankie squealed with delight and tore it open. "Something borrowed and something blue. You'll have to figure out the rest. Z."

Katie unzipped the bag, and Frankie pulled out a vintage turquoise fascinator. It included a small birdcage veil made from iridescent thread and a peacock feather.

Frankie placed it on top of her head backward, and the veil covered the back of her head.

"Give me that, you fashion disaster!" Katie said, laughing, pulling it off her head and flipping it around. She held it in place while Frankie looked at her reflection in the mirror. "See?"

"Oh!" Frankie laughed at herself, letting out a snort. "That's much better."

Katie set it down while she watched Frankie pull out a turquoise hand-beaded backless gown. She held it up in front of her torso (also backward) surveying her reflection with dismay. "Whoa! This is too J-Lo at the Grammy's for me," she admitted, glancing down at her cleavage. "She put the tits in titillating, but my girls are crepey and droopy. They need more coverage." Laughing, Katie flipped it around.

"Doh!" Frankie snorted again, laughing at herself. "Jeez Louise! This glam stuff… I'm terrible at it."

"You are," she agreed. "Speaking of your girls, I think you're gonna need these."

She pulled out an adhesive bra.

"What is it?"

"A sticky bra."

Frankie wrinkled her nose at it.

"Here. Let me show you." Katie opened her robe and peeled the backing off the adhesive, pressing each cup firmly into place. Then she tugged and fastened them together. "Ta-da!" she exclaimed, waving her hands in front of her.

Frankie batted Katie's newly voluptuous breasts

together. "Forget the fact that you're a witch, this is the real magic."

"I packed an extra set for the bride!" She handed them over to Frankie, who disappeared into the bathroom and emerged triumphant a few minutes later. "My rack has never looked so good! I might wear one of these jobbies every day."

"Maybe you should wait to make that decision until after you've peeled them off." Katie laughed knowingly and mumbled the rest. "Along with most of your skin."

"What?"

"Nothing." Katie laughed. "Ready for the dress?"

"Yes!" Frankie squealed. Katie gathered up the heavy fabric and held it over Frankie's head, as she slipped through the opening and shimmied into it. Katie let go and the skirt fell down to the floor. The keyhole back needed both of her hands to fasten the clasp, but when she did, the result was perfection.

"Oh, Frank," Katie said, her eyes moistening with tears. "You have never been more beautiful."

"It's all downhill from here," she agreed as she twisted back and forth, gazing with a dreamy expression at her reflection in the mirror. Leaning forward, she smoothed the front. "Look at that! I have actual cleavage!" She turned toward Katie. "Did you know Zoya was going to send this?"

Katie nodded. "I might have. You looked great in the dress you brought. But a woman deserves to feel like a princess on her wedding day, and this dress was made for you." Katie opened her arms and squeezed Frankie tight. "I love you, girl." She felt herself tear up and pulled back to wave the tears from her lashes.

"Let me put on mine and I'll order the Uber."

Twenty minutes later, they were speeding toward the chapel. When they got to the parking lot, Katie got a glimpse of shaggy hair and her stomach flipped. Taking a deep breath and forcing on a smile, she helped Frankie get out of the car and tipped the driver. Then Katie's nervous gaze flicked over to Brody.

"Dammit," she whispered under her breath when she realized how handsome he looked up close in his suit jacket and dress pants.

Harry was pacing in front of the chapel. When he laid eyes on Frankie, he raced toward her and pulled her into his arms. "God, you're a sight!" Frankie giggled as he nuzzled her neck, depositing kisses on it.

"Are we ready?" Katie asked, avoiding eye contact with Brody but feeling an undeniable pull. She felt her inhibitions weakening in his presence and knew it was Zoya's doing.

"We're still waiting for my mom," Harry said. "Her plane got delayed, but she should be close."

"Okay." Katie looked at the couple. "Why don't we give you two a minute?"

"Yes, please!" Harry waggled his eyebrows and pulled Frankie toward a gazebo lit up with LED lights.

Taking the opportunity, Brody stepped closer to Katie. "You're beautiful," he told her. "I hope it's okay to say that."

Katie nodded and cocked her head, looking at him.

She'd had just enough Mimosas to soften her resistance. "You don't look too shabby yourself," she whispered.

"I never thought we'd live to see the day Frankie became a wife."

A smile teased the corners of Katie's mouth. "Me neither. But she looks amazing and I know she's happy. They *are* a perfect pair."

His warm eyes drilled into hers, and she tuned in to his stream of consciousness.

So are we.

The thought startled her, even though it was never uttered aloud. She felt her resolve weaken, and her eyes darted shyly away. Brody reached out to gently squeeze her elbow.

She didn't recoil. That's progress.

Katie leaned closer, feeling warmth flood her heart when a yellow taxi stopped and a harried woman rushed out. She was plump and her long pink dress was sufficiently rumpled. "Sorry to keep everyone waiting!" she called out as she tipped the cab driver.

"Mom!" Harry rushed over to her side and pulled her into an embrace. Katie was happily distracted by the exchange since it gave her an excuse to put space between herself and Brody. She walked over to where Harry and Frankie were speaking to his mother and extended one hand.

"Katie, this is my mother, Rose."

Rose turned to Katie and shook her hand. Katie faltered as the colors intensified, swirling around them. There was a deep sadness in the older woman's eyes and an underscore of tension from being late to her son's wedding. Rose forced a smile on her face and Katie got a flash. A man holding a puppy while a little girl reached out to stroke its soft fur. A truck barreling down a deserted country road. A young girl crying and the scent of sage so overpowering she gasped.

Katie pulled back. The flashes were so vivid, but for once, it wasn't confusing at all. Her next assignment from Karma revealed itself, and she knew without a doubt what she was supposed to do. This one was personal.

"Ready to do this?" Harry asked Frankie, and it pulled her focus back to the moment at hand. Her best friend's wedding.

"I thought you'd never ask." Frankie grinned up at him and squeezed his hand. Brody and Katie opened the doors for them to walk into the chapel. Still in a daze, Katie followed behind, barely registering the chunky Elvis with mutton chops who was decked from head to toe in flashy gold lamé and thousands of sparkling rhinestones.

Her gaze drifted over to Rose watching the happy couple with tears in her eyes, and she could feel her internal struggle as if it were her own. It was Harry's wedding day, and half of her was absolutely thrilled, witnessing her son enjoying one of the best days of his life. The other half was devastated, missing the one who wasn't there. Katie knew Rose was feeling the void more deeply during this life-changing milestone event. She felt a deep desire to restore what had been lost, from one mother to another. It would be the ultimate wedding gift for the happy couple, and she couldn't wait to get started.

————

Thank you for reading "In a Flash: Midlife in Aura Cove." Check out the final thrilling installment of this hilarious and heartwarming series! Flash of Love: Midlife in Aura Cove. Order here.

In the riveting climax of the Midlife in Aura Cove series, the delicate balance between the mortal and supernatural worlds teeters on the brink of a new era.

Karma assigns Katie a mission hitting close to home. Guided by the flashes, she embarks on a poignant quest to reunite Harry with his long-lost twin sister, Jessica, and mend the shattered pieces of his family.

Katie's joyful anticipation of her first grandchild

turns to dread as the supernatural ramifications loom over her family.

Desperate to reunite with her beloved, Salvatore Lombardo, Zoya gambles her future for a chance to reunite with him. Will she succeed in proving her redemption to the eternal coven and secure her shot at reincarnation, or will she be condemned to an eternity of despair?

With heart-wrenching farewells and heartwarming new beginnings, Katie and her loved ones navigate through trials and tribulations, discovering that love is the ultimate legacy.

This is book 6 of the Midlife in Aura Cove Series— a little Florida town with big secrets.

Order Flash of Love Here.

Also Available on Amazon, BN Nook, Apple iBooks, Kobo, Google Play and many international booksellers. Or request it from your local library.

Like FREE Books? Enter to Win a Gift Card to My Bookstore   https://tealbutterflypress.com/pages/join-our-email-list-and-win

There's a new winner every week!

READ MORE BY THIS AUTHOR

Use the QR code below to access my current catalogue. **Teal Butterfly Press is the only place to purchase autographed paperbacks and get early access.** Buying direct means you are supporting an artist instead of big business. I appreciate you.

https://tealbutterflypress.com/pages/books

Also available at Barnes and Noble, Kobo, Apple books, Amazon, and many other international book sellers.

Find My Books at your Favorite Bookseller Below.

Books by Ninya

Books By Blair Bryan

About the Author

I've always been a risk-taker, so at 44 I decided to write and publish my own books. It has been a roller coaster ride with a punishing learning curve, but if it were easy, everyone would do it. I write under the pen names of Ninya and Blair Bryan.

I love to travel and a trip to Scotland with a complete stranger was the inspiration for my memoir. I also seem to attract crazy experiences and people into my life like a magnet that gives me a never-ending supply of interesting storylines.

If you love a good dirty joke, a cup of coffee so strong you can chew it, and have killed more cats with your curiosity than you can count, I might be your soulmate.

Visit me online www.tealbutterflypress.com

Let's connect in my facebook reader group, **The Kaleidoscope: Teal Butterfly Press' Official Author Fandom**

Made in United States
Orlando, FL
16 June 2024

47936806R00243